THE IPPOS KING

GRACE DRAVEN

The Ippos King
Wraith Kings Book Three
by Grace Draven

The Ippos King - Copyright © 2017 by Grace Draven

IS POD Edition ISBN: 978-1-64197-224-6

ABOUT THE IPPOS KING

The Ippos King
Wraith Kings Book Three
by Grace Draven

The demonic horde that threatened to devour the world has been defeated, but at great cost.

Plagued by guilt and nightmares, Serovek Pangion sets out to deliver the soulless body of the monk Megiddo to the heretical Jeden Order for safekeeping. Accompanying him is sha-Anhuset, the Kai woman he admires and desires most—a woman barely tolerant of him.

Devoted to her regent, Anhuset reluctantly agrees to act as a Kai ambassador on the trip, even though the bold margrave known as the Beladine Stallion gets under her skin like no other, and Anhuset fears he'll worm his way into her armored heart as well.

But guilt and unwelcome attraction are the least of their problems. The demons thought vanquished are stirring again, and a warlord with blood-soaked ambition turns a journey of compassion into a fight for survival. When the Beladine king brands Serovek a traitor, Anhuset must choose between sacrificing the life of a man she's grown to love and abandoning lifelong fealty to the Kai people.

A tale of loyalty and acceptance.

This book is dedicated to Patrick (Mr. Draven), who wore shackles, pretended to be an insect, and battled a vacuum cleaner to help me write this book. Thank you, handsome, for rolling with the punches.

CHAPTER

ONE

S erovek swung out of bed and padded naked to the wash basin and pitcher on the table near the shuttered window. Sleep eluded him and *galla* dogged his dreams. In the suffocating darkness of his bedchamber, he imagined their ravenous gibbering ghosted against his ears.

He cracked open the shutters to let in the fading moonlight cresting the tops of stately firs that marched in ranks down the slopes of the mountain into which High Salure was built. Its pale illumination allowed him to light a candle with a piece of char cloth. The wick sputtered to life under his hand, casting a small pool of light onto the table.

A crackling noise inside the pitcher warned that the cold pebbling his skin, steaming his breath, and making his toes curl against the stone floor was deep enough to skim a layer of ice on the water. Serovek tilted the pitcher and filled the basin before plunging his hands into the water and splashing his face.

The bracing cold made him gasp but also obliterated the last lingering threads of the nightmare still entangled in his mind. The revenant whispers of vanquished demons disappeared with them.

This wasn't the first time he'd abandoned the comfort of his bed or the occasional bedmate to contemplate the sliver of horizon just beyond the rocky terrain of his mountain home. Then, as now, Serovek wished the illusion of easy-going strength he cultivated was real. He strove not to crouch in a corner, knife in one hand, as the memory of malevolent shades swarming the ruins of Haradis in a cacophony of screeching madness pursued him. On the worst nights, he wanted to screech right along with them.

Long months had passed since he'd returned to High Salure, human once more, whole in body if not necessarily in mind or spirit. The *galla* were gone, immured in their ethereal prison by the efforts of five warriors and the sacrifice of one. Cold reason was not enough to extinguish the guilt that sacrifice engendered.

Dawn peeked around the mountain's edge as he dressed in a heavy tunic and breeches, tugged wool stockings onto his chilly feet and slipped on a pair of worn boots. The bed, with its pile of soft covers, didn't tempt him. He'd simply toss and turn again or lie on his back staring into the dark until the restlessness drove him mad.

A flicker of motion at the corner of his eye caught his attention, and he strode to the small scribe's desk set in one corner where an array of scrolls and ink bottles spread across its surface. An unfurled sheet of parchment, trapped under a river stone at one corner, shivered in the draft whirling in from the partially open window.

Serovek tapped it down with one finger to hold it still. The scrawl of words in black ink were barely visible in the predawn gloom, but he didn't need to read them to know what they said. Their message remained burned in his mind from the previous evening when he'd read it before the hearth in his hall.

Lord Pangion,

I hope this message finds you in good health. Since your return of my brother's body to his family's care, we have received a request from the Jeden Order to have him brought to the monastery there. We wish to adhere to this request as we feel the monastery was more Megiddo's home than my estate, which he only occasionally visited.

Unfortunately, we don't have the means or the people to spare to transport Megiddo to the Lobak Valley where the monastery resides. As such, I ask this favor of you, a comrade of my brother in the galla war: provide an escort of your men from your garrison to accompany Megiddo's body to the monastery, where we hope his spirit might find some measure of peace in knowing he's among his brethren.

Your servant,

Pluro Cermak

The message, polite and to the point, offered nothing on its surface that might inspire nightmares—other than Megiddo's name and that of the *galla*. If he were honest with himself, Serovek had suffered many a sleepless night prior to the letter's arrival. What was one more in the long procession?

He traced the curves and loops of Pluro Cermak's script across the parchment with one finger, lost in thought. He suffered no reluctance at providing the escort Megiddo's brother requested. It was the least he could do, though he wondered what had inspired the monks of the Jeden Order to ask for the body. Was it simply because they valued one of their own? Even caught as he was between the living and the dead? Did they not have enough to concern them with the valley's simmering unrest?

The news of the warlord Chamtivos's defeat and the return of the valley to the monastery's control had managed to reach as far north as Belawat. Chamtivos's bid to invade and control the area had been thwarted by the combined forces of the local population, the Nazim monks of the Jeden Order and a small contingent of Ilinfan swordmasters. Peace came at a high cost, and Belawat had issued a warning to all its traders to exercise caution when traveling to and from the valley.

Bringing Megiddo to his religious brethren carried risk to his living but soulless body protected by magic and to those who would bring it back to the Order. Unwelcome guilt coursed through him. He had men to spare who would do an able job of bringing the monk home and returning to High Salure unscathed. Still, it somehow felt both wrong and unfair that he not be among their contingent. The monk deserved' the respect and recognition of being accompanied by a high-ranking Beladine, especially one who had fought beside him and failed to save him from a horrific fate.

A quiet tap on his door pulled him from his grim thoughts. "Enter."

The door opened with a creak, revealing a servant carrying a tray with a steaming pot of tea, a cup, a plate of bread with butter and a cellar of salt. "Fair morning, my lord," the man said as he placed the tray on the table where the candle dripped a slow death into its shallow holder. "Something to break your fast." He reached up to close the shutters.

"Leave them." Serovek ignored his puzzled expression. "I won't remain long enough in here to bother starting a fire in the hearth, and the chamber could use an airing." Only innocent shadows, fading with the growing morning light, lingered in the corners, yet he fancied they flickered and gleamed in spots as if eyes watched him from their darkness and waited.

The servant bowed. "Will you require anything else, my lord?"

Sounds rose from the bailey below the window, the early rising of High Salure's garrison. A hodge-podge concert of soldiers' boisterous and often vulgar conversations, the whistles and commands to the horses, the clop of hooves on cobblestones, the hollow exhalation of the forges brought to life in the smithy. . . so many everyday sounds he'd grown accustomed to during his many years as margrave in this mountain fortress. They were the stuff of life, of breathing men and women, of hard work interspersed with light-hearted revelry or annoyed bickering, drunken brawling, and practice fighting. He recalled Haradis once more, shattered to its foundations, a silent mass grave once the *galla* were herded back to the nightmare realm from which they had emerged.

"My lord? Is there anything else you need before I leave?"

He'd forgotten the servant standing nearby awaiting his reply. Serovek waved him away. "No, that will be all."

The man bowed and backed out of the room, closing the door behind him with a quiet click. Serovek scrubbed a hand across his cheeks in a weary gesture. His beard was sorely in need of a clipping, and with the hesitant arrival of spring, he might as well just shave it off completely to stay cool for the summer months. One of the three garrison barbers had already set up his chair and knives in the bailey, hawking his services to those soldiers going about their morning tasks. His voice was loud enough to wake the sleeping mountain gods, and Serovek wondered why no one had yet dumped the man in one of the horse troughs to shut him up.

He returned his attention to Cermak's letter, considering. While Brishen Khaskem had no control or say in Megiddo's continuing fate, Serovek knew he'd appreciate news of the man who fought beside him against the *galla*. The prince regent had his hands full with raising and training the infant queen regnant while trying to keep the traumatized Kai kingdom she'd inherited from her slaughtered father from completely falling apart or falling into civil war, but Serovek believed Brishen would want to know.

He dragged a stool to the desk and sat down. The cold made his hands stiff, and he blew on them to warm his fingers before reaching for a quill. Tantalizing aromas of herbs and spice drifted to his nose from the still hot teapot, but breakfast would have to wait a little longer.

The ink in the inkwell had thickened to sludge, and he held the glass over another lit candle until the flame warmed and thinned the ink. He looked forward to writing this letter. Brishen had replied to the previous letters to him with an invitation to visit Saggara and partake of its hospitality. Belawat might consider Bast-Haradis an uneasy neighbor at best and a possible enemy at worst, but Serovek considered Brishen Khaskem a friend and looked forward to seeing him once more.

His lips turned up in a smile as he wrote. Winter had enforced a near total isolation for the garrison. Except for the necessary descent into the lowlands for patrol, those of High Salure had stayed close to home to wait out the snows and avalanches. It had been three months since Serovek crossed into Kai territory to visit the Khaskem and his pretty human wife.

And his magnificent second-in-command, sha-Anhuset.

The quill paused in its scratching on the parchment. Serovek rubbed absently at his midriff, a habit these days he hadn't bothered trying to break. Every so often his muscles there would contract— memory of a moment when the Kai woman had rammed a sword blade into his gut with all her formidable strength before wrenching it free on a gush of agony and blood. The act hadn't been one of aggression but of brutal necessity, and he knew, down to his bones, that were the Kai able to weep as humans did, tears would have welled in sha-Anhuset's firefly eyes when she stabbed him.

He sighed and returned to writing. Mooning over the dour Anhuset only served to distract him from his purpose, and he put her from his mind to concentrate on his message to Brishen. When he finished, he sanded the parchment, folded it closed and sealed it with a wax stamp of his family crest.

There were plans to be made and his own trusted seconds to meet with, men who had held High Salure for him when he left to battle the *galla* and would do so again when he brought Megiddo's body to the monastery where he once served as a heretic cenobite of Faltik the One.

His lightened mood, brought on by the anticipation of visiting friends at the new Kai capital, darkened once more. He blew out the candle, watching as black smoke from the extinguished wick rose in a serpentine spiral. Some of the *galla* moved like smoke, sinuous and choking. Others jittered and splayed like skeletal puppets pulled by a madman's strings, their twisted limbs and black-fanged maws dancing to a discordant tune that made the ears of the living bleed.

He clapped a hand over his midriff a second time, remembering the feel of the *galla* swarming him and the spectral *vuhana* he rode. Even now, a crawling sensation purled along his skin and up his spine.

Galla had swarmed the lower chamber where the wound of the world pulsed and birthed the abominations as fast as he and his fellow Wraith kings butchered them.

Serovek's heart tripped several beats at the memory of Andras's desperation as he tried to claw the monk free of the *hul-galla's* grip. The horde wrapped around Megiddo's body like murderous lovers, a gleeful, writhing, gibbering mass. But it was Megiddo's expression—that bleak acceptance of his horrific fate—that haunted Serovek most, his last word, a dirge that threaded his darkest dreams.

"Farewell."

TWO

The sharp crack of a *silabat* stick against armor sounded loud in the room, as did the curses that followed. Ildiko Khaskem careened into the wall before ricocheting back into the arms of her attacker.

Anhuset caught her neatly before pushing her back to the center of the imaginary circle in which they sparred. She spun the offending *silabat* in her hand with a casual flick of her wrist and offered the scowling *hercegesé* a faint smile. "You're slow this evening, Highness. Maybe you should tell my cousin to leave you be for a day."

Such familiar teasing didn't go beyond the chamber's closed door. Outside, Anhuset adhered strictly to the protocol of address and rank. Here though, with the human duchess as her student and she the teacher, Anhuset relaxed her rigid rules a little. And the *hercegesé* seemed to enjoy it.

At least most of the time. For now, Ildiko scowled at Anhuset and rolled the shoulder that had taken the brunt of Anhuset's strike. She wiped away the perspiration beading on her forehead with the back of her hand before dropping into the familiar half crouch, her own *silabat* at the ready. "I only wish that had been the reason for my lack of vigor.

The poor nursemaid and I were up all day with Tarawin and her sickly stomach."

Ildiko did look particularly haggard this evening, and it wasn't the weariness that came from spending hours indulging in pleasurable bedsport. Her heavy eyelids and the shadowy crescents under her eyes spoke of no sleep for an extended time. Anhuset recognized the signs. She'd pulled more than her fair share of long watches and guard duty. The boredom alone exhausted a person, though she suspected caring for a sick baby wasn't so much tedious as it was challenging. She didn't envy the *hercegesé* or Brishen the burden of parenthood.

The *hercegesé* dropped into the ready stance Anhuset had taught her: knees slightly bent, feet shoulder-width apart, body turned to the side to make herself less of a target. She gripped her pair of *silabats* in her slender hands, one raised perpendicular to her chest, the other elevated to her hip. The sticks acted as sword and shield. "Again," she said.

Anhuset gave a nod of approval before mimicking her student's stance. She lashed out, a calculated move that Ildiko parried with a quick block of one of her *silabats*. Anhuset didn't give her time to counter-attack, going on the offensive with several more strikes that had Ildiko dancing across the room, grunting and cursing under her breath as she parried her teacher's attacks.

"Better," Anhuset said, landing a particularly hard strike against Ildiko's crossed *silabats* that made the other woman stagger. "Hold with your forearms, not your wrists, unless you want them broken."

They fought along the chamber's perimeter, Anhuset continuously advancing, Ildiko retreating but successfully blocking each blow Anhuset attempted to land on her upper body.

Ildiko's grim features lightened with a tiny smile, one that fled when Anhuset abruptly changed tactics, swung low, and struck Ildiko's outer thigh with a *silabat*.

The *hercegesé* hopped to the side with a yelp and held up a hand to halt their bout. She rubbed her padded leg while glaring at Anhuset. "I thought you were just focusing on my torso."

Anhuset arched an eyebrow. "Did I say that?"

Ildiko's tone changed from indignant to wary. "No."

"You assumed it, *hercegesé*. I repeated the same movement several times…"

"So I would assume wrongly." This time Ildiko's scowl was for herself. "You did say predictability was a blade with two edges."

Anhuset nodded, pleased with her student's echo of her words. As a novice at *gatke*, Ildiko made every mistake Anhuset expected her to make, but she listened closely to instruction and committed them to memory. The pain of that strike, and the bruise sure to follow, guaranteed Ildiko wouldn't make the same mistake twice.

"You learn from your enemy; your enemy learns from you. Surprise them with the unexpected by teaching them to expect the same thing."

Ildiko wiped her brow with the back of one hand and blew a stray tendril of vibrant red hair out of her eyes. "I don't think I'll ever master this stick fighting of yours."

"Every student says that until they do."

"Even you?"

Anhuset answered Ildiko's doubtful smile with a toothy one of her own. "Even me, and I had a lot more bruises to show for it than you ever will." She pointed her *silabat* at Ildiko. "Enough chatting. Stance. Widen your feet a little more. Forearms instead of wrists."

A brief tap at the door interrupted their next round. Ildiko gave Anhuset a questioning look, one returned with a shrug. The entire fortress knew not to disturb the *hercegesé* and her teacher during *gatke* lessons. To do so risked the formidable wrath of Anhuset. So far, no one had been that brave or that foolish except one man.

"Might as well open it," Anhuset said, relaxing out of her stance. "He'll just keep knocking until you do."

Ildiko creaked the door open, a wide smile blooming across her mollusk-pink features at the sight of her husband standing on the other side. "Just in time, Brishen. You've saved Anhuset from yet another beating. I've trounced her at least a half dozen times this lesson," she cheerfully lied.

Brishen smirked as he crossed the threshold into the chamber, but Anhuset didn't miss the way his gaze swept his wife's form, looking for wounds beneath the distortion of her padded armor. Confession time.

"She'll wear a bruise on her left thigh for a week or so." She flinched inwardly when his eyes narrowed. "She's slower this evening than usual. I hear the queen kept her up all day."

Anhuset silently congratulated herself on turning Brishen's disapproval back toward his wife. His gaze settled on Ildiko's face, noting, as Anhuset had, the dark circles under her eyes. "Where was her nurse?"

Ildiko stood on tiptoe to brush a conciliatory kiss across his frowning mouth. "Right beside me. We took turns coaxing Tarawin to settle down and finally go to sleep."

"Bring in more nurses."

She laughed. "How many people do you think we should cram into that nursery just to get Her Majesty to go to sleep?"

Brishen slid an arm around Ildiko's narrow waist to draw her against him. "As many as it takes. I don't like waking up and finding you gone from our bed, even if it's in service to the little tyrant."

"Who has you dancing on a string just like she does the rest of us."

"I dispute that notion."

Ildiko laughed. "Of course you do."

Fascinated by the interplay between her cousin and his human wife, Anhuset idly wondered what it might be like to have such a connection with someone. She and Brishen trusted each other implicitly. She knew without a doubt her cousin would sacrifice himself for her, just as Anhuset would for him. They were cousins but closer than siblings, more accepting of each other than just friends, and her loyalty to him would remain steadfast until she died.

But it wasn't the same type of devotion she witnessed now between the *herceges* and his *hercegesé*. This affection burned bright with passion, with desire. There existed between them an unspoken and private language only the two of them understood and shared with no one else.

A vague ache pulsed somewhere under Anhuset's breastbone, and it took her a moment to realize the feeling was both wistfulness and no small amount of envy. What was it like to know someone so well that it seemed like they walked within your spirit and you within theirs?

She mentally shook off the emotions and the question they inspired. Such idle thoughts were a waste of time and not for her. She was pleased for her cousin. After all he'd suffered, he deserved this happiness. It didn't mean she needed, or even wanted, the same thing.

"Was there something you needed, *herceges*?" The dry tone of her question drew his attention away from Ildiko and onto herself. A half smile, faintly annoyed, faintly apologetic, played across his lips.

He bowed. "I can take a hint, cousin. Forgive me." He reached inside the tunic he wore and fished out a letter, its parchment neatly creased and its seal broken. He fluttered it before both women. "Serovek will be here at the end of the week. To discuss something to do with Megiddo's body."

A pall settled over the chamber, and a pitying look chased away all humor from Ildiko's features. "That's all he said? No other detail?"

Brishen shook his head, his own features grim. "I think he wishes to save those for when we speak in person." He skated his fingertips down her sleeve. "Can you see to it a room is made for him? Maybe now that Saggara isn't so overcrowded with Kai families seeking shelter, he'll be willing to stay in the manor house itself instead of the barracks."

Anhuset's stomach fluttered at his words. She frowned at the involuntary reaction. A visit from the Beladine margrave should have no effect on her, but it did, and she resented it. She hadn't seen him in months, and even when memories of his teasing smile or the feel of his mortally wounded body collapsing in her arms rose unbidden and unwelcome in her mind, she ruthlessly pushed them away. With the exception of Ildiko, she barely tolerated humans. Serovek's surprising attentions unnerved her, made her react in ways she didn't anticipate or understand, and she resented him for it.

"Of course," Ildiko said. "Did you want me to order scarpatine pie for him when he visits? I'll need to tell Cook now so she can prepare."

"It's his favorite." He raised an eyebrow at Anhuset's scoffing snort. "I'll want you at both supper and any meetings we have with him," he told her, his tone warning off any argument she might put forth. "I value your advice."

She bit back a protest. "As you wish."

Ildiko's gaze centered on the letter Brishen held. I wonder what this news is about Megiddo?"

He leaned down to kiss her forehead. "I have no idea. I wish I did." He saluted Anhuset, offering a warning that was as much serious as it was jesting. "Don't kill my wife. I'm rather fond of her."

A brief bow and he left the chamber, closing the door softly behind him, but not before Anhuset caught a glimpse of something that pumped ice water through her veins. For the space of a heartbeat, Brishen's yellow eye had glowed ethereal blue.

"You saw it! I know you did." Ildiko's own strange eyes were wide, her gaze flickering from the door back to Anhuset in a way that made Anhuset's skin crawl. "I can tell by your expression."

Anhuset kept her tone neutral. "Saw what, *hercegesé*?"

"Stop playing coy," Ildiko snapped. She pointed to the door. "The glimmer of blue in Brishen's eye."

"A trick of the torchlight." A wishful thought more than an answer. She hadn't imagined what she saw. Nor had the *hercegesé*.

Ildiko thumped the tip of her *silabat* against the floor, frustration and no small amount of fear threading her voice. "No, it wasn't. I've seen it in the dark as well."

Chills rose along Anhuset's arms. That unnatural blue, sign of a Wraith king's magic, had no place here, shouldn't exist anymore except in the blade once wielded by Megiddo, and that weapon was hidden away. "This isn't the first time?"

Ildiko shuddered. "I could only wish. I've seen it at least a dozen times before this. The first was after he woke from a bad dream. He called out Megiddo's name."

"Why didn't you say something before now?" Anhuset's leg muscles twitched with the urge to yank open the door and chase after her cousin, peer into his face, and demand he tell her why a Wraith king's magic still manifested inside him.

The *hercegesé* gave her a disgusted look. "And who would I tell? The Elsod? That old woman is holding onto life by the tips of her claws at Emlek, wondering how she can keep the entire Kai history from collapsing in on itself now that there's no one able to capture mortem lights." She waved away Anhuset's warning hiss. "I'm not saying anything everyone in this kingdom doesn't already realize." She spun the *silabat* back and forth in her palm, the movement highlighting her agitation. "Brishen barely sleeps as it is. His niece has inherited a country teetering on collapse, its capital shattered, its people still in shock, robbed of their magic for reasons unknown." Her voice shook then, thickened with sobs that turned her eyes glassy. "I can't put yet another burden on his shoulders."

The two women stared at each other, bound together by a mutual love for the Kai prince and the terrible secret of his sacrifice which demanded he rob his people of their very birthright: their magic.

Anhuset understood and agreed with the hard choice Brishen had made, but she felt the loss of her magic keenly, an emptiness that couldn't be filled, although her skills had been small compared to most and confined to practical things that others had mastered as juveniles. There were times when she envied humans like Ildiko, who never possessed magic of their own. You didn't mourn the loss of something you never had.

She mentally sidled away from the melancholy her thoughts wrought in favor of worry for her cousin. "Why would Brishen dream of the unfortunate monk?"

Ildiko shrugged. "Regret maybe? Guilt? Who knows. But for a moment, when he woke, Brishen's eye burned blue, just like now. Just like the several times before it." Her features paled beyond their usual pallid shade. "What if the spell used to turn them back from wraith didn't work completely? Is he becoming wraith again?"

A seeping horror filled Anhuset, the emotion reflected in Ildiko's strange eyes. She batted it away, unwilling to believe, or even accept, that such a thing was a possibility. "No, he is not," she said, and Ildiko took a wary step back at the low-voiced fervor of her reply. "This has something to do with Megiddo, and if ancient Kai magic still lingers, it's due to the monk's sword being housed here at Saggara. Brishen would do well to get rid of it."

"I agree. I'll talk to him about it, though I think he'll be reluctant to put it somewhere other than Saggara. Maybe you can mention something as well."

If Brishen heeded anyone's advice most, it was his wife's. He was a reasonable man, thoughtful and measured in his decisions, but that sword held the last vestiges of Kai magic in its purest, most ancient, most powerful form. She doubted he'd be moved by even Ildiko's considerable influence, much less her own arguments. She kept that opinion behind her teeth and gave Ildiko a quick nod. "I'll do my best."

They sparred a few more rounds, half-heartedly now that their thoughts were on Serovek's upcoming visit and the manifestation of wraith magic that had touched Brishen before fading. Once their session finished, they parted with the promise to keep a closer eye on the *herceges* and report to each other if the manifestations of magic increased in either occurrence or intensity or both. Anhuset hoped neither would happen. House Khaskem had enough to contend with trying to hold the fragile Kai kingdom together.

She spent the remainder of the week leading patrols, training new soldiers, and taking reports from Brishen's spies regarding the mood of so many displaced Kai. No one had ventured back to the ruined capital of Haradis. Memories of the *galla* still plagued people in their worst dreams, and many now considered the city cursed. Even Brishen physically recoiled when Anhuset suggested she lead a small expedition to Haradis to explore whether or not any portion of it was habitable.

"Not yet," he'd said in a voice thick with the recollection of ghosts. "Not yet."

She hadn't pushed, her offer to go spurred more by a sense of duty than by a macabre curiosity. Memories of Haradis being overrun by *galla* didn't haunt her dreams. She'd been in Saggara when it happened. Still, there had been more than a few days when she'd awakened to find her own claws tearing through her blankets, the image of Brishen impaled on the ensorceled sword that would transform him into a Wraith king, the Beladine margrave his executioner.

The equally grotesque memory of Serovek's resolute face and grim smile when he asked her to deal his own death blow to start his transformation destroyed her sleep just as often. Her reason told her such an act of violence had been necessary. Her guilt assured her that it didn't matter and ate at her insides. This man had once saved her life and the life of her cousin. She'd repaid him by plunging a sword blade into his gut.

That thought worried at her like an angry hornet, and by the time the week was done and Lord Pangion scheduled to appear at Saggara, Anhuset was in a foul mood, wishing she'd never agreed to participate at supper or the meeting Brishen had scheduled afterwards.

She had just left the training arena, drenched in sweat and short-tempered despite a grueling practice session with other fighters, when a flurry of activity near the redoubt's main gates caught her attention. The Kai clustered there either waved, bowed, or simply stared as Serovek and two of his retainers casually guided their mounts through the entrance and past their observers.

He was still as ugly as she recalled. A big man on a big horse, he sat in the saddle with the practiced ease of someone who probably spent more time there than on his own two feet. The flickering light from the torches set around the bailey gilded his dark hair where it trailed over his shoulders. The last time she'd seen him, he'd sported a beard that blunted the angles and hollows of his face. He was clean-shaven now, skin paler than she remembered, likely from more time spent inside during the harsh mountain winters.

In profile, his beardless features looked carved from stone, not with a sculptor's chisel but a hunter's skinning knife. If she looked upon him as just a construct of facial bones, she understood why Ildiko said he was handsome, but the awful human eyes and horse-toothed smile ruined his visage, just as it did every human Anhuset encountered. She bore no resentment toward humans who reacted in similar fashion to the Kai. They shared a mutual revulsion of each other's appearances.

Still, there was something about this man that fascinated her, despite her disgust at the notion. Anhuset wouldn't hesitate to admit or agree that Serovek Pangion was bold, courageous, and possessed a nobility of character that was often in short supply in both the Kai and human races. He had saved her and Ildiko from capture and death by raiders and their mage hounds, tended Anhuset's wounds and participated in Brishen's rescue. And he had volunteered to become a Wraith king and fight alongside the Khaskem against the *galla*.

And yet you dislike him, an inner voice admonished her.

Another added a mocking rebuttal. *Because he's dangerous. He makes you feel.*

"Be quiet," Anhuset muttered aloud, surprising a passing Kai soldier who gave her a puzzled look before darting away at her warning glare.

The small crowd of Kai paced alongside the visitors' horses, some calling out greetings in Common tongue. The three Beladine responded in the same language, bending to clasp clawed hands with their gloved ones, smiling their square tooth smiles. Someone said something Anhuset was too far away to hear, and the margrave tilted his head back to laugh, the sound echoing through the bailey. He had always been comfortable around the Kai, unfazed by their more feral appearances.

And he had never made any secret of his attraction to the dour sha-Anhuset.

Anhuset scowled and purposefully maneuvered her way through the bailey so that she could observe without being seen by Saggara's newly arrived guests. The last thing she wanted was Saggara's curious

Kai watching as Serovek tried to charm her with his teasing smiles and frank admiration.

He motioned to his retainers and they all dismounted to stand amid the growing crowd. The retainers disappeared from her view, but Lord Pangion didn't. The Kai were a tall, lithe people, taller than most humans, yet he stood taller than those surrounding him, his broad shoulders enhanced even more by the heavy clothing he wore to ward off the cold. For all his size, he moved with surprising grace, and that acknowledgment sent odd flutters through her ribcage. An irritated hiss whistled between her teeth. Handsome to others. Not to her.

A subtle change in both his expression and his stance made Anhuset instinctively slip into the narrow space between a tower of hay bales and one of the walls belonging to the redoubt's cooperage. His eyes narrowed, their quick flickers from side to side as he scanned the yard making her shudder a little. A warrior well trained, he'd sensed he was being closely observed, regarded with an intensity far greater than those who stood much closer to him.

His gaze passed over the spot where she hid. . . gods' bollocks, she was hiding from the Beladine Stallion! The realization made her lurch out of the concealing spot, her back snapping straight, chin up as she glared at the man who had neither seen her nor spoken to her, yet had already managed to practically set her hair on fire from annoyance.

Serovek didn't pause in his reconnoitering of the bailey, but once more his manner changed, shoulders relaxing, eyes still narrowed but with amusement now as a faint smirk played across his mouth. The uncomfortable certainty that he'd seen her lurking behind the horse fodder made her growl. She straightened her tunic with a jerk, prepared to march across the yard and, as Brishen's second, formally welcome him to Saggara.

She never got the chance. The crowd moved as a single wave, carrying Serovek and his men away from her on a crest toward the palace's entrance from which Brishen and Ildiko emerged. The prince regent and his wife greeted their guest first with formal vows, then more affectionate clasps of forearms and embraces. Brishen clapped

Serovek on the back, ushering him inside. Just before they disappeared from view, the margrave glanced over his shoulder and unerringly found Anhuset among the milling crowd. A quick tip of his head and another of those teasing smiles told her he'd known she was there all along.

Before the supper gathering that evening, she stood in her small bedroom in the main barracks and glared at the chest holding the garb she kept in reserve for more formal occasions. Were it strictly to her preference, she'd attend tonight's feast wearing her usual everyday clothing of homespun and leather in muted colors of brown, gray, and black. Fashion never interested her, and she was far more inclined to admire the temper of a well-made sword than the cut of a finely sewn tunic or the sparkle of a necklace.

The lone candle in the room provided just enough light to illuminate the delicate embroidery on the fold of emerald green fabric in the chest. Anhuset reached inside and pulled it out, shaking the cloth so that it unfurled into one of the court tunics she'd worn on those rare occasions when she'd been summoned to make an appearance before her uncle, King Djedor.

She shrugged. It would do as well as anything else in the chest, and at least she didn't have to tolerate the contemptuous stares of a herd of useless Kai aristocracy or the malevolent scrutiny of Queen Secmis. The *galla* had almost wrecked the Kai kingdom, and many had died in the onslaught, but Anhuset didn't grieve the deaths of the old court, especially its monarchs. She had watched in silent triumph as Brishen, as a Wraith king, destroyed his mother, the queen, once and for all. Good riddance.

After a hasty sponge bath and a futile attempt at taming her hair into something a little more elaborate than a simple plait or queue, she dressed and finally paused to stare at herself in the cloudy mirror she'd bought from an itinerant trader years earlier. She'd ceded the battle to tame her hair and left it loose except for a pair of tiny braids at her temples. The tunic's color emphasized the silver of her hair, the garment's cut, her height. A wide leather belt, replete with buckles and metal rings from which to tie sheaths and carry weaponry, circled her waist. Protocol and civility demanded she leave her sword behind in favor of carrying two daggers. Plain black trousers and ankle boots favored by the Kai completed the ensemble.

Anhuset smoothed a hand down the tunic, chasing away non-existent wrinkles. This was as good as it would get. She was no court lady, nor was she a great beauty, and gatherings like these were ordeals to be suffered rather than enjoyed. She attended to please her cousin, nothing more. Still, she fiddled with the tiny braids and adjusted the belt before giving her reflection a dour smile. "Just Anhuset," she said. "Nothing more, nothing less."

The bailey was sparsely populated as she made her way to the manor house and the great hall where Brishen planned to host the supper in Serovek's honor. To avoid being formally announced by the steward, Mesumenes, she skirted the main entrance in favor of the one that took her through the kitchens and down a set of corridors, exchanging quick greetings with servants as they hurried back and forth between the kitchens and the hall. A familiar voice calling her name brought her to an abrupt halt.

"Why the hurry, sha-Anhuset?"

Ignoring the flutters dancing within her ribcage, she schooled her features into an impassive mask before pivoting to face Serovek. She bowed. "Margrave," she said, congratulating herself on the blandness of her tone.

He strolled closer, his steps light on the stone floor despite the boots he wore. He raised a palm in question. "What? Not Serovek? Or even Lord Pangion?" Laugh lines crinkled the skin at the corners of his eyes. "We each shared an end of the same sword once."

At his reference to the time she stabbed him, her back went so stiff, it audibly cracked. The amusement that often graced his features when he spoke to her disappeared at her reaction, and a line creased the space between his black eyebrows as he met her slitted gaze.

"Your humor leaves much to be desired," she growled before

turning her back on him and striding away. The weight of his stunned silence followed her the entire length of the corridor.

Supper lasted an eternity. Brishen had invited a few of his ministers, those whose enclaves bordered the Beladine lands Serovek governed. The discussions at the tables, carried out in Common tongue for the benefit of their guests, revolved around the coming spring planting on either side of the border, reassurances from both Brishen and Serovek that no *galla* had been seen, the ever-present dangers of those who raided across both territories, stealing livestock or food stores, what neighbors battled over water rights to a particular stream or a communal well. There were inquiries into the infant queen's health and that of Ildiko, who had stepped into the role of motherhood. No one spoke of abandoned Haradis or the fact the Kai still reeled from the sudden and unexplained loss of magic for every male old enough to grow his first beard or female who'd had her first bleed.

The first was still a raw wound, the second a secret Anhuset suspected every Kai instinctively knew to keep from any human. She had no doubt that word of this particular disaster would get out eventually, and the human kingdoms surrounding Kai territory would find a way to exploit it.

She picked at the food on her plate, dividing her attention between the talk around her and the activity of all who entered or exited the great hall. If Ildiko were sitting next to her, she'd sternly remind Anhuset that she was no longer on duty. And Anhuset would brush the admonishment aside. She was always on duty.

As much as she tried to resist the temptation, she couldn't help but turn her gaze to where Lord Pangion sat beside Brishen, deep in conversation with all those who sat nearby. Those Kai who were meeting him for the first time were obviously impressed not only with his eagerness to eat scarpatine pie, but his ability to filet the hostile insect without getting pierced by its nasty barb and shot full of venom.

He watched her as well, his stare falling on her numerous times throughout the meal, even as he answered the many questions Brishen's ministers peppered him with regarding Belawat's plans for a new dam farther upstream or its willingness to trade with the Kai farmers with homesteads on its borders. Anhuset looked past him, pretending that deep blue gaze didn't draw her.

As the meal progressed and finally came to an end, her anger waned. Her reason told her he hadn't meant to offend her in any way, that he was likely puzzled by her reaction to his teasing. There was no way he could know how much that terrible moment they shared bothered her.

Once supper concluded and the various guests went their separate ways, Brishen motioned for Anhuset to join him, Ildiko, and Serovek in a small antechamber he typically reserved for more private meetings.

She was the last one in and closed the door behind her with a soft click, staying nearby to listen for any lurkers outside who might decide it was a good idea to eavesdrop.

The other three took seats at the table in the center of the room, and Ildiko served tea from a steaming pot a servant had delivered.

Brishen toasted his guest. "Tell us more of this letter you received from the monk's brother."

Serovek fished a folded parchment from an inner pocket of his vest and passed it to Brishen to read. "He doesn't go into detail, only saying the Jeden Order has asked that Megiddo be returned to them. No explanation as to why."

Brishen quickly scanned the correspondence before glancing up. "You told me once the Jeden Order worships a single god and are skilled in warfare. Anything else?" He set the letter down and refilled his cup, offering to do the same for Ildiko, who declined with a quick shake of her head.

Serovek didn't refuse, holding up his cup for a second pour. "Besides the fact they tread on heretic territory? No."

Anhuset spoke up then, addressing Brishen. "He is one of theirs. Why wouldn't they want him back?" Though she didn't mention it, she hoped Megiddo's sword might be returned to the monks along with his body. Nothing good would come of remnant magic spun up from the spellwork of a long-dead Kai wizard dabbling in necromancy.

An arrested expression passed over her cousin's face. "Maybe," he said in a studied, noncommittal voice. "Maybe not."

She frowned, slipping into bast-Kai. "He isn't your responsibility, Highness."

He returned her frown. "I disagree. He's bound by Kai magic."

"Which you…" Anhuset paused, the words "no longer wield," heavy on her tongue before she rolled them back. "Can't control with him because his soul is no longer in this world." She met Ildiko's worried gaze, remembering the phantasmal blue glow that had passed through Brishen's eye earlier.

Serovek refused a third helping of tea and pushed his empty cup away. "Your *sha* is right, Brishen," he said in Common tongue. "I wanted to tell you about the message but not to place some misbegotten guilt on your shoulders. The monk's order and his family agree he's best residing with the other monks. Is it our right to refuse the request?"

Brishen remained frustratingly unmoved by the argument. "Possibly. The Jeden Order is located in a strife-ridden area. You said so yourself. The monks reclaimed their territory stolen by the warlord Chamtivos, but there are still skirmishes there."

Serovek waved away his concerns. "I'll have a contingent of troops with me to accompany Megiddo's body to the monastery. Why anyone would want to make off with a soulless body defies reason, but they'll have to work hard and be willing to bleed a great deal if they want him."

Anhuset saw her chance. She left her vigil by the door to stand on the opposite side of the table from Brishen. "I can go with them to represent the Kai so the Beladine, and the monks know we honor the sacrifice one of their own made for us. I can also take his sword with us as well and deliver it to the monks."

The words were barely out of her mouth before Brishen said, "Absolutely not. The sword stays."

There was a finality to his tone that made even Serovek's eyebrows climb. Brishen was a genial man, yet there was in his voice a reminder that he was also a toughened warrior, a man who had destroyed his own mother's corrupt soul without hesitation and battled abominations born of Elder magic. The prince regent of Bast-Haradis.

Again, Anhuset sought Ildiko's gaze. The *hercegesé* gave a faint shake of her head, her features pale and disappointed, but she chose not to argue Brishen's edict. Megiddo's ensorceled sword would remain at Saggara.

In an obvious attempt to break the tension in the room, Serovek turned to Anhuset, a smirk tilting the corners of his mouth a little. "A Kai warrior in our party. We won't exactly blend in when we travel."

She snorted. "When have you ever blended in?" She'd seen it for herself. Lord Pangion's size alone commanded attention, but it was his demeanor that drew the eye more than anything. Despite his ugly human face, he possessed a presence that assured he'd never pass through a crowd unnoticed.

He chuckled, giving her a slight bow. "I yield the point to you. It will be a privilege to have Saggara's famed sha-Anhuset join us."

No longer stiff in his chair as if he braced to do battle, Brishen shook his head and gave his second a dubious look. "Try not to kill him before you're halfway there," he said. "I've been out of a war for less than a year. Don't thrust me into another one by dismembering a Beladine margrave."

Anhuset opened her mouth to assure him she could control her temper, but Serovek interrupted her. "And I'd prefer to keep all my arms and legs attached to the rest of me, thank you." He laughed at her narrow-eyed glare. "I can't win every battle with just this handsome face."

Forgetting her unspoken promise to rein in her temper, Anhuset growled and pointed a claw-tipped finger at Serovek while glaring at Brishen.

"My Lord Pangion," Ildiko said, her wide grin exposing small, pearly horse teeth. "You do enjoy courting danger."

Brishen echoed Serovek's amusement with a laugh of his own. "My wife has the right of it, friend." He passed the letter from Megiddo's brother back to Serovek. "I can send a company of troops along with Anhuset. I'd go myself except I'm needed here more." A vague thread of regret wove through his voice.

"That won't be necessary." Serovek tucked the letter back into his vest. "A bigger party than ten, and we'll be seen as something more threatening than travelers, especially with a group of toothy Kai accompanying us. One will be enough to make anyone think twice about annoying us. More than that, and we might have difficulty reaching our destination without a brawl or two." He offered another half bow to Anhuset. "And I've seen your second fight. She's worth at least three soldiers. We'll be well defended."

She didn't preen under so obvious a compliment, but it was difficult. He'd always been forthright in his admiration for her, and his praise in her martial skills set a small fire to burning gently in her gut. "I'll do all in my power not to shame the Khaskem during our journey," she said in carefully neutral tones.

Both men snorted at that before Brishen said, "That has never been in question, cousin. And never will be." He turned back to the margrave. "When do you wish to leave, and where shall Anhuset meet you?"

"It'll take about five days to ready everything and leave instructions with my steward. Send sha-Anhuset to High Salure any time during then. We'll travel from there to Cermak's estate to retrieve the monk. Is this agreeable to you?"

Brishen looked to Anhuset, who nodded. "Yes," they both said together.

Ildiko was the first to rise from her place at the table. "You'll spend the day with us, my lord? I have several rooms readied for guests. Saggara is finally empty of the crowds. You have your choice of chambers."

Anhuset clasped her hands behind her back and adopted a bored look. Inside, she warred with herself, one part hoping he'd take up

Ildiko's invitation, the other hoping he declined. She refused to give credence to the bubble of disappointment when he declined.

Serovek rounded the table to take Ildiko's hand and bowed over her knuckles before straightening with a smile. "Tempting as that is, I'll take the hours to return to High Salure. I'd like to get this done without delay." He glanced at Brishen. "Though if you don't mind, I'll pay my respects to the little queen regnant before I leave."

The prince nodded. "Of course. I'll take you to see her. Ildiko is the only human she's seen so far. She'll be fascinated."

Or frightened, Anhuset thought, but kept her silence.

Serovek saluted Ildiko. "As always, it's a pleasure to see you again, Highness. Your hospitality has no equal." He turned to Anhuset. She half-expected that teasing smirk, but he only saluted a second time, his voice serious. "Sha-Anhuset. Until we meet again."

Anhuset returned the salute, disappointed by the lack of his good-natured taunting. "Margrave."

The two men exited the room, leaving Ildiko and Anhuset alone. Anhuset stared at the closed door for a moment before speaking in a low voice. "There is no possible way you'll claw that sword out of Brishen's grip. Did you see his expression when I suggested it?"

Ildiko sighed. "I did. It will have to stay here for now, though I wish it otherwise. This isn't surrender just yet. Let me see if I can talk him around to the idea of at least taking the sword to Emlek or giving it to Serovek to house. Anywhere but at Saggara." She rubbed her arms as if chilled. "No good can come of storing the blade here. I can feel it."

The two women parted ways then, Ildiko to join Brishen and Serovek, Anhuset to return to the barracks where she hastily stripped out of her formal garb for her more comfortable everyday wear. She bound her hair in a quick loop knot at the back of her head, shouldered on a cloak with hood to protect her eyes from the day's coming sunlight, and left her room for the redoubt's stables to join a contingent of others for guard duty along the shores of the Absu.

She found Serovek in the stableyard, giving direction to his men before they headed home to High Salure. Despite her concealing hood, he spotted her and waved her over to where he stood next to his horse.

"You should have taken the *hercegesé* up on her offer," she said. "You'll fall asleep in the saddle before you reach home."

"Not like it hasn't happened before." He patted the horse's neck. "Magas here can find his way home blindfolded." He raised one of those expressive black eyebrows. "Are you asking me to stay?"

He was back to teasing her. She bristled. "No."

He heaved a dramatic sigh. "Ah well. There's no joy without hope, even when it's dashed."

"You're going to vex me the entire trip to the monastery, aren't you?"

He grinned. "I hope to charm you the whole way so that you fall into my arms by the time we arrive."

"If you still have arms by then."

Stop it, she silently admonished herself. *You're only encouraging him with the repartee.*

To her surprise, his expression turned serious again. "I wish to offer you an apology."

That really did startle her. "For what?"

He scraped a hand down his face as if trying to find the right words. "For my clumsy humor earlier. I know I tease you, and I know it raises your hackles, but obviously I crossed into forbidden territory when we were in the corridor earlier. I didn't mean to offend."

They were on uncomfortable ground here, at least for her. While he provoked her in a playful way every time they crossed paths, she knew how to respond. Snarls and snaps and warning growls that only emboldened him. It was a dance where she knew the steps, a game in which she understood all the rules. This was neither of those, and she scrabbled for how to respond to his sincere regret.

"You didn't offend, not in the way you think. That time, when we all stood among the menhirs, when noble men were stabbing each other as a last resort to save the rest of us...no humor can be found in that, not even gallows·humor. As a soldier, I know what it is to take a life and have the act leave its scar, but stabbing you was different. What connects us is an awful thing, better to be forgotten than jested about."

She clamped her lips shut after that, certain she sounded like a bumbling fool unable to string three coherent words together. But she didn't look away from him as he stood there considering her in the punishing morning light.

His homely features softened, the blue of his eyes darkening until they were almost black. "Does it truly bother you so much?"

"Doesn't it bother you?"

He patted his flat midriff. "Well, I get an ache now and then to remind me you have good aim and a strong arm. But otherwise, no." He didn't reach out to her, but he drew closer until they were nearly toe to toe. "We did what needed doing, Anhuset." His voice was soft, mild. "You're a seasoned fighter, a *sha* in the Kai military. I always assumed you, of all people, understood that what's necessary can sometimes be brutal."

She did understand. "This was different."

His voice was even softer now, a caress across her forehead. "How so?"

The bailey was nearly empty, with only a minimal crowd of Kai going about the business of guard duty or clean-up as the redoubt settled down to slumber. The margrave's retainers lingered near the gate, politely looking elsewhere as they waited for their lord to complete whatever business remained with his Kai hosts. To Anhuset, it felt as if only she and Serovek occupied the space.

"It just is," she said. "I can't explain it, but I accept your apology."

She itched with the urge to spring away, far from this strangely enthralling human who annoyed and beguiled her by turns. The laugh lines that added such character to his features fanned from the corners of his eyes once more as he grinned. "I'm glad to hear it. We've a long journey ahead of us. I didn't fancy sleeping with my back to a wall every time I closed my eyes."

A betraying twitch of her mouth made her nostrils flare as she bit back an answering smile. "I only accepted your apology. I didn't promise not to tear your arms off before we reach the monastery."

His booming laughter made heads turn. Serovek stepped back, looped the reins across his horse's neck and swung gracefully into the saddle. "Farewell, firefly woman," he said from his lofty seat. "I look forward to our meeting again in a few days."

Anhuset remained in place as he and his retainers rode through the gates and away from Saggara, watching until they disappeared in the sun's radiance. His valediction echoed in her mind.

Firefly woman.

CHAPTER
THREE

Serovek watched the lone rider guide her horse up the steep path toward High Salure's barbican. Even were he not expecting her arrival, he would have recognized her anywhere simply by her posture in the saddle—tall, confident, and graceful. She was bundled against the cold in a heavy cloak with a hood to cover her hair and shield her face and eyes from the winter sun. High boots sheathed her legs to her lower thigh, adding extra warmth to the layers of trousers and tunic she wore. Her cloak shifted with the horse's motion, revealing glimpses of her hunting leathers. Her hands were bare. Gloves didn't work well when you possessed claws at the ends of your fingers.

That Brishen's second-in-command had volunteered to accompany him on the journey to deliver Megiddo's body to the Jeden monastery still surprised him, but he was no less pleased for it. The last time he'd been in sha-Anhuset's company for any length of time, they'd prepared to face a horde of ravenous demons, and she'd skewered him on the length of his own sword. He looked forward to hours less horrific and bloody spent with her and her acerbic wit.

As if she sensed his scrutiny, she raised her head. The yellow shine of her eyes glittered in the shadows of her hood as her gaze unerringly landed on him where he stood on the battlements, braced against the wind that howled down the mountainside and through the col. She lifted a hand in greeting before nudging her horse to a faster gait.

He left his frigid perch, taking the stairs that led down to the great hall in a narrow spiral. A wave of heat buffeted him as he passed the lit hearth. The candles in their sconces and the lamps hung from chains cast a welcoming glow across the room. Newly laid rushes smelled of dried lavender, combining with the scents of supper being prepared in the kitchens. For all that this was a military fortress in service to the Beladine kingdom, it was a lavish place much spoken about by the local gentry. Serovek, Lord Pangion, had spared no expense in turning High Salure into a stately home as well as a formidable fortress.

He met Anhuset at the entrance to the barbican, where a contingent of his men had gathered to observe the Kai woman's arrival. Some called out greetings, a handful meeting her halfway to walk beside her horse as they escorted her to the barbican. These soldiers had patrolled borders with her and the Kai who served with her, and several had aided in rescuing her liege from raiders paid to torture and kill him.

Sha-Anhuset had ever been forthright in her opinions regarding humans. They were hideous to look upon, possessed strange customs, and suffered from questionable culinary preferences. More than once, Serovek had choked down laughter at her obvious revulsion for human expression and behavior.

Despite that, she was also a warrior with an understanding and admiration for those who served in the role of soldier as she did, be they Kai or human. She returned his men's greetings, calling those she recognized by name, and wishing them good fortune in Common tongue so all could understand.

He saluted her when she finally stood before him, holding her horse's reins in one hand, and a decorative box in the other. "Sha-Anhuset," he said, not bothering to disguise his pleasure at seeing her here in his home. "Welcome to High Salure."

Faint consternation flitted across her sharp features. For all that she was graceful in her movements, she gave a stiff bow before offering him the box. He took it, cursing when it jumped in his hand. He almost dropped the thing before tightening his grip. Something inside the container thrashed against the sides and the top, scrabbling for a way out.

Anhuset's yellow eyes, without noticeable pupil or iris, lightened a shade, and her mouth turned up at one corner. "Margrave. A gift from the *herceges* and the *hercegesé*. A delicacy at a Kai table, as you've witnessed yourself."

Serovek edged open the lid for a peek, before slamming it closed when an armored tail tipped with a stinger that dripped black fluid jabbed at him. A collective gasp rose around him, and every soldier surrounding them took at least three steps back. He raised an eyebrow at Anhuset, who continued to watch him with that twist of amusement playing across her lips. "I'm very fond of scarpatine. And a female at that. Even better."

He didn't lie. A notorious dish favored by the Kai and served at celebrations, dinners of state, and to important guests not too terrified to attempt eating it, was indeed one of his favorites. This was Brishen's nod to him in recognition not only of friendship, but also brotherhood. The only thing that confused him was the scarpatine itself. The Kai rarely used the females in the pie, only the males as the females were difficult to subdue and kill without getting stung, and their venom could be deadly. Were he not fast friends with Brishen and trusted him completely, Serovek might have wondered if the *herceges* weren't trying to do away with him.

As if she heard his thoughts, Anhuset gestured to the box. "I'm to relay the message from the *herceges* that he couldn't think of anyone more suited to battling an enraged female while enjoying the fight."

His laughter echoed through the bailey, while his men snickered around him. The box with the angry scarpatine inside jumped in his hand. "I've always liked your cousin. Now to convince my cook I pay him enough to make the pie." He held out the box to the soldier closest to him. "Take it to the kitchen."

The man hesitated, glancing from one side to the other, as if silently asking for volunteers to take on the task. None of his cohorts stepped forward. He gingerly reached for the box before grabbing it with both hands. It jerked in his grip, the scarpatine's tail striking the sides of the box with hard taps. The soldier took off for the kitchen at a jog, eager to be rid of his burden.

Another soldier offered to take Anhuset's horse for stabling. She untied the satchel from its place behind the saddle and slung it over her shoulder before leaving her mount to the man's care. Had it been any other woman, Serovek would have offered to carry her burden for her, but this was Anhuset. He didn't relish having his hand bitten off for the effort.

She paced him as they passed under the barbican and into the bailey. A busy place full of clamor and chaos, only the briefest pause in the noise marked her arrival before resuming.

"Watch your step," he told her, pointing to the depressions in the soft ground where rain had gathered from the day before, then iced over sometime during the night. Even with the sun high, those pools in the shade remained frozen. Winter had been long this year and spring slow to arrive.

He had never known her to be a chatty woman, though she never hesitated in expressing herself. Serovek was familiar enough with the Kai to know her taciturn manner was an individual trait and not one representative of the Kai in general. He didn't mind carrying the conversation. Anhuset didn't say much, but she had an expressive face and revealed a lot more than she was probably aware of and would be horrified to learn, especially from him. He bit back a smile.

"Did you have a good journey to High Salure?"

She shrugged. "Good enough. No one tried to kill me on my way here, though it's damn bright today."

He ushered her to the citadel's main entrance. "Let's get you out of the sunlight."

Someone on the other side had been waiting for them. The doors opened the moment Serovek's boot touched the threshold. One of his servants had snuffed out half the candles and lamps while he'd been outside. The great hall was no longer ambient but tenebrous, with most of its illumination emanating from the fire roaring in the hearth.

Beside him, Anhuset gave a small grunt. "You need not go through this trouble for me. I'm used to guard duty during the day. The brightness is an annoyance, that's all."

"Are you sure that's something you can cope with for a prolonged period? We'll be traveling by day, resting at night."

"I'm not human." By her tone, she might well have said, "I'm not diseased."

Serovek chuckled. "Implying you're not weak. Rumor has it the delicate Ildiko Khaskem took down one of your Kai assassins with a shutter pole. By herself."

They both paused at the foot of the stairwell. Anhuset dipped her head in acknowledgment of his strike. "Point taken." She raised an eyebrow when he stared at her. "Don't look so surprised. Just because you have a talent for annoying me like no other doesn't mean I won't recognize you as victor in an argument."

He let out a long, slow whistle. "Sha-Anhuset, you will never cease to amaze me."

The look she gave him would have withered a lesser man to a desiccated husk. "It isn't that momentous, Lord Pangion," she said in the driest tones.

Despite the bleak purpose of their trip, it promised to be an entertaining one. Serovek grinned. Anhuset's sharp wit fascinated him as much as her appearance and demeanor. That fascination only strengthened with each interaction they shared. "Come. I'll show you to your room."

They ascended the tightly spiraling stairwell to the second floor, where the space opened up to a corridor lined in closed doors. Serovek led her to one and pushed it open to reveal a sumptuously appointed chamber illuminated only by the light spilling from the fire dancing merrily in the corner hearth. The windows were shuttered against the daylight and the cold, leaving shadows to pool in the niches and under the wall hangings.

"Will this suit?" he asked. "If not, there are other rooms to choose from. My staff can have another ready for you in short order." He'd inspected this space once it was readied, hoping she'd approve. Anhuset, though, often surprised him.

A flicker of unease darted across her face as she took in the room's trappings. "You went to too much trouble. I would have been fine with a bed in the barracks."

He had half-expected such a reaction. The Kai woman was far more comfortable among humbler surroundings, but something had urged him to offer her the best at his disposal. Maybe a vanity on his part. He didn't dwell long on the niggle of disappointment.

"If you'd prefer the barracks, I'll see to it something is made ready for you, but I hope you won't decline an invitation to have supper with me."

Anhuset shook her head. "This is fine. No need wasting someone's labor and making them work to prepare a second place for me to sleep." A slight turn of her head alerted him she watched him from the corner of her eye. "I despise frivolous nitwits who'll put a household in an uproar just to appease their whims."

"Then we're of like minds. But you still haven't said if you'll dine with me."

"What are you serving?"

The unmistakable note of dread in her voice made his eyebrows rise. He couldn't resist teasing her. "Join me and find out. Or are you afraid?"

Her own silvery eyebrows crashed together. "Name the hour."

They agreed to meet in the great hall at sundown. While he would have liked to spend the rest of the day with her, offering himself as tour guide to the citadel, he had last-minute preparations and plans to make with his steward.

Anhuset dismissed his apology with a flick of her hand. "Not necessary, margrave. I've been here before as you know. I'm familiar enough with the grounds." She set her satchels next to the curtained bed and scraped back her hood to reveal her hair, white as new-fallen snow and gleaming even in the dim firelight. "Your *marhskalk* owes me a chance to win back money I lost to him in the last dice game we played together."

For a moment, Serovek fiercely envied his master-at-arms, Carov. He'd much prefer to spend the next few hours in Anhuset's company himself, engaged in a friendly game of chance, even if she managed to clean out his treasury. He'd especially welcome a sparring match with her. She was a formidable fighter—he'd seen that firsthand—and would make a worthy opponent.

He accompanied her downstairs and into the bailey where she joined Carov and a group of soldiers training in the practice yard. A few called out to her, inviting her to participate in a mock battle. Her yellow eyes caught fire. She bowed briefly to Serovek, promising to meet him at their appointed time for supper.

He left her to meet with his steward as she shrugged off her cloak, draping it on a nearby post, to reveal she was well-armed and ready for combat. Serovek jested with his men to keep the injuries to a minimum.

His steward Bryzant waited for him in his study. An efficient man and an ambitious one as well, Bryzant was a high-born younger son from one of the more prominent Beladine families. He'd gladly accepted the position of steward in Serovek Pangion's remote citadel. High Salure was far away from the Beladine court and its hub of social and political machinations. Few would want to spend years in the kingdom's hinterlands bordering Bast-Haradis, even in service to the highly respected margrave. Serovek had been surprised by Bryzant's enthusiastic response to his invitation to become his steward.

Now, ten years into the role, he had proven himself invaluable, making sure the fortress's day-to-day administration ran smoothly. He'd been the one to oversee the non-military tasks when Serovek left to fight the *galla* alongside Brishen and the other Wraith kings. Serovek intended he do so again while he made the journey to deliver Megiddo's ensorceled body to the Jeden Order.

"My lord," Bryzant said, trying to bow as he entered the study, arms filled to overflowing with scrolls. "I need signatures from you for supply requisitions, among other things."

Serovek neatly plucked several of the scrolls out of Bryzant's arms and set them on the nearby table. By the look of it, he was in for hours of unavoidable drudgery. Too bad he couldn't put his signature and seal on documents while on horseback.

The two men sat across from each other, Serovek with quill in hand while Bryzant passed him the first of many pieces of parchment. "I've sent requisitions in as you requested for additional leather, wool, and food stores. We're waiting for three bids to come in for all of them." Bryzant pointed to the list of names on the sheet. "Two are local, one is from the capital. That one will be more expensive, of course."

"But possibly better quality, unless the vendor assumes we're ignorant provincials and tries to gouge us with high prices for poor product." Serovek scowled. "Have you seen examples of the others' goods?"

Bryzant shook his head. "Not yet. I wanted to wait until you left for the monastery in case you needed anything beforehand." He set the vendor list aside, replacing it with another sheet of parchment, this one with a much longer list to review. "Do you know how long you might be gone, my lord?"

Not long enough, Serovek thought, eyeing the parchment in front of him with resigned distaste. While the administration of High Salure mostly fell to his steward, leaving Serovek to the tasks of defense of the borders and diplomacy with his Kai neighbors, Serovek kept a close eye on things. He'd witnessed and heard of too many instances in which a dishonest steward robbed his overlord blind or sent him into penury through mismanagement.

Given the choice, he would much rather spend his time on patrol, sparring, or battling demons alongside the Kai *herceges* or, even better, playing a cutthroat dice game with sha-Anhuset. He disliked the drudgery of stewardship. He disliked the notion of thievery under his very nose even more. Bryzant had done a fine job in the role these last ten years, giving Serovek no reason to doubt his honesty, his fealty, or his abilities. Still, it was best to remain diligent.

"No more than a month, I think," he replied to Bryzant's question. "I doubt the monks wish to act as our hosts any longer than necessary, and the Khaskem will want his *sha* back in short order."

The sun was well on its way toward the horizon before Serovek finally broke free of his steward as well as those other officers of his household, including one quietly seething cook who demanded to know how exactly he was supposed to cook and serve the vile insect bestowed upon him earlier and not die from the effort. Serovek's puzzled shrug and short "Just bash it with a club," didn't calm the man's outrage. Certain the cook contemplated every manner of butchering him behind the slit-eyed stare he leveled on Serovek, the margrave chose strategic retreat and left the kitchen to find his guest.

He had no compunction to disguise his interest in sha-Anhuset. From the first moment he met her, she'd drawn him like a moth to a blazing lamp, and he didn't care that he might burn to ash if he got too close. She was prickly—at least with him—as well as dour. Unwavering in her devotion to the Kai regent, she represented the Kai military and the physical prowess of the soldiers who served at Saggara in the finest manner. She wore her strength and her confidence as easily as she wore her armor, and Serovek sometimes wondered if any weakness existed behind her fierce expression and distinctively beautiful features. Should she ever choose to bond with a husband, the man would have to possess an iron-plated backbone to equal her.

His effort to break free of administrative shackles failed in the end. He'd only made it to the front entrance's threshold when he heard Bryzant shout his name. He turned to see the steward racing toward him, pale and wide-eyed with panic.

"My lord! My lord, wait! We have a problem!"

His plea was joined by a chorus of shouts and screams erupting from the direction of the kitchen, along with the dissonant bang of pots and pans slamming into furniture or the floor.

"What in the gods' names is going on?" Serovek met Bryzant in the hall's center and just as quickly strode past him as he hurried toward the source of the commotion. The steward jogged to keep up.

"The scarpatine," he said between pants. "It's gotten loose."

Serovek halted and glared at the man. "Are you serious?" At the other's nod, he cursed loud and long and charged into the kitchen.

Chaos greeted his arrival. Overturned pots and broken ceramic lay scattered across a floor made slippery from puddles of spilled soup and trampled vegetables. Three of the scullery maids stood atop one of the preparation tables, all armed with weapons that included a cleaver, a skillet, and a raw goose leg.

Those still on the ground joined the cook in ransacking the rest of the destroyed kitchen, lamplight glinting off their knives as they hunted for his lordship's lethal delicacy. No one noticed Serovek's presence.

He leaned down to speak softly to Bryzant. "Stay here and make sure no one accidentally stabs or clubs themselves or each other. And keep the door closed. I'll return in a moment."

Bryzant nodded, his eyes darting around the room as he searched for any suspect movement amid the destruction.

Serovek eased out of the kitchen, closing the door gently behind him before bolting for the bailey. He found Anhuset in short order, sitting amid a cluster of soldiers, a small heap of coins beside her as she watched Carov roll a set of bone dice into the center of their makeshift circle.

She glanced up and instantly gained her feet, abandoning the game without hesitation. "What's wrong?"

"The scarpatine has escaped." He expected at least a huff of derisive laughter from her at her host's carelessness, but all she did was bend to gather and pocket her winnings. "Any idea what room it's in?"

"Still in the kitchen." He gave a brief nod to the soldiers who'd risen as well and motioned for them to stay where they were. "The maids are standing on the tables, and the cook is stabbing at anything that moves. What's the best way to catch Brishen's fine gift?"

As tall as she was, Anhuset had a much easier time matching his pace than Bryzant did as they headed back to the fortress. "Use yourself as bait. I'll do it. I've done it before. It's easy enough if you're quick."

That sounded ominous, and Serovek wanted to ask her what she planned to do and how often scarpatines terrorized the kitchen staff at Saggara, but they reached the scene of mayhem before he had a chance.

The kitchen was in an even worse state than when he left it only moments earlier, and Bryzant had joined the maids perched on the preparation table, his weapon of choice, a rolling pin.

At Anhuset's sharp whistle, everyone froze. All gazes settled on her as she held up a slender finger tipped with a sharp black claw. Her eyes shone like gold coins. "Stay still and quiet," she said. "Otherwise I won't be able to hear the scarpatine."

No one argued, and all watched with wide eyes and bated breath as Anhuset pulled a knife from a sheath on her belt and made a shallow cut on the underside of her forearm. Blood trickled from the wound to splatter on the floor in crimson drops. She walked a few steps in one direction, leaving the sanguine equivalent of breadcrumbs in her wake. The silence in the kitchen breathed even when the occupants did not.

Her patience and bloodletting were rewarded when a scrabbling, clicking noise rose from under the shelter of a corner cupboard. A pair of black pincers emerged first, their ends snapping together. The scarpatine inched forward, revealing the rest of its armored body, including a tail that arched over its length, venom dripping from the tip to drizzle down the segmented carapace. Its back legs were longer than the front to accommodate a pair of venom sacs the size of hen's eggs. Five pairs of eyes on short stalks swiveled in multiple directions before locking onto the drip trail of blood Anhuset had left on the floor.

A mass shudder swept the crowd. Even Serovek, who thoroughly enjoyed the Kai delicacy that was scarpatine pie, swallowed back a knot of revulsion when the insect's proboscis emerged from a space between its jaws to suck up the blood.

Anhuset spared a glance for the cook, who stood nearby. "Hand me your apron very slowly," she said in a quiet voice. At his uncomprehending stare, her tone sharpened. "Now."

Serovek tensed when the man did as she ordered, but in quick, jerky motions. The movement alarmed the scarpatine, which whipped around with a hiss to face this new threat and leaped at the cook.

Once more, pandemonium erupted as people not already standing on the furniture leaped to any elevated space they could reach. A few tried to escape the kitchen altogether, only to find themselves facing Serovek's daunting form blocking the door. His glare dared them to try and shove past. There was no way he'd open the door and chance the scarpatine escaping into another part of the citadel. They'd never find and capture it.

The creature was fast, but Anhuset was faster. She darted after the scarpatine, leaping over upended chairs and broken crockery while eluding the flailing elbows of terrified scullions.

A pounding on the kitchen door vibrated the wood against Serovek's back. Voices called from the other side, inquiring, demanding entrance. "Margrave, what's happening?"

Serovek held the door shut and narrowed his eyes in warning as three of the younger scullions—lads no more than twelve or thirteen—considered their chances at going through him to get out of the kitchen. Their fear of the scarpatine was fast overriding their deference to their liege. "All is well," he bellowed over his shoulder to Carov on the other side. "Just give us a few moments."

Anhuset had cornered the scarpatine not far from the hearth. Its tail struck at her, flinging droplets of black venom to sizzle on the floor planks. She danced out of the way, avoiding most of the splatter. The droplets that landed scorched the leather of her boots, leaving behind an acrid scent and tendrils of oily dark smoke. Woman and insect feinted with each other, she avoiding the nasty barb on the end of the scarpatine's tail, the scarpatine dodging the apron she snapped toward it.

Suddenly, the scarpatine lunged at Anhuset. The maids screamed, the cook shouted, and the door smacked hard against Serovek's spine.

Anhuset twisted to the side and cast the apron like a net toward the creature. And missed. It darted back at the last moment, hissing its victory at avoiding the trap.

It lost no time in renewing its attack, launching once more at the Kai woman. This time Anhuset snatched the rolling pin out of a startled Bryzant's grip and brought it down like an executioner's ax on the scarpatine.

The insect burst under the impact, splattering guts, venom, and shattered carapace in every direction. A rancid odor, reminding Serovek of a battlefield under a summer sun, filled the kitchen.

People covered their noses and mouths with their hands or aprons. The unmistakable sound of retching replaced the shouting. Serovek, who was rarely plagued with a weak stomach, even at the most gruesome sights, felt his somersault in warning.

Unfazed by the smell or the slimy detritus of smashed scarpatine, Anhuset tossed the ruined rolling pin into the hearth and inspected her boots where wisps of smoke drifted off new scorch marks left by the venom splatter. She glanced at Serovek. "You owe me a new pair of boots, margrave." She didn't wait for his answer, but turned her attention to the others.

"Check your clothing." She pointed to her boots to emphasize the importance of that command. "If any of the venom is on it, don't touch it with your bare hands. Cut your garb off if you have to. As you can see, the venom burns anything it touches. And someone get me a shovel so I can scoop this up and bury it." She waved a casual hand at the smoking insect carcass as if it were as harmless as a dust ball.

"Can't you just throw it in the fire?" Bryzant asked, still perched on the table.

"Only if you want to vomit up your insides once it starts to burn and make Lord Pangion's home uninhabitable for a week." She returned her attention to Serovek. "I'm afraid there will be no pie for you, Lord Pangion. Smashed scarpatine means spoiled meat."

He straightened from the door to give his guest a quick bow. The kitchen looked like the aftermath of a whirlwind's visit, but it was now at least safe to open the door. "We've squandered the Khaskem's generous gift," he said. His statement earned a few disbelieving coughs as well as an indignant snort or two. "But we thank you, sha-Anhuset, for taking care of the problem."

As soon as Serovek shoved aside the bar holding the door closed, Carov and a half dozen soldiers stampeded inside, brandishing an array of weapons to save their master and his servants from the monster menacing them. They halted as a group just inside the threshold, awestruck.

"My gods," the master-at-arms breathed out, eyes wide. "What happened?"

"A hard-fought battle with supper," Serovek replied. "Sha-Anhuset won."

The meal that evening was a more humble affair than he originally planned. After the disaster in the kitchen and the colossal cleanup that followed, it was a wonder they ate at all. He considered it prudent to simply avoid the cook and his many knives before the man decided it might be a fine idea to serve his lordship's own heart back to him and his Kai guest on his best platter.

Anhuset sat to Serovek's left at the table, the only two people brave enough to linger in the great hall. She contentedly cleaned her plate and went back for seconds, despite an initial hesitation that had her sniffing suspiciously at some of the covered dishes the servants set before her.

"I had hoped to offer you a more laudable feast than this," Serovek said, gesturing to the plates of cured meats, eggs, cheese, bread and butter. A humble repast and one guaranteed to garner disdainful sniffs from even the lowliest Beladine gentryman.

Anhuset was not Beladine gentry. She shrugged. "There's nothing wrong with anything here. It's good food." Her features pinched into a disgusted scowl. "I'm just thankful you didn't serve those vile, maggoty things humans seem to favor with their supper."

He blinked. Maggoty things? He tried to recall what common food resembled something as repulsive as a cooked maggot. Nothing came to mind. "We don't eat maggots, at least not that I'm aware of."

"They aren't really maggots." She downed a swallow of ale before continuing. "They just look like them. Hand-sized with a thin brown skin that hides a soft inside, which turns to a white mush when it's cooked. It reminds me a little of candle wax and tastes like dirt." She shuddered. "Brishen almost didn't survive his wedding day because of them. His entire retinue contemplated assassination because we had to eat them so as not to insult our Gauri hosts."

An image of the food she described filled his mind, and a burst of laughter escaped him. "You're talking about a potato!" The bland, common potato. The Kai viewed it with the same aversion that most humans viewed scarpatine pie. Serovek laughed even harder at the notion.

"Whatever it's called, it's revolting. The entire ride here, I worried I'd have to eat another one at High Salure. I was prepared to claim a puny gut and skip supper entirely." She speared half an egg with her eating knife and held it up to him in salute. "I thank you for the small mercy of not serving one to me."

Serovek returned the salute with a lift of his goblet. "I thank you for saving my servants from the scarpatine."

A tiny smile flitted across her mouth. Her lips drew back a fraction, exposing the white points of her teeth. Like her claws, they were among the more obvious and intimidating reminders that she wasn't human, but a member of the last Elder race still occupying these lands. Indomitable. Fierce. Fading with every generation born. The last wasn't common knowledge, and Serovek only knew of it from his stint as a Wraith king. He'd be surprised if, in a few centuries, there were any Kai left. The thought saddened him.

"You've gone from laughter to melancholy in less time than it takes me to drain a good ale," Anhuset said. "You never before struck me as moody."

Truth be told, he wasn't the same man he'd been a year ago. He still appreciated a good joke or turn of phrase, still enjoyed a good romp between the sheets with an enthusiastic bed partner and a fast gallop on his favorite horse, and could still laugh easily at the odd humor of life itself. But a darkness ran through him now, a shallow stream of gloom he couldn't shake off, no matter how much he tried. He knew its source: Megiddo's ghastly fate and his own guilt in not being able to save the monk.

He pushed aside the haunting memory of Megiddo's eyes as the *galla* dragged his eidolon into the void of their prison. Serovek shook away the thought. There lay the stuff of nightmares, and they had no place here at his table.

"I'm as predictable as the sunrise," he told Anhuset and chuckled at her snort. "I was just thinking you don't smile much. You should. Your features are made for it." He didn't fabricate. There was an austerity to her face that was softened by her toothy smile, and unlike many, he wasn't intimidated by the sight of her pointed teeth.

"Like this," she said, baring her ivories to the back molars in a wolfish grin.

Serovek rolled his eyes and coughed his laughter into his goblet when she reared back in her seat, grin evaporating. She stared at him as if he'd suddenly grown a third arm or an eye in the middle of his forehead.

"Are any of you aware of just how hideous doing that makes you?" she said.

He toasted her a second time. "Only to the Kai, sha-Anhuset."

The expression of annoyance was so common among humans, no one thought anything of it. Until he witnessed Brishen's involuntary reaction to Ildiko's eye rolls, he'd never even noticed the habit. He'd been careful since then to guard his own expressions whenever he visited Saggara. In the comfort of his own home, he'd forgotten. Anhuset had reacted with the expected loathing.

Serovek shrugged inwardly. She wasn't a fragile thing. She'd recover and adjust. He had no intention of tiptoeing around her on this trip or demanding his men do the same. She would resent it if he did.

After supper, he invited her to join him in the same study where he'd met with his steward to discuss the route they planned to take to the monastery. Once there, he unrolled a detailed map on the table for their perusal, pointing to various landmarks that dotted the way.

Anhuset stood beside him, studying the map as he traced the meandering line that marked the flow of the Absu river along the borders shared by the Kai and the Beladine before it turned east toward Bast-Haradis.

"We'll take a barge down a portion of the Absu and then up one of its tributaries until that branches at a shallower stream. From there, it's by horseback all the way. We can transport Megiddo by wagon and then by sled if necessary. There will still be snow in some places."

"I have better sight in the dark than you do," she said. "If we travel by day, I can scout ahead at night once we stop so we know what's ahead at daybreak. I can sleep in the saddle if need be while we travel."

Her statement wasn't a boast. Any soldier worth his sword could sleep on horseback when necessary. He'd lost count of the times he'd done so himself. "Do you want an extra scout? I have one who's good in both daylight and at night."

She tried—and failed—to hide her pique at the suggestion. "No. I'll cover ground faster on my own."

"Fair enough." He didn't insist. She had her pride, and he trusted her abilities. "Should you change your mind, don't hesitate to say so." He'd grow old and die waiting for such a thing, but the offer was there. She gave a quick nod, her stance relaxing a little as she returned to studying the map.

They spent another half hour discussing the distance they wanted to cover each day and when they expected to return to their respective homes. Despite the sudden clenching in his gut at the idea, he extended another offer to Anhuset.

"The fork in the Absu that will take us closer to the monastery is just north of Haradis." She visibly flinched when he spoke of the Kai capital. "If you wish it, we can sail a little farther south so you can reconnoiter the city and report its state back to Brishen. It will be a simple thing to bring the barge around and sail north again to the river's fork. We'd lose a day at most, and the monks haven't specified an exact date for when they want Megiddo."

She stilled next to him, deep in contemplation. Her eyes were pools of firefly light when she fixed her gaze on him, a hesitancy in her expression he'd never seen before. "You wouldn't mind?"

"No." A whisper of memory grazed his mind. Sibilant laughter formed of ancient malice. "I wouldn't have offered if I did."

"Then yes, and I thank you for it." She gave him the Kai salute of rank and file to a commander. "I won't linger, and the Khaskem may find what I learn useful."

When they finished with their planning, he invited her to join him on the balcony that led off the large solar at the other end of the corridor from the study. "The view is worth suffering my company," he said and winked.

She sniffed. "I find you annoying, not insufferable. Yet."

Serovek stopped a servant with a request that wine be brought to the balcony. He pretended not to hear Anhuset's faint gasp when she stepped onto the balcony and the expansive view of the mountainside from High Salure's towering perspective.

A clear night and a bright moon cast the landscape into sharp silhouette, turning the tops of the evergreens covering the slopes into claw tips that jutted skyward. Torches lit in the bailey below flickered like jewels. To the north, the snow-capped Dramorins fenced the lands that separated the kingdom of Belawat from the flat plains of Bast-Haradis's hinterlands in the east. The liquid ribbon that was the Absu slithered through the landscape, the umbilicus of trade between three kingdoms and numerous cities and towns.

Serovek never grew tired of this view. If he actually lived to old age, he hoped his last days would be spent here, looking out at such grandeur, as glorious in the darkness as it was in the daylight. "What do you think?" he asked his silent companion.

She didn't answer him right away, and he took the time to admire her profile. The frosty moonlight sharpened the angles of her face so that her facial bones looked as if they had been carved from the shards of a dark mirror. Her long nose complimented the curve of her cheek-bone, and the hollow below it. She wore her hair shorter than the waist-length tresses Beladine women favored. Hers fell just below her shoulders. Fly-away strands caught in the wind that scoured the slopes to partially obscure her jaw. A few strands stuck to her lower lip before she pulled them aside with the flick of a claw tip.

Sha-Anhuset wasn't beautiful. Not in the way of Beladine women or even human women in general. Not even in the way of Kai women. But she was sublime, as majestic and unyielding as the distant Dramorins. And just as unconquerable. The first time Serovek had seen her at Saggara, he'd been awestruck. He was no less so now. Maybe even more as he learned more about her and had glimpsed the stalwart heart that beat beneath the armored breastplate.

Her lamplight gaze shifted to him. "Impressive," she finally said. "And easily defended."

He snorted. "Planning an invasion, madam?"

"Hardly. Brishen keeps me too busy at Saggara to make plans for conquering High Salure." A worry line marred her smooth forehead for a moment, though she said nothing more.

"I've no doubt of that. We'll all be experiencing ripple effects of the *galla* infestation, the Kai kingdom most of all." He didn't envy the Khaskem. That the kingdom of Bast-Haradis hadn't yet disintegrated was a credit to Brishen's even-handed rule as regent.

A statuesque study in light and shade, she turned to face him fully. "All the Kai owe you a debt of gratitude for fighting alongside the *herceges*. You sacrificed much. Suffered much."

Her voice echoed with memory. He knew what she recalled in her mind's eye because he saw it in his own. Her steady grip on his sword pommel, the resolute horror in her face when she'd skewered him on the blade and embraced him in her strong arms so he wouldn't fall. A shared intimacy of purposeful savagery in the service of a man trying to save a world from destruction. Nightmares of that moment still plagued Serovek. He suspected they plagued Anhuset as well.

"Not nearly as much as some."

"Megiddo."

He nodded. "And others. I've heard rumors. The Kai unable to capture the mortem lights of their dead, a loss of magic. All of that has something to do with the *galla*."

She'd gone stiff as a spear shaft while he spoke, and her expression closed as tightly against him as the door he'd barred to the kitchen earlier.

"I suppose so," she said in a flat voice. "If you're inclined to believe rumors."

He didn't press her to expound upon his commentary, and the tightness around her mouth warned him he'd find the endeavor a futile one if he tried. She had, however, confirmed what he'd begun to suspect. The *galla* were defeated and once more imprisoned, but that triumph had come with more than the price of Megiddo's sacrifice. The demons spawned by the ancient Gullperi had left their mark on the Kai in ways beyond the razing of Haradis.

She caught him by surprise when she abruptly changed the topic. "You're a wealthy margrave with influence. Why haven't you married?" Her sharp teeth gleamed white in the darkness at his wide-eyed stare.

He recovered quickly enough and matched her smile with a wry one of his own. Subtle verbal deflection wasn't her strong suit. "Who says I haven't?"

His question took her aback. He saw it in the way her fingers tightened on the stem of her wine goblet and the slight jerk of her shoulders. "Well then, are you or aren't you?"

Tonight was obviously a night for recollection. None of it cheerful.

He stared into the black pool of wine in his goblet, seeing the vision of a sweet face and brown eyes. He had cared for but not loved the woman he'd married. He'd instantly loved but never had a chance to know the daughter she bore him. He still grieved them both. "I was," he said. "A decade ago. She was proud. Beautiful. Long hair that she wore tied back with silk ribbons."

Anhuset's features eased, and she tilted her head to consider him as if he were suddenly a brand new enigma to her. "You like soft women."

He chuckled, welcoming her comment. "I like strong women. Soft…" He bowed to her. "Or not."

They were both quiet for a moment, staring at the shadow-shrouded mountainside that even the bright moon no longer illuminated.

"I'm not sure I'd know what to do with a hair ribbon," Anhuset finally said, addressing the stars above them.

"Probably strangle someone with it."

She choked on the wine she'd just sipped, and Serovek thumped her on the back until she quieted. Then she laughed, and he was lost.

There was the magic of the Kai, and then there was the sorcery of Anhuset's laughter. The purr of a cat mixed with the promise of a warm fire and the sleepy seduction of a satisfied lover, all bound together into a sound that rolled out of her throat and rasped past her lips to bewitch him.

"I will take that as a compliment and bid you good evening, margrave," she said, setting her half empty goblet down on the balcony's railing cap. "I'll see you at dawn?"

He remembered to nod, even as all the blood in his body rushed toward his groin. He'd bless the darkness for its concealment except for the fact his companion saw better at night than she did during the day. "Shall I send a servant to fetch you?"

She declined the offer and wished him a peaceful sleep. He watched her until she disappeared from sight.

Serovek groaned under his breath. "Peaceful sleep. Not likely," he muttered. He drained the contents of his goblet and did the same with Anhuset's. He didn't remember the last time he'd indulged in such a luxury as restful sleep, but maybe this time his dreams wouldn't be of a doomed monk but of a silvery-haired woman of imposing gravitas and firefly eyes. One could always hope.

CHAPTER

FOUR

"P luro Cermak's farmstead." Serovek gestured to a stretch of fallow fields sleeping under a thin blanket of new-fallen snow, the treeless landscape dotted by a large house and several barns. "Megiddo rests there."

Shielded from the sun by her hood, Anhuset still squinted for a better look at the place where the monk's body, alive but soulless, slept protected by ancient Kai magic. Her horse's breath streamed out in misty clouds that hung in the cold air, obscuring part of her view. A year ago, Anhuset might have sensed the presence of sorcery. No longer, and the reminder of what she—and all the Kai—had lost in the *galla* war deepened the hollow inside her.

She and Serovek had departed High Salure just before dawn, accompanied by a half dozen of his soldiers as they descended from the mountain fortress to the flat plains at its feet. They had ridden a half day, finally stopping on this small hillock overlooking the farmstead. The rattle of a bridle and occasional creak of a saddle as someone shifted in their seat mingled with equine whuffles and the far-off call of the first birds returning north in anticipation of spring. Otherwise, their party was silent, waiting for their leader's next instructions.

Serovek's face was grim as he gazed down at his vassal's holdings. Anhuset had seen the margrave flippant and teasing, an unabashed flirt who never failed to raise her hackles with his glib wit. She'd also seen him brave and self-sacrificing, displaying more nobility than sense on occasion. He was charming, ruthless, and calculating. A man of many facets who'd dug an arrowhead out of her shoulder with gentle hands, executed a murderer with those same hands, and ridden into battle alongside a man his own king considered a possible enemy. She'd never seen him like this: remote, forbidding, as if the task of returning Megiddo's body to the Jeden monks was a trial to be endured.

"Is the monk's brother willing to give him up to his order? Or is this a thing he's obligated to do?" She'd assumed the first, but the death of a loved one, especially an unnatural death like this, sometimes made people react in strange ways and hold on to that which had already left them long ago.

Serovek maneuvered his mount to start down the slope. Anhuset stayed abreast of him as the others fell in behind. "My impression from his letter is that he welcomes the monastery's willingness to take over guardianship of his brother's body. He simply needs someone else to take Megiddo there."

A man bearing a strong resemblance to Megiddo, only older, met them at the door. A woman, coiffed and layered against the cold, stood next to them. Both bowed stiffly, and their gazes shuttled back and forth between Serovek and Anhuset, lingering on her the longest.

"Welcome, my lord." Pluro Cermak offered a second bow. "We're most pleased to have you guest with us. Come in from the cold."

Anhuset didn't follow Serovek across the threshold. The invitation had been for the vassal's lord, not his escort, and she considered herself part of that group. They would wait outside until Lord Pangion had spent time with Cermak in courteous fraternization.

Serovek was having none of it. He half-turned, scowled at her and the soldiers with her, and motioned them forward. "Hurry it up. You're letting all the heat escape just standing there."

Cermak's wife gaped at them like a caught fish, eyes wide as she huddled behind her husband while the margrave and his party hustled into the hall. Anhuset entered last, using her heel to shut the door behind her.

Pluro motioned to the fire roaring in the hearth at one end of the room. As startled by the twist in social protocol as his wife, he still managed to remember his hosting duties. "Please warm yourself by the fire. I'll have food and drink brought." He turned a severe look on Lady Cermak, who fled for the kitchen.

Soon, a parade of servants, led by Lady Cermak, brought out cups of warm ale and hot tea, along with boards of bread and dried fruit set on a table not far from the hearth. Anhuset nursed a cup of the tea, warming her hands around the heated ceramic.

"I hate it when he does this," one of the soldiers closest to her muttered. "We're better off in the kitchens flirting with the maids."

Another elbowed him. "Stop complaining. It's a sight better than standing outside freezing your balls off, and the ale isn't half bad."

Not part of their conversation, Anhuset kept her thoughts to herself, but she agreed with the first soldier. Every state dinner or social gathering she'd ever been forced to attend at Saggara had been an exercise in awkwardness. Brishen and Ildiko, raised among the intricacies of court machinations in Haradis and Pricid, navigated those dangerous waters with effortless finesse, and she'd witnessed Serovek do the same when he visited Saggara. She, however, lurched and stumbled her way through such interactions. The humble kitchen seemed a much more inviting place to her as well, even if it was in a human household where the gods only knew what horrors lurked in the stew pots suspended over the cooking fires.

She grumbled under her breath but adopted a neutral expression when Serovek waved her to where he stood with Cermak and Lady Cermak. The woman's eyes grew wider with every step Anhuset took, her face paler. Had Serovek's master-at-arms been present, Anhuset might have put a wager forward over how long it took for the lady of the house to bolt, certain if she didn't, she'd be eaten.

As if a Kai warrior accompanying his entourage was an everyday event, Serovek casually introduced her to his vassal. "This is Anhuset, the Kai regent's second, what they call a *sha,* similar to Carov, only with more power and more responsibility. She's agreed to accompany us to the monastery as a representative of the Kai kingdom."

Anhuset pushed back her hood so their hosts might have a better look at her and gave a short bow. "I am honored," she said, careful not to expose too much of her teeth. Usually, she made extra effort to grin at any human she crossed, just for the sport of eliciting a reaction. That had no place here, especially since the lady of the house was twitchier than a rabbit and on the verge of banking off the walls at the merest ripple of her own shadow.

A small meeping noise escaped Lady Cermak, and though her throat visibly worked to exhale breath or words, nothing else escaped her mouth. Her husband had better luck. As pale as his wife and shackled to her by the death grip she had on his elbow, Pluro still managed a polite greeting. "Welcome to Mordrada Farmstead, sha-Anhuset. We appreciate the regent's acknowledgment of my brother's service to him."

More dull pleasantries passed between them until the tea was gone and the food eaten. Anhuset hoped they wouldn't linger much longer. They'd come for Megiddo, not to while away the day in stilted conversation with his brother. They still had several hours on horseback ahead of them before they stopped for the night at a riverside village Serovek had pointed out on his map the previous evening.

He set his cup down on the table. His men followed suit as did Anhuset. "I thank you for your hospitality, but we've a long journey ahead of us. If you'll take us to where Megiddo rests, we'll place him in the wagon we brought and be on our way."

A quick, silent conversation passed between Pluro and his wife, words conveyed only through long looks and fast blinks. Lady Cermak, still mute, still nervous, finally spoke, and only to excuse herself from their company. Anhuset had the impression she'd just abandoned her husband to a fate of which she wanted no part.

Pluro straightened his quilted tunic and flexed his shoulders if he prepared for a confrontation. Serovek's eyebrows crawled toward his hairline though he said nothing. The vassal motioned to the hall's entrance. "If you'll follow me, please."

Whispers of inquiry exchanged between those in Serovek's escort reached Anhuset as they all trailed the two men out of the manor and back into the cold outdoors. Serovek fell back a step or two until Anhuset came abreast of him. Pluro didn't wait but strode ahead, skirting a flock of roaming geese and a pair of hay carts parked nearby. Lines of wash flapped in the cutting breeze.

"What do you think?" Serovek asked her, his voice quiet.

She tried not to dwell on the pleasurable warmth that coursed through her at his request for her opinion. "I didn't expect the monk not to be in his brother's house."

"Nor I." He signaled to the rest of his men. "Wagon," he said. They saluted and broke away to retrieve the wagon they'd brought to transport Megiddo.

When they approached the smallest of the farmstead's three barns, Serovek's harsh "Surely, he's jesting," echoed her own thoughts. There was no possible way Pluro had stashed his own brother in a barn with the livestock. However, the man never changed directions, and soon they entered the dark, pungent structure.

Occupied by a few head of cattle, two mules, and a small number of sheep, the barn was a little warmer than outside, but their breath still steamed in front of them. Weak sunlight bled through splits in the building's cladding and flooded the entrance, illuminating the space enough for the two men to see without too much trouble. Anhuset saw everything clearly, including the ominous thunderhead that had descended over Serovek's countenance.

Pluro led them to the very back of the barn, past the stalls, hay racks and shelves of tack and tools, to another closed door partially covered in an array of webs spun by busy spiders. The webbing spread across the hinges and surrounded the latch and handle, signs that it had been some time since anyone had disturbed their labor by opening the door.

Anhuset and Serovek waited as their host paused to light an oil lamp before brushing away the webs and freeing the latch. Hinges squealed as he pushed the door inward. The newborn flames inside the lamp stretched fingers of light into the ink-dark room. Shadows fled at their encroachment, and soon the flickering illumination spilled onto a bier on which a man lay in peaceful repose.

Anhuset took in the sight with a heart that slowed its beat and breath that hovered in her nostrils. Beside her, Serovek sighed softly, a reverent sound laced with regret. Five men had sacrificed much to battle *galla* and save a world. One of them had paid an even more terrible price.

Megiddo Cermak breathed but slept the slumber of the dead, his soul trapped in a *galla* prison while his body, kept alive and protected by Kai sorcery, waited for his soul's return. He wore armor similar to Serovek's but plainer, its only nod to decorative elements a border of runes etched into the steel around the collar of his breastplate.

The bier on which he lay was a simple affair of wooden slats laid adjacent to each other, their ends fastened at either side to rails that ran the length of the platform. Designed for ease of transporting the dead, the bier acted as Megiddo's transparent coffin as well for now. The last remnants of power Brishen had drawn out of his own people with necromantic spellwork, flitted across the width and length of the bier in tiny blue sparks that faded as fast as they ignited.

A year ago, Anhuset would have sensed Megiddo's presence even before she reached the barn, felt the pull of sorcery similar to her own, albeit feeble, magic. No longer. Now there was nothing. No twinge or draw, no prickle along her spine. Not even a strip of gooseflesh to signal an awareness of magic.

She'd known the moment it happened, when the desperate Khaskem had stripped every adult Kai of their magic in order to save them from total annihilation. A hollow had opened up inside her and remained. Neither rage, nor grief, nor acceptance of the necessity of Brishen's devastating act filled it. Anhuset stared at Megiddo—more simulacrum than living man, despite the fact he breathed—then looked away.

She focused instead on Serovek, whose features had gone so pale, he fairly glowed in the dark. His nostrils flared, reminding her of an angry bull, and his hand clenched on the pommel of his sword as if he were tempted to draw it.

"Why is your brother's body in one of your barns with the live-stock instead of in the house?" He bit out each word from between clenched teeth, his tone quiet but no less menacing for its lack of volume.

Pluro blanched. Anhuset took a quick step back just in case the man's fright twisted his guts enough that he retched up his stomach's contents. He crossed his arms, not in confrontation but in defense, as if the pose might somehow save him should Serovek decide to split him from throat to bollocks with his blade. His explanation came out in a long, stuttering string of words sprayed into the cold air.

"It wasn't always so, Lord Pangion. Megiddo was in the house for a time. We had no choice but to move him here. Strange things happened when we kept him there. Voices whispering when no one was in the room. Odd lights without fire or candle to birth them." He shivered, and not from the cold. "All of us dreamed terrible dreams, nightmares to wake you in a sweat. Our servants refused to sleep in their rooms any longer, and some refused to work inside. My wife needs the help, so I thought it best to move Megiddo here. I didn't see the harm. After all, he's unaware of his surroundings. He wouldn't know or care. Once I did so, everything returned to normal. No voices, no nightmares, no lights."

His description sent a splinter of unease down Anhuset's back. She recalled her conversation with Ildiko about Brishen's dreams, had seen herself the shimmer of sorcerous blue that had edged his eye, as if the dark magic that had turned him eidolon still lingered inside him, tied somehow to the deathless warrior lying motionless before her.

What Pluro described wouldn't have been enough to convince her Megiddo belonged in an isolated barn, forgotten. Unlike the vassal, however, she hadn't seen the *galla* firsthand. He had, and from her observations of her own countrymen who'd fled Haradis before the *galla* horde, the experience left the lingering stain of terror on the soul and the mind. She didn't approve of his actions, considering them weak, but she didn't condemn him for them either.

Serovek wasn't as forgiving. He glared at Pluro so hard, the man should have caught fire. "You deserve a thrashing," he said in those same quiet, seething tones. "Get out of my sight before I decide to give you one."

Pluro fled without a word, nearly falling over his own feet to escape the barn. Anhuset watched him go before turning back to Serovek, who stared at Megiddo's still form with an expression both furious and haunted.

"His brother saved him twice, and this is how Pluro repays him," he said. "Megiddo should have let the *galla* have him."

She touched his arm with one claw tip. "Strength isn't always a gift shared between blood. The gods blessed one man with the courage of two. Your vassal's failing isn't that he's evil; it's that he's craven."

Serovek stared at her for a moment, his flinty expression softening a little. "You never cease to surprise me, Anhuset. You're far more lenient about this than I am. History has proven more than a few times that evil is often the spawn of cowardice."

"I wouldn't expect you to be forgiving toward Cermak. Megiddo rode beside you into battle, suffered through the bloodletting required by the ancient spellwork just as you did. You saw firsthand what happened to him. In your place, I might not have held back from carving Pluro into pieces at the knowledge he put Megiddo here."

His mouth quirked a little. "Saw that, did you?"

"You were hardly subtle." She moved closer to the bier. "He looks peaceful. You all did once the spell that made you eidolon took hold. Do you think he feels pain?"

Serovek shrugged. "His body? No. His soul? I wish I could say no to that as well, but I think it otherwise." Guilt and regret seeped into his words.

She turned fully to meet his eyes, so dark against his winter-pale skin. "It wasn't your fault."

He went rigid once more. "I never said it was."

"You didn't have to. Many who escaped the razing of Haradis are eaten alive with guilt over their own survival, even when they know there was nothing they could do for those who perished."

Serovek's breath steamed from his nostrils on a long exhalation. "Sometimes I think we stand easier under the yoke of our own sacrifices than we do under the yoke of someone else's."

How well she understood that sentiment. The image of his expression at the moment she had stabbed him to trigger the magic that would turn him eidolon remained emblazoned in her mind. Agony, shock, even when he knew what to expect and joked about it until the moment the sword entered his body. She remembered the feel of severed muscle clenching involuntarily around the blade as she drew it out, the weight of his body when he collapsed in her arms, the hot gush of his blood saturating her midriff as she held him.

He had never forgiven her for that violence because he had never blamed her for it. She carried enough self-blame for them both. He had saved her once. Her gratitude had been brutal.

Footsteps entering the barn intruded on her dark thoughts. The tread didn't belong to Pluro Cermak. It was confident instead of diffident, and without fear.

Jannir, one of the High Salure soldiers, appeared at the doorway. His gaze flickered briefly to Megiddo before settling on Serovek. "The wagon is right outside, margrave. We're ready when you are."

Serovek nodded. "Let's get to it then. No need to linger here any longer than necessary."

The room was too small for more than two people to maneuver the bier and carry it through the doorway. Serovek didn't question whether or not Anhuset was strong enough—for which she was most pleased—only instructed her to stand at one end of the platform while he stood at the other and lift.

They carried the bier into the main part of the barn where

Serovek's men waited to take a position on either side and act as pall-bearers. Anhuset gave up her spot to one of the soldiers to follow them outside, where the wagon was parked just beyond the entrance.

Except for a clutch of hens loitering nearby in case someone chose to scatter feed on the muddy ground, the yard was empty. She eyed the manor house and caught a glimpse of faces peering from the windows in both the ground floor and upper stories. Servants, most of them, but Anhuset would have bet her favorite horse that Pluro Cermak and his skittish wife hid among the watching crowd.

They put Megiddo's bier into the back of the wagon and strapped the platform down with rope so it wouldn't move as they traveled over rutted roads. One of the men brought a large blanket and cast it over the monk. The fabric didn't fall directly onto his body but draped above it as if Megiddo lay within a box whose sides and lid the blanket now covered. Serovek spoke briefly to the wagon driver for a moment before turning to the rest of their escort.

"Mount your horses. We're done here."

Anhuset guided her horse until it stood alongside Serovek's. "No farewells for Megiddo's brother? He hasn't even seen fit to come out and bid you good journey or thank you for making the trip."

The margrave's upper lip lifted in a sneer as he raked the manor house with a hard stare. "He's probably too busy trying to find where he misplaced his spine. Gratitude and good wishes from a sniveling coward like that is worth less than his silence." He tapped his heels to his horse's sides, and the animal stepped high into a brisk walk. "We ride," he called to the group.

By unspoken agreement, the riders arranged themselves into a chevron around the wagon with Serovek taking point lead and two riders behind him and in front of the wagon. Anhuset joined the remaining three soldiers in the back. Megiddo, his bier strapped down securely in the wagon, slept undisturbed.

They traveled the road that wove back and forth across both Kai and Beladine lands until it curved toward the banks of the Absu to run parallel to the shore. The remains of a wooden bridge stood on either side where the river was narrow, its piles cut away by ax or saw where they would have supported the pile caps, stringers, and deck.

The soldier riding in front of Anhuset spoke. "I think every bridge that crosses the river has been destroyed. I'll bet some of Cermak's men turned this one to kindling when they were running from the *galla*."

The land on this side of the Absu had been protected from the *galla* invasion by the river itself. Water acted as a barrier against the demons, and the only way they could cross was by bridge, either natural or man-made. Cermak's farmstead had lain on the wrong side of the river, vulnerable to the galla. Their household had been lucky to escape with their lives. Anhuset was surprised that Pluro had returned to re-establish his farmstead, even knowing the Wraith kings had rid the world of the demons' threat.

They rode past the bridge's remains. Farther down the river, a small towboat and barge serviced the small farmsteads in the area. It was large enough to transport the wagon and its cargo down the river along with its escort in two trips. It was at that crossing they'd stay the night in the Beladine village of Edarine.

Taciturn by nature, Anhuset was content to simply listen, without commenting, to the idle chit-chat the three men riding beside and in front of her swapped between them. She spent the time dozing in quick catnaps as the sunlight carved paths in the clouds overhead and warmed her shoulders. These were the hours she normally slept when she wasn't on patrol or guard duty, and her horse's easy gait made her even drowsier. She blinked, focusing her attention on Serovek's broad back as he rode ahead of them.

The memory of his revelation from the previous evening worried at her. He'd been married once. To a beautiful woman who wore ribbons in her hair. Affection had laced his voice when he spoke of her, along with old grief. Curiosity for this nameless wife plagued her even now, though she'd cut out her own tongue before she asked for details. She allowed herself a tiny smile, remembering his quip when she told him she wouldn't know what to do with a hair ribbon. He'd always been forthright in his admiration for her dry humor. Maybe because he possessed the same at times.

The trip to Edarine remained uneventful, though the towboat captain asked more than a few questions as to what was under the blanket in the wagon. While Anhuset considered threatening the man into silence by offering to cut out his tongue, Serovek patiently fielded each question, keeping up a steady stream of conversation without ever answering a single one of his inquiries.

Once they disembarked, they traveled a drover's path and reached the outskirts of the town just as twilight chased the sun westward. Serovek sent one of his men ahead to secure lodgings for the night, then turned and called Anhuset to join him up front. "Edarine hosts a good market, even in the cold months," he said. "We'll purchase more provisions tomorrow for the trip. There's an inn with clean rooms and a tavern that serves decent ale and food." He chuckled at her involuntary recoil at the mention of food. "Don't worry. I'll make sure they don't serve you the potatoes."

She dreaded what supper might have in store, vowing only to taste enough as a gesture of goodwill in case it was foul, which she fully expected. She gestured to the wagon behind them. "What will you do with the monk?"

Frown lines marred his brow for a moment. "I'll be guilty of hypocrisy for a night," he said. "Carrying him into the inn so he can stay in a room will bring more attention on us than I care to have. We'll leave the bier in the wagon and rent a stall in the inn's stables."

"I'll stand guard," she volunteered. "I can eat in the stables as well. Me at your table in a common room will draw all the attention you're hoping to avoid." It only made sense that she keep watch through the night. Nor did she much relish the idea of pacing the confines of a room in an inn crowded with so many humans.

"I'm happy to put you on guard duty," he said. "I can't think of a more vigilant protector, though you're always welcome at my table, wherever that may be. Curious eyes be damned."

His praise sent another of those awful, embarrassing blushes crawling up her neck to her cheeks. She gave him a quick salute and trotted back to her place behind the wagon, adopting such a forbidding expression that none of the men riding with her dared ask what she spoke about with the margrave.

Except for a cat that paused in its hunting rounds to watch their group ride past, the streets of Edarine were deserted after dusk. Lamplight filled the windows in the houses lining the main thoroughfare, and a few faces appeared behind them, curious as to who rode through the streets at an hour when the shops were closed and most travelers had found their lodgings for the night.

The inn where they planned to stay stood at the other side of the town, a two-story structure from which spilled light and music. Several wagons were parked nearby, and numerous horses crowded the yard of the adjacent stables. A figure emerged from the inn to greet them, the soldier Serovek had sent ahead to secure lodgings for them.

"They had two rooms remaining, my lord. The rest are taken. The innkeeper has said he and his wife are happy to give up their bedroom to the margrave for the night."

Serovek snorted. "Generous but not necessary." He dismounted and tossed the reins to the man. "I'll speak to the innkeeper. Get the horses settled. Did you find a place for them and for our cargo?" At the other's nod, he crooked a finger to the wagon's driver. "Klanek, have Weson show you where to park the wagon and where to unload. Sha-Anhuset will accompany you."

The stall reserved for them was spacious, clean, and tucked far in the back of the stables, away from the main traffic of stablehands and riders coming and going. Judging by the size and the pristine conditions of the space, Anhuset guessed Weson had spent quite a bit of Serovek's coin for it. Fresh straw covered the floor in a thick carpet, and someone had brought in extra saddle padding as bedding, along with an extra unlit oil lamp if needed.

She, Weson, and two more of their escort carried Megiddo's bier into the stable, setting it down gently alongside the stall's back wall. She straightened the blanket in spots where their movements had dislodged the cover to reveal some of what lay beneath. A few of the stablehands had paused in their tasks to watch them pass, but their attention had been solely on Anhuset instead of what she and the others transported.

After assuring her companions that not only was she comfortable in the stall but happy to be there by herself, they left to join Serovek in the inn. The lamp remained unlit, an unnecessary convenience for her and more of a fire hazard than anything. The stablehands drifted away once their work was done, and soon the stable grew dark. Anhuset sat down not far from the bier and reclined against the wall, happy to soak in the darkness and listen to the whuffles and snorts of the horses in the adjacent stalls.

Hints of blue iridescence shimmered under the blanket covering Megiddo. Anhuset leaned over to slide back a corner of the cover for a look at his still features. Had she no knowledge of how he came to be in this predicament, she might have thought him only asleep.

She'd first met him months earlier when he had arrived at Saggara with Serovek, volunteering his sword and his soul to fight the *galla*. Anhuset might have said all of a dozen words to him in the very short time she'd known him, but he'd left her with an impression of ascetic dignity. Even now, his features, expressionless in soulless, ensorceled sleep, retained a certain gravitas that made her want to bow to him in a show of respect.

The murmur of voices on the other side of the stable wall reached her ears. She stood, passing along the stall's back wall until she found an opening where one of the boards had warped enough to create a space between it and the board next to it. She glimpsed the silhouettes of three people, one tall and brawny, the other two much shorter and slight. One of the voices belonged to Serovek. The other two were feminine, full of smiles and flirtatious laughter. As their figures moved closer to the stable, their change in positions highlighted more details.

Serovek headed in the direction of the stable's entrance, a woman on either side of him, attached to his elbows like arm ornaments. He carried a wrapped parcel in one hand and a tankard in another. His deep voice floated in the night air, amused, seductive, teasing. The women laughed, one nestling his arm into her generous cleavage while the other flipped her hair back to show the graceful line of her neck to its best advantage.

An annoying spasm in Anhuset's right eyelid made her rub at the spot. She did her best to ignore the sharp flare of irritation, turning away from the narrow view of the trio to resume her seat next to Megiddo's bier. It was no business of hers what the margrave of High Salure got up to or with whom. She was here only as Brishen's representative. Nothing more. A trill of feminine laughter taunted her. She clenched her jaw and hummed a Kai drinking song to herself to drown out the sound.

She kept her seat when the smaller entrance door to the stable opened, then shut. Only one set of footfalls headed toward her, barely discernible, especially for such a big man. His were the only steps, and Anhuset watched the stall entrance for his appearance with narrowed eyes, still annoyed by the unsettling pang lodged in her chest at the sight of him with the women. She declined to name the feeling though that same inner voice which called her a liar was more than happy to do so.

Jealousy, it whispered in her mind.

Anhuset growled low in her throat.

The footsteps halted. "Tell me that's you greeting my arrival with great joy, Anhuset."

She snorted, amused. "It's me."

"Damn black as the bottom of an inkwell in here," Serovek groused. "I'm probably about to walk into a horse."

Glad he chose not to bring his admirers with him into the stable, she repaid the kindness by reaching for the flint and steel in the small pouch belted at her waist so she could light the lamp she'd left unlit. The flare of the broad wick made her blink, eroding the finer edges of her vision with its brightness. She placed the lamp atop the stall's midrail, scraping away the straw on the floor underneath it to create a small firebreak just in case it toppled.

Serovek entered the stall, mouth turned up in a smile. He held up the cloth-wrapped package and the tankard. "Supper, if you're willing to brave it." He sat down beside her and slid the parcel and tankard toward her. "I promise there's no potato in there."

It smelled delectable. Salt, roasted meat, the underlying sharpness of spicy peppers, and the rich dairy scent of hot butter. Despite her misgivings, her mouth watered, and she untied the cloth with eager fingers. A savory pie—one that didn't squirm about under the crust— lay in the center of the kerchief, a spoon next to it.

Serovek chuckled at her appreciative inhalation as she closed her eyes and breathed deep. "No doubt, this will be a boring meal for you. You don't have to battle the contents to see who's going to eat whom."

"Believe it or not," she said, "but I'm not always eager for a scuffle, especially when it involves my supper." She snatched up the spoon and dug into the pie. "You have my eternal gratitude, margrave," she told Serovek after the first piquant spoonful.

"I'm pleased you're pleased," he said before echoing her earlier pose to lean back against the stall divider. He closed his eyes and stretched out his long legs, crushing straw beneath him.

Anhuset ate the pie and finished off the ale he brought in silence, glad that Serovek wasn't a man who found it necessary to carry on a conversation during a meal. She rewrapped her empty pie plate and set it aside, along with the tankard. Belly full, she shifted her position, this time to recline against the bier so that she faced her companion, who appeared to have fallen asleep while she supped. She took the opportunity to look her fill.

As much as she was reluctant to admit it, only his strange, human eyes were truly repulsive to her. They darted here and there in their sockets, reminding her of mice caught in bone traps. She'd never understand how Brishen had grown used to seeing it with Ildiko. When, however, Serovek lowered his lids, hiding that particular hideousness, the beauty of his features bloomed before her. And her annoyance and fear bloomed right along with it.

"What are you staring at, sha-Anhuset?" A thread of humor wove through his question, as if he could hear what she thought and found it amusing. He didn't bother to open his eyes.

She scowled, mortified at being caught gawking at him like some love-sick juvenile. "Your ugly face," she snapped.

He opened his eyes this time, deep water blue with black pupils like whirlpools at their centers. His lips parted in a grin, revealing white teeth, square as a horse's. So utterly different from a Kai's own sharp ivories. He gestured to the bier behind her and the still Megiddo recumbent upon it. "He's far prettier than I am."

Anhuset cocked an eyebrow. "And he's mostly dead. Doesn't say much for your looks, does it, Stallion?" She instantly regretted the harsh words. He hadn't deserved them. He frightened her, twisted her into knots with emotions she couldn't understand and didn't welcome, and she'd gone on the attack.

His eyebrows arched before his eyes slitted, and he raked her with a gaze that could have sliced flesh off bone. "It seems your teeth aren't the only sharp things in your mouth," he shot back.

He gained his feet in one graceful motion, picked up the pie tin and tankard, and exited the stall without a word, leaving her to brood, with only the horses, a near-dead monk, and her own remorse to keep her company.

Bound to her duty as guard, she didn't chase after him. Bound to her pride, she didn't call out to him to return so she could apologize. Recognizing her own ineptitude with the more subtle signals of social interactions, especially with humans, she'd likely muck that up too. She stood and began to pace the stall's confines. "What is wrong with you, Anhuset?" she admonished herself. No one answered.

She killed the lamp's flame, grateful for the returning darkness, and had just settled back in her original spot when the stable door opened a second time.

"Oh for gods' sake, not again." Serovek's footsteps, slower and more careful now, drew closer. "If I end up pitchforking myself because I'm fumbling about blind here, I put the blame entirely on you, Anhuset."

She scrambled to relight the lamp when he reappeared in the stall, this time carrying a handful of mint. He gestured for her to hold out her hand and dropped a small bundle of the leaves into her palm. "That ale left a sour taste on the tongue. The mint will help get rid of it." He popped a few leaves in his mouth and chewed before spitting the pulp into a corner of the stall. "I found it growing wild along the inn's south wall. Even old crone Winter can't kill the stuff."

"Thank you," she said, pleased beyond reason he had come back, puzzled as to why. The mint was astringent on her palate but worked as he claimed.

This time she didn't change positions when he resumed his earlier spot, and they sat together hip to hip, her legs nearly equal in length to his. He'd be even taller if he didn't possess the horseman's bow. Anhuset wondered from which of his parents he'd inherited his impressive height and size. Not only was he tall, he was big, with a personality to match. No one would overlook him in a crowd.

"You're pensive tonight," he said. "Missing Saggara already?"

He'd given her an easy excuse, one she could embrace as a perfectly reasonable explanation for her ruminating. She might be clumsy with the interplay between them, but she wasn't dishonest, and Saggara had only crossed her thoughts once and only in terms of what she had to do there once she returned.

She forced herself to meet his inquisitive gaze. "I owe you an apology." His blatant astonishment might have been amusing if it weren't so irritating. "You needn't look so shocked," she huffed. "I overstepped the rules of civility with my insult earlier. You did nothing to deserve it."

He tilted his head to one side, studying her. "Then why did you say it?"

I was jealous. Embarrassment locked in her throat. Relief made her lightheaded when he answered for her.

"I think you still carry a lot of anger toward me from the ritual at Saruna Tor," he said.

That made her pause. The grim memory of Saruna Tor remained a wound on her spirit she didn't think would ever heal, and she hadn't been one of those made eidolon there. Even when Serovek had practically begged her to be his executioner on that hill, guilt over stabbing him still burdened her. Anger toward him did not, nor did she remember it ever being so. "What are you talking about?"

A faraway expression settled over his features. "The moments after you stabbed me, you said 'I will never forgive you for this.' I carried those words into battle with me so that I might return and ask that you reconsider."

She gasped, forgetting for a moment to keep her emotional guard up around him, avoid more of the invisible grappling hooks he tossed at her every time they crossed paths that drew her inexorably to him, half step by half step no matter how hard she fought against it. She looked away from his sudden, intense scrutiny, sympathizing in that moment with Pluro Cermak's skittish wife and the desire to bolt for safety.

"I might have meant them at the time, but I shouldn't have said those words either." Her fingers throbbed from how tightly she'd laced them together, and her throat ached with the effort to speak. "You saved me and the *hercegesé* from Beladine raiders and their mage hounds, took care of my wound, gained the information we needed to find Brishen and his abductors, and risked yourself and your men to help me rescue him. Putting a sword through your belly was no way to clear such a debt. I owe you more than I can ever repay in this lifetime or a dozen more beyond it."

Complaint or confession. If asked which it was, she'd have a hard time deciding, and it might well have been a little of both, but somehow she felt lighter by speaking aloud of this shame, no matter how ridiculous it might appear to others, that had weighed her down these many months.

Serovek snorted, mouth tight with disapproval. "You shoulder an anvil of your own making." His lips softened with a hint of a smile at her surprise. "I asked you in particular to run me through because I knew you to be strong enough to see the deed done and not falter. I laid a terrible task at your feet, and you took up the gauntlet. Don't think I'm unaware of what I asked of you." His gaze flitted from her face to her hair, slowing to travel the length of her body before returning to her face. "If we were keeping a tally of who is in debt to whom, every breathing person on this side of the Ruhrin ocean would owe their lives to those of us who rode against the *galla*. *If* we were keeping tally. We aren't. And you owe me nothing. There's no debt between us. There never was."

"I like strong women, soft or not." He'd said that while they stood on the balcony of his study, overlooking the steep slopes of the mountainside. Ribbons and swords, she thought. So different yet both made admirable in his eyes by the hand that wielded them. He was a man like no other, Kai or human, she'd ever met before.

"What was your wife's name?" she asked in a soft voice, a reverence she could offer for what she suspected was still a lingering grief.

He bowed his head a fraction in acknowledgment of her change of subject. "Glaurin. Our union was arranged, but we'd been childhood friends so were familiar with each other when we married. She bore me a daughter we named Deliza."

A child. The idea tied her confused emotions into tighter knots. Somehow, Anhuset had no trouble imagining Serovek as a loving father. "What happened to them?"

A shadow of sorrow descended over his features. "Plague."

He didn't have to say more. Anhuset remembered the plague outbreak from a decade earlier. It had swept through the human kingdoms, killing thousands. The Kai, afflicted by their own sicknesses, had suffered no effects of the disease that ravaged their neighbors. Gauri and Beladine alike had fallen like chaff beneath a thresher's flail.

She grazed his arm with her claw tips, the barest touch. "I'm sorry."

He stared down at her hand for a moment before covering it with one of his, palm callused and warm. "So am I." They were both quiet a moment before he spoke again. "And you? No spouse or children?"

She'd taken lovers. Sometimes for a day, sometimes for a week or a month. Most had been sparks of warmth to ease loneliness, or a few hours of entertainment with no emotional attachment, sometimes even hazy memories captured only in the foggy aftermath of a day spent drinking far too much Peleta's Kiss. None had ever incited a longing for something more profound or long-term. Occasionally she observed Brishen and Ildiko together and wondered at the depth of their bond. She envied it, but no one so far had moved her in such a way to make her actively search for something similar.

As for children, they were strange, puzzling creatures. Usually loud, demanding, and bordering on feral. She'd rather keep a scarpatine as a pet.

Serovek didn't need to know all that. Anhuset had vomited up enough of her inner demons for one evening. "I'm uninterested in either one," she said with a shrug. "Even if I were, I'm not considered a worthy catch by a Kai seeking to elevate himself through an advantageous union. Nor am I the easiest person to get along with most days, if you can imagine that."

That elicited a chuckle from him. "Oh, I can imagine the second just fine." Serovek's wide grin coaxed an answering one from her. "I am, however, stunned by the first. You're closely related to the Kai queen regnant and the regent. Surely, Brishen must be fighting off a line of suitors trying to take his valuable second from him."

"Those connections don't make me any more desirable. I'm *gameza.*"

She watched as he searched his internal cache of bast-Kai words for translation, but nothing came to mind. "What's *gameza?*"

"Bastard. I'm the illegitimate daughter of the old king's sister. My father, so I'm told, was a handsome stablehand as well hung as the horses he tended." *A reputation much like yours, margrave.* She kept the thought to herself.

Serovek blinked, his grin still in place but softened by her revelation. "You're always refreshingly blunt. It's one of many things I admire about you."

The damn blush crawled up her neck and into her face yet again.

Anhuset prayed the stable's near darkness would hide the reaction his compliments continued to spawn.

He crossed his long legs at the ankles and pondered his boots. "Let me guess. Your mother committed double sacrilege. Not only did she bear a child outside of a marriage sanctioned by the sovereign, she bore one of a man not even of royal blood, tainting the bloodlines." He rolled his eyes, and Anhuset twitched.

She tilted her head to one side, considering his words and the contemptuous tone in which he uttered them. "Does human royalty feel the same way about *gamezas*?"

"In my experience, yes." He shrugged. "Personally, I think a good shot of stablehand blood into some of those murky pools is exactly what's needed. It seems like the Kai aristocracy suffers the same prideful blindness the human ones do." He smiled at her quiet huff of laughter.

"I'm glad to be *gameza*," she said. "Were I not, the regency would have fallen to me while Brishen fought the *galla*. I'm not fashioned for such a role. I'm a soldier first and foremost."

"And one Brishen depends on at every level. As does his *hercegesé*. I'm sure Ildiko was grateful to have you with her while she held the Kai kingdom together."

Anhuset suspected Ildiko would have managed just fine on her own were it necessary. The human *hercegesé* had assumed the role of regent in her husband's stead, never once wavering, though Anhuset had seen the doubt and the fear Ildiko had tried her best to hide from everyone, including Brishen.

"The *hercegesé* surprised a lot of us, I think. I was simply her sword and shield."

He studied her for a moment, brow stitched into a frown. "I don't think you give yourself enough credit." She didn't get a chance to argue with him before he turned the subject back to her parentage. "Do you resent your mother for her indiscretion?"

It wasn't an unreasonable question. The lot of a nobleman's or noblewoman's bastard was often a hard one, at least in Kai societies, where family connections and alliances held more value than affection or emotion. To them, a bastard was valueless and often shunned for the sin of their parent's carelessness.

Anhuset raised one eyebrow. "No. She birthed me and turned me over to nursemaids who didn't know how to handle me."

"To no one's surprise, I'm sure."

She tipped her nose up and gave a sniff to show her disdain of his teasing. "I followed in her footsteps. Tried out a stablehand or two myself when I was older."

It was his turn to arch an eyebrow. "Is that disappointment I hear in your voice?"

She waved a hand as if brushing away an annoying gnat. "Just because they cared for stallions didn't mean they were stallions themselves." Some small demon whispered temptation in her mind, and in that moment she gave in to it. She slanted Serovek a long look and lowered her voice, challenge implicit in every word. "The typical empty boasts shattered by unforgiving reality."

Serovek straightened from the slouch he'd adopted. The deep blue of his strangely colored eyes had darkened so that she no longer saw the distinction between iris and pupil. He leaned toward her a fraction, his face still as if he sought to mesmerize hers with the power of his stare. "I'm not typical, firefly woman," he practically purred at her. "Nor do I toss out empty boasts."

The blush-heat that had settled on her neck and face now spread throughout her entire body at the name he gave her. That heat bore all the hallmarks of anticipation, fascination, and to her chagrin, lust. "You aren't a stablehand either," she said before rolling out of reach. If she didn't put some physical distance between them now, she'd regret it.

Obviously, humans brewed a stronger ale than the Kai did. Surely, it explained why she was seriously considering cutting the laces on the placket of Serovek's trousers with her claws, crawling onto his lap and learning whether or not he lived up to the reputation of his nickname.

He didn't try to stop her when she scooted even farther back. She pretended not to see the smirk turning his mouth up at the corners.

Straw dust stirred up by her movements made her eyes itch, and she used that excuse to close them against the image of the Beladine Stallion once more reclined against the stable wall, all power, muscle, and grace.

"Don't you have a nice comfortable bed to sleep in tonight?" she said. "Courtesy of the innkeeper and his wife?" Serovek could sleep in the saddle as easily as she did, but his men would expect him awake and alert when dawn came. Staying up all night with her here in the stables did no one any good.

Her heartbeat stuttered mid beat when he said, "I'll be sleeping here tonight. I'll feel better with two of us keeping an eye on him." He waved a hand at Megiddo's bier.

Indignation swamped her. Anhuset lunged to her feet to loom over the margrave and glare. "You don't trust me." The idea that, despite his assurances, he might not have faith in her ability to protect Megiddo stung. Badly.

He stared up at her, face bland and guarded, as if he had expected such a reaction from her at his news. "I trust you implicitly. This has nothing to do with you and everything to do with the monk." The haunted look briefly touched him before flitting away. "I owe him my presence, my assurances that he isn't forgotten or shunted aside as his brother did to him."

Her outrage bled out of her like water from a sieve. She regarded him, sitting in the straw, looking for all the world like a man without a care. Until one looked deeper into the blue of his eyes and saw the shadow of melancholy there. "You said no one was keeping tally."

The lines at the corners of his eyes furrowed deeper with his half smile. "I did, didn't I?" He flicked a piece of chaff at her. "If you must know, there's a running wager going on at this moment as to whether or not I'm swiving you or will be swiving you here in the stables."

He'd danced away from the tangle of emotion the subject of Megiddo seemed to inspire and found steady ground in the irreverent teasing which so often drove her mad. This time Anhuset welcomed it.

"Is that so? And the odds?"

"Four to one in my favor."

"Wait. There are seven of you all together."

"I want to live to see morning," he declared. "I abstained from the wager."

"Such faith your men have in your prowess." Anhuset recalled the two tavern maids attached to him as he made his way to the stables. That faith wasn't exactly misplaced. "Who wagered against you?"

"Ogran. He said if I had any sense, I'd spend my evening charming the prettiest alewives instead of chatting it up with a dead monk."

Knowing what she did about Ogran in their short time on the road, Anhuset easily pictured him saying such a thing. She also heard what he didn't say but certainly thought when she'd caught him staring at her. Why would the renowned Beladine Stallion want to spend his evenings with an ugly, sharp-toothed, eel-skinned Kai woman?

"I may not remember telling you I wouldn't forgive you for having me stab you, but I do remember you boasting that if you survived the *galla*, I'd share your bed when you returned."

Every speck of humor fled Serovek's expression, and the blue eyes went black in an instant. He didn't change position, but every muscle, relaxed just the moment before, fairly quivered with tension now. "I recall that boast as well." He almost growled the words.

Anhuset crouched in front of him, allowing him to see her gaze touch on various parts of his body, lingering on his wide shoulders and trim waist, the muscled thighs and especially the impressive erection now ridging the laced placket of his trousers. Beladine stallion indeed. "I don't indulge when I'm on guard duty," she said in her most no-nonsense tones. "Nor am I a reward for your victory over the *galla*, though you have my greatest admiration for your bravery. Maybe one day instead, I'll have *you* in *my* bed."

He didn't miss a blink, and the smile he turned on her was meant to slay. In that moment, Anhuset was very glad she was Kai and could focus on the strangeness of his looks instead of their seductiveness.

"You once said I wouldn't survive you," he teased. "While you were saying hello to my bits with your hand."

She abandoned her crouch to take a seat in a spot that was a less tempting distance than the one next to him. "Keep that in mind should I ever extend the invitation." She closed her eyes against the sight of him across from her and tried not to imagine him naked. "Since you plan to stay here and pester me, margrave, you might as well try to sleep and leave me in peace. Besides, I want to dim this lamp before I go blind."

He caught the extra blanket she tossed him, gave her a salute, and turned on his side away from her. "Goodnight, firefly woman," he muttered before pulling the blanket over his head.

Anhuset shook her head. Silly nickname. Uttered in tones of affection. She dare not dwell on that too long.

She lowered the lamp's flame a second time, sighing with relief at the returning darkness. Serovek stayed quiet, and she listened to the slowing rhythm of his breathing as he fell deeper into sleep, his ready willingness to embrace slumber wordless proof that he did indeed trust her. They still had hours before dawn, so she took the time to explore the stable's interior before making a quick reconnoiter of the stableyard and the grounds immediately around the now dark and quiet tavern.

A rustling reached her ears, and she stilled in the shadows, lowering her eyelids to hide her eyeshine as two figures slunk around one corner of the tavern. They skirted the open space of the stableyard with its revealing shards of moonlight reflecting on the ground and kept to the darkness thrown by the inn and two outbuildings before stopping not far from the stables. They didn't draw closer, only stared as if noting the placement of the doors and high windows shuttered for the night.

Their efforts at concealment were for naught. Anhuset got a good look at the two. Ragged men with the hard-edged mien of the scavenger about them, they wore knives on their belts and tucked into their boots. One was bearded, the other beardless, and both in desperate need of a bath. They used hand signals to communicate with each other, and while she wasn't familiar with that particular language, she didn't have to be fluent to understand the gist of the exchange.

The one without the beard tried to coax his companion into entering the stable. The other man shook his head, hands making slashing motions in the air as he argued against the idea. The slap of palm to palm for emphasis, an exchange of shoves, and the two came to an agreement before stealing away toward the town's main road.

Now that was interesting. Either she'd just come across two horse thieves looking to help themselves to someone's mount and trying to figure out the problem of her presence inside, or they'd seen Serovek's party arrive and assumed whatever required an escort of heavily armed soldiers was likely valuable and prized in the left-hand marketplace.

Fortunately for the thieves, they chose not to try their luck tonight. Anhuset would have dealt with them as nuisances. Serovek would have seen their thievery as insult. Hers would have been the more merciful punishment.

She scanned the area a final time before returning to the stable's interior. No thieves lurked in the corners, and every horse was accounted for. However, things were not as she'd left them. The animals nickered and tossed their heads, agitated. Their eyes rolled as she passed.

Her pulse surged when she came upon the stall where she'd left Serovek with Megiddo. The blue sparks of sorcery flickering earlier under the blanket covering Megiddo now encased the entire bier in a halo of luminescence. It spilled onto the ground, spreading in a pool that surrounded Serovek. The margrave lay on his back, face contorted into an expression of agony, jaw clenched. He breathed hard through his nose, and his eyes squeezed shut as if refusing to gaze upon some horror that faced him in the most terrifying of dreams.

He muttered a string of words, all of them nonsensical. Anhuset reached for him, intent on bodily dragging him away from the bier and out of the stall where the magic pulsed and swelled. She froze in mid-crouch, every hair on her nape standing on end, as laughter—insane, unnatural, and otherworldly—echoed throughout the stable.

CHAPTER
FIVE

Demons danced in the maelstrom of Serovek's nightmare. He stood in a whirling darkness, hemmed in by a miasma of smoke that shrieked and gibbered. If evil had a voice, it sounded like this. Icy horror spilled over him. He knew that sound. It had filled his ears as he, a monk, a chieftain's son, an exiled nobleman, and a Kai king battled their way through the ruined streets of Haradis to reach the chamber whelping *galla* like a diseased womb. This wasn't the chamber from which they spilled; it was the womb itself.

Something slithered against his shoulder while something else flitted along his fingertips—thin, sharp, like the edge of a razor. He recoiled, jerking to one side. A mad gibber abused his ear, and the smoke spun and whipped around him, tattered veils caught in a hard wind. Within the gloom, he spotted pinpoints of crimson and cerulean light that flickered and darted to and fro. Eyes, he thought. They were eyes, and they watched him with the predatory stare of the ravenous.

Laughter rebounded off invisible walls, echoing back, with one peal fading only to be replaced by another. Serovek gasped at the unearthly, inhuman scream above the mad cacophony. An awful, agonized shriek of despair, it built and built until he thought its reverberation might shatter his skull into a thousand pieces.

Instead of running from the ghastly clamor, he raced toward it. Desperation roiled in his gut to reach the source of torment and stop it. He batted away unseen hands tipped in claws as pointed as any Kai's. Sinuous tethers wrapped around his legs and grasped his arms as he hurtled in the direction of the ungodly screaming. The hovering feral eyes followed, watching him with a palpable hunger.

He plowed through shield walls of shadow thick as the morning mists that purled over High Salure before the sun burned them away. The sun didn't reach this unclean place to immolate its disease and never would. Mantle after mantle of convulsing darkness tore beneath his hands as he struggled to reach the voice of penultimate suffering. He stumbled, almost falling, when something firmer than shadow glanced off his side, leaving a burning sensation along the ladder of his ribs.

The tortured voice was louder now, closer, and where he'd heard only guttural screaming before, Serovek now made out words along with sobbing. Pleas for mercy, for surcease from the pain. Prayers not to many gods, but to one. Another tide of horror cascaded over him. He recognized the god's name and the voice of the man whose beseeching cries fell on a deity's deaf or uncaring ears.

"Megiddo!" he bellowed into the heavy gloom, and the gloom spasmed at the name before taking up the call in a venomous chant.

"Megiddo! Megiddo! Megiddo!"

The screaming halted just as Serovek burst through a drape of darkness into a pallid twilight. What greeted made him want to shriek as well. Megiddo hung before him, impaled at numerous points on a scaffolding of short spikes, a corona of blue light shimmering around him. He didn't bleed, but his skin bore the look of earth trapped in drought, fractured and fissured to reveal more of the cerulean luminescence.

Shadows spiraled around him, fluid and quick, revealing monstrous visages with gaping maws and glowing eyes that glittered with a twisted kind of glee. They capered through and around the scaffolding, a construction of polished blackness that reminded Serovek of obsidian and reflected the light spilling from Megiddo's eidolon. The shadows wrenched the structure one way and then the other, creating a torsion that wracked the captive monk's body in every direction until the snap of bone echoed amid the victorious squalls of cavorting *galla*. The monk groaned, the sound animalistic in its torture.

Serovek lunged for Megiddo, sprinting toward the scaffolding. But for every step he took, the distance between them tripled. And the *galla* laughed and laughed. He reached for his sword, enchanted by Kai sorcery, to hack through the foul creatures, but there was nothing at his hip to unsheathe and wield.

The *galla* didn't cease with their attentions. Unsatisfied with breaking bones, they turned to the fissures marking Megiddo's body. Serovek cursed them all, bellowing his rage and his torment as they peeled the monk like a grape, consuming his suffering as if it were a pleasure elixir. His wails filled the gloaming, and the blue light pouring from his exposed insides coruscated in a column that pulsed around him.

The *galla* ebbed away for a moment, not in fear but in anticipation, as if they knew what would happen next. The light around Megiddo contracted, knitting itself together in delicate filaments under the hands of an unseen weaver until it bound him in a tight shroud that flashed once, twice, brilliant and bright before fading back to a dull glow, leaving the monk hanging as before but whole again, his eidolon unbroken, his skin no longer flensed away. He raised his head slowly, as if the weight of all the world rested on it, and stared at Serovek with glowing blue eyes made abyssal by despair. "You shouldn't be here," he whispered in a thready voice. "You can't help me. Save yourself. Go."

As if his warning sounded an alert, the *hul-galla* surrounding him suddenly turned its attention on Serovek, a malevolent scrutiny comprised of a thousand baleful stares. Serovek quashed the instinctive urge to run. There was nowhere to run, and he dared not turn his back on the horde. Megiddo begged him to leave, and in that moment Serovek wanted desperately to obey, but his nightmare held him in its grip, in this gods-forsaken place with a man whose spirit he couldn't help and whose torment clawed its way into Serovek's own soul.

From the corner of his eye, he caught a flicker of more light, white instead of blue. A meandering seam no wider than a strand of hair but bright as the sun. And clean. An antithesis to everything in this accursed domain. He sensed it down to his bones. It drew him like a lodestone, like Anhuset's rare and sultry laughter. The *hul-galla* set up a screeching to make his head throb. As one writhing, smoky mass, they surged toward the thread of brightness.

"Get out," Megiddo commanded in a voice no longer thin but forceful, adamant. "Get out before they do!" He threw his head back against the scaffolding, driving one of the short spikes through the newly healed flesh of his neck, and roared.

The sound trumpeted above the *hul-galla*'s screeching, a blast that buffeted them aside and away from the shining seam. The monk howled a second time, uttering words Serovek didn't know but that lifted him off his feet and flung him backwards, into the heart of the shadow, through it, to the edge of his nightmare where a voice waited to yank him across to the other side of consciousness.

"Wake up, margrave, before I punch you awake!"

Serovek hurtled out of sleep, Megiddo's tortured screams still ringing in his ears. He awakened to the sight of Anhuset's grim expression and her narrowed yellow eyes blazing brighter than a lamp. He clutched her arms, breathing as if he'd tried to outrun his horse on foot. "Megiddo," he gasped, gaze sliding to the bier on which the monk's soulless body rested, enveloped in a shimmering blue corona.

The light pulsed in shallow rhythm as if mimicking a racing heartbeat. Unsettled neighing from the horses in their stalls and the hard crack of hooves against wood rails filled the stables. Anhuset stared at Serovek, silent and unflinching as his fingers burrowed into her muscular arms while he tried to rid his mind of the echoes of *galla* laughter and Megiddo's suffering. Cerulean luminescence played off her angular features, sculpting her high cheekbones into more pronounced relief and sharpening her jaw. A Kai under a blue sun. Beautiful. Deadly. Not human.

"A man caught between worlds strives to reach you in this one." Her yellow eyes flared with a greenish tinge under the spectral haze. "Are you truly here with me?" At his nod, she pried his fingers off her arm, slid her hand up his forearm, and pulled him to his feet. "Wake fully, Lord Pangion, and plant your spirit in the world where you now stand."

Her command snuffed out the last of the echoes, but not the memory of the monk crucified on a scaffold of black bones. He stared at Anhuset, concentrating on her features. "Can you hear them at all? The *galla*? I dreamed them, but I swear it was more than a dream."

"I believe you." She left him to rummage through one of her packs, returning with a small hand mirror. "Take a look," she said, handing it to him.

He held the mirror up and swallowed back a gasp as horror flooded him. The blue luminescence hadn't confined itself to a corona surrounding Megiddo's bier. Serovek stared at his reflection with eyes flooded in the same shimmering hue. His natural eye color was blue as well, but of a more natural shade. His dead wife had once likened his irises to the deep of a cold ocean. Now they glowed with the ethereal strangeness of a Wraith king's power, like the simulacrum *vuhana* he'd ridden into battle against the *galla*. As he continued to stare, the light faded, his sclera becoming white again, even as his irises darkened, losing their definition to pupils dilated from the dimness of the stables and the last vestiges of his nightmare. "Gods," he breathed, before thrusting the mirror at Anhuset.

Her claws scraped across the glass as she took it from him. Her eyes glowed as well as she regarded him, but from the nature of her heritage instead of sorcery. "How long has this been happening?"

Serovek shrugged. "This is the first time I've seen it."

"But is it the first time you've looked?"

"No."

This was the worst nightmare he'd had about the *galla* or Megiddo so far, but not the only one. Each time he'd awakened, the shuddering aftermath left him bathed in a cold sweat. He'd dealt with battle sickness when he was younger, less inured to the savagery of war. This wasn't battle sickness. No one's eyes glowed ethereal blue when they fought their own inner demons.

Anhuset put away the mirror, switching it for a flask. "You look like you need a drink. If this doesn't chase away the echoes, nothing will."

Serovek ran the flask under his nose, rearing back when his eyes watered at the familiar smell. Peleta's Kiss. He saluted Anhuset, took a healthy swig and braced for the burn as the spirit scorched a path over his tongue, down his throat, and into his stomach where it ignited with a heat to melt the last splinters of ice coursing through his veins. This time the shudder that threatened to break his joints loose had nothing to do with the nightmare and everything to do with the flask's contents. Clear-headed, with a warm glow burning in his belly, he thanked Anhuset for her offering and returned it to her. "The spirit that cures all ills," he said.

She nodded and tucked the flask back into the satchel where she'd stashed her mirror. "Nectar of the gods." Her mouth curved. "For when they want their insides set on fire." The amusement softening her features faded as she eyed him. "I've had bad dreams, but yours was worse than what most of us suffer, I think." She inclined her head toward Megiddo. "And him being here has something to do with it obviously. Do you wish to speak of it?"

He liked that she didn't demand he tell her what he dreamed, though holding such a nightmare close did the dreamer no good. "Not really, but we both know this was more than a dream. I think it was a warning and probably something you should relate to Brishen when you return to Saggara." Her features remained expressionless as he recounted the grotesque visions and the sounds of the *galla* as they tortured the Nazim monk. Only her eyes changed, their yellow brightening or darkening as he spoke of the hairline crack of light in the writhing darkness and Megiddo's desperate command that Serovek get away.

When he finished, she turned to stare at the monk's bier and the body lying peacefully under the blanket. The blue light had disappeared completely. "How long have you dreamed of the *galla* and Megiddo?"

It felt like several lifetimes. "Since a couple of months after returning home from Haradis. They've grown progressively worse as time passed but nothing like tonight." He followed Anhuset's gaze to the bier. "Then again, this is the first time I've been in such close proximity to him since I turned him over to his brother for safekeeping."

His anger over Pluro keeping his brother's ensorceled body stashed away in a rundown barn lessened at the memory of the man's explanation for doing so. Nightmares, he'd complained. Horrific nightmares that aged you a decade in a night. If Megiddo's nearness spread night terrors like plague to anyone sleeping nearby, he couldn't so harshly condemn Pluro for exiling his brother away from the house.

Either his musings played across his features, or Anhuset thought as he did at that moment. "We may have rushed to judgment about your vassal's actions. The dream you just woke from had you downing Peleta's Kiss like water. If Pluro Cermak and his household fought such battles in their sleep more than once, he probably couldn't get his brother out of the house fast enough or far enough. And who could blame him?"

Serovek twitched back a corner of the concealing blanket to gaze at Megiddo's peaceful, austere face under the transparent shell of protective sorcery. "He hung on some kind of scaffolding, begging for mercy while the *galla* flayed the skin from his body in strips no wider than reins. And when they were done, they healed him and started over again."

It wasn't the sight of such gruesome cruelty that made Serovek's hand shake when he covered Megiddo's face again, but the memory of his voice, the hopelessness in those screams for mercy. The madness.

A sudden thought occurred to him, making him frown. "Has

Brishen complained of bad dreams in which the *galla* and the monk play a part?"

"If he has, he's not shared those complaints with me," Anhuset replied, her features serene, her voice mild.

Unlike human eyes, which gave away numerous tells in the shift of a gaze or the dilation of pupils, a Kai's eyes gave away very little. He'd discovered through years of careful observation that they actually did possess pupils, but they were the same color as the iris and the sclera: yellow upon yellow upon yellow. They moved and shifted just like a human's eyes, but the monochrome coloration obscured such movement instead of highlighting it. Anhuset's citrine stare didn't reveal anything, but her studied composure did. He knew her well enough now to know she was, by nature, neither serene nor mild. She'd dodged his question with an answer that wasn't a lie but also not quite the truth.

Serovek chose not to push. Sha-Anhuset's devotion to the *herceges* was absolute. He could do to her what the *galla* did to Megiddo until the end of time, and he'd not get a word out of her until she chose to share one. Besides, if he were honest, he prayed Brishen slept untroubled in his human wife's arms and what Serovek dealt with now was merely a mind trying to rid itself of poisonous memory.

Pray hard, an inner voice told him.

He turned his attention to his silent companion and gave her a short bow. "I'll not be rolling up in my blanket again, and I doubt you're one to while away the hours in chit-chat." He laughed at her derisive huff. "I propose either a round of dicing or sparring. Your choice, though I'll have to go back to the inn for the dice and my waster."

Those yellow eyes flared bright, and Serovek didn't bother hiding his amusement at the delight overtaking her expression. He might have known that the way to charm Anhuset wasn't with compliments or flowers but the offer to brawl or gamble.

She raised a hand, signaling him to wait before she bent to rummage through her gear. "No need. I have a waster and a *silabat* with me. The second will work as a waster as well. I also have dice, but I'd much rather spar."

"Eager for the chance to beat my arse?"

Anhuset presented a wooden practice sword and the *silabat*, offering both for him to choose his preference. Her half smile briefly revealed the points of her teeth. "Absolutely."

He took the *silabat* and saluted her with it.

She questioned his choice with a raised eyebrow. "You know how to use one of those in sparring?"

A few of his men scoffed at stick fighting—until someone with a mastery of the martial form sent them limping and bleeding out of the practice yard. Serovek's own trainer, a grizzled warrior with three fingers on one hand and no mercy in his soul, had taught Serovek how to fight with numerous weapons, the stick being a favorite.

He spun the *silabat* in his hand, admiring its balance and weight. Whoever carved this one knew what they were doing, and in the skilled hands of a fighter like Anhuset, it was lethal. "I can manage," he said.

No doubt the waster she held was nearly as deadly as her real sword, lacking only the edge and point to equal them. She grasped the practice sword with the typical Kai hold—partially open palm with the thumb pressed against the grip on one side, the middle and forefinger held straight on the other side. He thought it odd the first time he'd seen it, a method unique to the Kai to accommodate their claws. "I always wondered why the Kai held a sword in such a seemingly unwieldy way until I tried the grip myself."

The waster, a graceful wooden copy of her steel blade, cleaved the air as she practiced a short slash. "And what did you discover?"

"A strengthened forearm and improved point control. I never questioned the Kai's ability to handle a blade. I've seen firsthand how your folk fight. I just thought the grip strange."

Anhuset raised the weapon to give him a better view of her hold on the grip. "You've a good eye. That's exactly how it works." She tapped the *silabat* he held. "As you're open to trying the grip on your own, I'm willing to hone your skill at it should you wish." This time she lightly tapped his knuckles. "Not that you'll need it since you've no claws of your own."

"A shortcoming, I'm sure." He couldn't help but tease her.

"Your words, margrave. Not mine." She adopted a shallow crouch, and motioned for him to do the same, waster held in a casual way that Serovek knew better than to underestimate. "I thought you said sparring instead of chatting."

He struck with the *silabat*, a move she easily countered. "So I did," he said and launched another attack. Soon they were battling up and down the stable's dimly lit center aisle, their audience a half dozen horses watching from their stalls while others dozed, undisturbed by the mock fighting.

They had fought together in true battle against Brishen's kidnappers and torturers. Serovek had witnessed her prowess in a fight, though he'd never battled her himself. Sparring her forced him to use every skill he possessed just to stay on his feet and not have her bash him in the head with her waster. She was ungodly fast, and he was reminded of how Brishen moved in a similar fashion, with a darting speed that tricked the unknowing into believing the quick were not the strong. The Kai were both, blessed with thick bones and naturally muscular physiques. Long-limbed Anhuset possessed the reach to successfully lay a bruise or two on him, every strike hard enough to send a spike of pain through his body.

He gave as good as he got, unconcerned that she might not withstand his most aggressive attacks or break through his staunchest defenses. She was more than up to the task, only snarling under her breath and baring those intimidating teeth when he managed to wallop her with the *silabat*.

Outside, winter still gripped the land, coating the grass with frost. Inside the stable it was warm and sweat dripped from Serovek's hairline into his eyes. Anhuset's gray skin glistened in the dull lamplight, a lavender blush riding along her cheekbones from the heat of the building and their own exertions.

Their sparring came to an abrupt end when Anhuset maneuvered close to the stall housing Serovek's horse. Ears laid back and nostrils pinched, Magas stretched his neck over the stall door and bit the Kai woman on the shoulder.

"Gods damn it!" Yellow eyes wide, Anhuset pivoted, ready to strike this newest attacker with her waster. She lowered her sword arm and glared at the stallion before turning the baleful expression on Serovek. "Did you put him up to that?"

Both man and horse snorted at the same time.

"Magas and I are close, and I'm good with horses, but not that good. He's probably annoyed that we're keeping him awake." Serovek leaned the *silabat* against one of the stalls before approaching. "Let me see the damage."

She exhaled an indignant breath but turned to present her back. "We should have listed a rule or two before we started. No biting." Before Serovek could respond, she dropped the waster and pulled her shirt over her head, baring her torso to his gaze.

He paused, swallowing a gasp at the sight of her long back, as graceful as he remembered. His thoughts scattered in every direction before he managed to catch one and hold on to it. Not that it did him any good. The notion he should have taken up sculpting instead of warfare just for the ability to carve this majestic woman from stone wasn't what he needed to dwell upon at the moment.

Anhuset glanced at him over her shoulder, a silvery eyebrow arched in question. "Well?"

Serovek had interacted with the Kai enough over the years to know they were more broad-minded about such things as nudity than many human cultures were and didn't assign it the same eroticism. Had the stables been too warm, he had no doubt Anhuset wouldn't have hesitated to strip and fight him, bare-arsed as the day she was born. With that kind of distraction, he would have lost the sparring match after her first attack.

She had a way of testing him at every level. This was just one more, and he shoved down the lust roiling through his veins to concentrate on the bite mark Magas left on her shoulder. A crescent shape of square indentations that marched along the top of her shoulder and through the scar left by the bodkin Serovek had dug from her flesh more than a year earlier, the bite hadn't broken the skin. The bruise it promised to leave would be impressive, one not even Anhuset's gray skin could hide.

"You'll live," he said, fingertips hovering just above the mark, the temptation to touch humming along his fingernails. Did his voice sound as hoarse to her as it did to him? Strands of her silvery hair fluttered across his knuckles. "That was a warning nip at most. He gets grumpy when he's sleepy."

"Stallions," she groused, shrugging her shirt back over her head and straightening the hem with a yank. "Arrogant, temperamental, and more trouble than they're worth."

He couldn't resist. "Not all of us."

It was a good thing he never underestimated her martial prowess. He snatched up the *silabat* just in time to deflect her strike with the waster. Nearby, Magas gave a disgruntled whuffle.

Anhuset's narrow-eyed gaze flared bright in the dim stables. "I was talking about your horse."

"Were you indeed?"

His mild taunt earned him a hard strike to the hip from her waster. He dodged her open-palmed blow, went low and managed to kick one of her legs out from under her. She stumbled but recovered just as fast. After several feints and counter feints, as well as exchanged blows, they ended up on the stable floor amid a flurry of straw.

Anhuset straddled Serovek's torso, hard thighs clamped against his sides like a vise, her waster's edge pressed to his neck. She gave him a glimpse of her pointed teeth when her lips parted in a smirk. "Now what, margrave?"

"I die from lack of air," he said on a soft wheeze. "My gods, woman, did you fall on me, or did Magas?"

She gave a scornful huff but shifted position to ease her weight on him. "Better now, dandelion?"

He inhaled a thin breath, still recovering from having his chest flattened. "Never let it be said the Kai are made of flower petals and wool rovings."

"I don't know how you weak humans ever got this far."

"We're cunning, feral, and afraid of dying."

Anhuset arched an eyebrow. "If that was praise toward your kind, it's the worst I've ever heard."

Serovek savored her considerable weight now that she was settled more on his midriff and pelvis. He glanced to the side at her waster. "Are we finished sparring, or are you planning to wallop me a few more times with your sword?" He didn't mind lying on the stable floor among a cloud of straw remnants, though a tickle in his nasal passages warned of a coming sneeze.

Anhuset tilted her head to one side, studying where the waster's blunt edge rode the ridge of his jugular. "Had this been a real sword and a real fight, I'd have cut your head off by now."

Her eyes rounded when Serovek gently poked her ribs with the *silabat's* tip.

"True, but not before I skewered you like a roasted chicken with this handy stick of yours."

Her chuff of laughter made him smile. He liked her laugh. From what he was learning about her, she was a solemn woman and her laughter rare. He'd once thought her humorless until she began trading quips and taunts with him. An endless cache of fascinating qualities lay behind those bright citrine eyes and dour expression, and he had every intention of discovering them.

Something in his face must have given away a hint of his thoughts. Anhuset's amusement faded, and the air around them pulsed with a different kind of tension. She pulled the waster away but didn't move from her spot atop him. A slender finger, tipped in a sharp black claw, speared a lock of his hair before twining it around her knuckle. "You're even uglier this close up."

The blood coursing through his veins rushed toward his groin. He dropped the *silabat* to rest his hands on her hips. "And you're just as beautiful."

Those firefly eyes narrowed. "I imagine that silver-tongued charm felled a battalion of women at the Beladine court." She gave his hair a quick tug before unwinding it from her finger. "I still won't swive you, margrave." She rolled off him and stood.

Serovek lay supine a moment longer, missing the feel of her weight and heat on him. "Ah, sha-Anhuset. You're a harsh woman," he teased. "Breaking my heart as well as my back."

"Don't tempt me, Lord Pangion. My threat to tear your arms off before this trip is over remains." She held out a hand, which he took and gained his feet. The yellow shading in her eyes flickered, and Serovek had the sense her gaze passed over him. "You're nimble for such a big man," she said, the faintest thread of admiration running through her voice. "Fast too."

He brushed straw bits off his clothes and out of his hair before giving her a wry look. "So to sum up, I'm big, ugly, and annoying."

Once more, the brief flash of pointed teeth in a smile that vanished as quickly as it appeared. "So sayeth you."

Unlike her, he didn't hesitate in showing her his grin, widening it even more when her nose wrinkled at the sight of his own square ivories. She had made him laugh, made him lust, and most of all made him forget the nightmares that plagued his sleep.

He bowed to her. "You have my gratitude," he said. "I'll be a walking bruise by daylight, but the sparring did what I couldn't do alone."

She took the *silabat* he held out to her. "And what's that?"

"Quieted the sounds of Megiddo's screams in my head." Just saying the words made him shudder inside, and he shoved down the echo of the monk's torture and the *galla's* laughter before it broke through the wall of silence he'd built with Anhuset's help.

She passed him to return the *silabat* and waster to their place among her baggage. "I've always believed there isn't anything a good brawl and a few bruises can't fix."

"I'm sure a little Kai magic never hurt either."

The sudden stiffness in her posture surprised him, and her expression turned wary. "I suppose," she said in a noncommittal voice that was a telltale sign itself, as was her abrupt change in subject. "You should try and sleep before the dawn comes. Even an hour or two will help."

This wasn't the first time she'd reacted in such a way to one of his casual remarks about the Kai's ability to control magic, and Serovek wondered at her reaction. That her people were born with such an inheritance was no secret. He'd warned his men countless times to be especially wary when dealing with Kai raiders crossing their borders. They were a physically tough people and hard to kill, and any magic they wielded, no matter how minor, made them even more so.

He tucked the observation away for later, when he could mull it over without the shadows of his recent nightmare clouding his thinking. Her suggestion to sleep before the following day's travel was a sound one. Still, the thought of returning to the stall where Megiddo rested didn't appeal to him, even now when the blue luminescence surrounding the bier had disappeared. "Maybe you should sleep instead. I'll keep watch until dawn."

She scooped up his blankets and tossed them at him. "Remember, your night is my day. I'm wide awake. If I need to sleep, I can do so while I ride. You're the leader of this expedition. You need your wits about you." She lifted her chin to indicate the empty stall across from the one they currently occupied. "Sleep there if you need or go back to the inn. A soft bed awaits you if you want it, and distance from the monk."

"I'm not Pluro Cermak," he snapped, affronted by her allusion to a need for posher surroundings or a desire to avoid the monk. "Megiddo might be in a barn again, but I'll not leave him here alone."

"He won't be alone, Lord Pangion." Anhuset's more formal address didn't quite disguise the sympathy in her voice. "And I doubt anyone would compare you to his brother under any circumstance."

He'd lashed out unfairly. The residual fury at discovering Megiddo's resting place in a ramshackle barn had ignited with Anhuset's suggestion. There'd been nothing beyond the remark other than practical advice. "Forgive me," he said, and offered her a second bow of the evening. "You didn't deserve my rancor."

Anhuset's shoulders lifted in a shallow shrug. "It's of no matter. I suspect you and I will brawl with words as well as wasters and *silabats* on this trip. You didn't try to tear *my* arms off. There's nothing to forgive."

Once more, she chased away his demons with her wit and made him laugh. Serovek left her with Megiddo and their gear to find a sleeping spot in a pile of mostly clean straw in the empty stall. Bedded down, with his back to his companions, he stared at the wall in front of him, counting the cracks marring its surface until his eyelids grew heavy. He was tipping over the edge of sleep when Anhuset's voice stopped him.

"Margrave?"

Some instinct, or maybe the tone in her voice, warned him to stay put and keep his back to her. "Hmm?"

"You're ugly, but your hair is soft."

A gust of more laughter burst past his lips and out his nostrils. The woman wouldn't know how to deliver a compliment if her life depended on it. He wrapped the blankets more snugly about him. "Then I've found favor in your eyes with one thing." he said. "Good night, Anhuset."

CHAPTER
SIX

Anhuset quickly learned that the conversation between human males worked better than any dream elixir brewed by the most skilled Kai apothecary. It was vapid, shallow, and so utterly uninspired she was in danger of sliding from a light sleep atop her horse into a stupor of boredom.

The late morning sun offered little warmth but a great deal of punishing light, and she was glad for the deep shadows of her hood that kept the worst of the glare off her face. She kept a slitted gaze on the wagon rolling ahead of her, Megiddo's blanket-covered bier tied down to keep it from sliding across the wagon's platform. As usual, Serovek took the lead in their caravan, flanked by two of his men, Jannir and Ardwin. She couldn't hear what they discussed over the inane bluster and gloating her companions swapped between them, each trying to outdo the other in their feats of prowess in a fight or between a bedmate's thighs.

Of the three who rode beside her, she knew Erostis best, having diced with him on those occasions she'd visited High Salure. An amiable man with a trickster's hand for rolling the bones and an accurate intuition for his opponent's weaknesses in a game, he'd lightened Anhuset's purse by several coins in gambling rounds. At the moment he lectured the more flamboyant Ardwin for his poor spending habits on wine and women.

"You keep buying a trio of whores for the evening, and you won't be able to afford scratching your arse before the week is out. And with the amount of drink I saw you put down last night, I doubt you had it in you to crawl on top of one of them for a quick fuck. They never made such easy money in a night."

Ardwin stiffened in the saddle, affronted by the admonishment. "What are you? My da? And just because you can't get a rise out of your own prick, old man, doesn't mean I can't."

Erostis's dry chuckle told her he'd taken no offense at Ardwin's defensive insult. It was the bluster of youth. Erostis was a good twenty years older than Ardwin and unruffled by such things. Anhuset suspected the two of them engaged in similar verbal brawls on a regular basis.

The rider to her right and just behind her narrowed the space between them, and her back prickled at the weight of a jaundiced stare on her. It wasn't the first time she'd felt this particular stare. Ogran edged closer, watching her with the sullen expression that seemed permanently stamped on his features. Unlike the rest of their party, he kept to himself, had little to say, and lacked any noticeable humor.

Anhuset considered none of these things a character flaw. She was laconic herself; her wit, when it made an appearance, sharper than most people liked. But there was about Ogran a mien of dangerous resentment, bubbling so close to the surface she could almost smell it. He never put voice to it on this trip, and whatever caused his malcontent remained a mystery. Still, she remained wary. His gaze, when it landed on her—and it did more often than she liked—held something much darker than mere curiosity or disdain. Human gazes were hard for her to read, their strange eyes too much a distraction to discern the nuances of subtle expression, but his scrutiny had a weight to it that didn't need discernment. He didn't approve of her presence among them and made little effort to conceal it.

"Your ears aren't pointed," he stated when he finally coaxed his mount to ride adjacent to hers. The debate between Ardwin and Erostis went silent.

The hood she wore kept the worst of the sun's brightness off her, shrouding her ears and hair, providing deep shadow and obscurity. He must have pondered over the shape of her ears from the previous day, when she'd been bareheaded. Anhuset accommodated his unwelcome observation and scraped back the hood so he might have a better look. When she turned to face him, he swallowed hard and reined his horse back from her.

His initial statement stoked her own curiosity. Humans were odd, and she had little use for them, but good strategy meant understanding even those one found puzzling or even unlikable, and for the next few weeks, she'd be the sole Kai among a contingent of humans. Ogran just happened to be one of the more unpleasant ones. According to Serovek, he was High Salure's best tracker and could sniff out spoor better than a hunting hound. Any traveling party benefited from the presence of someone with those skills, though tracking seemed the only positive thing about him. "No, they aren't," she said. "Why would you think they'd be so?"

He shrugged. "Well, your teeth are pointed."

"Oh for fuck's sake, Ogran," Erostis muttered. "How much of a lackwit can you be?"

Ogran offered a rude gesture in reply but otherwise ignored the other two soldiers.

Anhuset blinked, surprised by the reasoning. Skilled tracker or not, if this was an example of Ogran's intellect, then she heartily agreed with Erostis. The man was a lackwit. Such rationale might have suggested he question his own physical characteristics. His teeth were square but his ears were like hers, curved with dips and shallows of cartilage and fleshy lobes from which both Kai and humans sometimes sported jewelry.

Images flashed across her memory, of Ildiko Khaskem crossing her strange eyes and the Kai's predictably horrified reaction when she did it. Anhuset stared at Ogran for a moment without answering and curved her lips into a grin so wide it squinched her eyes and made her cheeks ache. The movement exposed her teeth to the back molars, and she nearly burst into a fit of laughter when Ogran's visage washed pale with terror. He shuddered so hard, his horse shied in reaction. Nearby, Ardwin's thin, breathy "Holy gods, save us," only emphasized Ogran's terror.

Erostis's initial flinch gave way to a grin of his own, though unlike her own ivory spikes, he possessed the typical squared teeth of his kind. He saluted her with a quick touch of his fingertips to his forehead.

Her attention flickered back to Ogran, and she lost the grin. "I don't bite with my ears," she said before turning away to tug the hood back in place. Ogran's horse quickly fell behind hers. Their conversation was over, and Anhuset silently thanked the absent *hercegesé* for the inspiration of her response. Maybe now they'd all shut up, and she could doze in peace.

She hoped in vain.

Ardwin soon resumed his debate with Erostis, the second baiting the first with gentle mockery. Anhuset gave up trying to sleep but pretended otherwise in order to dissuade the others from including her in their conversation. She focused on Serovek's broad shoulders as he rode ahead. His black hair fluttered in the chilly breeze, falling down his back to rest between his shoulder blades. Sunlight caught the silver threads woven through his locks. She wondered how old he was. Powerful, and muscular in build, with the marks of a life defined by both joy and tragedy etched into his features, he seemed neither young nor old but a man in his prime. He wore the mantle of leadership with ease, though she'd never witnessed tyrannical behavior from him. Most of his men offered him respect that bordered on reverence.

Once she'd believed he was simply a human possessing lusty appetites, martial prowess, and a singular ability to annoy her until she gnashed her teeth. He'd obliterated those assumptions when he dug an arrowhead out of her shoulder and helped save Brishen from his abductors, when he volunteered to fight by the Khaskem's side against the *galla*, and when he fearlessly handed her his blade to spill his blood on an ancient tor. There were depths to Serovek Pangion deeper than oceans she'd only glimpsed from far shores, so much more than teasing innuendo and damn fine horsemanship.

He struggled with the tragedy of Megiddo's fate, reason not always conquering guilt at having survived the *galla* when the monk had not. She'd seen it in his expression when he woke from sleep plagued by what she suspected was more than bad dreams and far more dangerous. The ethereal luminescence which Ildiko had seen in Brishen's eye had surfaced in both of Serovek's, along with a horror that faded as he grew more awake. Still, its shadow had lingered in the midnight blue of his gaze, along with the cobalt light that turned his gaze spectral and haloed Megiddo's soulless, ensorceled body.

Did ancient Kai magic still linger in those Wraith kings who'd returned to their human forms after they defeated the *hul-galla*, trace ribbons of it revived by proximity to Megiddo's body or his sword? And if so, what terrible thing might it visit upon those who'd fought so bravely and emerged triumphant thanks to the sacrifice of one of their own?

The questions whirled in her mind like dust spinners on a hot summer day, along with a yearning to know more about High Salure's margrave, peel back those endless layers that revealed a man she'd grown to admire more and more every day. Admire and crave.

She growled under her breath, tightening her grip on the reins hard enough that her mount slowed from an ambling walk to a near stop. She loosened her grip and tapped the animal's sides. The horse resumed its leisurely pace. Her three companions hadn't noticed or heard her displeasure at acknowledging the weakness of such unfortunate attraction. Serovek Pangion was ugly, irritating, and far too cocksure of himself, especially regarding his presumed attraction to the opposite sex, including her.

And his hair cascaded through her fingers like silk.

A second growl rumbled in her throat when he glanced over his shoulder at her, gave a quick smirk, and turned back around, as if to signal he'd heard every one of her thoughts and dared her to deny them.

Twilight hadn't yet crawled across the sky, and there was still plenty of light to set up camp when Serovek signaled a stop. Anhuset roused from her light doze for a better look at her surroundings. She recognized the wooded landscape with its mix of still-dormant oaks and firs so dark a green, they etched black silhouettes against the sky. Close by, the Absu tumbled and rushed in a loud whisper. A melancholic pang settled beneath her ribcage. Dead Haradis lay not far from here, less than a day by boat.

Their group split the work between them, building a fire, unloading a few supplies, hunting for supper, taking care of the horses. Erostis returned from his foray into the wood, not with a brace of hares, as she expected, but a line of fish taken from the river. "I'm a better fisherman than hunter," he said, holding up his prizes with a triumphant smile.

The fish, roasted on spits, accompanied flat bread cooked on a round sheet of metal Ardwin had unloaded from their wagon, all washed down with cups of tepid ale. Nightfall brought a dip in temperature, and the group sat huddled around the fire, wrapped in cloaks. Anhuset stayed farther back to avoid the worst of the light and noticed no one looked directly at the flames.

"You wear an odd expression, Anhuset." Serovek had abandoned his spot and sat next to her. "What are you thinking?"

Her nostrils flared. He wore the scents of the forest and camp smoke. Earthy smells that made her blood warm and her skin tingle. She quaffed the rest of her ale, wishing for something more bracing like Peleta's Kiss, where the burn would stave off images of what the margrave might look like naked and sheened in sweat from a bout of hard lovemaking. She scowled into her empty cup before answering. "I see neither you nor your men stare into the fire. Smart."

One dark eyebrow rose, and Serovek's mouth turned up at the corner. "I'm glad you approve. Men blinded by firelight can't fight well if attacked in the dark. It's one of the first things I and my commanders teach the novices. I'm guessing this isn't a problem for the Kai."

"No, though we still give our novices similar warnings since we're even more sensitive to light than humans." She rolled the cup between her palms, considering her next words. "In many ways, you aren't so different from us."

This time both of his eyebrows climbed, and Anhuset braced for his usual teasing. He surprised her when he poured some of his ale into her cup, then clinked his cup against hers in a silent toast. "I couldn't have said it better myself."

He steered their conversation toward other things—the trip itself, what they expected from early spring's unpredictable weather. Surface topics that didn't require internal questioning or inspire thoughts in her mind that made her twitch with either doubt or an uncomfortable desire. He was good at casual conversation, shouldering most of it while she preferred to listen, and quietly attentive when she did speak.

While they conversed, she grew aware of an intense scrutiny from the other side of the fire. She darted a glance in that direction, glad for the fact the solid color of her eyes and their glow hid their movement from the others. Ogran stared at her and Serovek, obvious dislike pinching his features much as they had earlier when he'd questioned why her ears weren't pointed. A flicker of sly malice sharpened his expression before disappearing. All of Anhuset's instincts came alive in warning.

She left her place to retrieve one of the ale skins and refill her cup. Serovek offered up his cup for a refill as well, as Ogran's stare became a bodkin point between her shoulder blades. Serovek's regard, in contrast, held a sensual interest that threatened to scatter her thoughts. A maddening trait.

"Tell me," she said softly. "How long has Ogran served under your command?"

He tilted his head to one side, obviously puzzled by the question. "As long as my steward. He came to High Salure with Bryzant as his servant, then chose to join my guard. He's a decent soldier, and as I mentioned earlier, an excellent tracker. Why do you ask?" He glanced at Ogran who instantly looked away, expression now studiously bland.

"Just curious." She continued watching Ogran, who peered into his ale cup as if it revealed his fate and fortune.

"I find that hard to believe." Serovek returned the scowl she gave him with narrow-eyed regard. "You don't say or do anything without purpose. Curious you might be but not for idle gossip. Something about Ogran has raised your hackles."

She bristled now, affronted by the idea she might be so predictable, especially to this man who possessed a terrifying ability to effortlessly see to the very heart of her. She abandoned the idea of hedging her answer.

"There's something about him beyond a sour demeanor. I have a sour demeanor. This is different. I'd never turn my back on him."

Once more Serovek's gaze fell on Ogran and lingered. "Not the friendliest sort, I'll agree, but in the years he's served High Salure, he's never given me reason to doubt his loyalty. I won't condemn a man for a wrongdoing he hasn't committed." Anhuset was about to protest that her observation wasn't a request to somehow punish Ogran, but Serovek stopped her. "However, I trust your instincts implicitly. Familiarity can blind a person to another's ill will. I'll keep a closer eye on him."

His words stunned her for a moment. Not the ones about Ogran, but those about her. She expected him to justify his choices regarding Ogran. She hadn't expected his blunt and total acceptance of her advice. "Why do you trust me?"

His slight shrugged matched his slight smile. "Because you're sha-Anhuset," he said, as if that alone explained everything. He rose, dumped out the dregs of his cup and bowed to her before leaving to speak with Klanek, who walked the perimeter around the wagon, checking the transport for any problems that might slow their trek the following day.

She would never understand him. Never.

Just look closer. Look longer.

"Oh, shut up," she muttered into her cup, wishing the internal voice had a tongue so she could rip it out.

That night, when all but she found sleeping spots not far from the fire and wrapped in blankets for warmth, she approached Serovek. He'd set up his makeshift bedding near the wagon, almost within touching distance from Megiddo's ensorceled bier. Even facing the probability of suffering from another round of bad dreams that were more than dreams and much, much worse, he refused to stray far from his fallen comrade, though it meant revealing to the others how the Kai magic that protected the monk also infected their stalwart leader.

His half smile held a question and a hope that refused to die no matter how she might scoff. "Decided to share my bed, firefly woman?"

"I admire your fortitude," she said. "And my answer is still no."

His quiet chuckle warmed her more than any fire ever could. "I'm also a patient man." He reclined back on his elbows, long legs stretched so that one foot rested against hers where she stood. "So why have you decided to loom over me?"

She had little skill with the diplomacy of words. Most of the time she preferred not to speak at all. Serovek didn't need a nursemaid, and Anhuset couldn't think of anyone less suited to the task than herself, but she could be of use to him beyond the roles of night guard, armed escort, and Kai representative. "Should you begin to dream, I'll be nearby to wake you." She kept her voice soft, once more feeling the weight of Ogran's grim regard on her back. No doubt he strained to hear whatever they said.

For a long moment, Serovek didn't answer. He glanced at the wagon adjacent to him before returning his gaze to her. The half smile was gone, allowing her to see the serious side she once thought him incapable of displaying. Shadows darkened the deep-water blue of his eyes even more. "I appreciate and accept your safekeeping."

She told him goodnight then and left to reconnoiter their campsite and the makeshift rope corral where they'd confined the horses. The forest around them rustled continuously with nocturnal foragers and the predators that hunted them. In the distance, a wolf's lone howl echoed through the trees and was soon joined by a chorus of others. The nearby river tumbled and murmured under a cold spring moon.

To her relief, the night hours remained uneventful, and if Serovek dreamed, they were easy ones that didn't trouble him awake or twist his features in anguish and horror. Megiddo's bier remained dark, no glowing aura of Kai magic to illuminate it or the wagon. When the sun broke across the horizon, she yawned, slid her hood over her head to shield herself from the brightening day, and greeted the yawning margrave with a quick nod.

His slow blinking and sleepy smile made her wonder if this was how all his bedmates saw him when they woke beside him. Made restless by the image her thoughts evoked and the sight of Serovek with the first rays of the sun gilding the silver in his hair, she turned her back and set to relighting the smoldering fire in preparation for the group breaking their fast.

Amid grumbling about the cold and bland road rations, they made short work of the morning meal before breaking camp and setting off once more toward the first dock where a towboat and small barge waited to take them down the Absu, passing the remains of Haradis, before heading farther east and south by way of one of the river's tributaries.

The captain and his crew waiting at the dock eyed their party with doubtful looks, settling briefly on the wagon with its blanket-covered cargo before resting on Anhuset, whose face was mostly obscured by her hood. She kept her hands tucked into the sleeves of her cloak, as much for warmth as to minimize the inevitable macabre curiosity humans had for the Kai.

"We can take the lot of you, but it'll be slow-going with the weight and all. Hope you aren't in a hurry." The captain smiled a yellow-toothed smile. "And the fare is more when I'm traveling such a distance."

"How close do you sail to Haradis?" Serovek counted out a pile of coins from a fat purse he kept tied to his belt.

The captain's face froze at the question. He dragged his gaze from the money dropping into his outstretched palm to frown at Serovek. "Too close to my liking, but to get where we're going, we'll have to sail within a quarter-day's walk from it before reaching the tributary." He scooped the generous fee into a pouch before tucking it into his tunic. He tugged on his tangled beard. "Nothing to worry about though. There's plenty of water between us and the city, and we can navigate right quick past it. You'll only catch a glimpse of the tower remains before it's at our backs and gone."

Serovek gestured to Klanek to bring the wagon forward and instructed the rest to start loading everything onto the barge. He nudged Anhuset's shoulder, and the two distanced themselves a short way from the rest.

"Here's where you decide if you want to stop at Haradis." His offer surprised her, one that instinct warned she should refuse, and loyalty to Brishen pressed she should accept. Serovek nodded to the crew. "The captain can sail to one of the narrow points of the Absu without docking. The river is calmer there and easy to wade, even if you can't swim. We can get to the shore and make our way to Haradis on foot."

"I'm familiar with the path." She paused, caught by a single word in his plan. "We?"

The teasing smile flickered across his mouth and was gone. "I'll accompany you unless you wish to go alone." He raised a hand as if to ward off an expected protest from her. "I know you don't need a protector, but this is Haradis." No amusement remained in his expression, and his voice carried a note that made the hairs on her nape lift a little. His gaze shifted to the direction in which the broken capital lay. "It isn't as you remember it. I'd discourage anyone from going alone."

Brishen had cut off every suggestion and offer she'd made to visit Haradis and report back to him of its condition. A man of mild temperament and monumental resolve, he barely listened to her arguments in favor of sending a scout. His face had taken on the same bleak look Serovek wore now, as if memory of battling the *galla* there was a blacker shade than all the dark dreams Ildiko claimed plagued his sleep. The margrave offered her the chance Brishen continued to deny her for reasons he refused to discuss; she'd be a fool not to accept. From a military standpoint, it was both wise and necessary. And Brishen Khaskem wasn't here at the moment.

"I agree with your prudence, but you're not obliged to me," she said, wishing she could read human emotion more easily. Serovek's face was a study in stoicism, but the tension in his body and her own instincts alerted her to the fact that visiting Haradis wasn't something he anticipated with pleasure. "You fought the *galla* there. Surely, that's no memory you wish to resurrect."

He shrugged. "We fought the *galla* many places before we defeated them. Haradis is the remains of a battlefield. The memorial of a tragedy. But neither I nor any of the Beladine lost a loved one there. We don't have a history with Haradis. You do."

Had it been Saggara destroyed by the *galla*, he'd be right. Like all the Kai, a part of her mourned the loss of the city and its inhabitants, but the ties that bound her heart lay elsewhere. "Saggara, not Haradis, has always been my home. I won't be troubled."

Serovek's forehead creased for a moment into a disbelieving frown. He sighed. "So you say. If the river and weather stay agreeable, we should reach the city's edge by late afternoon."

The captain balked at first when Serovek relayed their plans, quieting only when the flash of additional coin passed in front of his eyes. Serovek's men protested even louder.

"I can go in your stead, my lord," Erostis offered. "I know nothing of Haradis, but with sha-Anhuset acting as guide, we can scout enough of the city and report back with useful information for both you and the Khaskem."

He grunted when Serovek landed a friendly swat on his shoulder. "You're more useful to me here. And with Anhuset and I both familiar with Haradis's streets, we can split up and reconnoiter in half the time and be finished before midnight."

His assurances stretched reality a little in her opinion. He might have fought his way through the streets of Haradis, but Anhuset doubted he remembered much about the city's grid, too busy cutting his way through *galla* to reach the palace. But she held her tongue and didn't argue. Erostis was a decent sort, and she liked him well enough, but if she had to have human company for this trip, she preferred the margrave. The small voice inside her gave a mocking laugh before she could silence it.

Once they were all aboard and the towboat and barge riding the Absu's waves under his steersman's guidance, the captain approached Serovek with a pair of filled pipes, offering one to Serovek. Close enough to hear their conversation, Anhuset leaned on the railing to unabashedly eavesdrop.

"The stop where I'd normally put you to disembark has changed." He puffed on his pipe before using it to point out some unseen detail of the geography on the passing shore. "A squire with holdings not far from here sent a small army of crofters and vassals to dredge the shallow spots. They're deeper and wider now, no drying up during the hot months, and they cut down every bridge and tore away every natural dam they found just in case you and the others missed a demon or two." He shot Serovek a challenging look, as if questioning the Wraith kings' success and believing more in their failure. "The landing is too deep for your horses and too treacherous for a swimmer. I can pull to shore about a half league farther back. You can hike in from there and meet us down river by a way-stop called Cat's Paw Hollow."

Serovek's gaze met hers over the captain's head. "Decision's still yours," he told her in bast-Kai.

She replied in the same tongue, much to the captain's consternation. "It'll delay the journey."

"Not by much and only if you want to pitch camp overnight in Haradis." A tiny shudder belied his casual tone. "I'm not much eager to avail myself of the hospitality."

Decision finalized, they made plans to disembark at the agreed-upon spot, leaving behind their horses and most of their gear, carrying with them only what they could transport in oilskin packs. For Anhuset, that meant going without her armor, her shield, and some of her heavier weaponry. It was much the same for Serovek.

They both watched the tow and barge for a moment as they sailed onward, leaving them on a spit of dry ground that stretched into the river like a pointing finger. A short footbridge had once stretched from this spot to the main shore, but the captain had spoken true. All that remained now were bits of cut rope and a few broken boards that hadn't been scavenged yet for firewood. The current tumbled slower there in the gap between land and river but was still something not to take lightly. People had drowned in waters shallower than these.

"I should have asked this on the boat, but just assumed it was so. You can swim, yes?" Serovek eyed her with part hope and part dread.

Anhuset bit back a laugh. She understood what he implied. If she couldn't swim, he'd have to carry her across, and if he did, they were in imminent danger of drowning. If she were to guess, she probably equaled Serovek in weight, and while he was impressively strong, carting another person across deep, fast-running water presented significant risk for both. "I'm an excellent swimmer."

His wide shoulders drooped in relief and his square teeth flashed white with his smile. "Is that a boast?"

She sniffed. "It's a fact, margrave. I'll even challenge you to a race across if you wish and promise not to tell your men that you lost. Badly."

His laughter carved the lines at the corners of his eyes a touch deeper. "As cold as that water promises to be, I wager I can walk on it just to keep from freezing my balls off."

Anhuset was growing to enjoy the look of his amusement. The sound of it too. It teased but didn't mock. She'd never known him to be cruel, though she'd witnessed his ruthlessness firsthand when he'd sentenced a brigand to die and carried out the execution himself without hesitation. Those who mistook his jovial manner as a weakness took their life in their hands.

She never made such a mistake with anyone, but she'd underestimated Serovek Pangion and the power of his charm. He was a man she could admire at every level. She didn't want to feel this way. Not for anyone.

"The Absu won't get any warmer with us standing here," she said abruptly, ignoring the puzzlement flitting across his face at her sudden gruff tone. She bent to remove her boots and strip off her clothing. Soon, she was bare to the wind and sun, with chill bumps covering every bit of skin. Her nipples ached from the cold, and she clenched her jaw to keep her teeth from chattering. A strangled sound reached her ears, and she paused from stuffing her clothing deep into the oilskin she carried to catch Serovek peeling off his trousers, leaving him as naked as she.

He was an impressive sight. Muscular and long-legged. A big man with a physique hardened by years of martial training and horsemanship. Her gaze drifted over him, stopping at his groin to stare admiringly at his endowments. "So the rumors were accurate," she said bluntly. "I wondered. And doubted."

He exhaled a combination of a cough and startled laughter before clearing his throat. "Did you now? I know I've said it before, but it bears repeating. You're refreshingly forthright."

The heat of a blush suffused her skin, chasing away the cold. She'd never been one to mince words, but there were times when it was better to keep one's thoughts to oneself. This was probably one of those times. But what was said was said, and she couldn't roll back time. "I don't know how else to be, Stallion."

"And I'm grateful for it," he replied. He swept a hand down his torso. "If it were warmer...well, you aren't seeing me at my best." He winked.

"I've seen you at your best." Her tongue had taken on a life of its own, refusing to heed the command of her brain which shouted at her to shut up. "On the summit of a tor, as an eidolon returned from battling demons, in a fight with those who tortured my liege. The gods were generous with you, but that isn't what elevates you or any man."

With that said, and the fires of mortification still singing through her blood, she didn't wait for an answer or rebuttal. Instead, she lifted her pack and shoes, inhaled a bracing breath and waded into the river.

All thoughts of Serovek's naked beauty fled her mind at the first lap of the Absu's icy caress on her skin. Every Kai curse word she'd learned from childhood to present day poured from her lips in a stuttering stream as she swam across the narrow channel, keeping the arm holding her gear above her head. Behind her, a litany of snarling Beladine invectives filled the air as the margrave joined her.

The Absu's waters were numbingly cold, never warming even after their vigorous swim. Once out of the water, Serovek shook like a drenched dog, scattering a shower of water droplets in every direction. "Fuck, it's cold," he declared through chattering teeth, accompanied by a shiver as he sloughed more water off his skin with his hands. His hair hung in a dripping horse's tail over one shoulder. The bracing cold had washed his complexion of any ruddiness. Anhuset found him almost attractive.

They hurriedly dressed in the still-dry clothes dug from their oilcloth packs. She almost groaned aloud at the blissful feel of thick dry wool wrapped around her. She'd left her cloak with her gear in favor of a padded tunic and a small cap she now pulled down over her chilly ears. It did nothing to shield her from the afternoon sun's brightness, but they'd be in the forest shade soon. She'd just have to squint until then.

Serovek fastened on his second boot and stood. He flexed one foot, frowning. "I think my toes have frozen together. At least we won't have to swim on the return trip."

"We don't have much sunlight left. We'll need to walk to warm up." Her back teeth clacked across her words. He was right. It was fucking cold, and standing about complaining wasn't going to make things any better. She did as he had, drying her feet and slipping on her boots before setting off toward the line of trees standing sentinel in front of them. Behind their shield wall lay a sun-dappled trek through a dense understory and beyond that, Haradis.

Serovek fell into step beside her, still shivering. He carried a long knife in one gloved hand and used the other to help clear a path. She carried a similar knife, the weapon serving as both slayer and scythe if needed. They cut through a barrier of crackling thorn bushes, still dry and brown from the last days of a clinging winter. "It's a good thing we aren't hunting or being hunted," she muttered. "We're making more noise than a herd of cattle, and I left enough blood on those thorns to paint a portrait."

The woodland twilight offered respite from the sun, drawing upon itself a deeper darkness as the day waned. Anhuset was grateful for the shade and not having to squint. She glanced at her companion, noting that he now squinted in an effort to make clear those things made obscure by the gloom. "We're closer to Haradis," she said. "I'm familiar with this area and can put us on an easier path than this one."

"By all means, take the lead," he said, gesturing for her to stride in front of him. "The darker it gets, the harder it'll be for me to see. I never thought I'd be in a hurry to return to Haradis, but I don't need to slow us down by stumbling my way through the woods half blind."

He was Beladine, raised in a society where women rarely held a leadership role, and she'd expected him to offer some token resistance to her leading the way. He did not, and she was glad for it and his practicality. At least there'd be no foolish arguing over who enjoyed the questionable privilege of being first to carve their way through a spiky bramble thicket.

Darkness had descended fully by the time she caught sight of the closest tower that flanked one side of Haradis's main gate. It rose above the treeline like a spear point, the small windows near the top nothing more than black spots from which no lamplight shone.

"The woodland breathes softly," Serovek said in quiet tones. "And carefully, as if it either waits for something to come forth or hopes it passes by once it finally does." The slight change in the way he held the cane knife alerted Anhuset to his rising caution.

She didn't scoff at his observation, feeling too a kind of unnatural hush that thickened around them, growing more and more stifling the closer they got to the city. No animal sounds, no scurrying for food, no howls or the crackle of dead leaves under creeping feet other than theirs. This forest was empty of its creatures.

The night held no mystery for her. She saw better in the shadow than she did in the light, and nothing looked out of the ordinary as they trekked closer to the gate. But the silence—it breathed, just as Serovek said, and Anhuset strained to hear some odd whisper or ghostly conversation float toward her. A burbling sound teased her ears, and she pointed in the direction from which it came, close to the city and growing louder as they walked.

"Water," Serovek said.

Anhuset frowned. "I used to go adventuring with the *herceges* in these woods when we were children. There's no water on this side. The Absu curves around the city's southeastern border before bisecting it."

"There was no stream on this side when we arrived in Haradis to fight the *galla*, but I know what I hear. It's the sound of water." He groaned softly. "And I'm just now warming up."

His good-natured complaint didn't lessen her increasing unease. A strangeness clung to these woods now, even without the wet whisper of running water that wasn't supposed to be nearby. It was as if each step closer to Haradis took her one more step away from the living world, where the stars glimmered above, and the shadows cavorted below as they had always done. This felt more like a falling away toward an abyss where everything that pitched into it fell and fell and never stopped. This wasn't her magic sounding a warning; her instincts recoiled ever harder from Haradis with each step taken.

"Anhuset."

They'd halted. Anhuset frowned. When had they stopped? Serovek stared at her, concern mingled with puzzlement carving lines into his forehead. "Can you feel it?" His voice was barely above a whisper. "Haradis is more than abandoned, more than destroyed. It's befouled. Those who died here...theirs weren't clean deaths. Are you sure you want to do this? We can turn back any time you wish."

Were he anyone else, she'd assume he either patronized her or considered her weak. Instead, she considered his words for a moment, knowing they were offered in empathy and a shared sense of wrongness suffocating the entire area. "I'm sure," she said. "Was Haradis like this when you were here?"

Serovek shook his head. "I don't know. The *galla* were spewing out of the heart of Haradis, thicker than a hive swarm. Maybe what we're feeling is the memory of the trees. Such evil leaves a smear on everything it touches. And lingers."

His conjectures were reasonable and only added to her sense of urgency that she scout the city and report back every detail to Brishen, despite his expected disapproval. She might tell him things he already knew or expected, but her instincts, which had always served her well and kept her alive, told her this was something far more sinister than the haunting tragedy of Haradis's ruin.

"You've done me the favor of delaying your own journey to give me this opportunity, margrave, and I'm grateful. You aren't obliged to accompany me into Haradis. I promise to be swift. In, a quick look around, and out again so as not to delay more. But I have to do this." As Anhuset spoke the words, sense of duty overrode instinct, and she barely controlled the urge to sprint out of the woods for the gate hidden behind the tree line. "I need to."

He eyed her for a moment without speaking, then lifted the long knife he held to regard it with a measure of disdain. "I doubt this will do much good against anything lurking in the city, but it's better than nothing." He swept a hand in the direction of Haradis and gave Anhuset a short bow. "Shall we, madam?"

Gladness sang through her that he chose to join her, but she pushed it down. Such foolery was reserved for the drunken hours after too many pints in an alehouse and no bedmate to help stave off melancholy self-reflection. It had no place here where the darkness that was more than darkness inhaled, exhaled, and waited.

She gasped at the sight greeting them. The last time she'd visited the capital had been when Brishen brought his new bride to face his parents and the royal court. Haradis, far from the sea, now perched on an island.

A series of canals dug by unknown hands in a spiderweb pattern channeled the water she and Serovek heard earlier. From her vantage point, she couldn't see their source, but the water's flow told her it came from the Absu itself. A small portion of the river had been redirected here—not for irrigating fallow fields but to isolate the city within the confines of a liquid labyrinth. A prison for the *galla*.

"Someone's been very busy," Serovek remarked beside her. "And very afraid. This took the labor of many, and they favored speed over neatness."

He was right. The canals were numerous but shallow, the main one completely surrounding the city with offshoots of others spreading from it in a disorderly fashion. The canals' sides were uneven, higher in some spots than others, undulating in places like a ribbon instead of a spear haft. But they were clear of debris. At no point was a channel blocked or bridged by bits of detritus built up by storms or animals. Whoever had constructed this watery barricade continued to maintain it, providing safe haven in shallow runnels for any who might flee the city from that which couldn't cross water.

Anhuset noted all of it in a sweeping glance before returning to stare at what remained of the once thriving, living city. Saggara was her home, where those who meant most to her lived, but she'd spent her childhood here. Unlike the Kai who'd fled the carnage as refugees, or Brishen, who'd fought the demons to their very gate, she hadn't experienced the horror of the *hul-galla*'s attack or seen the havoc they'd wrought firsthand. Haradis didn't have an emotional grip on her the way Saggara did. She'd believed it true when she declared such to Serovek. She was wrong.

A few seasons had passed since the *galla* had swarmed the capital, devouring thousands in a single night. She'd expected a place abandoned if not forgotten. She wasn't prepared for this.

Haradis squatted on its island, a decaying carcass of crumbled buildings half hidden behind what little remained of its fortifications. The once formidable palace, with its spear-point towers and sweeping bridges reached for the unforgiving moon with broken fingers, half of its façade gone to reveal split timbers dressed in bits and pieces of ragged clothing lifted by a long-gone wind and tossed into what remained of the rafters. They resembled funerary flags for the dead whose mortem lights were lost forever to the Kai. The wreckage of more modest structures—shops and hovels—revealed a devastation which didn't spare anything or anyone regardless of status. Haradis wasn't just a ruined city; it was a corpse. Desecrated. Violated. The *galla* had not only consumed its citizens, they'd sucked the life out of the very stone and wood from which the city was built.

She heard a keening noise, shocked to realize it came from her own throat. Haradis wasn't Saggara, but it was Kai to its bedrock, just as she was. Brishen's adamant refusal to come here or send scouts in his stead made sense to her now. Traumatized by what he'd been forced to do to become eidolon, he'd realized what his fellow Wraith kings hadn't, what the Kai themselves refused to acknowledge: The *galla* had shattered the Kai kingdom and the spirit of its fading people in ways the human kingdoms could never understand and must never know. Saggara represented a sliver of hope of what survived. Haradis was the culmination of all that had been lost.

Serovek remained quiet, a solid, comforting presence, as Anhuset continued to keen low in her throat, a soft dirge for all the Kai, both living and dead. She turned to her companion when she finished. Sympathy softened his expression though he didn't offer meaningless platitudes, for which she was grateful. Her unexpected grief still threatened to swallow her.

"We stand before an open grave," she said. "I'm glad I took your advice and chose not to come alone."

"I would have followed had you chosen to do so. Even the strongest shouldn't bear the sight of this place in solitude."

She shook her head. "I didn't think it would be so..." She trailed off, uncomfortable with revealing her turbulent emotions, even when they threatened to burst from her in a despairing, raging scream.

"How could you?" Serovek's voice sounded as heavy as her spirit. "More than lives were lost here. You have the right to grieve, but your grief will have to wait."

His practicality worked its own particular magic on her, and the horror freezing her in place faded. "True." She physically shook off the lingering effects of shock. She was here to scout, not to mourn. "I think we should wait to split up. Haradis may be dead, but it may not be abandoned."

They entered cautiously, picking their way across rubble scattered across moonlit streets. Anhuset spared a glance at Serovek, noting the tight set of his mouth and hollow expression. He might not have suffered the shock she did at the sight of Haradis's current state, but he carried with him the memory of it overrun by the *galla*.

There were places in the world ancient or haunted or both. Remnants of Elder magic spun by the long-vanished Gullperi lingered there, along with ghosts unable to break the tethers that bound them to the life their bodies had forsaken. Haradis was old but not ancient, and the magic of the Kai had been drained by sorcery that made five men eidolon. From what she could tell, it wasn't haunted either. Even the dead didn't loiter in Haradis. It was emptiness profound—except for her instinctive certainty, she and Serovek weren't alone.

"Are you looking for anything in particular or just noting things to report back to Brishen?" Serovek asked the question in the same low voice, his gaze sweeping back and forth across the wrecked landscape.

"The latter." Her instincts continued sounding an alarm that there was something here to find, but as of yet, it chose not to make itself known. She kept a tight grip on her knife, even knowing the weapon might be useless against whatever hid from sight.

Serovek followed her to one of the market squares, once a lively place whose perimeter was lined with stalls and interior enjoyed by visitors strolling under starlight and children playing on a manicured lawn. The grass was dead, the stalls collapsed heaps of debris. Bits of clothing littered the square. Anhuset paused in front of a cluster of rags. On first glance, it looked as if a washer woman had dropped her basket and left the spilled contents where they lay. Frocks and tunics, a cloak, even shoes and boots lay within the heap, all stained with dark splotches.

"I won't describe what seeing a full *hul-galla* in one place is like,"

Serovek said as he squatted next to the heap. "But I think seeing this was worse, and it's everywhere in Haradis."

Confused by his comment and the scene before her, Anhuset poked at a dress hem with the tip of her knife. "But what is 'this?' All I see is a pile of dirty, discarded clothing and shoes."

Serovek turned to stare at her, the expression of sympathy on his face from earlier transformed now to one of awful pity. "Ah, firefly woman, Brishen shared very little of our battle here, didn't he? And I'm guessing the refugees refuse to speak of what they saw." He gently pushed the hand holding her knife away from the clothing. "The stains you see on the clothes, they're all that's left after the *galla* consume their victims."

Anhuset's heart vaulted into her throat and she leaped away from Serovek and the gruesome memorial to Haradis's dead. The horror she'd beaten back outside the gates nearly overwhelmed her once more. "I didn't know," she said in a tight voice. The memory of her cousin's face, the flicker of horror in his eye when anyone mentioned Haradis by name had been the only tell or reaction he revealed. "My gods, the burden Brishen shoulders."

The margrave stood and closed the distance between them. "It's a heavy one indeed. Think hard as to whether or not you want to share with him your visit here. If you do, I'll offer my own observations as well. If you don't, and we find nothing of import, then it will be our secret."

"Why would you do this?" He had no reason to ally himself to her in this way, no obligation to keep any secret for her.

"Because Brishen is my friend, and I suspect he, like Megiddo, came away from the *galla* war more scarred by it than the rest of us. Why add to the burden you say he carries?"

They left the square then, Anhuset sick to her soul by every proof of Haradis's complete annihilation. She tried not to look at the numerous mounds of clothing dotting the streets. Instead, she scanned the few shops and dwellings that remained standing, peering inside with the conflicting hopes of finding something and finding nothing.

She was spoiling for a fight, a way to bleed off the angry despair engulfing her. The gods help any human or Kai scavenger who might be looting their way through what was left. She'd carve them into pieces small enough to fit inside thimbles.

A thin echo of bone-chilling laughter drifted on the wind from the direction of the palace. Ice water trickled down Anhuset's spine. The laughter was like nothing she'd ever heard and prayed she'd never hear again.

"That's the sound of *galla*," Serovek said. No pity or sympathy remained in his expression. Dismay had replaced both. Dismay and fear. The laughter pealed once more, this time closer and just as terrifying. "Water," Serovek snapped. "Run for water."

They sprinted back the way they'd come, toward the crumbled walls and broken gates and beyond that the safety of the canals and the prison they made of Haradis. More of the gibbering laughter sounded, nearly on their heels, and Anhuset stretched her legs for all she was worth to reach the gate. Serovek kept pace beside her, a swift runner despite his size.

She caught a roiling motion from the corner of her eye and glanced to the right. "Fuck!" she shouted, and the abomination rushing toward them on a writhing cloud of shadow shouted back in a voice that mimicked hers.

"Fuck! Fuck! Fuck!" The shout pitched higher until it became a scream that made her ears throb and teeth grind.

Suddenly Serovek veered away from Anhuset, sprinting directly across the *galla*'s path. Both Anhuset and the *galla* shrieked, she in shock, it in triumph as it darted toward its victim.

"No you don't, you bastard," Anhuset snarled, unsure if she spoke to the *galla* or to the margrave, figuring it applied to both.

Desperation pushed her to greater speed. She reached Serovek before the *galla* did, grabbed his wrist and yanked him toward a broken fountain set in the middle of a rubble-filled courtyard. They hurtled over the fountain's ledge, splashing ankle-deep into stagnant water deposited there from previous snows or rain.

The *galla's* gleeful shrieking changed to unearthly howls of rage at finding its prey snatched out of reach. It twisted and writhed midair, collapsing in on itself in a miasma of oily smoke before bursting outward to reveal a jumbled mess of every kind of body part as well as misty images of faces, mouths wide in silent screams.

"I thought the Wraith kings forced them all back into the void and sealed the gate." The idea that they'd failed made her stomach knot itself into a ball of nausea.

Serovek kicked a spray of slimy water onto the *galla*, slinging even more as the thing recoiled out of reach. "So did I."

Anhuset seized his arm. "Enough. You keep doing that, and we'll be standing in a dry fountain with no protection." She let go of the margrave and kept an eye on the *galla* who'd retreated but didn't flee. So began a waiting game, and all the odds lay in the demon's favor.

She'd saved herself and Serovek from being devoured for now, but he was far from appreciative. The thunderhead of a scowl descended on his features. His dark eyebrows lowered, and for the first time since she'd met him, he bent the full weight of his disapproval on her in a withering stare.

"Never do such a thing again," he said, practically baring his teeth at her. "If not for that foolish stunt, you'd be through the gate and safe among the canals right now."

"And you'd be a bloody stain on those fine clothes you're wearing," she snapped back. "I don't need a hero to save me," she continued in a milder voice. "Though what you did was heroic and brave. And stupid."

"Sha-Anhuset." He said her name in such a way that Anhuset forgot about the *galla* for a moment, startled into silence by what she saw. "You misunderstand me. One of us has to survive this little trip to warn Brishen there's at least one *galla* frolicking about Haradis. Between the two of us, I'm probably stronger, and I know you're faster. Strength isn't what would save us from that thing." He waved his knife toward the *galla*, and it lunged at him, snapping four sets of newly formed teeth.

"Your eyes," she said softly." He blinked at her, confused by her comment. "They glow like your *vuhana's* once did. Like they did when you dreamed in the inn's stables and said you saw Megiddo."

His demeanor changed, posture stilling, and his face took on a far-away look as if he contemplated some inner question with countless answers. "But I'm awake, and Megiddo isn't close by." A hard shudder shook him. "There are still *galla* in Haradis. Maybe there is still eidolon in the five of us. Perhaps enough to bind us all together."

An awful possibility to contemplate, but it made sense. "You don't know that for sure, and even if it were so, you aren't eidolon enough to resist a *galla* attack. We have to figure out a way to get to the gate before any of your men coming looking for us." An ugly thought reared its head, and she buried her claws into the back of Serovek's thick tunic, holding tight. "Don't do it," she warned.

A growl erupted from her throat at the false innocence in his expression. "Do what?"

"Leave the fountain and run toward the city's heart to draw the *galla* away. If you think I'll leave you so that thing can feed on you, think again. Run, and I'll simply chase after you, and my death will be on your hands."

Pure extortion with a slathering of guilt, and she wielded it with unapologetic glee.

It was his turn to growl. "If you were my second, I'd remove you from command."

"If I were your second, we wouldn't even be having this conversation."

He gusted out a frustrated sigh and raked his free hand through his hair. "Then we're at a stalemate. Any suggestions?"

She was out of ideas at the moment. The fountain's sanctuary was a stroke of luck. She'd caught the glimmer of moonlight reflecting on a liquid surface as they'd raced for the gate and prayed to every god paying attention that the reflection floated on life-saving water. For now, they were relatively safe, but the *galla* had all eternity to wait them out.

Serovek jerked in her grasp. Afraid he'd ignored her warning and planned to bolt, she tightened her grip on his tunic and prepared to knock his feet out from under him if necessary. Instead, he pointed in the direction of the derelict palace. "Look."

A crackling streak of light arrowed toward them, pulsing in colors of cerulean, scarlet and viridian. Anhuset automatically bent her knees and raised her knife in a defensive stance, even knowing that steel likely wouldn't work on this newest threat.

The *galla*, a gibbering, cackling chimera of gruesome and constant transformation, halted its contortions, emitted a mad scream, and shot away from the fountain. The luminescent quarrel hurtled after the demon, piercing the center of poisonous darkness. The *galla* screamed again, a raging cry for help as it convulsed in the grip of an expanding brightness that blinded Anhuset completely. She closed her eyes and turned her head. A flash erupted across her eyelids and silence fell.

Anhuset dared a squint. The world remained a flare of outlines without details, only imprints of brightness. She felt Serovek close beside her. He asked a question, a single word, a single name.

"Megiddo?"

She strained to see, cursing under her breath at the struggle. Another voice broke the silence, a far echo where the distance between life and death was the span of a breath and the measure of eternity. A voice familiar, but also strange.

"Run."

She was lifted off her feet, set down on dry ground just as abruptly and yanked forward so hard, she thought Serovek might tear her arm off as he launched them both into a dead run. "I can't see!" she cried out, trying not to stumble.

"Keep running! I won't let you fall."

He was true to his word, guiding her along clear paths as they sprinted through Haradis. She only stumbled once, and he caught her, hand on her waist to keep her upright, never slowing in their dash to safety. Her vision slowly recovered from the flash-fire brightness that blinded her, and by the time they splashed into the first canal, Anhuset could make out the true shapes and colors of her surroundings.

They stood knee-deep in freezing water, Haradis a gutted carcass behind them. She prayed she might never revisit it and suspected Brishen prayed for the same thing in the privacy of his thoughts or in the arms of his devoted *hercegesé*.

Serovek pressed his hand to her shoulder, coaxing her to face him. His eyes no longer held the ethereal glow, though she found them just as disconcerting with their movements as he scanned her features. "Stop that," she said.

He blinked. "Stop what?"

"Moving your eyes so much. I keep waiting for them to jump out of their sockets and run off."

He burst out laughing, and the hand holding her shoulder squeezed in an affectionate grip before he let her go. "Seems your sight is returned without issue."

"It is." She offered up a faint smile, enjoying the sight of his amusement and the fact she was the one who'd amused him. "You're almost not ugly when you laugh, margrave."

He snorted, shaking his head. "Only you can wrap a compliment inside an insult and present it as a gift with all sincerity." He bowed. "I thank you, madam. Stay with me a little longer, and soon you'll find me breathtaking."

She sniffed. "The Kai don't live that long."

More laughter, and this time she joined him, a delayed euphoria singing through her that had little to do with their ridiculous banter and everything to do with the fact they'd survived an encounter with the *galla*. No small thanks to an arrow of ethereal lightning and a one-word warning from a heretic Wraith king trapped in a world of demons.

Once their laughter faded and they waded across the canal to solid ground, she spared a quick glance at Haradis. "What happened to the *galla*? I was blinded right as the light spear struck. I only saw flashes behind my eyelids."

Serovek's gaze followed the same path as hers. "It grew from a spear to a net and swallowed the *galla* whole before disappearing."

Anhuset recalled Serovek saying the monk's name, a question full of hope, of uncertainty, of regret. "Do you really think it was Megiddo?"

He shrugged. "I have to be careful to see what is there instead of what I want to be there, but yes. At least a manifestation of him. He found a way to cross back into this realm and save us."

If that were so, then she and Serovek owed Megiddo a life-debt, one she hoped she might one day repay, though such a thing seemed impossible, at least in her lifetime. And after what she just faced in the broken city, she'd discourage anyone from trying to access the *galla*'s realm for a rescue mission. Too many had suffered too greatly in order to shove the horde back into the cesspit from which they'd spawned. Even now, the idea that there'd been one running free in Haradis made her skin crawl and her chest tighten.

"Do you think there are more *galla* free in there?"

"No." His answer surprised her. "I think however it landed on this side, it was alone. *Galla* don't split off from one another. They're more like a hive. If there had been more than one, we'd have faced them as well."

"But how did it get free? And will others follow?"

Another shrug. "I wish I knew. The Beladine and the Gauri record stories of stray *galla* brought across by necromancers with more ambition than brains, hoping to enslave one to do their bidding. It never ends well. The necromancer is eaten, as are his nearest neighbors, until a team of wizards come in and exorcise the thing back to where it came from. I wouldn't be surprised if just such a thing happened here. Haradis as it stands now might keep out the Kai and the usual looters, but a necromancer would see it as a treasure chest to be opened."

She scowled. "Such foul magic has no place in this world." The moment the words rolled off her tongue, she regretted them. Necromantic magic had allowed living men to die, to resurrect, and to lead an army of the dead into battle against the *galla*.

Serovek's half smile held a hint of melancholy. "It has its uses from time to time."

Anhuset reached out and laid her hand on his chest. His heart, as noble as the moon was fair, beat strong and steady under her palm. "Forgive me. I meant no malice or insult toward you."

He covered her hand with his. He'd always been forthright in his admiration for her as well as his attraction to her, but the fond expression gracing his visage now was something else, something greater and deeper. "There's nothing to forgive. You, of all people, know firsthand what it took to win against the *galla*. You're right; there's no place for such twisted sorcery in this world. If it didn't exist, neither would the *galla*."

Her lips thinned. "Pull another stunt like you did in there, and I'll kill you myself."

She didn't stop him when he lifted her hand to his mouth and pressed a kiss to her palm. A hot tingling purled up her arm to suffuse her entire body. She only pulled her hand away when he released her fingers.

It's just the aftermath of relief at avoiding death, her reason told her turbulent emotions. Her emotions guffawed and told her reason to kindly fuck off.

She took three obvious step backs to put distance between them, ignoring his faint smirk in favor of staring at Haradis. "With it sitting on an island now, any *galla* that might still be in there can't leave." Or so she hoped.

Serovek's smirk vanished and his reply revealed his doubt matched hers. "Maybe. You have to tell Brishen everything when you return. You can set off for home with the others once we've reached the agreed-upon landing spot."

The implacable flatness in his tone made her stiffen, and his words sounded alarms. "I don't understand."

His shoulders went back and his legs tensed, all the signs of someone bracing for a physical altercation. "I'm taking Megiddo to the monastery alone. The magic remaining in his body is somehow tethering us to each other. I wouldn't be surprised if it drew that *galla* to me like a beacon. I won't risk my men or Brishen's sha to transport him to the monks."

That noble heart of his was a damn annoyance at times. Anhuset bared her teeth. He didn't even flinch. "My task," she bit out. "My duty, is to accompany you and the monk to his order. I will complete that task."

"I relieve you of that duty. Go home to Saggara."

"Just like that?" she scoffed. "A little hand-waving from you, and I march off to do your bidding?" She crossed her arms and gave him a thin smile. "You can neither relieve nor dismiss me. I'm the Khaskem's *sha*, not yours. If you don't wish me to ride with you and your men, so be it. I'll just follow behind you, but I'll see this journey through to its end."

He raised his hands and his gaze to the night sky, as if beseeching divine help. When he returned his attention to her, it was to glare her into submission. She raised one mocking eyebrow. "My gods," he muttered. "Do you ever yield?"

"Not if it means abandoning my duty." She might not always read his expressions easily or correctly, but she clearly heard the surrender in his voice.

He tried one last tactic. "Don't you think Brishen would find your observations regarding Haradis more valuable than you acting as a Kai ambassador to a group of heretic monks?"

"Considering it was probably Megiddo's eidolon who saved us in Haradis less than a half hour ago, getting his body safely to the monastery is of utmost value. Besides, I can draft a message which one of the others can deliver."

One long-suffering sigh that tempted a grin from her, and he tightened the pack on his back "Let's get on with it then. We'll have daylight soon enough, and I wouldn't put it past the captain to leave us behind if we're late."

To Serovek's surprise, Anhuset wasn't the only one to resist his plan of splitting their party. They'd hiked to the agreed-upon meeting place and reboarded the towboat where it and the barge had docked for the remainder of the night. Except for the nightwatch, the crew was asleep. Serovek's men, however, were awake, their lamps held high as they called greetings to the margrave and the Kai *sha*. The boat was crowded, dirty, and loaded with the bare minimum of necessities to keep passengers comfortable, especially overnight. After the foray into Haradis, he was happy to see it floating on the Absu, waiting for them.

He fielded the rain of questions, held back a yawn, and glanced at Anhuset. She looked haggard. She'd slept little over the past few days, and while resilient, even she wasn't immune to exhaustion. "We'll tell you everything in the morning," he promised the others. "For now, I'm off to bed and you should be as well." He stepped closer to Anhuset. "That includes you. The towboat has a nightwatch as does the barge, and the crew knows this river better than any of us. I need you alert and refreshed if you plan to finish this journey with me."

She didn't argue, only gave a quick nod, fished her cloak out of her stash of gear left on the boat and stretched out on the deck away from the walkways. Wrapped in the cloak, she was a still silhouette under the stars. Serovek wished he could join her.

Before he found his own bed, he checked on Magas and the other horses. The stallion whickered to him and nuzzled Serovek's hair while demanding more scratches along his neck. Serovek breathed deeply of the scent of horse and river. Despite their pungency, they were pleasant smells, a mark of the natural that traveled along paths adjacent to the unnatural.

He gave Magas a few more affectionate pats before returning to the part of the boat his comrades had taken for sleeping. Someone had reserved a spot for him not far from Anhuset, using his gear as a marker. Serovek would much rather have shared her space or have her share his, but such preferences would have to remain wishes. For now.

The captain approached him as he laid out his bedroll. "Haradis still surrounded by the canals?"

Serovek didn't miss the worried note in the man's inquiry. He sat down to remove his boots and dug through his main satchel for a pair of stockings to warm his still frozen feet. He was tired, not so much from the trek back to the boat, but from the aftereffects of terror and the scrape with death in Haradis. "Still surrounded," he said. "You weren't dressing it in frills when you said the landscape had changed. Who dug those canals? The squire who took out the bridges? Because that isn't the work of the Kai."

The captain shrugged. "Every Beladine within walking, riding or swimming distance gathered to dig them." He shivered. "I hear tell from those who live closest or ride the river that on some nights you can hear the ghosts of the Kai who died there screaming." He eyed Serovek, who didn't comment. "Could be fanciful storyteller's tripe to scare everyone, but I'm glad the water's there."

He paled when Serovek said, "So am I."

The two bid each other good night, and Serovek lay on his back, contemplating the heavens while he waited for sleep to claim him. One *galla*. Only one lurking in Haradis, trapped by water and eager to devour anything or anyone unfortunate to cross its path. *We thought we got them all.* The idea that they missed one sickened him. The possibility that they hadn't and somehow one had escaped its prison again lodged his heart in his throat.

The rough canals offered a small measure of fortification against another—gods forbid—*hul-galla* escaping the city, but he feared it wasn't enough. Not now and definitely not in the long-term. He understood Anhuset's insistence she accompany him and the others to the monastery. The dazzling bolt of cerulean light which speared then enveloped the shrieking *galla* before disappearing with it was Megiddo. Even had Serovek not heard or recognized the voice that commanded them to run, he knew the bright arrow's source, had felt the essence of the man's existence in his very bones. Somehow, the monk's eidolon had crossed ethereal barriers to capture a *galla* and drag it back to its pit.

Serovek suspected Megiddo's ability to do so was directly tied to the existence of his still-breathing body in this world—a lifeline that allowed the eidolon access to the reality in which his physical form abided. Keeping his body safe had become more than a mission of respect for a fallen hero: it was now an absolute necessity. If another *galla* swarm somehow broke free again, every breathing being would depend on a circle of water and the imprisoned soul of a monk to save them. Had he been standing at the moment, the weight of such an awful scenario would have brought him to his knees.

Brishen needed to know what was happening at the old Kai capital and possibly organize a brigade of workers to deepen, widen, and reinforce those canals. And if the Kai wouldn't do it, Serovek would find a Beladine who would. He'd redirect the entire mighty Absu until Haradis drowned under her waters if necessary. Such an act might start a war between his country and Brishen's, but dealing with the *galla* exacted a greater price. Friendships throughout history had been tested by difficult decisions. Some survived, some didn't. One lived with the consequences of doing what was necessary.

Snores and muttered bits of dreams from his comrades surrounded him. Sleep didn't elude them as it did him. Serovek abandoned his observation of the stars to regard Anhuset where she lay on her side away from him, a long silhouette. He'd never forget her expression when she gazed upon Haradis, wrecked by the *galla*.

He'd always considered her a fiercely beautiful woman, even with the yellow eyes and intimidating teeth. His first sight of her had stopped him in his tracks, and he'd gawked like a young lad while she bent a contemptuous scowl on him. Everything about her fascinated him, and despite the emotional armor she wore, even more difficult to penetrate than that made of leather and steel, he'd swear before any and all that underneath was a woman as vulnerable as she was powerful. He'd glimpsed that vulnerability as they stood before Haradis's broken gates. It had taken colossal effort not to reach out and draw her into his embrace, to offer some token of sympathy or comfort.

She would have broken his arms for his presumption. Instead, he'd waited beside her as she rode out the shockwave of grief. Later, practically drunk on relief at escaping the city still alive, he'd dared to kiss her palm. Those claws of hers would have shredded his cheek with a single swipe had she wished to harm him. Her hand had been cool on his face, the skin toughened in places with calluses. Not the delicate palm of a pampered lady, but one of a warrior who wielded sword and spear and carried a shield.

What would it be like, he wondered, to gain sha-Anhuset's affection? That unswerving devotion she gifted to Brishen and, by association, to his wife Ildiko?

He put aside the question and other useless pondering about the enigmatic Kai woman and closed his eyes. An image of the stray *galla* in all its shadowy madness rode along the edges of slumber, making him shiver. Somehow the monk, tortured and flensed on an iron web by a mob of the demonic, had broken free and become a hunter of his torturers.

Serovek hadn't given any thought to the death awaiting him when he used himself as bait to give Anhuset a slim chance of safely reaching the canals. He'd simply reacted. Thank the gods she'd cut off his noble, reckless gesture at the knees by chasing after him, then dragging him into the fountain's stagnant waters. But it had been Megiddo who'd ultimately saved them both. Could they do no less for him? Do more than just leave his body at the monastery and be on their merry way? The question grated against Serovek's soul until sleep finally overtook him.

The two crafts continued their way up the Absu's tributary the following day, traveling toward the territories troubled by the warlord Chamtivos. Serovek stood with his men at one end of the boat. Anhuset was not among them. She remained where she'd bedded down the night before, still fast asleep. He'd chosen not to wake her to break her fast or join this meeting. She already knew of his plan; they'd discussed the details on the trek back to the landing. After several days with minimal sleep, she needed the rest, and he needed her alert for the remainder of the journey.

Earlier, he'd enjoyed a smoke from his pipe and watched from a spot nearby as Ogran passed Anhuset, paused, and walked backwards to stand beside her. He slid a foot toward her slumbering form as if to shove her awake.

Serovek lowered his pipe. "Ogran," he warned in a soft voice. The tracker froze. "Unless you want your head used as fish bait and your entrails decorating the barge, I suggest you rethink that idea."

Ogran gave a careless shrug before continuing on his way to where his comrades sat with the crew for their morning meal. Serovek eyed him now, standing apart from the others as he usually did, a faint sneer on his mouth and his eyes constantly shifting from one person to the next without ever meeting their gazes.

Had he always possessed such a sly mien, or had Anhuset's suspicion influenced the way Serovek viewed him? Ogran had never given him or his commanders any trouble in the years he'd served at High Salure, and his tracking skills had come in handy numerous times. Serovek had brought him on this trip because of those talents. Ogran's surly manner was of no concern to him as long as the man didn't stir discord among the other soldiers or display insubordination. The tracker had done neither so far, though he obviously disliked Anhuset.

The Kai woman, as brusque in her own way as Ogran, wouldn't care if some human disapproved of her, so her questions stemmed from something else, something more worrisome.

He didn't have the luxury of mulling over the idea for long. A brief recounting of their adventure in Haradis and the encounter with the *galla* left him fielding numerous questions all focused on just how effective the canals were in keeping the thing and any of its ilk imprisoned in the city.

"They've trapped the *galla* so far. Who knows how long it's been lurking in there. No reason to think it can get out now, especially if there's some ghost or guardian making sure it doesn't get out." He hadn't divulged his belief in the idea of Megiddo manifesting as the arrow of light. His men were already disquieted by the monk's breathing but soulless body.

"I thought you and the other four got rid of all the *galla*, commander." Weson turned to look over his shoulder in the direction of Haradis, growing more distant with each bob of the boat. The shadow of fear lingered in his eyes when he turned back to stare at Serovek.

"So did I. So did we all. And I believe it to be true. This wasn't a *galla* missed but one somehow escaped. Either there's another breach between worlds or some idiot sorcerer trying to make a name for himself sneaked into Haradis, managed to summon one and ended up being eaten by the thing."

Serovek conjured the last scenario on the spot, wishing that such were true instead of the possibility of a breach. His soldiers latched onto the idea with enthusiasm. He didn't blame them. It was a far less terrifying scenario.

The wagon driver, Klanek, suggested posting a warning marker at the city's edge on their return trip. "Maybe it would keep people out of there and from causing more trouble," he said.

"A sign like that would start a panic." Erostis punched a hole in the idea before Serovek could. "All it would take is one person to see it, make the usual wrong assumption, and set rumors flying. Next thing you know, Belawat would be at war with Bast-Haradis and no one clear as to how it all got started."

Serovek was very glad he'd brought the sensible, cautious Erostis with them. "Agreed. And that brings me to the main reason for this meeting. We didn't plan to encounter a *galla*, but it's happened. And I didn't expect to see a canal system surrounding Haradis, but I have. Circumstances have changed, and we have three tasks before us now. The first, to get Megiddo Cermak to the Jeden Order. The second, return to High Salure with instructions for Bryzant to find me an engineer. The third, get a message to the Khaskem at Saggara. I'll have to split our party three ways to get it all done."

Numerous sputtered protests greeted his announcement. Erostis, spokesman by silent agreement from the others, spoke above the noise. "No disrespect intended, commander, but your plan doesn't seem all that sound. If Chamtivos wasn't still making a nuisance of himself in the Lobak Valley, I'd have no concerns, but it's still dangerous territory because of him. We're safer together as a larger party."

Serovek nodded. "True, but our numbers also draw undue attention. We may only be eight, but we're eight, heavily armed, escorting a wagon carrying mysterious cargo. Two or three of us would be seen as no more than a family hauling goods or produce."

"Then just send one of us to High Salure and one to Saggara," Erostis argued.

"Or send the Kai woman home if you don't want attention." Ogran's smirk gave his features a decidedly rattish cast. He thrust his chin in the direction where Anhuset slept. "If anyone is drawing attention, it's her with those wolf eyes and claws. Not to mention the teeth."

Erostis closed his eyes, and his shoulders slumped. "Ogran," he muttered, "Do us all a favor. Pretend you're smarter than my horse's backside and shut up."

Snorts and smothered laughter disguised as coughs greeted his comment. Ogran lost his smirk in favor of a snarl, and his hand dropped to the dagger at his belt. The amusement died instantly, and the tension in the group rose fast as the rest of the men mimicked his action.

"Stand down," Serovek said. "All of you."

To those listening, his tone was no different nor his voice any louder than a moment earlier when the conversation was far friendlier, but to a man, they obeyed instantly. Even Ogran, though he glared mute promises of retribution at Erostis.

"Ogran is right," Serovek continued, hiding a smile at their surprise. "Sha-Anhuset does attract notice when she's bare-headed and uncloaked, which has mostly been once we're camped for the night and not in a village." He then cheerfully wiped away Ogran's self-satisfied expression. "Who among us has witnessed a Kai warrior in a fight?" All but Weson and Ogran raised their hands. Serovek pinned the tracker with an unblinking stare. "A single Kai with martial training, like sha-Anhuset, is worth three of us in combat." He was pleased to see Erostis's, Klanek's, and Ardwin's enthusiastic nods. "Which means her value as a guard on this journey outweighs the risk of curious stares and a few awkward questions."

Erostis resumed his role as mouthpiece for the others. "Then who do you wish to stay and who returns with messages to High Salure and Saggara?"

For just a moment, Serovek entertained the idea of keeping Ogran with the group traveling to the monastery, then thought better of it. He didn't relish the idea of burying bits and pieces of the man because he inevitably crossed Anhuset the wrong way one too many times.

"Sha-Anhuset and I will take the monk to the monastery. As Klanek's the wagon driver, he goes with us. Erostis as well, to act as rear guard." Ogran's glower turned even darker when Serovek continued. "The remaining four of you can decide between you who pairs up and who goes to Saggara and who goes to High Salure." He gave a quick nod to Weson. "I could send one messenger, but as you said, a group is safer, and two are safer than one on any journey." He glanced to where the captain stood. "We'll reach the next stop shortly after noon. Have your decision made by then and your gear packed. Sha-

Anhuset will have a message ready to give to whomever goes to Saggara."

He left them to confirm the time of the next stop with the captain and discovered Anhuset awake, seated against the railing. She huddled in her cloak, the hood pulled far forward to shield her face from the late morning sun. She held a bowl of the steaming gruel the boat's cook had served for breakfast and stared at it as if she'd spotted a horse dropping floating there. She brought the bowl close to her nose for a sniff, gave a disgusted grunt and set it down on the deck as far from her as she could shove it. Her eyes glowed like bright lamps in the hood's shadow when she lifted her head to stare up at him.

"Humans eat the foulest things," she declared.

Not one to let perfectly good gruel go to waste, Serovek scooped up the bowl and sat down next to her, where he proceeded to wolf down the contents, much to her undisguised revulsion. He set the bowl down between his feet and winked at Anhuset. "You missed out," he said. "The boat's cook makes a fine porridge."

"By all means," she said in her driest tones. "Help yourself." She nodded toward the group clustered at the stern. "I see you advised them about your plan. What did they say?"

Serovek shrugged. "The usual arguments about traveling in a larger group, reluctance for playing the messenger." He chuckled. "I think they've convinced themselves we'll be babes among fiends without them to guard us."

"I'm surprised one of them didn't consider me a fiend." She waved one clawed hand at him.

"Ogran was the first to suggest you deliver your own message to Saggara."

"You'll forgive me if I don't find that surprising." The yellow of her eyes swirled in countless shades from burnished gold to daffodil, mesmerizing Serovek. "I pity whoever has to pair with him on the trip, though not enough to suggest you have him stay with us."

"The rest are used to him. They'll just ignore his sourness as usual."

A frown line creased her brow. "Margrave, would you grant a request?"

His eyebrows rose. This was unusual coming from Anhuset. "Of course."

"Send Ogran to High Salure. I'll have my message for Brishen prepared for when we split up, but I want someone other than him to deliver it."

The thought had crossed his mind as well. He saw no reason for Ogran to shirk his duty were he one of the pair chosen to travel to Saggara, but if it eased Anhuset's mind to assign the task to someone else, Serovek had no issue. "As you wish. You may have to scrounge for parchment. I doubt the captain keeps a stock on-hand, but it won't hurt to ask. If there's none to be had, decide what you want to tell Brishen and repeat it to the men. Between the two of them, they'll memorize and relay it."

Her deepening frown told him she wasn't thrilled at the second choice, but their options were limited, and the next village or town near a boat landing was another day's travel and another delay if they waited to buy writing supplies before sending messengers to their destinations.

Anhuset finally nodded. "I'll keep it short either way." She eyed the empty bowl, then Serovek. "I can't believe you ate all of that vile slop."

He grinned. "And it was my second bowl." She shuddered. "If you threaten the cook enough, he might be willing to part with some of the fish he's saved for the midday meal."

"I'm not that hungry to go through the trouble." The brief touch of her claws on his arm sent a pleasurable tingle across his skin. "I thank you for letting me sleep, though you exaggerated how I would have reacted to Ogran waking me."

"I wondered if you were awake." He'd suspected as much. Exhausted or not, she'd never be one to sleep deeply. "And I disagree. Look me in the eye and tell me you wouldn't have eaten his liver if he'd shoved his foot in your back to wake you."

She wrinkled her nose, eyes glowing bright in the hood's darkness. "I don't want to look in your eye. It moves too much and is strange."

The tiniest smile played along her lips. "I've no doubt Ogran's liver would have tasted a lot better than that gruel you just shoved down your gullet."

The crew and his men all turned toward Serovck at his laughter, some with puzzled looks, others like Erostis with a considered scrutiny that moved from him to Anhuset and back again. Serovek knew what they thought. What about this taciturn, intimidating Kai woman fascinated him so?

Everything.

While Anhuset composed her message, he spent the time reviewing the map he'd brought with him of the Lobak valley. The wagon and its precious cargo precluded leaving the roads for a shortcut through rougher country. Several of the paths marked on the map were hardly more than drover roads, and they'd be lucky if they didn't have to stop more than once to repair a broken wheel. Ogran, who hailed from this part of the Beladine hinterlands, had assured him before their trip that the wagon could make it.

"Some spots will rattle your brains, especially if the local folk have driven cattle or sheep through after a hard rain and it's dried since. We'll just have to go slow and nurse the wagon along. Once we cross the Dulgrada bridge, we'll be on a main road that's nearly as smooth as a royal courtesan's backside."

Serovek was more worried about the bridge than the roads. The Dulgrada was a spandrel bridge instead of one of the more numerous suspension bridges. Sturdy, wide and built to provide safe passage for foot and transport traffic over the narrow but deep ravine that marked entry into the Lobak Valley, it provided a shorter, less circuitous route to the monastery. A safer one too, where Chamtivos wasn't causing trouble. Serovek hoped the map, which showed the bridge, was still current, and they'd have an easy crossing.

By the time they'd reached the next landing, Ardwin, Weson, Ogran, and Jannir had their gear packed and had negotiated among themselves as to who would return to High Salure and who would travel to Saggara. Serovek had rightly guessed Ogran wouldn't volunteer to travel into Kai territory when another choice was available to him. Anhuset would be satisfied.

The four men disembarked, Jannir carrying the note Anhuset had written for the Khaskem on a ragged piece of parchment she'd bought from the captain for a sum equal to highway robbery.

With their numbers reduced to four and Megiddo for the remainder of the journey, and most of their road rations sent with the others, they were low on supplies. Feeling generous after making a nice profit on a bit of blank parchment and some ink, the captain gave them some helpful information.

"When you leave, go a half league west. It'll take you off your path a small ways, but there's a village with a decent market where you can purchase more provisions. I'll give you directions and the names of the better vendors."

"Let's hope they sell onions cheaper than you sell parchment," Anhuset said in the driest voice.

Once the captain left, Serovek tutted and gave a sigh of mock disapproval. "Not much in the way of diplomacy there, firefly woman."

She shrugged and set to work packing the last of her satchels in preparation for disembarking. "I let him rob me and didn't eat him. That's diplomacy."

He thanked the gods for the blessing of having her here. Her acerbic remarks made him laugh, made this journey less grim, and the dangers not so burdensome. She was good for his soul. He would miss her mightily when they parted ways at High Salure and she returned to Saggara.

It didn't take long after they traded the river and barge for land and horseback to reach the village the boat captain recommended. A small but bustling place acting as a hub for other smaller villages, the center square was crowded with people and stalls selling everyday goods and produce. What luxury items there might have been, Serovek couldn't guess. His interest was only in resupplying their provisions to last until they reached the monastery.

He and Erostis were the only ones to travel into the village itself. Anhuset stayed with Klanek and the wagon just outside of the settlement. Before they'd left, Serovek asked her if she wanted him to bring back any specific fruit or treat for her. She'd shaken her head. "I'll eat whatever is there." She scowled the moment the words left her lips. Before Serovek could tease about her statement, she pointed a finger at him. "No maggot potato things. I might as well eat dirt. It'll taste better."

While they didn't have Anhuset with them to draw a crowd's attention, Serovek himself garnered more notice than he anticipated. Even garbed in the hard-worn travel clothing in need of laundering and days of road and river dirt on him, people had guessed a nobleman of importance was visiting. Vendors fawned over him in the hopes he'd be generous with his purchases. Some of the village elders invited him and Erostis to supper at their homes, and a yeoman's beautiful wife made it clear she'd be happy to introduce him to the village's other hospitalities.

Another woman tucked a bundle of dried herbs bound in ribbon into one of the satchels he carried along with the packages of dried fruit he'd purchased from her. "For your lady-love," she told him with a smile and a wink. "And if you don't have one of those, you can always make yourself a nice cup of tea with it."

They returned with bulging saddlebags. "We bought potatoes," Serovek announced, grinning when Anhuset winced. "There isn't much available in the way of fresh stuff with everything just coming out of winter, and Erostis has assured me he knows how to cook these 'maggots' in such a way that you'll come to love them."

She gave Erostis an arch look. "Don't go to extra trouble on my account. I'm not convinced those things are meant to be eaten as food in the first place."

They loaded and secured the cumbersome packs into the wagon. Serovek took the brief time to scan his map and the route they'd take to the bridge. Movement from the corner of his eye caught his attention, and he glanced up to spot Anhuset pausing before bending down to stare at something on the ground. Whatever she dropped, she scooped up and, with a quick sleight of hand, tucked it away in her tunic.

He would have thought nothing of it except for the arrested, almost guilty expression on her face when she did it. When they were once more on the road, he considered asking her but thought better of it. It was one thing to inquire out of concern, another to pry.

For this leg of the journey, Erostis rode in the front next to Klanek, where the two swapped stories of various escapades when they were children that made Serovek pity their parents. He rode behind the wagon next to Anhuset, content to enjoy the quiet.

She surprised him when she broke the companionable silence with a question. "Why is the Lobak valley so desired by this Chamtivos?"

"Because owning land is possessing power. Owning a great deal of land is having a great deal of power, but you must fight hard to keep it. Chamtivos was the youngest son of a minor Beladine nobleman. To keep the holding intact, the lord bequeathed all of it to the eldest son, to be inherited upon his death."

She gave a soft whistle. "I'm guessing whatever brotherly affection existed until then vanished."

"That's putting it mildly," he replied. "What Chamtivos lacked in status, he made up for in ambition and ruthlessness. He killed his father, his brothers, and their progeny so there'd be no claim but his to the holding. According to him, the hard hand of fate had dealt harshly with his family. A drowning, hunting accidents, an unfortunate fall from a cliff, a difficult childbirth. He then traveled to the capital and petitioned the king not only for recognition of his right to the fiefdom but to the lands bordering the Jeden monastery and beyond."

"A man so driven makes a dangerous vassal. One who'll murder his own family to rise in status will think nothing of murdering anyone else, including sovereigns. Nor will they remain content with ruling a castle and farmland, no matter how rich." Her features hardened. "Even the Khaskem, as even-tempered as he is, would have Chamtivos either imprisoned or put to death."

On a slope overlooking the plain surrounding Saggara, with an army of the dead behind him, Serovek had watched as Brishen's eidolon embraced his mother's twisted spirit and obliterated it. He'd done it without hesitation or regret, much like Chamtivos, but for entirely different reasons. He had no doubt Brishen would do exactly as Anhuset claimed.

"As he should. As King Rodan should have done. It would have saved countless lives and himself a lot of grief had he done the same." He shrugged. "Instead, he strung Chamtivos along with bait and false promises for who knows what reason, then gifted the entire valley, including those holdings, to the Jeden Order, believing the monks would be defenders of the territory for the crown instead of contenders for it as Chamtivos would."

"But are they not considered heretics?"

Some of the more zealous Beladine, strict in their orthodoxy, often called upon the king to outlaw the Nazim monks and proclaim all their orders as heretical, including the Jeden Order. Such cries fell on deaf ears, especially when the warrior monks proved themselves so useful in furthering the king's interests.

The wagon had rolled farther ahead of them while he and Anhuset chatted, their horses content to amble along while their riders were distracted. Serovek tapped Magas's sides with his heels to close the gap between him and the transport. He replied to her question once they caught up to the other two, who were now close enough to hear their conversation.

"To the devout among us, they are heretics, but the king isn't a religious man. His philosophy has always been pay the crown tax, tithe your soldiers and vassals to his army in times of conflict, and remember your place. You're free to worship as you please as long as it doesn't threaten his rule."

Her expression turned inscrutable, her mouth becoming pinched. "It's well known among some that the king of Belawat will do what he believes is necessary to hold the throne."

Had Serovek not been directly involved in Brishen's rescue from Beladine raiders who'd tortured the Kai prince and would have killed him, he might not have caught the oblique accusation in Anhuset's comment. She and others, himself included, suspected King Rodan had a hand in the two attempts on Brishen's life and that of his Gauri bride. He glanced at Erostis and Klanek, looking for any indication that one of them had heard what she implied. Both only looked mildly bored.

Unlike them, Anhuset didn't look bored at all. Tall in the saddle, she sat tense, waiting for his reply. He could almost feel the heat of her rising anger at the memory of what the raiders had done to her cousin. While there was no solid proof of his involvement, she obviously laid the blame for Brishen's torture and disfigurement at King Rodan's feet.

"He's always been a wily sovereign," Serovek said, careful with his choice of words and eager to turn the focus back to the warlord. "Letting Chamtivos live was one of his few mistakes, and one I doubt he'll ever make again. Were it not for the monks' fighting ability and help from Ilinfan swordmasters, he'd still control the Lobak valley. They wrested most of it from him, and he's gone into hiding, though he remains a boil on Rodan's arse."

His mention of the Ilinfan swordmasters acted like an incantation, instantly diverting her attention away from Rodan's ruthless machinations to something she embraced with fervor: sword fighting.

"We in Bast-Haradis know of your fabled swordsmen," she said, a touch of admiration in her voice. "I've always wanted to spar with an Ilinfan swordmaster."

"The monks are indebted to them," he said. "They're the pride of the Beladine kingdom, though the king barely tolerates them." Rodan trod a thin line with the various factions in his kingdom, from religious orders with impressive martial skills to renowned swordsmen whose true loyalty most believed lay with their brotherhood and their leader they called the Ghan.

"Possible threat to the precious throne?" Once more her voice had taken on that studied neutral tone.

He approved of her caution. "There are always threats to the throne."

Slouched casually on the wagon's driver seat with the reins loose in his fingers, Klanek joined their conversation. "I got to see an Ilinfan swordmaster fight once. Some years ago during Delyalda at the capital." He grinned. "Beat the shit out of the king's champion, then refused to be the replacement when it was offered to him."

Anhuset nudged her horse closer to the front of the wagon. "Did he live up the reputation of swordmaster?"

The driver snorted. "And then some. It was an exhibition match, but we all wondered about that when it was over. Alreed, the champion then, was spitting blood, tongue, teeth and was half dead by the time the king called the match. The swordsman never said a word, never strutted about. Just bowed to the king, said something to his patron Lord Uhlfrida, and left the arena."

"A man who knows the worth of his skill doesn't need to brag of it or seek praise for it," Serovek said.

Anhuset nodded. "Fighting such a warrior would be a privilege."

Klanek echoed aloud Serovek's silent reply. "If you lived to tell of it."

That night they camped not far off the main road. As Serovek promised, Erostis worked culinary magic over the fire to turn the humble but much-loathed potato into a delectable dish that had his mouth watering for a plate piled high with the vegetable.

Anhuset's nostrils flared as Erostis handed her a plate to pass to Klanek. She held it for a moment, eyeing the golden-brown cuts of potato with their crispy edges and generous sprinkling of salt and herbs. Her eyebrows slowly climbed as she stared at the plate, then Erostis, then the plate again. "This is the same maggot potato thing?"

He preened, delighted by her obvious amazement. "It's all in the technique, madam. I can make your shoes taste delicious given enough time and spices."

Serovek hid a smile as Klanek gazed longingly at the plate Anhuset held. "If you don't mind passing that over, *sha*, before it gets cold, I'd appreciate it." Serovek noted the driver dared not reach for the plate. Smart man.

She reluctantly gave up the plate, nostrils still flared to catch the smell of herbs and smoke infused into the potatoes. Serovek motioned to Erostis to fill another plate as Klanek took his from Anhuset, his gaze hard on her clawed hands as if he feared she'd change her mind and snatch his supper back from him, taking his arm with it.

"Care to brave the roasted maggot? It won't try to kill you like scarpatine." Serovek couldn't resist teasing her. "Or if you don't wish to take so big a risk, I'll be happy to share a few pieces of mine with you." He raised his plate in offer.

Her glare might have set him on fire had it stayed on him longer, but the helping of supper Erostis handed her proved a more powerful distraction. All three men watched as she brought the plate up to her nose, indulging in a long inhalation before spearing a potato chunk with one claw and popping it into her mouth. As she chewed, her lamp-light eyes widened and rounded.

"This can't be the same disgusting heap of dirt-tasting mush I had to swallow at the Khaskem's wedding dinner," she declared once she swallowed. She speared another piece, this time eyeing it with a specu-lative look.

Her audience's laughter coaxed a smile from her, much to Serovek's delight. "One and the same," he said. "Erostis's boast wasn't an empty one. He's a good cook."

"Why do you think I'm here?" the soldier added, giving Anhuset a wink. "It isn't because the margrave thinks I'm pretty to look at."

Anhuset embraced her conversion from hater to lover of the previ-ously despised vegetable with gusto, wolfing down three heaping serv-ings before announcing she intended on abducting Erostis to take him back with her to Saggara so he might share his culinary secrets with the Kai cooks.

Erostis gave his liege a pained look. "Sorry, my lord, but I'm not learning how to cook that bug pie abomination you like to eat if I go there. I have my limits."

After the destruction of High Salure's kitchen as half his garrison waited outside the doors to do battle with an escaped scarpatine, Serovek agreed with him. "I think it best to leave the preparation and consumption of such a dangerous meal within Kai territory, where the staff knows how to handle one of the creatures in most situations."

"No pie for you at High Salure, margrave," Anhuset said with mock sympathy.

"It just means I'll have to visit Saggara more often, madam," he replied, waiting for her expected scowl at the idea of seeing him. His heart knocked briefly against his ribs as her expression turned pensive instead, nor did she fire back a sharp rebuttal.

Anhuset further shocked him by setting her plate down and announcing she was off to scout the area. If he didn't know better, he'd suspect the fierce Kai *sha* had found a ready excuse to flee.

She returned just as Serovek finished brushing down Magas for the evening and checked the ropes of the makeshift corral he and Erostis had strung earlier between a grouping of trees. The firelight behind her edged her silhouette in a ruddy corona. Her silvery hair challenged the moon's grace, and the bright tapestry of her eyes glowed in the darkness as she approached him. "I wondered if you'd still be awake when I returned."

He met her halfway. "Did you discover anything odd?"

She shook her head. "No." She dragged out the word, and they both paused in their trek back to the fire, stopping next to the wagon.

Serovek frowned. "There's a wealth of reservation in that one word, Anhuset."

Her lips turned down at the corners. "I could just be twitchy thanks to our trip to Haradis." She nodded toward the dark barrier of trees from which she'd emerged. "I found three sets of tracks heading in the direction we're traveling, following a line of trampled brush and trails of blood. Boar tracks too. I think a trio of hunters was tracking a wounded hog. The spoor wasn't fresh, but I followed it for a short time until it faded. Nothing of interest really."

"But?" She might well be twitchy as she claimed, seeing an enemy behind every tree, under every rock, and lurking in every shadow. It didn't matter. He trusted her instincts, and something about the spoor had raised her hackles.

"It feels purposeful." She blew a strand of silvery hair away from her face, and her foot tapped the ground in a sign of her frustration. "I'm not explaining this right. Old tracks, old blood. An ordinary hunt. But like someone went to the trouble of making it look that way."

He gazed beyond her shoulder to the shadowy wood. They weren't far outside contested territory, and even in places where peace mostly reigned, raiders and brigands of every sort still presented a threat to travelers. If miscreants followed them with the intent to rob, they were in for a nasty surprise. Even with their numbers halved, Serovek's party presented a formidable fighting force. Erostis and Klanek were experienced soldiers and had seen their fair share of skirmishes, and he almost pitied anyone who'd challenge a Kai *sha*.

At his prolonged silence, she raised an eyebrow. "Do you doubt me? You're welcome to see for yourself."

"I'm not that big of a fool, Anhuset. If you suspect there's more to those tracks than meets the eye, I believe you. We've known to be on our guard since the outset of this trip. We'll continue as we are. If we're being tracked by thieves who think us easy prey, they'll learn differently soon enough."

She gestured to the wagon. "Who'd guess an ordinary cart pulled by ordinary horse flesh would draw so much attention? You'd think it's a monarch's sedan and stallions from Nadiza's lightning herd."

Serovek walked to the wagon, and Anhuset followed. He leaned over the center board and folded back the blanket covering Megiddo's ensorceled bier. The thrum of Elder magic tickled his fingertips when he did. The monk's face, peaceful in repose, carried none of the blue corona Serovek had half expected to see when he moved aside the covering. "It isn't the wagon itself or the team that pulls it. It's the fact the cargo is covered and accompanied by an armed escort."

"Such inspires curiosity," she said. "It doesn't necessarily incite robbery. There's something more at work here." He felt the weight of her curious gaze before it settled on the bier. "For no reason I can explain, it's difficult not to stare at him. Even when he was alive—still awake and aware—he drew the eye."

Serovek gazed at her profile from the corner of one eye. She'd gathered her hair in a loose knot at her nape, exposing her graceful neck and the sharp line of her jaw. He liked her face with its high cheekbones and swooping eyebrows as white as a snowy owl's feathers, the curve of her lips that were so parsimonious with their smile. She wore a contemplative expression as she studied Megiddo, an expression tinged with admiration. "You find him handsome, then?" A nettle of unwelcome jealousy spoiled even more with a touch of envy pricked his insides. How he'd love to garner such an expression from her for himself.

Her quick, derisive snort answered his question before her words did. "Hardly, but even ugly can be arresting."

Her remark gave him hope. She'd been stingingly blunt regarding her opinion of his appearance. Anhuset, like most Kai, considered humans ugly, and the sentiment was returned by most humans. Still, he'd never taken her harsh honesty personally. Even had she thought him as impressive as Megiddo, or as handsome as the handsomest Kai man, it wouldn't matter. This was a woman whose affections would be hard won if won at all, and they wouldn't be obtained through surface attractiveness.

He flipped the blanket edge back into place, hiding Megiddo's face, and turned to his companion. He studied her as she studied him, her lamplight eyes bright in the darkness, the emotions there hidden in depths of numerous citrine shades. "And beauty is a quality defined by more than appearance," he said softly. "Good night, Anhuset." He bowed and left her at the wagon.

Her reply, just as softly uttered, trailed after him. "May your rest be peaceful, margrave."

The following day they rode parallel to a deepening ravine, their pace slowed by the topography's gradual ascent and the degradation of the road. The smooth packed earth of the market roads gave way to rocky, uneven ground, and Klanek dared not push the horse team to a faster pace and risk breaking an axle.

Serovek consulted his map twice, searching for a bridge that crossed the ravine and allowed them to reach the other side and the entrance to the Lobak Valley. The map showed two bridges adjacent to each other; the beam bridge and a primitive footbridge. The footbridge came into view first. And last. No other bridge stretched across the ravine beside it.

He reined Magas to a halt and signaled the others to do the same. "Fuck," he muttered, scowling at the rickety footbridge, just wide enough to allow two people to cross side-by-side if they were willing to risk the sway and swoop of frayed ropes at the mercy of a howling wind.

Erostis and Anhuset stopped on either side of him. The soldier stated the obvious. "There's no beam bridge."

"I can see that." Serovek unfolded the portion of the map showing the bridges. It hadn't changed since his last study of landmarks. Two bridges, not one, and he was certain they hadn't taken a wrong turn. The way here had been mostly a straight track.

Anhuset leaned toward him for a look at the map. "Your map says to cross here?" One eyebrow slowly climbed as she changed positions to stare at the footbridge. "You'll not get one horse across that death trap, much less a wagon and team. It looks ready to snap under the weight of a rat."

He nearly bit his tongue to keep from snapping at her in frustration. He held up the map. "The mapmaker I purchased this from is reliable and renowned. There's supposed to be a beam bridge here as well as the footbridge."

"Maybe we took a wrong path after the village or the forest." Erostis turned his mount in a circle as if to search for some hidden road whose markers they'd missed.

Serovek shook his head. "No, we're traveling in the right direction." He coaxed Magas toward the footbridge, buffeted by the ravine's chilly gusts as they rode parallel to its edge. As he got closer to the footbridge, the discrepancy between map and reality revealed itself.

The map was correct, as was their direction. A beam bridge had once spanned the ravine, but no longer. Someone had destroyed it, tearing the anchor bolts from the cliff walls. Bits and pieces of spandrels and parapets not fallen to the river far below hung on narrow outcroppings, providing sanctuary for bird's nests. The bits of stone looked like broken teeth against the cliff's dark rock.

"Well, that explains why there aren't two bridges," Anhuset said behind him, her remark snatched away by the spiraling wind.

"Aye," he replied as they rode back to where Klanek waited with the wagon. "I'll wager those who destroyed all the other water crossings we've seen had a hand in its collapse."

"But why not take out the footbridge as well? A quick swipe with a scythe on the ropes, and it's done. Much easier than the beam bridge."

He'd questioned the oversight as well for a moment until he gave the footbridge more than a passing glance. "Whoever it was, they were wise not to cut that one. It's an escape route. Someone fleeing the *galla* can still cross the ravine, and the demons can't follow." He gestured toward the bridge. "Gaps between the boards. Too narrow to trip a person, but enough space between them that you see water. The demons can't cross."

Klanek's face wrinkled into deeper worry lines when Serovek relayed the news about the collapsed bridge to him. "If we can't cross here, we'll be forced to take a different route to reach the valley, and that means going through what's left of Chamtivos's territory."

Serovek was about to tell the driver he'd love to hear any alternative options when Anhuset straightened from her casual slouch and pointed to a spot behind him. "It seems your map missed a third bridge, margrave."

He twisted in the saddle, then wheeled Magas around for a better look at this newest surprise. While the spot where they stood had cleared of morning fog hours earlier, dissipated by sun and wind, it still clung to a part of the cliffs in the distance—a gray shroud whose folds now parted in ripples to expose a magnificent beam bridge of swooping arches, decorative spandrels, and graceful parapets constructed of ivory stone.

"That one isn't on the map, is it?"

Startled by the unexpected discovery but hopeful the gods had just bestowed a mercy upon them, Serovek bit back a smile at Erostis's almost forlorn question. "No, it isn't, but that doesn't mean it can't be crossed. We might as well scout it before we decide to take the longer route." He didn't relish traveling through Chamtivos's territory, and if this new bridge offered a way to avoid that, he'd gladly take it.

They set off toward the bridge, and Serovek felt a splinter of unease the closer they came to it. How a map maker could capture the details of a footbridge but miss a beam bridge of this size and majesty made no sense. Judging by the depressions in the cliff walls where the other beam bridge had been anchored, it was wide enough to accommodate all types of traffic, with a lane dedicated to each side crossing instead of having to wait for clearance.

This bridge dwarfed the collapsed one, easily three times its size and wide enough to allow full battalions and cavalry to cross, along with wagons of every size. Tendrils of fog wound through the parapets and floated just above a bridge deck partially covered by a carpet of tightly twisted ivy. The greenery wrapped pilasters and spilled over the deck's edge in long garlands. More of it draped statues twice the height of a man that lined the bridge on both sides.

Where bridge deck met cliff edge, a set of pavers carved in arcane runes marked the transition from ground to bridge. Their party halted, and Serovek dismounted for a closer look at the carvings. He stretched out a hand to trace one of the symbols in the air. The abrupt change in temperature made him step back before reaching out a second time to test the air.

"What is it?" Anhuset had dismounted as well and came to stand beside him and Magas.

"Put out your hand," he instructed her. "Just over the line where the bridge starts."

She hesitated for a breath before doing as he asked. Like him, she yanked her hand back. Unlike him, she didn't try a second time, electing instead to wipe her hand on her leg. "It's warm. Summer-warm compared to where we're standing."

Serovek had assumed the runes carved in the pavers were either wards or a greeting and was inclined to believe the former rather than the latter. Therefore he wasn't overly startled when his hand slipped across an invisible barrier that separated the hard cold of a lingering winter still gripping the land from the heat of a day in high summer. No wonder the ivy draping the bridge was so lush and green. An enchantment protected it from the elements.

What made him pause was Anhuset's lack of awareness of or sensitivity to the sorcery. The Kai he'd known, blessed with a heritage of magic, could sniff it out when it was nearby. She'd said nothing nor given any indication she'd felt its presence, even when they stood at the bridge's entrance.

"Did you not sense the magic as we got closer?" he asked her in a low voice, keeping his tone light and conversational.

Her entire body stiffened, an infinitesimal tensing. If one wasn't watching her closely, they'd have missed it, but Serovek had been watching, and the reaction told him his question had touched a raw spot.

Her expression as well told him more than she realized. Studied. Distant. An indifferent mask. "It's human magic," she said in a bland voice. "The Kai don't always sense the sorcery your kind wield."

Your kind.

Had she slammed her shield down between them, her message couldn't have been clearer. He trod where he wasn't welcomed with his question, and she warned him with those two words that he'd be wise to back off from any more inquiries.

He held up both hands, palms out, in a gesture of surrender before turning his attention to Erostis and Klanek. "We don't know what these wards do or if the bridge's apparent stability is just an illusion. I'll walk it first..." Three sets of protests went up so that he had to raise his voice above them. "Then come back so we'll go as a group." He scowled at Anhuset and the two men as they all readied to launch into another spate of argument. "I'm not asking you. I'm telling you."

"I'm going with you," Anhuset returned his scowl. "My magic

might have missed the first ward, but it may catch something else before you stumble into it."

Her suggestion gained an enthusiastic nod from Erostis. "It's a good idea, margrave. Better than you going alone or me and Klanek with you. The *sha* would know what to avoid if there's anything unseen lurking on the bridge."

Serovek's faith in Anhuset's sorcerous senses had been tested one too many times now. It was no longer as strong as Erostis's, but he didn't argue the point. He passed Magas's reins to him instead and motioned to Anhuset to do the same. "Leave your horse. We'll keep the risk to a minimum."

When they stepped onto the bridge, a tilting sensation made him sway, and his ears popped as if he dropped suddenly from a greater height. He widened his stance to keep his balance and saw that Anhuset did the same. The sensation passed as quickly as it struck, leaving behind a cloying heat and the scent of decaying vegetation.

Dressed for winter, the two shed their heavier layers of clothing, but even down to a thin shirt, he still broke a sweat. Beside him, Anhuset wore a sleeveless tunic. A fine sheen of perspiration already glossed her arms, defining long muscles, and she squinted without the protection of her hood. She'd unsheathed one of the knives she wore at her belt, the blade catching the dull gleam of sunlight on its edge.

She stretched out her arm, inviting him to lead. "Ready for a stroll, margrave?"

Up close, the bridge was even more dilapidated. Age and abandonment had left their marks, as had the purposeful defacement by long-vanished vandals. Even half choked in the creeping ivy, it was still a magnificent structure of lavishly carved stone. The statues he'd seen lining the parapets towered above him, standing on plinths engraved with epitaphs in an unknown script. The sculptor or sculptors had rendered the rich texture of silk and delicate embroidery from stone in the garb worn by the effigies, and the crowns they all wore told all who looked upon them that these were kings and queens. Larger than life in both marble and flesh and blood, they loomed over their lesser subjects with haughty majesty.

Anhuset's voice beside him startled him from his contemplation. He'd been so distracted by the sight of the statues he hadn't heard her approach. "I can forgive a mapmaker for overlooking a bridge, even one as grand as this, but an entire city?" She pointed to the other side of the ravine where the mist hung thick as a barrier wall, obscuring everything at the bridge's opposite end. Until now.

The impenetrable gray had fractured in spots, creating gaps in the mist wall to reveal a true fortification complete with imposing gate, battlements, and turrets. Towers claimed by more of the ivy soared skyward behind the walls. The crumbling remains of graceful sky walks once connected a few of the towers, their spans dismembered. In the sun, the city gleamed alabaster pockmarked by lichen and mold.

As much of a ruin as Haradis, this nameless city perched on the cliff's edge in equal silence. Serovek fancied he still heard the faint echo of voices and the creak of wagon wheels as they rolled over a bridge deck clear of ivy and crowded with people.

Unease crawled down his spine. What lay behind the mist and fortifications? Was the silence born of a place devoid of inhabitants or one that simply hid a quiet predator? A *galla* waiting to ambush the unwary if they walked through the gate?

He turned to Anhuset. "Have my eyes changed?"

Alarm flashed briefly across her face. She glanced over the parapet to the Absu river, a pale blue ribbon winding a path at the bottom of the ravine. Water. The barrier which no *galla* could cross unless there was a solid bridge. Just like this one.

"No," she replied. "Only one part of your eyes is blue, and that is the blue you were born with. Deep water, not eidolon."

They both looked back to where Erostis waited with Klanek and the wagon carrying Megiddo. No strange light leaked out from the blanket covering the bier nor shimmered around the wagon itself.

Serovek exhaled a relieved sigh, returning his attention to the city. "If there were *galla* here, we'd have known it by now. So would half the countryside. I don't know why the map doesn't show the city or the bridge, but one looks sturdy enough to cross and will get us to our destination quicker."

"Not a sound from the place," Erostis called to them. "A dead city, or an abandoned one."

"Old ruins are as plentiful in this country as freckles on my favorite pub wench's skin," Klanek argued. "I'm surprised we've only come across this one and Haradis so far."

"Call it fortune." Serovek took several steps across the deck. Only the heat bore down on him. "If no one's there, we won't be overwhelmed by beggars when we enter the gate or crowds when we travel through the city." More steps and only the wind to whisper his name while the statues ignored him in favor of staring at each other with empty gazes.

Solid beneath his feet, the bridge still vibrated under the hard gusts purling beneath its spandrels and joists. "Don't cross until I give the signal it's safe to do so," he instructed the two men. More sure of the bridge now, he and Anhuset started a basket weave motion as they scouted the bridge, walking the sides, then crossing paths at the center to walk the opposite side, then doing the same again and again, skirting tangled mats of ivy as they went.

Serovek eyed the statues as he traveled the deck pausing at one unlike those on either side of it. The difference lay not in the sculptor's hand but in the vandal's. Hammer and chisel wielded by an enraged hand had savaged this particular king, hacking away at the face, breaking the crown, and defacing the epigraph on the plinth until the mysterious words were obliterated.

"The others are mostly untouched," Anhuset said as she crossed the bridge to reach him.

Serovek leaned toward the damaged statue despite his better instincts warning him against such an action. "Whoever he was, he was hated." He stretched out a hand toward the plinth.

"Don't," Anhuset warned.

"I've no intention of touching it," he assured her. The words no sooner left his lips than a tiny bolt of lightning arced from the stone to jolt his fingertip. Serovek leaped back with a yelp, narrowly avoiding trampling Anhuset.

"I warned you not to touch it," she snapped.

"And I didn't," he snapped back.

He glared at her and she at him until a thought occurred to him. Something in his expression must have forewarned her of another one of his uncomfortable questions for the scowl disappeared behind that stoic mask she erected like a shield wall.

"The statue is warded," Serovek said. "I'm guessing they all are. Human sorcery or not, I'd think a Kai possessing even a drop of Elder magic would sense it, yet you didn't. Again."

He'd heard rumors in the months following the *galla*'s defeat of Kai unable to capture the mortem lights of their dead. For a people whose history relied on the stored memories of the dead to record their history, such a calamity was catastrophic, unprecedented, and as far as he knew, unexplained.

"You've lost your magic, haven't you, firefly woman?"

Her lips thinned into a mulish line, while her yellow eyes lightened until they were almost white.

Annoyance, he thought. Anger. The hostile emotions paled a Kai's eyes while the benign ones turned them gold.

Her hand clenched on the knife she held before loosening, and her shoulders relaxed. When she spoke, her voice carried nothing of her momentary fury, only a faint thread of sadness. "I have."

"Will you ever tell me why?"

"No."

Serovek had expected such an answer. She'd maneuvered around his oblique questions until he'd asked her outright. Still, she only confirmed what he'd already ascertained and nothing more. Sha-Anhuset was a woman judicious with her words and possessive of her secrets. This one he sensed affected far more than a single Kai. "If there's a way I can help you regain it, I hope you'd tell me."

Her posture slumped a little more, and the hard angles of her faced softened. "Ask me nothing else about it," she said. "You know enough now to realize the *galla* was attracted to you, that while I can be an extra sword on the bridge, I can't sense sorcery. I inherited very little Elder magic to begin with, but my sword arm is strong, and I'm enduring. Let that be enough."

"It's always been enough." He wanted to gather her in his arms, stroke her silvery hair and apologize for his prying. He bowed to her instead. "No more intrusions," he promised. "I was wrong to meddle and beg your forgiveness."

"Done," she said, eyes darkening once more to their citrine shade.

Quick to bristle and just as quick to pardon, she was a creature of dichotomies in character and appearance: dark and light, harsh and merciful, dour and humorous, secretive and forthright. And he lusted for her mightily, even now as they traveled across an ancient bridge toward a strange and empty city.

They continued methodically weaving toward the opposite side, reaching the deck's center. Anhuset stopped to stare down its length. "What malice is this?"

The mists veiling the city suddenly thickened to a dense, roiling mass before spilling like a waterfall onto the bridge, rushing toward them in a gray tide.

A low-hanging cloud did no more damage than get someone wet, but this was far more than weather, and Serovek wanted nothing to do with a repeat of Haradis. "Run!"

He never had a chance to lift a foot. His command acted as a catalyst for invisible listeners. The ivy, wild and thick, turned into a writhing, whipping mass. Vines, slender as threads and stout as broom handles lashed upward and out with serpentine speed. Serovek fell to one knee as several leaf-covered ropes snaked around his ankles and calves, wrapping so tight his feet went numb.

Anhuset's expletives singed his ears as more of the ivy coiled around her as well, even managing to encircle her wrist and yank her knife out of her hand before tossing it into one of the heaving mats of vegetation. The blade sank out of sight, devoured by the feral foliage.

"That was my favorite knife, you pile of pig shit," she snarled, straining against her bonds.

Shouts behind them made Serovek's heart seize. He twisted enough in his shackles to shout at Erostis, who'd mounted his horse to ride toward them. "Stay there, gods damn it!" His shout ricocheted off the cliff walls and echoed back to them. He turned his attention to Anhuset, her lips pulled back from her teeth as she growled and fought against her bonds. The vines climbed higher up her body, twining around her thighs and hips, weaving a cage of greenery around her lower torso.

"Anhuset, stop." She paused long enough to stare at him. "Stop," he repeated. "The more you move, the higher they'll go and the tighter they'll get." His own tethers hadn't traveled any farther up his body than his calves and were loose enough that he regained his footing and stood.

Her eyes rounded at the sight, and she halted her thrashing. The vines stopped their creep as well, though they didn't retreat or loosen on her. "So we're stuck here while whatever that is..." She tilted her head toward the mist only a stone's throw away from them. "Consumes us."

"Pray that isn't so," he said. He wouldn't offer any false reassurances. He had no more idea than she what lay in store for them.

The preternatural mist had slowed its rush to a slow lap, dissipating in spots until it no longer resembled a ground-hugging cloud.

Serovek's lips parted in a silent gasp. "Lover of thorns and holy gods," he breathed in a whisper.

He'd prayed never to see this very sight ever again, yet once more a vast crowd of the dead stood in front of him, their regard far heavier than the vaporous forms they wore.

Icy fingers of panic closed his throat for a moment, rendering him mute. The necromantic magic he was sure still lingered inside him had somehow managed to attract restless ghosts without his knowledge or control.

"Anhuset." He forced her name past his teeth. She turned her head just enough to give him a quick glance without taking her eye off the host of apparitions watching them in return. "Have my eyes changed?"

Her scowl darkened even more, not with anger but puzzlement. "No. They're still the same. Cold-water blue and just as strange as they always are."

He might have chuckled at her comment were they in different circumstances.

The throng of spectral watchers rippled before him, tattered shapes whose details sharpened for a moment into men, women, and children. There were thousands of them crowding the bridge deck, some gliding away from the main group to flutter along either side of and behind him and Anhuset until they were surrounded.

"Who are you?" He wondered if they'd speak as those who'd followed the Wraith kings into battle had done.

One shape in the front and center of the shifting mist separated from the rest to drift toward him. A woman, lithe and nearly as tall as Anhuset. Her nebulous features hinted at a comeliness bordering on the sublime. In life she must have been breathtaking to behold.

As she drew closer, Serovek inhaled sharply. He recognized her. One of the statues behind him wore her face. A queen, crowned in a diadem whose jewels had been pried out by a long-dead thief. As he'd done with the faceless king, Serovek had paused to admire her image. He hadn't expected to confront her specter.

She didn't speak, but nonetheless a voice sounded clear in his mind in a tongue he understood. "A dark song is your spirit, Wraith king, a hymn of the broken. We heard its dirge across the ravine." Her phantasmal gaze passed over him, leaving frost ribbons on his clothes where it touched. "A general of the dead with the taint of the damned on him."

There was no condemnation in her words, no judgment, yet Serovek briefly closed his eyes, sick to his soul at their truth. When he opened them again, she was still in front of him, and beyond her Anhuset watched him with a wary, puzzled expression.

The queen had addressed him by the title given to the five who'd fought the *galla*. "How do you know me?" he asked. "Did you and yours serve under my banner?" The Kai dead had followed Brishen while the human dead had answered to Serovek, Andras, Gaeres and Megiddo.

Again, only a voice in his mind answered. "We serve no one. All of the dead heard the summons of a son of the Old blood."

This time the ghostly throng behind her spoke aloud, repeating in hollow unison ancient Kai words once uttered by Brishen's eidolon on Saruna Tor.

"Rise and come forth, ye sleepers and ye wanderers. Come forth and prepare for war. Rise. Rise."

"Oh fuck." Anhuset's face had gone the color of a dead fish. "All my wealth for a sword and shield right now."

Serovek shuddered hard enough that he would have fallen to his knees had the vines not held him upright. Those words had seeded more than a few of his nightmares, always preceding grotesque images of Megiddo tortured by the *galla*. He shoved aside the guilt and abiding horror to concentrate on the queen.

"We wished only to cross to the other side as a faster way to the Lobak valley," he said. "We've no interest in exploring your city, only passing through it."

She shook her head. "The dead and the damned already reside in Tineroth, Wraith king. There's no welcome for you and yours here." The spectral queen smiled a sad, bitter smile. It faded, and behind her the court of phantoms sighed, the sound like the last gasp of the dying. "We've come to warn you. The guardian of Tineroth waits at the gate. Those who enter don't leave. Go back the way you came."

He was about to reassure her that was exactly what he intended when Anhuset pulled on her bonds in an attempt to free one arm. "Margrave, look to the far battlement right of the gate." Serovek did as she instructed, spotting a lone figure perched like a raptor on the battlement's narrow ledge. "Whoever that is," Anhuset continued. "They aren't a ghost."

She was right. The wind howling up from the ravine whipped the figure's pale hair around their head, partially hiding their face. They were too far away for Serovek to make out any specific features, but the dull gleam of sunlight on steel told him the watcher wore armor, and the pole arm casually tucked into the crook of their elbow spoke of a warrior's ease with weaponry.

Like the bridge and the city it led to, something about that distant figure raised internal alarms, even if the phantom queen's words hadn't already done so.

"We can't stop you from entering Tineroth," she said, her voice no longer strong in his mind but more of a resonance heard in a deep well. "But you, like others before you, will die there if you do."

Serovek was no stranger to war, against the living, the dead, and the demonic, but a shorter path to the monastery wasn't worth risking their lives more than necessary, and his instincts told him the guardian the queen warned him about was more than a solitary warrior with a sharp blade.

She gestured with a pellucid hand, and the vines fell away from his and Anhuset's legs, retreating with a loud hiss as serpentine as their movements. "Your choice," the queen said. "Farewell." Her form faded, the last bits of mist shredded by the wind. The crowd of ghosts accompanying her lost shape and definition, melting into the obscuring fog that rolled back toward the city before enveloping it entirely in a gray shroud.

Serovek no longer saw the guardian, though he was sure they still watched him and Anhuset with malevolent intent.

Anhuset strode to where her knife lay on the deck, no longer covered by the vines. "What did the ghosts say? I could tell the one was speaking to you in your thoughts."

"Turn back and live or go forward and die," he replied. "I'll give you and the others details once we're off this bridge and back on the road."

She wiped a hand across her sweating brow, no longer scowling now that she had her blade back. "I was hoping you'd say that. I'd rather face Chamtivos than keep company with ghosts and whoever watched us from the battlement." A quick look back over her shoulder toward the mist wall. "Not a ghost," she said. "But I think someone or some *thing* I'd not want to cross if I didn't have to."

Her remark put to rest any hesitation he might have harbored about taking the long way through contested territory. It spoke volumes that the fierce Anhuset wasn't keen on journeying into the eerily silent city the queen called Tineroth.

He was done with ghosts and *galla*, and his feet craved solid ground. "You boasted you're a fast swimmer." He gave Anhuset an arch look, grinning a slow grin when she returned it. "But how fast can you run?"

"Faster than you, margrave," she scoffed.

"Care to wager on that?"

"Any time, any place," she said and launched into a sprint for the spot where Erostis and Klanek waited.

Serovek raced after her, uncaring if he lost a handful of coin to her, relieved to leave behind the dead and the grim words of their monarch.

"A dark song is your spirit, Wraith king, a hymn of the broken."

CHAPTER
EIGHT

Anhuset lay on her back looking up at a star-studded sky as she worried a dirty silk ribbon between her thumb and forefinger. She preferred being on guard duty, but she obeyed Serovek's edict that the four of them would take short shifts through the night so they were all mostly rested and alert during the day. No more napping on her horse while they rode through contested territory.

Despite the stains and fraying edges, the ribbon still slid smoothly between her fingers. One of her companions was asleep, the second tending the fire, and Serovek himself taking this round of the watch. None would see her stroking the ribbon.

She'd rescued it from a burial in the mud when the herb bundle it wound around had fallen to the ground by one of the wagon wheels. Arms full of newly purchased supplies, she'd stared at the cluster before nudging it out of the way with one foot. Once she loaded supplies into the wagon, she scooped up the bundle. The trailing ends of the ribbon binding the herbs together had once been a pristine white before the fall in the mud had stained them brown. Serovek's words, spoken in affectionate tones as he recalled his wife Glaurin and her preference for ribbons, echoed in her mind.

"She was proud. Beautiful. Long hair that she wore tied back with silk ribbons."

She'd stared at the ribbon, finally unwinding it. The ruined herbs went by the wayside and the ribbon into the pouch she kept on her belt. Guard duty had provided her the privacy to fidget with the ribbon, first to try weaving it into her hair under the heaviest locks where no one could see it. Her attempts met with failure, and she'd hurled the ribbon away, only to rescue it from the thorns of a berry bush. Serovek was right. She'd do a much better job of strangling someone with the ribbon than decorating her hair. She was no Glaurin Pangion, proud and lovely. She was sha-Anhuset, proud and fierce.

Since then, she'd kept the ribbon in the pouch until she was alone, using it like prayer beads instead of hair ornament. She didn't pray, but the ribbon's silky feel on her fingertips relaxed her. Tonight she hoped it might lull her into a quick nap.

"Whatever you're worrying between your fingers, Anhuset, it's a wonder your claws haven't shredded it yet."

A quick sleight of hand and she shoved the ribbon into her tunic sleeve. Serovek, relieved of guard duty by Erostis, approached her, his smile deepening the lines in his face, lending his handsome features an even greater attractiveness. Anhuset lurched upright, the breath trapped in her throat at the horror of that thought.

Serovek's smile slid away. He paused in front of her. "What's wrong? You look like you've just seen a *galla*."

She scrambled for some explanation for her action and settled on changing the topic. "Is it my turn for guard duty? I wasn't asleep." A poor save, and one that made Serovek arch an eyebrow.

"No, you're after Erostis. Remember? Then Klanek after you."

"Shouldn't you try and get to sleep now that your watch is done?" He saw entirely too much. The last thing she wanted was for him to ask to see what she'd just tucked out of sight. The image of his knowing expression made her cringe inside.

"I will soon enough. I saw you were still awake and couldn't resist seeking out your sunny company." He winked, not waiting for an invitation before sitting beside her.

Not long ago, she would have snarled at him for his teasing, flummoxed by his humor and overt flirting. Now she simply reclined back on her elbows and stretched out her legs. "I've been accused of many character flaws. That one's a first."

He grinned, the creases etched into his skin at the corners of his eyes fanning wide. "You do make me smile, firefly woman. I'll sorely miss this when our journey is over and we part ways."

I'll miss it too, she thought. To admit aloud she might miss his company was even worse than accepting it internally. No one, Kai or human, had ever affected her the way this Beladine nobleman did, and it terrified her. She didn't want to like him, and gods forbid she desire him!

She changed the subject once more. "Our history doesn't have a record of a city called Tineroth, at least not that I'm aware of. Not unusual as those ghosts were human, and the Kai have little interest in the affairs of humans unless they affect the Kai."

"I've never heard of Tineroth either. A city that size reached by a bridge of such grandiose size and design would be well known by those living in the area and appear on every map, even as ruins. Care to wager that if we returned there tomorrow, both would be gone?"

After the events on the bridge, there'd been no debate over whether or not to journey through the territories plagued by Chamtivos and his band of raiders. It was a dangerous route, but no one wanted to attempt a crossing through the haunted city, not even Erostis or Klanek, who'd only seen some of what occurred on the bridge.

"You already lost our bet over who was fastest across the bridge," she scoffed. "Are you trying to beggar yourself to me with these bets?"

He chortled. "I have a feeling I'd win this particular wager. That city was no more anchored to earth than the mist covering it."

She agreed. "And exactly why I won't take that bet." In other circumstances she might not have beaten him across the ravine. Serovek was a big man, but also a surprisingly fast one. Still, after hearing phantom humans chant ancient bast-Kai in sepulchral voices, she'd practically sprouted wings in her eagerness to get far away from the restless dead.

Serovek left her for a moment, returning from his sleeping spot with his pipe. "Care to join me?" He held up the pipe in offer.

She declined, content to watch him prepare the pipe for smoking. There was something about his actions that soothed her, and she turned on her side to face him.

He had good hands, deft in everything they did, from controlling a horse and wielding a sword to extracting a bodkin point from her shoulder and snapping a man's neck as punishment for the crime of murder. His fingers were straight, with short, clean nails. She'd known the feel of those hands clasped with hers, on her shoulders in a stable after Magas nipped her. What would it be like to have that strong, capable touch on other parts of her body? Did he seduce his lovers with a caress that promised even greater pleasure? The stars above winked back at her but offered no insight or answers.

"What weighty ponderings have painted such a black scowl on your face, Anhuset?" Serovek held the unlit pipe in one hand, his head tilted to one side as he regarded her. The fire limned his face and body in flickering light.

Anhuset would die a thousand deaths before revealing her speculations to him. She asked a question guaranteed to redirect his attention. "Why have you not remarried?"

His eyes widened before narrowing in silent amusement. He unfolded his big frame to stand—all grace and size and hard muscle. "You always manage to surprise me, firefly woman. Give me a moment, and I'll satisfy your curiosity."

He left a second time, returning from the campfire with his pipe lit. He resumed his seat beside her, drawing on the pipe and exhaling smoke rings before he finally spoke. "Are you making an offer of marriage?" he asked, no hint of teasing in the question.

She sputtered and sat up. "No!" She glared at his widening grin, which stretched even wider when she harrumphed and resumed her lounging position. "You're the worst sort of tease," she grumbled.

"Oh, my beauty, you have no idea. I hope one day to enlighten you." He raised a hand in surrender when she opened her mouth to scold him. "No more teasing," he said. "I promise."

"You still haven't answered my question. You're a wealthy Beladine nobleman with land and vassals, an army you can field for your king, and a reputation as an outstanding lover that's gone beyond Beladine borders. Even the Kai have heard of your prowess. I've seen for myself how human women vie for your attention."

The inner voice she wanted so badly to thrash into silence chose that moment to mock her. *Not just the human ones. You're beginning to see him with their eyes.*

Serovek blew a thin stream of smoke into the air. The cloud swirled upward in fragrant wisps. "Why do I suddenly feel like the fatted hog?"

"Because a rich, unmarried nobleman of any country is a prize to be won as soon as possible." A sudden thought occurred to her. "You aren't *gameza*, are you?"

"A bastard?" He shook his head. "No. Even if I were, it wouldn't matter. I'm the lord of a prosperous estate and have the support of King Rodan. I remain unmarried because I choose to."

Her thoughts whirled, along with her emotions. Confusion over his lack of motivation in expanding power, wealth, and status through an advantageous union, relief that he showed no preference for some Beladine beauty with strange eyes and small square teeth, who could weave ribbons into her hair with the same ease that Anhuset could handle a sword.

"Do you still grieve your wife?" Maybe that was why he chose not to remarry. Loyalty to a dead woman. Anhuset had never known such depth of feeling for a lover. It seemed to her an awful, vulnerable thing.

Serovek regarded her in silence for several moments before answering. "Delving deep tonight, Anhuset."

"Tell me to stop and I will." She strove to understand the heart and mind of this man. Melancholy shadowed his former easy humor, a lingering taint left by his time as eidolon, fighting the *galla* alongside Brishen.

He shrugged. "I've nothing to hide." Smoke rings floated around them as he drew on the pipe and exhaled. "You never stop mourning those you loved and lost. Glaurin was a good wife. I honor her by remembering her fondly, all those things about her that gladdened my spirit, instead of those which might have annoyed me. She paid me the compliment of being my wife and giving me a daughter." A half smile lifted one corner of his mouth. "If you're asking if she's the reason I haven't remarried, the answer is no."

The insidious inner voice poking a sharp stick at Anhuset continued its harassment. *Why then?* Instead she said aloud, "Who chose Deliza's name? You or your wife?"

"I did." An abiding sorrow filled his voice and darkened the deep blue of his eyes. "It means 'hope' in old temple language."

There it was, the vulnerability she feared. How long did the living suffer from the loss of the dead they loved? What wreckage did such loss leave behind and was it worth the pain? Did it make her weak for avoiding such attachments and Serovek strong for embracing them? For he was strong, inside and out. He'd proven that strength over and over to her. What did he see when he stared hard into her soul? A warrior tough and unyielding or simply a woman too frightened to care too much?

She tried to imagine him with children. It wasn't hard. A stillness settled over him when she rested her hand on his forearm and gave a gentle squeeze. "I've no doubt you would have made a loving father."

He gazed at her hand before covering it with his, his callused palm rough on her knuckles. That deep-water gaze lifted to hers. Were she not so wary of his effect on her, she might have fallen into it, succumbing to his allure. "Thank you, Anhuset."

His gratitude carried the ring of a prayer offered to a beloved deity, and Anhuset felt her face—nay, her entire body—light up at the words. Her heart tripped a beat in double time. Was this how Brishen came to see Ildiko as beautiful instead of hideous? Through glimpses into her soul? Or was it a gradually expanding knowledge of her character that seduced him and made her desirable? Brishen Khaskem had never been weaker than when he fell in love with his wife.

Nor as strong, argued the internal voice.

"No thanks necessary. I only speak the truth," she told Serovek before rolling onto her back and closing her eyes, too afraid to look any longer upon his face, or worse, have him look upon hers and see past her outward serenity to the turmoil within.

A companionable hush descended between them. Anhuset breathed the sweet smell of pipe smoke as Serovek burned through the bowl of herbs and leaf. She kept her eyes closed, denying the temptation to look at him. Despite her certainty that she'd stay awake through the night, drowsiness claimed her.

"You are truly the most beautiful woman I've ever beheld."

Perched on the edge of sleep, she wondered if she imagined Serovek's compliment. She didn't bother to open her eyes. "I don't understand why you think so," she mumbled.

His voice caressed her, body and soul. "And I don't understand why you do not."

Anhuset drifted off, waking not long after for guard duty, and discovered a blanket tossed over her. Serovek had returned to his pallet while she slept and now lay on his side facing her. Dawn light gilded his hair, bronzing the red highlights there, silvering the gray ones. His black eyelashes fanned against his cheeks. In slumber, he looked younger, the refined angles of his face softened. If he dreamed, it was of something far more pleasant than the tortures of Megiddo.

Not so ugly this morning, the inner voice mocked.

"Shut up," she said aloud and tossed off the blanket to stand and stretch. Klanek waved to her from his place by the fire pit. He'd taken the previous watch and now stoked the fire in preparation for an early breakfast.

Serovek neither looked nor acted any differently than he had days or months before, yet that day Anhuset found it difficult not to stare at him. Maybe it was seeing him surrounded by ghosts and holding silent conversations with spectral queens or hearing him recall his wife and daughter with a far-away voice of affectionate memory.

He hadn't changed, but something profound in her had. She'd once thought him a brave but shallow man, arrogant at times, with a peculiar gift of annoying her like no one else could. Except for his courage and her annoyance, she'd been so very wrong about him.

She took up her usual spot as rear guard of their small caravan, with Erostis riding beside her. They weren't long on the road when Serovek trotted back to them and bade Erostis to trade places with him.

"I have a question for you," he said as Magas settled into a leisurely walk that matched her mount's.

Her alarm bells sounded. He'd knocked her sideways on the ghostly bridge when he asked up front if she'd lost her magic. She hadn't lied when she confirmed his suspicions with a single word, but she would do so if he wanted to know more. That Brishen had stripped all but the youngest of the Kai of their birthright wasn't her secret to tell, but it was hers to protect, no matter the cost. "I don't promise to answer it," she replied.

Fortunately, he chose not to pursue the subject. "You say you haven't married because you're *gameza*, but the purity of a bloodline is typically only important to noble families scrabbling for power and status. Their offspring are pawns. Even as *gameza*, you hold a great deal of influence with the Khaskem. You're his *sha*, even more trusted than his closest counselors. Was there no lover who tempted you into a permanent bonding?"

She nearly wilted in the saddle from relief. An easy question with an easy answer and no need for lies. "No, not a single one," she said cheerfully. "I can barely stand their company after a few nights, much less years or a lifetime. I'd make a terrible wife."

He laughed. "You say that with such passion."

"It's the truth." One truth, at least. No Kai had ever remotely tempted her to make such a commitment. Her heart remained her own, her devotion reserved for Brishen, and through him, his human wife and the child queen regnant. "I make a better *sha* than a wife."

"Brishen is fortunate to have you as his *sha*, especially now. Saggara is much changed since it's become the new capital."

He didn't know the half of it. "It was once the old one," she said. "Before the monarchy moved it to Haradis. Saggara wasn't prepared for the return to its original role."

Saggara's population had exploded overnight with the *galla* invasion, straining resources, space, and tempers. A goodly portion of the refugees displaced from Haradis had dispersed to other towns and villages once the *galla* were defeated, but the redoubt's permanent population was still twice the size it was before Haradis's destruction, with fewer Kai leaving and more coming in now that the queen regnant was in residence.

"He'd benefit from having several *shas*," she said. "I spend more time breaking up fights over who gets what parcel of land or grain ration than I do riding patrol."

"It'll calm down in time," Serovek assured her. "Especially under Brishen's regency. He would have made an exceptional monarch. He'll make an exceptional regent for young Tarawin." He studied her as he always did before asking questions that made her squirm. "Do you miss things the way they were before the *galla*?"

Her magic had never been much to speak of, but it was an essential part of her, and now it was gone forever, leaving behind a wound that would never heal. "We all do. The *galla* changed everything." She attempted to turn the topic back on him. "And you? When did your dreams of Megiddo start?"

The narrow-eyed look he gave her told her she'd been less than subtle. "Not long after I left him with his brother. At first, I thought it was simply guilt. Even when you know the decision made—the sacrifice given—was the only choice, your soul will still shout down your mind."

He'd given her insight into the guilt burdening him over Megiddo's fate, a burden that seemed to grow heavier every day. Unwarranted, unfair, especially with such bent reasoning. "Megiddo wasn't given. He was taken. And he was the one who severed the Gauri exile's hand to free himself. If anyone gave the monk to the *galla*, it was the monk." She answered his silent, questioning gaze. "Brishen told me and the *hercegesé* what happened."

Serovek sighed, turning his face up to the sun with closed eyes. "So many lives lost and still no one knows what brought the demon horde down upon the world. I suppose we'll never know." He glanced at her, as if sensing the weight of her consideration. "What?"

Layer upon layer, this man. Like the forging of a blade under a swordsmith's hammer. Folded steel and the fire of suffering. He was strong inside and out, with the ability to bend and not break, draw blood, and still gleam in the light. "I don't think I've ever seen you truly melancholy until now. Cheerful, ruthless, cold-blooded, horrified even. But not this."

"Didn't you? These days I find myself more maudlin than I like." This time his smile was wry. "An unfortunate weakness arising with my advancing age."

She huffed. "You can't use the excuse of dotage. You're a man in his prime. Besides, it isn't a weakness to feel sadness. Whoever boasts they haven't been touched by sorrow or tragedy is lying. We grieve because we still remember what it is to feel." And why she did her best not to feel too much.

"Wise words. Practical ones too. What do you grieve for, Anhuset?"

"Those things whose burdens are easier borne if I don't speak of them." She wasn't ready to bare her soul to him. Even knowing he'd pass no judgment on her, it felt trivial somehow to reveal her own lesser desolations when his experiences had been so much worse than hers.

"One day," he said softly, "you'll trust me enough to gift me with a glimpse into that guarded heart of yours."

She surprised herself, and possibly Serovek, by staying quiet instead of denying his statement. To her relief, he didn't push for more from her.

While they remained wary as they traveled along drover paths snaking through the contested territories, most of the trip remained uneventful. They still shared the nighttime guard duty so that at least three of them were awake and rested at all times.

Only one thing caused them all to draw swords and push the wagon team to a faster pace. Two leagues out from the entrance pass to the Lobak valley, they traveled through marshland, riding over a rutted road partially submerged in spots by water lapping sluggishly across its surface. It was an ordinary road through an ordinary wetland except for the slender poles embedded in the ground at regular intervals that ran the road's length on either side.

Carved with arcane symbols that glowed dully in the gray light of an overcast day, the poles were attached to each other by shimmering bands of the same luminescence to create a border that hummed a wordless tune.

Anhuset had halted her horse at a suspicious splash, the sound made ominous by the sight of four huge scaled humps breaching the still water and hinting at something colossal gliding just below the surface. A wake, of a size comparable to that left by a ferry or other large craft, rippled the surface behind the swimmer.

"Weapons at the ready and stay in the center," Serovek instructed them. "I've no doubt this fence was erected to keep whatever is in the water from attacking those who take this road, but no need to tempt fortune by testing its effectiveness. Keep moving."

The heavy mist blanketing the marsh followed them even after they left the road for higher, drier ground. Damp and chilly, the fog drifted belly-high on the horses, and Anhuset caught herself peering hard into the miasma, looking for ghostly crowds or a phantom queen who ruled them.

Late afternoon saw no respite from the cloudy gloom. Grim and frowning, Serovek rode a slow circle around their party as they tightened the distance between riders and wagon. "I don't like this," he said. "We're traveling blind through this soup but stopping to camp is a worse alternative." He rode closer to Anhuset. "How good are the Kai at seeing through fog?"

"Unfortunately, no better than humans," she said.

"I was afraid such was so." He addressed all three of them. "Keep moving and your eyes and ears open. We'll journey until full dark and get as far as we can before we stop to make camp. With any luck, this will have burned off or faded, and we'll have clear weather."

As fate would have it, luck laughed at Serovek's optimism. The fog only thickened and rose higher until the wagon and team were vague shapes in front of Anhuset and the riders with her as phantasmal as the ghosts on the bridge they'd left behind days earlier.

"Methinks this stuff is thick enough to walk on." Erostis's muffled complaint hung in the clinging mist, disembodied and far away though Anhuset knew him to be just ahead of her.

"I might as well be blindfolded for all I can see where I'm driving this team," Klanek added.

"Hush." Anhuset's command silenced them instantly. She reined her mount to a stop and listened. Almost indiscernible from the clop of horse hooves and the creak of wagon wheels, the faint sounds of movement teased her ears. The slide of leather on leather, the bend of wood from the draw of a bow. A furtive step. A careful inhalation.

"Close in," she said, hoping her party heard her near whisper. "Shields."

The hard thunk of an arrow hitting flesh, followed by Klanek's pained cry, set off a chaotic melée between their group and a half-glimpsed band of silent attackers. Obscured by the mists, they targeted the horses first.

Anhuset's horse squealed its terror as the tip of a whip snaked through the fog to land a welt across its rump. The animal bucked beneath her, thrashing even when a second whip crack heralded a strike across its withers, leaving a bloody welt.

Anhuset fought the reins with one hand and slashed at a shadowy figure darting toward her.

"Defend the wagon!" Serovek, invisible in the mist, commanded.

She was useless to help at the moment, working hard to control the half-mad equine under her. The horse reared, arching too far back to come back down on its front hooves. Anhuset leapt from the saddle to avoid being crushed as the horse fell backwards. She still held her sword, but lost her shield.

More shapes hurtled through the mist, swarming them. Three rushed her, solidifying into men armed with blades and an ax. Undaunted by their number, she took the first man down with a quick cut to the torso, disemboweling him. Blood splashed hot across her arm and hand. The second she decapitated. The third reversed his charge and fled. Anhuset grabbed the ax the headless attacker had dropped and flung it, sinking it between the man's shoulder blades. He fell, disappearing into the mist without a sound.

"Anhuset!" Serovek's bellow carried to her, followed by a curse and more shouts before abruptly going silent.

She bolted in the direction from which his voice had come, praying she wouldn't stumble over a downed horse or worse a dead Serovek. She glimpsed the wagon, abandoned by both driver and team. She dared not shout in return and give their attackers her location.

Her caution came to naught. The slide of a rope sounded right at her ear before one looped around her neck and was jerked so hard, her head snapped back, and she lost her footing. The ground rose up hard and unforgiving, driving the air out of her lungs in one thin, constricted whoosh.

She worked at the rope collaring her, trying to slide a claw between it and her throat to keep from being strangled. The noose tightened even more, choking off her air. Rough fibers cut into her skin as she thrashed on the ground, this time reaching back to find her killer and sink her claws into him. Her hands met only air and the end of a long baton to which the rope was attached. Whoever held it was far out of her reach.

The gray of the mists became the gray of strangulation that finally closed over her eyes in a black curtain, and she knew no more.

CHAPTER

NINE

She woke with a muffled gasp, wincing at the fiery pain flaring in her throat, as if she'd swallowed a live ember. A thick cloth gag covered the lower half of her face, muzzling her. An attempt to stretch resulted in muscles cramping in protest. She was bound in a fetal position, wrists to ankles, the leather strips wrapped so tight her fingers were numb. Forced into a hunch and unable to straighten, she was afforded only a sliver of view of her surroundings.

A cluster of horses gathered nearby, shuffling away as human legs strode back and forth. Raucous voices filled the air, all male, some joking, others angry, a few drunken.

Anhuset twisted her shoulder and craned her neck, trying to see better. She lay in the middle of a camp surrounded by strangers who, for the moment, hadn't noticed she'd woken.

There was no sign of Serovek, though she thought she caught a glimpse of Magas half hidden behind the large tent at the edge of her line of sight. Sadness weighed on her as she remembered the sound of an arrow striking a body, then Klanek crying out in pain. Was he dead? Was Erostis? Serovek himself? And if so, why had their attackers chosen to keep her alive for now?

The pain in her throat was nothing compared to what swelled in her chest and threatened to choke her more effectively than the lasso someone had noosed around her neck to strangle her into unconsciousness. The margrave who'd battled and won against the *galla* surely hadn't met his end at the hands of a bunch of roving marauders and thieves.

She tugged on her bonds, testing their strength. Her captors had trussed her more thoroughly than a pig set for slaughter, and if her blurring vision and pounding head were clues, they'd drugged her for good measure.

A pair of muddy boots suddenly planted themselves in front of her. Anhuset arched her neck for a better view of their wearer. He crouched in front of her, revealing a boyish visage with a sweet smile and the empty-eyed stare of a murderer. She didn't have to be human to discern the trappings of madness lurking behind his eyes. Whatever stared at her from black pupils and hazel irises, it made her think of the *galla* in Haradis. Every hair on her nape stood on end.

"Finally awake," he said in Common tongue. "I'm surprised you aren't dead with as many darts as we shot into you once you fainted. There was enough sleep elixir on those points to drop a warhorse. It really is true what they say about the Kai—as strong as you are hideous."

He was less than subtle with his baiting, and Anhuset didn't rise to the insult. She met his stare with an unwavering one of her own until he stood up and put some distance between them. He motioned to someone standing nearby. "Remove her gag."

"What if she tries to bite?"

Count on it, she thought.

The chill in the killer's tone would have frozen a lit brazier. "Then I suggest you don't get your fingers too close to her mouth."

Coward. For all his posturing and the dead gaze, this man was craven. Was he the group's leader? And if so, what idiot followed a commander who ordered his men to do what he wouldn't do himself?

Another man skirted a wide circle around her until he stood behind her. A painful jerk on her hair, and the gag fell from her mouth. This time when the first man squatted in front of her, he wasn't nearly as close. "Sha-Anhuset of the Kai." Her eyebrows arched, and his satisfied smirk made her want to slap it off his face. "Yes, I know your name. You're the first Kai I've ever seen this close. Eyes that glow like a wolf's in the dark. If the rest look like you, then you're an ill-favored bunch. I pity the Gauri woman who married your regent. Poor bitch. Terrible fate being fucked every night by ugly Kai cock."

Anhuset had heard worse remarks from better adversaries. "Where's my horse?"

"That's what concerns you? No worries for the great man himself or the rest of your party?" He shook his head, clucking his disappointment. A crowd had gathered behind him. He addressed them this time. "Aren't you lads glad you don't have this unfeeling cunt to lead you? More interested in her nag's fate than her comrades'." A chorus of jeers met his remark. He turned back to her, his sneer aging his youthful features. "Your nag is unharmed, tethered not far from the margrave's stallion. You'll not be needing it."

She had no intention of letting him see her worry for the others so he could use it against her. "You know who I am." This time she allowed a matching sneer to creep into her voice. "I can't say the same about you. Why did you attack us?"

He waved another man over to stand with the one currently hovering behind her. "Sit her up. I'm tired of bending down to have this conversation."

The pair did as he ordered, yanking her roughly from her recumbent position so that she sat, still hunched over, her back aching from the strain, her hands still numb. The bright sun making her squint hung in the sky, arcing toward the west. Early afternoon. She'd been insensate almost a day, brought down first by strangulation and kept that way by a sleep elixir administered via darts.

Her captor loomed over her, arrogant and bloated with triumph. She'd hand over a decade of her lifespan to a god for the chance to split him from throat to gullet with her sword, her knives, or her claws. She wasn't picky.

"I was paid a hefty sum to capture you and the margrave," he said. "And expect an equally nice ransom for the enchanted monk." His shoulders went back and his chest out. "I'm Chamtivos Havonas, lord of these lands." He scowled. "Or so I was before the Nazim monks stole them from me."

So this was the infamous warlord who wrought havoc in the Lobak valley and surrounding areas. A boil on the arse of many, if the gossip she'd overheard among the ferry crew was anything to go by. His revelations answered some of her unspoken questions. Serovek was still alive, though in what condition she could only guess. Megiddo was likewise somewhere in the camp, though from her limited vantage point, she couldn't tell if his body still lay in the wagon or had been removed. No mention of Erostis or Klanek, and she feared the worst.

"If we're still alive, then you want something," she said. Captives were troublesome to hold, expensive to keep alive. Even paid handsomely to take them captive, Chamtivos said nothing about ransom for her or Serovek. She wondered who'd paid the warlord and why. Her first guess was Ogran, but a lowly tracker in the service of his lord didn't possess the funds needed to entice someone like Chamtivos to attack a margrave and hold him prisoner.

Chamtivos beamed his approval. "I like the way you think, Kai woman. Those bastard monks will pay a fortune to have their brother returned to them. You and the margrave? Well, he's someone's inconvenience, and you're a challenge. The two of you will offer me and my men a good bit of entertainment before we get rid of you."

His foreboding explanation didn't surprise Anhuset. She was astonished he'd allowed her and Serovek to live this long, but their time ran short. If she didn't find a way to escape and help the margrave do the same, they'd die, and she suspected their dying would be prolonged and gruesome.

The warlord, frustrated by her indifference to his ominous hints, gave up his attempts to bait her. He walked away, pausing briefly to speak with another man, their voices too quiet and distant to make out what they said. They soon parted, Chamtivos toward the tent she'd spotted earlier, the other man toward her.

He carried a cup in one hand. She expected to see a weapon in the other, but there wasn't one. Like Chamtivos, he crouched down just out of striking distance in case she tried to lunge for him. Tall and rangy, he moved with a feline grace. Blessed sanity stared back at her from his eyes. As one of her captors, he was her enemy, but he didn't make her recoil the way Chamtivos did.

"Water," he announced, holding up the cup. "Dasker poison always makes a person thirsty once they're awake. I'll give you a drink, but if you try to bite me, I'll make you eat the cup."

His warning, issued in a mild-mannered tone carried no less impact than if he'd snarled it at her. Given half a chance, she'd kill him in her bid for freedom, but were their positions reversed, she'd have told him the same thing. And she was terribly thirsty, her tongue practically sticking to the roof of her mouth every time she spoke. "No biting," she said. "I swear it."

They studied each other before he nodded and carefully tipped the cup to her lips. She drank, resisting the temptation to guzzle the water and spill half of it down her chin. Once she emptied the cup, he set it aside.

"I'd give you more, but to drink your fill now will only make you vomit it all up later. Let the poison's effects fade a little more, and I'll bring you another. Do you have to piss?" Puzzled by and wary of his consideration, she nodded. He whistled and called out names. Three men answered his summons, all carrying either a bow or crossbow. Each one nocked an arrow as they drew closer. "I'm going to partially unbind her," he told them. "If she even twitches toward me, shoot her."

Grim nods and drawn bows aimed at Anhuset made her pray she only twitched in the right direction.

"Don't make me regret my kindness by kicking my ribs in or my jaw loose," her dubious benefactor warned as he worked at her bindings. "Forget modesty and take care of your needs. Try anything else, and they'll turn you into a pin poppet."

"Understood," she said.

He worked the straps loose, freeing her wrists from her ankles. Blood rushed back to her fingers, and she stood on wobbly legs, still dizzy from the poison's lingering effects.

Relieving her bladder in front of onlookers didn't bother her. Running off into unknown wilderness just to hide your bare arse from others was foolish when you were on patrol or guard duty. She was no fine lady to worry over such notions, though the reality of having three broadheads trained on her while she answered nature's call wasn't to her liking.

Her partial freedom only lasted as long as it took her to finish. She was once more escorted back to her spot in the mud where Chamtivos's man retied her in the same position, though this time he didn't do it so tight that her fingers went numb. She glared at the gag cloth he held up. "Don't tell me you expected differently," he said, one eyebrow arched. "If I had a mouth full of teeth like yours, I'd be gnawing on my bindings every moment I wasn't observed."

He knotted the gag at the back of her head and left her with a pair of guards, taking the same path that Chamtivos had to the tent. Was Serovek in there as well? It was the only place in the camp itself big enough to hide a person. Everyone else had pitched small lean-tos hardly big enough to cast a square of shade or didn't bother with one at all. That tent served more than just the purpose of luxury for the group's leader.

She'd have to bide her time and strategize a way out of this dilemma before Chamtivos decided to enact whatever *entertainment* he had planned. It would mean leaving Megiddo behind, but the monk had something neither she nor Serovek did: value. He'd be safe for a short time.

Cramped, cold, and hungry, she shifted from side to side to keep the blood flowing through her limbs. Several escape plans played through her mind, each one ending with her either shot, skewered, or dismembered for the attempt and Serovek still held captive. She gave up temporarily, allowing her racing thoughts to settle. Her guards didn't talk to her or pay her much attention. She listened to their idle conversation. And learned.

For all his swagger and self-importance, Chamtivos wasn't particularly well liked by those who followed him. These were peasants and yeomen under the command of a nobleman's youngest son. They'd been loyal to his father and transferred that loyalty to Chamtivos out of respect for his dead sire. She wondered how many of them knew or suspected their current leader had committed both patricide and fratricide to seize the position he now held. The two guards set to watch her questioned whether the effort in attacking their party and taking Megiddo hostage had been worth the sacrifice of the seven men who'd died in the attack.

Anhuset could account for three of those deaths. She wondered how many of the remaining four Serovek had been responsible for. If he were lucky, none. Otherwise, whatever punishment Chamtivos chose to mete out to the margrave, it would be brutal.

She pretended to nap so her guards would assume her asleep and loosen their tongues even more. The remainder of their conversation was as dull as listening to grass grow, though she learned that the man who'd given her water was Chamtivos's second-in-command and named Karulin. From what little she'd gleaned from her interactions with both men, Karulin seemed more suited to the role of leader than Chamtivos, and she wondered why so measured a man had chosen to serve one so malevolent and erratic.

Made groggy by boredom and cold, she snapped alert at the approach of a new visitor. Anhuset lifted her eyelids enough to observe the man who greeted her guards and paused to loom over her, wearing a nasty smirk.

Conversation ceased, replaced by an expectant hush. She forced her muscles not to tense, and kept her eyelids lowered as she waited to see what her observer might do. He didn't carry a weapon unless one considered the stench wafting off him deadly enough to kill a person with a single whiff.

He unlaced the front of his trousers, and Anhuset nearly gave herself away by the disbelieving snort she swallowed behind her gag. Did he think to rape her? With the way she was bound, he'd have to exercise considerable effort to get her clothes out of the way without cutting them off her. He'd fail and die for trying. She was bound, not helpless.

Her disgusted snarl held an equal amount of shock when instead of a rape attempt, he pissed on her. She rolled away, barely avoiding a face full of the reeking yellow stream.

Howls of laughter rang out from her guards, and saliva filled her mouth as her stomach heaved. The stench of urine flooded her nostrils as she fought to hold down the bile creeping up her throat. Whistles and catcalls joined the laughter. Her tormentor grinned and swiveled his hips in a lewd motion, waving his dripping prick at her. He finally tucked his bits into his trousers and replaced the placket, then strutted back and forth in front of the growing audience, raising his arms to coax more cheers from their ranks, as triumphant as any conquering hero claiming victory over the vanquished.

He'd signed his own death warrant with that act of humiliation. Anhuset swore to herself no matter what it took or how long, she'd kill this man, carve him up into small pieces, and toss his remains into a midden for the rats to feast on.

Unsatisfied with his shallow victory and the attendant cheers from the crowd, the idiot chose not to walk away from the scene. Instead, he moved closer to her, leaning down to say something or maybe spit on her. She didn't wait to find out and used all her strength to lunge forward and slam her forehead into his face.

Bone crunched and screams replaced the gloating snickers as the raider fell backwards, hands clutched to his face. Blood seeped through his fingers, cascading in rivulets over his knuckles as he rolled on the ground, bellowing in agony.

Still seeing stars from the hit, Anhuset wasted not a moment in protecting herself as best she could, tucking her head between her arms and curling even tighter into the fetal position as punches and kicks rained down on her head, shoulders and back from those who sought to punish her.

An angry voice rose above the snarls and curses accompanying the blows. "Back off before I geld every last one of you."

They obeyed instantly, and Anhuset, never a religious sort, thanked any gods listening for the respite from the battering and for the return of the one the guards called Karulin.

"Explain," he demanded. "Lie, and you'll regret it."

Both men spoke at once with a few from the crowd interjecting their accounts before going silent under Karulin's glare. A chorus of gasps went up when he tugged Anhuset's gag down to her neck without hesitation or concern he might lose his hand. His nose wrinkled when he caught the smell on her. "Are you bleeding anywhere or having trouble breathing?"

She was tempted to say yes and beg him to untie her so she could check, but instinct told her he'd know she was lying, and his warning to her guards echoed in her mind. "Just a few bruises," she said.

He nodded and left her to see to the man whose screams had weakened to pitiful moans. Anhuset couldn't make out what Karulin said, but when he returned to her, he eyed her with renewed caution and a faint approval she was certain she didn't imagine. "It seems there's no part of a Kai that isn't dangerous," he said. "You shattered Lewelis's nose and knocked out three of his teeth. You'll have a knot on your brow for the doing, and you stink worse than a dead weasel, but you didn't come out the loser."

Soaked in piss, tied like a hog, and held captive by a mad bastard eager to make her the focus of some future and no doubt violent game didn't feel much like winning, but at least now Chamtivos's men would think twice before trying to make sport of her a second time.

Chamtivos returned from the tent to join their little gathering. After listening to Karulin's summary of events, he tutted, gave Anhuset a once-over glance filled with revulsion, and left her to help Lewelis to his feet. He listened to the man's complaints of her ill-treatment of him with an attentive expression and a few sympathetic nods. Even she gasped along with the others when he suddenly pulled a knife and slashed Lewelis's throat in one swift arc.

Chamtivos turned away before the body hit the ground, and once more she caught a glimpse into the cruelty-laced madness lurking behind the boyish façade. She stiffened when he walked toward her. The crowd backed away, except for Karulin, who eyed his master as warily as he did Anhuset.

The warlord wiped his blade clean on a bystander's sleeve. That person dared not utter a word of protest. "The Kai woman is my captive," Chamtivos said in a strangely cheerful voice. "Not yours. Mine. And while she lives, I think of her as one of my possessions." He offered them all a sunny smile that made everyone take at least two steps back. "I don't like people touching my things without my permission. Do it again, and you'll join Lewelis there, feeding the vultures and the worms."

His gaze settled on Anhuset. "You're a vicious cunt," he told her. "Ogran was right when he said you were worth three humans in a fight. Day after tomorrow promises to be an exciting day indeed." The maniacal glee in his voice sent splinters of ice through her veins. She didn't ask him to clarify or expound. She wouldn't give him the satisfaction. He'd only drop more obtuse hints as a way to torture her, hoping to seed her fear and drink it like a poisoned nectar. Instead she focused on his last statement. Ogran.

Her suspicions had borne out. He might not have the funds to bribe a warlord to murder a margrave, but he was just as involved in its planning.

Chamtivos gestured to the group in general. "Get her rinsed off. It's bad enough having to look at her. I don't want to have to smell her too."

He strolled away but not before Anhuset spotted blood on his clothes and his hands. Dried blood that didn't belong to the dead Lewelis. Her heart thudded heavy. Serovek.

She clenched her jaw under the dousing of ice water, nearly breaking her back teeth in the effort not to screech from the shock of cold pouring over her. The shivers she couldn't control. They worsened every second until she almost convulsed from muscle spasms. At least she no longer smelled like a dead human's piss.

Karulin came to her rescue yet again, this time carrying a blanket. "My gods," he muttered as he dragged her to a dry patch of ground. "You're a lot heavier than you look."

You're just a sad, weak human, she thought, unable to stop her teeth from chattering long enough to speak.

Rescuer he might be, but Karulin was also cautious. He draped the dry blanket over her wet form, then pulled another strip of cloth from a pocket of his tunic. This time he didn't have to say anything for the attending guards to nock arrows and take aim.

"Chamtivos says no food. He doesn't want to waste provisions on you." Karulin looped the gag cloth through his fingers as he spoke. "But you're allowed more to drink if you want it."

Something in the way he dropped his chin and stared at her made her hesitate in accepting the offer. It wasn't what he said but what he didn't say that decided her. The water wouldn't just be water. "I'm not thirsty." She reared back when he leaned forward to tie the gag cloth over her mouth. "Why?"

As she guessed, he understood the rest of her unspoken question. His features hardened though his voice remained mild, vaguely bored. "I believe in a fair fight. What's to come won't be fair."

He knotted the cloth just above her nape, muzzling her before she could interrogate him more and pulled the blanket firmly around her shoulders. He stood with the same lithe grace that hinted at speed and agility. "No one will bother you tonight. You have my word."

He was as good as that word. No one accosted her for the rest of the day and through the night. Only once was she moved, and then by Karulin himself who untied her enough so she could heed nature's insistent call and also ease the painful kink in her back.

Dawn came with a thin frost glazing everything exposed to the open air. Anhuset's hair crackled as she curled in on herself for any scrap of warmth. Her ears were numb as was the tip of her nose and her hands. The blanket she huddled under offered little in the way of a barrier between her still damp body and the morning cold. As a Kai, she actively avoided the sun. Now she eagerly looked forward to its rise and the heat it offered.

A flurry of activity at one end of camp near the tent made her peek out from the blanket's cover. She forgot about the cold and discomfort, the bruises and backache. Chamtivos emerged from the tent, followed by two of his men carrying a limp, bloodied Serovek between them. His feet plowed shallow furrows in the dirt as they dragged him to a waiting horse. Dark hair, matted with what looked like blood partially obscured his face, but not enough that she didn't see the swelling misshaping his features or the way both of his eyes were blackened and scabbed shut. A thread of crimson drool stretched from his mouth before breaking to splash on the ground.

Her emotions spun in a whirlwind. Relief that he was alive, rage at his mistreatment. In her mind, she cried out his name, a wailing that would have carried for leagues had she given voice to it.

As if he heard her, he slowly lifted his head, turning it in her direction. She growled long and low behind the gag. Her guards tensed and dropped their hands to the knives at their belts. There was no way he saw her, not with those eyes. His face, once handsome by human standards, was a horror of welts, cuts and purple bruises. He looked like Magas had danced on his face with all four hooves.

Anhuset glared at Chamtivos as he gave instructions to the pair holding the margrave. The warlord left them to heave their burden onto the horse and approached her. "Stand up, princess," he said. "We're going for a ride." He waited impatiently for her guards to release the bonds that kept her hunched before shoving her toward a second horse. Instead of freeing her legs so she walked instead of shuffled and could mount the horse on her own, they lifted her, tossing her across the saddle like a sack of grain, feet hanging off one side of the animal, her head and shoulders off the other. The position caused pressure to build behind her eyes.

Chamtivos squatted so they were eye level with each other.

"Remove her gag," he ordered an unseen lackey. Karulin joined him, and it was his hands that carefully untied the gag and tossed it aside. Anhuset thought the warlord's unexpected consideration strange until he told her, "Riding a horse like this will make you sick, and I don't want you choking on your own vomit before I've had a little fun with you."

You'll be choking on your own blood when I'm finished with you, she wanted to say. Instead she asked questions she doubted he'd answer in any meaningful way, but she had to try. "Where are you taking us? Why did you beat the margrave?"

He chuckled, rubbing his hands together like a child anticipating a treat. "You'll see. As to your second question, the margrave refused to tell us how to break the enchantment protecting the monk. We used a little persuasion. He's much more stubborn than he is intelligent."

He couldn't have been more wrong in his assumption. Serovek's intelligence far outstripped his obstinacy. "He won't tell you because he can't. He doesn't know how to break it. Only the Khaskem does. If you'd asked me instead, I could have told you that and saved your men the trouble of trying to beat it out of Lord Pangion."

Chamtivos gave a blithe shrug. "A few lessons in humility either builds character or breaks it. We'll see which it is for his lordship once he wakes."

Talking while draped across a horse made her stomach roil. Her skull began to throb. She tried another tack. "He'd make just as valuable a hostage as the monk. The Beladine king will pay generously to have one of his military governors returned to him alive and mostly unharmed."

"Maybe. But someone else has already paid me a king's ransom to capture him, and I'll gain something even better—power—if I dispose of him. A certain steward rises in the world if the margrave doesn't make it back to High Salure. Pangion isn't nearly as valuable alive as he is dead."

The shock of his words left her almost as speechless as the ice water dousing she'd endured the day before. Bryzant had planned all this? Serovek's steward who'd stood on a kitchen prep table holding a rolling pin like a club while she chased an angry scarpatine around the scullery? Her thoughts reeled. Why? And what did Ogran hope to gain from the alliance and the betrayal?

A cascade of grim possibilities made her scowl. He was one of the four sent back to High Salure and Saggara with messages. Had only Ogran made the journey back alive, and if so, what message did he deliver?

Her neck hurt from keeping it arched so she could look into Chamtivos's deceptively innocent features. "Why haven't you killed him already? And me as well?"

"As I told you before, you're entertainment." He smiled. "I like a challenge and am fond of the hunt. The Kai have a reputation for being strong, fierce fighters. I'm told you're equal to three men in a fight. You'll make for challenging prey."

There it was again, the comparison between her and specifically three humans—an echo of what Serovek had told Ogran while they decided how to split up their party and who would return and who would continue to the monastery. Karulin had referenced it first, and even had he not mentioned Ogran's name, she would have known it was him.

Chamtivos's revelation of his plans for them was anticlimactic, at least for her. Anhuset had imagined something far worse than being hunted by him and his minions, though she wouldn't make the mistake of underestimating their prowess, especially with Karulin in their party. Every instinct she possessed told her that despite his kindness toward her, he was likely the most dangerous adversary in this group.

Done with conversation, Chamtivos left her to issue more orders and soon a party of twelve, along with her and a now unconscious Serovek rode out of the camp. Her sense of time told her they hadn't traveled more than an hour before they halted again, but her balking stomach and pounding head protested it was a lifetime. The smell of water teased her nose, and she heard the sound of gently lapping waves tumbling against a shore.

She was afforded a better view of her surroundings once they hauled her off the horse and dropped her in a heap onto a pebbled beach. She struggled to her knees before managing to stand. A lake, with an opposite shore in the far distance and an island rising from its center lay before her. She recalled Serovek's map. There'd been a body of water marked on the map whose location was parallel to the path they'd planned to take to the monastery. If her sense of direction was correct, this lake was that body of water.

Were Chamtivos and his men planning to drown her and Serovek? She discarded the idea. The warlord had stated he planned to hunt them. She eyed the island in the lake's center, noting its shape like a hump with a significant incline that rounded off to a gentle summit. The land itself was covered in a conifer forest, nearly black against the gray sky and matching the lake's serenely dark surface.

Two boats sat beached nearby, just large enough to transport their entire party to the island. Chamtivos took no chances and ordered Karulin to muzzle her again. The grim expression Karulin had worn was now black with disapproval. He tied the gag snugly, but not so tight that it cut into her cheeks. She swore a flicker of apology danced across his features before he guided her to one of the boats.

They split into three groups. Two men stayed behind to set up an overnight camp on the shore, while the others divided their numbers between the boats. "Put his lordship in the boat with me and the Kai bitch in the other with Karulin," Chamtivos ordered.

The slap of the oars on the water as they skimmed across the lake was the only sound. The water itself was dark, with the vague outline of a drop-off that began not far from the shore and plunged into depths no sunlight reached. This was a deep, deep lake. Surface waves lifted and dipped them gently, and more than once Anhuset spotted undulating shapes cresting above the water in scaly, serpentine arches. The creatures moved counter to the waves, leaving broad, flat wakes behind them as they glided parallel to the boats. She was a good swimmer and didn't fear drowning should some accident occur and she fell in the water. But whatever patrolled just below the surface promised a death more savage than a drowning.

They reached the island's leeward side without incident. A man from each boat hopped into waist-deep water with bow lines and towed the boats, always watching the deeper water for any sign of the creatures that had followed them. Once they turned the boats so that the bows faced out toward the lake and set both anchors and spikes, the rest of the group piled out. Anhuset muttered under her breath as she plunged knee-deep into the water. She'd just started drying out and warming up.

Karulin kept a steady hand on her arm as she shuffle-waded to shore. Two others dragged Serovek to where she stood, dropping him at her feet. A faint groan escaped his lips.

Chamtivos faced her, gesturing for Karulin to remove her gag. "You've the rest of the day and night to prepare. Tomorrow morning, we return for the hunt. I'm much looking forward to pitting my skills against you, Kai woman."

This was a petty man driven by childish malice and an overblown sense of his own importance and entitlement. How he managed to gain and keep a fighting force willing to die for him in a war with the Nazim monks puzzled her greatly.

Karulin moved from behind her to scowl at Chamtivos. "This is wrong. All of it. When did our purpose drift from fighting for our lands to chasing defenseless captives through the forests for fun?"

Chamtivos lost the smirk he wore. Something neither human nor Kai nor anything belonging to this world stared back at her and Karulin. They both retreated a step. "It isn't your place to protest or judge. Here I am king."

He didn't wait for a reply but strode to where the other men gathered, making plans for the following day and exchanging wagers over who'd make the first kill and how they'd do it. Karulin bent to pick up the gag he'd dropped to the ground. He held it out to her, face hard with a quiet fury and equally resolute. "Do you want this?" She nodded. Cloth strips came in handy for numerous reasons. He folded the gag neatly, tucking it under Serovek's prone form. "You can retrieve it once I'm not so close to you."

His actions were odd, as was his statement. Bound as she still was, her mobility was severely limited.

"Will you be one of the hunters tomorrow?" Anhuset hoped not. She'd regret killing him and only him. He might be as twisted as the master he served, but she trusted her instincts and her judgment, and they told her Karulin was nothing like Chamtivos.

His lips thinned. "That depends on whether or not Chamtivos requires me to prove my loyalty to him." He shrugged. "I'm an adequate hunter and better with a sword than a bow." Her eyes widened at these key details he shared with her. His voice, already low, softened even more. "There are four archers among us who are far more skilled than the rest. Without them, you might survive." He backed away. "Good luck, sha-Anhuset."

He returned to the boats where the others had already begun boarding. Chamtivos regarded him from his place at the bow of one boat, reminding Anhuset of a snake studying unsuspecting quarry. Karulin ignored him, and she guessed he'd not turn his back on his master, figuratively or literally, any time soon.

She watched them row away, leaving her and Serovek without provisions or weapons of any kind. She'd expected no less. Wrists and ankles still bound, she'd have to find a way to cut herself free, otherwise she was useless to Serovek and herself. A small, triumphant cry burst past her lips when she discovered a treasure folded into the creases of the gag cloth tucked under Serovek's shoulder: an eating knife. Small, easily hidden, and just as sharp as any fighting blade she normally carried.

Chamtivos had a traitor in his midst, or at least a man who felt it necessary to even the odds a little more between predator and prey. Karulin had managed to wrap the knife in the gag cloth without anyone noticing, including her, relying on the hunch that Anhuset might want the cloth as either a bandage or a weapon. He was her enemy, her adversary, but at least an honorable one, unlike that craven dog to whom he gave allegiance.

She cut her bonds away and used the gag cloth to create a makeshift sheath for the knife. Chamtivos might have stripped her of her weapons, but she wasn't without. She had teeth, claws, Karulin's knife, her training, and her wits. They'd not find her easy prey to hunt and kill.

Serovek was another matter. Up close he looked in even worse shape, battered and bloody. No doubt she'd find more contusions and worse under his clothes. His breathing was quick but not labored, a good sign, that. Even if his captors had broken a rib or two, they hadn't punctured a lung.

She lifted a few strands of his hair, sticky with blood, away from his abused face. "The cruelties of lesser men inflicted upon a greater one. I'm sorry, Serovek." The sight of his injuries seated a cold fury deep in her gut, and she almost wished Chamtivos and the gutless lackeys he commanded would turn their boats around and start the hunt now just so she'd have the pleasure of ripping their heads off and feeding their bodies to whatever lurked in the lake's depths.

It was late morning, and she had less than a full day's cycle to get herself and Serovek to some form of shelter and plan how they might survive. "Come on, margrave. We can't stay here forever."

They were exposed on the beach. The conifer wood covering most of the island offered the camouflage of shadow as well as darkness that she saw far better in than her human adversaries. There would be places to hide. Small caves, outcroppings or niches, swales overhung by tree branches with deeper ditches that could serve as ambush trenches. Anhuset hoped the island dwellers were less menacing—and smaller—than what she'd seen in the lake itself.

She eased Serovek onto his stomach, wincing when he emitted another groan. "This is only going to get worse for both of us before it gets better," she assured him.

Kneeling at his head, she hooked her elbows under his shoulders and clasped her sore wrists at his back. He sagged in her arms, dead weight, his head resting between her breasts.

"And humans complain the Kai are heavy," she muttered. "I think I could carry Magas easier."

Widening her stance, she slowly raised him to his feet, using her legs to support him. With his feet still dragging the ground, she wedged her thigh between his legs, grabbed his left hand with her right and draped it over her shoulder. Every punch and kick she'd taken after head-butting Lewelis made itself known in the sharpest way when she pressed her head to Serovek's side, squatted and curved him over her back for a lift off the ground.

Sweat trickled down her face and dripped into her eyes as she took one staggering step, then another and another toward the tree line.

She adjusted her weight and that of her burden until she had her legs solidly under her and could walk without staggering. Soon, she adopted a steady pace, Serovek heavy on her but not impossible to carry despite his considerable bulk.

Heated by her exertions, she welcomed the shade the towering firs offered. She'd miss the warmth later, but for now the chill helped as she climbed the island's slope.

Thorny underbrush clawed at her clothes. She wove through a labyrinth of majestic trees, their needle-shaped leaves whispering to her while they swayed and creaked in the steady wind coming off the water. Serovek grew heavier on her back with every step, and the air in her lungs scorched a path on the inside of her bruised throat with each breath she took.

Exhaustion conquered her halfway up the slope. Dizzy, gasping, and in danger of dropping her burden, she staggered to a spot mostly clear of the rapacious underbrush but still padded with a carpet of fallen fir needles.

The process of lowering herself to the ground and rolling Serovek off her shoulders and onto his back left her seeing double. She collapsed next to him, listening to the thunder of her heartbeat in her ears.

Once her heart stopped racing and her lungs no longer threatened to catch fire, she checked Serovek. He still breathed, the rhythm deeper, slower as if he sensed that for now he was safe in the company of a friend instead of among enemies. Anhuset gained her feet to explore their immediate surrounds. The conifers, statuesque and close together, bound the forest in an endless twilight. Mushrooms and lichen grew in abundant patches on the forest floor and on flat rocks.

Luck smiled down on her when she spotted an expanse of stone with a shallow indentation in its center, a water-catch that still held a gathering of morning dew hidden from the sun. She didn't have a cup to scoop up the water so unwrapped the gag cloth from the knife and saturated it until water trickled through her fingers as she held it in her palm.

Serovek's bloodied lips parted as she squeezed a stream of water into his mouth. He swallowed everything she offered, the tip of his tongue swiping over his lower lip to catch the last drops. Anhuset used the damp cloth to lightly swab his face and break the crust of blood sealing his eyelids shut.

He regained consciousness gradually, his eyes moving back and forth beneath the thin skin of his lids, and his breathing changed once more. One eye finally opened to a bare squint, his gaze made even more hideous by the blood threads marring the whites of his eyes.

"Ah gods," he said in a rough voice. "We made love, didn't we? And I don't remember any of it." He shifted position, cursing from the pain it caused him. "You weren't jesting when you said I wouldn't survive you."

He was a sorcerer in his way with his ability to coax out her amusement in even the direst of circumstances. Pleased more than she could express at his revival and his humor, she pushed his hair back from his forehead with a careful caress. "Obviously, you aren't dying."

"I'd probably feel better and hurt less if I were."

She used the cloth again to finish cleaning his face. He flinched away when she touched a particularly sensitive spot on his cheekbone. "Hold still," she ordered. During her ministrations he'd managed to open his right eye more, though his left remained closed. "How much can you see?"

"Blurry on the right side. I'll let you know about the left when I can open it." Poor vision notwithstanding, he didn't miss the marks of her own stay with Chamtivos and company. "You're wearing a few bruises and lumps yourself, not to mention that rope burn around your neck." He attempted to scowl but thought better of it. Still, his voice betrayed his anger. "They noosed you."

She nodded. "Rope looped at the end of a pole."

"Then there's a Kuram in their midst." He expanded his remark when she shook her head to indicate she wasn't familiar with the term. "Horseman out of the Glimming. The Kuram are herders and use *guras* —what was used on you—to capture wild horses." He pointed to her throat. "When did they give you that?"

"When we were first attacked. They shot me full of darts dipped in dasker poison to keep me that way until they reached camp. How did they take you?"

"Sheer numbers," he said. "I killed a few, but they swarmed me like hornets." He reached up to touch a spot on his scalp. "Someone with a club got in a lucky shot, though I don't think the lump on my head is as impressive as the one on your forehead."

She'd forgotten about that injury. "Courtesy of one of Chamtivos's henchmen. I head-butted his face after he pissed on me."

This time Serovek's ferocious scowl defied any pain he might have suffered from the expression. "He's first on my list to kill, then."

"You'd have to wait your turn behind me," she said. "Besides, Chamtivos already did it. Cut the lout's throat for causing trouble and mistreating what Chamtivos considered his property." That statement made her want to tear the warlord's arms off. And his legs for good measure.

Serovek regarded her, trading his frown for a half smile. "Battered and pissed on, you're still beautiful."

"And I didn't think you could get any uglier."

His smile grew, accompanied by a wince. "Does this mean I can't coax you under me?"

"The beating has made you delirious. I doubt you can even stand at the moment." Her mind recognized his jesting, but her body reacted otherwise, sending a hot blush flowing under her skin. Her heart, barely slowed after the climb, resumed its previous heavy beat.

Serovek waved a hand in a careless motion. "Some bruises, a few cracked ribs. They didn't geld me."

"Don't think the idea didn't occur to them. And you didn't mention the black eyes. Your nose is broken too. You're in no shape for a swiving."

He snorted. "I'm beaten, not dead. I'd suggest you be on top, but you weigh as much as my horse. You'll break the rest of my bones those shit maggots didn't get to." A chuff of laughter escaped her. "Ah, there it is," he marveled, as if he'd turned back a threadbare cloth to reveal a valuable jewel.

"There's what?" Her question was rhetorical. She knew to what he referred.

"Your smile. There's no finer sight than a smile from sha-Anhuset, unless it's a smiling, *naked* Anhuset." He wiggled his eyebrows.

Anhuset rolled her eyes. "Feeling better by the moment, I see."

She sat down next to him, watching as he turned his head to take in their surroundings. His amusement was gone, the jovial manner with it. "What happened to the others? Klanek, Erostis?" His voice dropped. "Megiddo?" He listened without interruption as she recounted the events from the attack until their current predicament and Chamtivos's plans to hunt them the following day.

"You've made an enemy of your steward it seems. He hates you enough to pay a fortune for your death and planned it over time I'm guessing."

His heavy sigh spoke of regret, sorrow, even a touch of embarrassment. "Bryzant has been my steward for a decade. It's never a joy to learn you've nursed a viper at your breast. He's capable and intelligent, but he needed help to execute this plan from a distance."

"Ogran?"

He nodded. "You were right to be suspicious of him."

It was her turn to sigh. "One of a few times when I wish I'd been wrong."

"He was a useful puppet. Not smart enough to coordinate such a plan on his own, and he gains nothing from my death, but show him enough coin, and he could be persuaded. Bryzant, on the other hand, has some things in common with Chamtivos. A younger son without inheritance or prospects beyond his service in my household. He was ambitious and, above all, patient. And he lacked Chamtivos's predilection for killing off family members. If he paid the warlord, he did so from funds taken out of my treasury. I might find it amusing if you weren't part of his machinations. Or Megiddo and my soldiers, for that matter."

"Did he tell you he plans to ransom Megiddo to the Jeden Order?"

He pressed a hand to his left side. "Every time his dogs used their fists on me."

For now, there was little she could do to alleviate his discomfort, nor could she stay here with him much longer. They needed water, and she needed to scout the island, learn what the terrain held in store and discover any hiding places or defensible spots they could exploit in preparation for tomorrow's ordeal.

"I'll have to leave you here for an hour or two while I search the area. There's no avoiding it." She handed him the eating knife Karulin had sneaked to her.

Serovek's mouth fell open. "They missed a knife on you?"

"Not mine," she said. "Chamtivos's second-in-command. The two are at odds. Karulin is a decent sort if you don't count attacking travelers and holding them hostage for ransom money. And compared to Chamtivos, he's sweetness, light, and sanity. He left the knife on purpose. It was either an act of rebellion or one of betrayal."

"It seems loyalty is hard to come by these days, no matter who you are," Serovek said in wry tones. He tried to return the knife to her. "Take it with you. You don't know what you'll cross in your exploration."

She pushed it back to him. "I have ten claws, sharp teeth, and can take down anything with the aid of a sturdy stick. I'm well armed. You need the knife more than I do."

"I've no argument for any of that," he replied.

She stood and brushed dirt off her trousers. "Good. Less time wasted." A thought occurred to her. She needed some way to know if he was in trouble while she was gone. "Can you whistle?"

His brow creased in frown lines and he pursed his mouth. A clear, near perfect mimic of a flycatcher's song filled the air, carrying through the trees where a chorus of bird calls answered with full-throated enthusiasm.

"Impressive," Anhuset said without a drop of sarcasm when he stopped.

"And hurts worse than being kicked in the balls." Serovek pressed a hand to his mouth. "If you're wanting me to whistle a tune for you before you go, forget it."

She resisted the urge to once more comb his tangled hair back from his face with her fingers. "Tempting but no. Whistle if you're in trouble. Something like a two-three-two pattern so I'll know it's you and not some bundle of feathers courting a female."

"Anhuset." Serovek crooked a finger and she leaned closer, admiring his long dark lashes and the swoop of his eyebrows. His mouth beckoned her despite its bruising and the remnants of blood in its corners. "Be careful. I don't want to lose you."

The words sent a bolt through her. Words not of lust or teasing but of deep affection for her, of fear for her. Anhuset almost replied she wasn't his to lose, but that was no longer true.

She, who'd never subscribed to delicacy of any type, stroked Serovek's swollen face in a delicate caress. "Worry not. I'll take care and return soon."

Her trek down the slope, through the forested labyrinth, was quicker than she anticipated. She didn't dwell on the question of whether she was leaving Serovek or fleeing from him.

CHAPTER

TEN

There wasn't a bit of flesh on him that didn't hurt, and his insides didn't fare much better. Serovek had been in more than his share of fights in his lifetime and wore the scars as badges, but he'd never endured the kind of beating Chamtivos and his men had doled out to him. If he didn't piss blood or spit out a couple of teeth, he'd be amazed. If he and Anhuset lived through this fun little excursion the warlord had planned, he'd consider believing in merciful gods.

Once assured he wasn't going to die on her in the immediate future, Anhuset had sprinted down the slope, fleet as a deer. Chamtivos hadn't extended his particular brand of hospitality to her with the same zeal as he did to Serovek. Though it galled him, Serovek knew he'd serve her best by staying behind. He had to clear his head, pry open both eyes, and make himself useful to the woman who carried him across her shoulders over difficult terrain to get him to safety.

"Ugly you might find me, firefly woman, but I think you're beginning to like me," he said to the stately firs surrounding him. Serovek smiled despite the pain it caused as he imagined Anhuset's expression had she heard him.

He took the damp cloth she'd used to give him water and clean his face, and soaked his right eye, glued shut by scabs. Hot threads of blood trickled down his cheek as he broke the scab and forced his eyelid up. The world remained blurry, but his depth perception was no longer skewed. He wondered if Brishen had dealt with the same when he lost his eye and how long it had taken for him to adjust.

Scooting closer to a young tree, he used the trunk as support to leverage himself first to his knees, then to his feet. He breathed hard, lightheaded from the exertion as well as the pain in his ribs, lower back, and face. Resting against the sapling for a moment, he rode out the first few waves of agony until his body accustomed itself to the discomfort enough that he didn't feel like bellowing with every movement. Leisurely convalescing wasn't an option. He had to move, had to walk, and at some point, would probably have to fight. He already considered himself a detriment to Anhuset. He wouldn't be the means by which Chamtivos would find it easy to kill her.

She'd left him the eating knife for defense, but knives were tools as well as weapons, and after what felt like a thousand years, he managed to scavenge a few sturdy sticks of decent length and thickness and staggered back to where Anhuset had left him. His mobility might be limited from his injuries, but his enemies hadn't broken his fingers. He settled down to craft crude but effective weaponry with the eating knife and sticks.

The day had aged into late afternoon by the time Anhuset returned, grim-faced but carrying an armful of items she'd scavenged during her scouting. She paused to eye the third spear he was whittling at, shaving off bits of wood to create a lethal tip at one end.

"A fishing spear," she said. "Nasty bit of work if you take one of those in the gut."

He honed one of the back-curved edges he'd whittled into the stick's tip, meant to hook onto whatever it grabbed and tear if prey tried to wriggle free. "I'm not inclined to show mercy to this group," he said dryly, setting the knife and stick aside for a moment. "I see you were foraging as well as scouting. What interesting things have you brought back?"

She dumped what was in her arms into a small pile at his feet: a short length of rope stained with mildew, a tattered shirt, and a moldy basket of smooth round rocks. She held onto the best item of all, a gourd full of water, and offered it to him. "You're surely parched, but I don't think I need to warn you about why you shouldn't guzzle it all down."

Serovek nodded his thanks, using the first sips to rinse the taste of blood from his mouth. The water was cold, and to his dry tongue and throat, sweeter than winter mead. "Water from the lake?" he asked between sips.

Anhuset folded in front of him, long legs crossed at the ankles, her knees bent so she perched like a butterfly with spread wings. A beautiful butterfly with the sting of a hornet. "Yes, though I kept an eye on the waves. Something or things patrols those waters. They're big, long like snakes and were very interested in our boats when we rowed here. They may not come ashore, but I wanted to be cautious, not eaten."

He raised the gourd to her in a toast. "Who wouldn't?" This time he swallowed a more generous gulp, his belly cramping in warning as the water hit his stomach like a stone. "I don't much like the idea of you risking your life that way, but I thank you for the water. Rest assured I'll savor every drop."

Was that a blush tinting the high ridges of her cheekbones? He hoped so. She didn't admonish him for laying on the charm, only nodded and slid the basket of rocks toward him.

"These are from the shore. I picked what I thought might work in a sling. Do you know how to use a sling?"

He almost chuckled but a twinge with the sharpness of a portcullis spike in his ribs changed his mind. "Since I was about four years old. My father taught me. When I was thirteen, I took down a charging boar with one shot landed between its eyes."

Her eyebrows rose and her eyes widened. Even if he couldn't read her eyes in the way he could read a fellow human's, Serovek was sure by her expression she wasn't disbelieving of his boast, only impressed. Trust. She was learning to trust him.

"So not just adept at seducing women, riding horses and swinging a sword, then." She tapped the basket. "I'm adequate with a sling, though I've never killed a boar with one. I prefer throwing spikes." She gestured to the knife he set aside. "When you're done with your spear, I'll take the blade and whittle a few spikes to carry with me. We can use the shirt and rope to make a sling."

He hefted the rope. There wasn't much of it, certainly nothing to use for climbing or netting something, but there was plenty to make a sling once he unraveled some of the fibers. "Besides the rocks, where did you find the rest of these?"

"Different spots on the island. Either we aren't the first unfortunates to be marooned here for Chamtivos's pleasure hunts or this island is visited by others who leave things behind when they return to the mainland." She reached for one of the two completed spears, inspecting it with a careful eye, testing its weight and balance in her hand. "You made this just with the eating knife?" At his nod, she smiled a wide, toothy smile guaranteed to turn most humans pale with fright. Serovek only wondered how he might kiss her senseless without having his tongue shredded to ribbons. "I can run back to the lake with one of these and try to spear something for dinner, but we'll have to make it a fast one. We can't stay in this spot much longer." Her gaze swept over him. "I can carry you again if needed."

His stomach recoiled at the idea. The water alone sat uneasy in his belly as it was. "I'm not hungry, and I can walk." He sounded more abrupt than he intended, but Serovek would crawl up the remainder of the slope on his knees before he put that burden on Anhuset a second time. "What else did you discover during your foray?"

Her grin fell away. "There's only this side of the island with a shore fit to land a boat. The other side is a sheer drop to the water. The best place to be is at the island's summit, but the slope is steeper the higher you climb, a lot of it muddy and hard going. If we had more time, drier ground, and a gentler ascent..."

"And me not injured."

She waved away that obstacle with an airy hand as if it meant nothing. "We'll just strategize around it."

Serovek admired her ferocity, her pragmatism, her indomitable will. She didn't give up or back down. Her sheer grit saved her from what, in any other woman, would be deluded optimism. Anhuset didn't need rescuing. She just needed help—someone to open the armory so she could choose the weapons that would allow her to resolve the problem. "The summit is out, but I'm guessing you found an alternative."

She nodded. "I found a spot under a shallow rock overhang closer to the windward side and not much farther up than where we are now. A hike but not a climb. From below, you can't see the overhang and the niche it creates until you're on top of it, but if you're in that spot, you can clearly see whatever's coming up the slope, even with so many trees in the way."

"It'll be hard covering our tracks, especially if they bring in a tracker."

She flashed him another toothy smile. "And why I made sure to lay down enough false trails that it looks like the island's been invaded by herds of cattle. Those arse-wipes will have a difficult time telling the real trail from the false ones, even with a good tracker in the party."

"Well done," he said softly. Once more a faint blush painted her cheekbones.

Anhuset cleared her throat, the yellow of her eyes flaring bright in the shadows. "We should leave now if you don't want to hike in the dark." She gathered her foraged items together and plucked the empty gourd from his hand. "Depending on how many participate in the hunt, they'll come in one or two boats. Someone will be left behind on the beach to guard them."

He took the hand she offered and levered himself upright to stand beside her. "Whatever we plan, it will require diversion, ambush, and speed. Unlike me, you can move quickly. You'll have to be the hunter yourself in this game."

"And you the bait."

Even in the woodland gloom, her hair shone silvery-white, a

beacon she'd have to hide before Chamtivos arrived. Serovek reached out to lift one of her locks and cradle it in his palm. Anhuset stilled but didn't pull away. His blood heated at the notion she might welcome his touch. "We work well together. But you leave me and see to your own skin should things turn against us. You must get Megiddo away from Chamtivos. Even if the monks pay the ransom he's demanding, he won't honor the exchange. They'll figure out a way to break Brishen's enchantment and butcher Megiddo's body for sport."

Her eyes brightened to the palest yellow. "We fought well together when we rescued the *herceges* from his captors. We'll do the same to save ourselves and Megiddo now."

Her resolve strengthened his, and they packed their small trove of found treasures in the tattered shirt. Serovek used one of the spears as a walking stick while Anhuset carried the other two. Their trek to the rock ledge and overhang was slow going as they laid down more false trails. Near twilight, they reached the spot she'd chosen. Serovek noted how the topography did as she described, fooling the eye for anyone climbing the slope and offering a good view for whoever occupied it. "You're a woman of many talents, Anhuset," he said as he pressed a hand to his side. A fire burned within his ribcage, and every bruised, abused muscle screeched a protest at his lack of mercy in traipsing across uneven landscape instead of resting in a soft bed to heal.

"Are you having trouble breathing?" Anhuset appeared in front of him, her gaze trained on his face, one hand covering his where it rested against his ribs. There was no misinterpreting or mistaking the concern in her voice. "Sit before you fall." She pointed to a flat section of rock half covered by leaves.

"I'm fine, Anhuset. Just sore and wishing for a glass of Dragon Fire, a hot bath, and a comfortable bed." *And you to share all three with me.* He didn't argue with her, though the aches and pains in his body didn't lessen; they simply switched places.

They settled into the scant fastness, preparing for both an uncom-fortable, cold night and the ordeal to come. Serovek prayed some of the hunters would take the bait he offered and head this way when they arrived. Anhuset, as superior a fighter as she was, would have a hard time of it trying to outmaneuver and kill a dozen or more hunters by herself.

While she built up a makeshift wall of brambles to slow down any charge up the slope and hide Serovek behind its screen, he split and unraveled the bit of rope, turning some of the fibers and a patch of the tattered shirt into a sling. The rocks Anhuset had gathered by the lake served as perfect projectiles. Bigger than a chicken egg but smaller than a fist, they were the right size for maximizing speed and accuracy without sacrificing impact. She'd admitted to not being as good with a sling, but the woman knew how to pick a good sling stone.

She gathered brambles for her wall and kindling for their fire while Serovek carved throwing spikes for her. Once they'd prepared as best they could, she surveyed their handiwork with a dour expression. "I could construct two-foot spike traps in the bramble to keep Chamtivos's men from getting to you without risking themselves, but you'd have as much of a chance at stepping on one as they would if you end up fighting hand-to-hand. And if I were them, I'd just use an archer to pick you off from a distance."

"How glad I am you'll be on my side in this hunt," he said without any sarcasm.

She snorted and left her inspection of the bramble wall for an even closer inspection of him. In the darkness, her features were merely hints of angles and curves layered in shadow, with her yellow eyes like twin suns flaring and darkening with her emotions. "Can you stand long enough for me to check your injuries?"

Her question made him even more determined not to be an invalid. He stood on more stable footing now, no longer dizzy or half blind. The sizzling pain under his ribs remained, but he'd grown used to the discomfort. "I'm just bruised and feeling my age."

"Let me see anyway. For my peace of mind." Her fingers were already tugging his blood-stained shirt up for a view of his torso.

He shivered, from the cold and her light touch on his bare skin.

"Your vision at night must be even better than I assumed if you can see a bruise in this blackness."

She didn't look up from studying the contusions decorating his body. "It's as daylight to you, just without color." Her fingers traced a delicate map over his side, making him twitch at the sensation. Her claws, as hard and strong as the points he'd carved into her wooden throwing spikes could have cut him deep, but they glided across his flesh in the most delicate caress. "Those bastards knew where and how to hit. Enough to make you hurt and bleed but not enough to kill you."

"Brimming with kindness." This time his sarcasm spilled into his words. Chamtivos and his lackeys had enjoyed doling out punishment when they couldn't convince him to divulge the secret to breaking Megiddo's enchantment. They could have beaten him to death without ever solving that mystery because Serovek didn't know it. Only the Khaskem knew how to break the spell he'd wrought on the monk. Even if Serovek did know, he would have died under their fists silent with the knowledge and Megiddo's enchantment unbroken.

"Anhuset." She raised her gaze then, alerted by something in his voice. "Our chances of surviving tomorrow are slim at best, even with our plans and preparations."

She lowered his shirt, quiet for a moment as if weighing her next words. She pivoted to stand before him, her features more defined with her much closer proximity. Her body heat warmed his front, and her eyes had darkened to the gold of coins in a king's counting house. Serovek's breathing turned labored, a labor having nothing to do with compromised lungs or injuries.

He resisted the temptation to close his eyes when she laid her hand gently against his cheek. "If the gods abandon us, I will be proud to die fighting at the side of Serovek Pangion, Margrave of High Salure and battle mate to Brishen Khaskem."

His heart galloping faster than a spooked horse, Serovek bent his head, tossing aside any lingering resistance to this fierce, courageous woman. He didn't have to bend far. She was nearly his height and slipped her hand to his neck to pull his head down to her.

He'd often imagined what kissing Anhuset might be like. All the scenarios had been variations of a passionate tangle of limbs, a hard press of mouths together, the score of her claws across his shoulders. They would gasp together and struggle, and pant, and fight each other for supremacy while they yanked each other's clothes off in a frenzy of desire.

This kiss was none of those things. The first brush of her lips on his was no more than a zephyr's whisper, the second a soft, curious tug on his lower lip, the third a luxuriant suckling of his upper and lower lips. The fourth kiss was a slow, thorough, glorious mutual exploration of the way her bottom lip felt a little fuller than her top one. Her breath tickled the sensitive corners of his mouth while her hand kneaded his nape. Her claws on his skin were a tantalizing contrast to the softness of her fingertips.

Serovek groaned, not from pain but from the dizzying euphoria of finally experiencing the fruition of a dream that had consumed his slumber many a night. He slid his arms around her to draw her closer, uncaring that his body twinged hard at her weight against the painful contusions decorating his torso. She copied his actions, the hand at his nape sliding down to the middle of his back while her other hand cupped one buttock for an appreciative squeeze.

He pulled back enough to look into her eyes, see that they were actually much like his, with sclera, irises, and pupils, all various shades of yellow that merged into the lamplight brightness so different from a human's. He grinned. "Had I known you liked my arse, I'd have invited you to squeeze it long before now."

She surprised him further by bending to nibble his chin. The playful touch lit a fire in his body as hot as if she stroked his cock. The touch was brief but powerful. Anhuset's own smile was a faint lift of one corner of her mouth. She gave him another squeeze. "It's an exceptionally nice arse, margrave. I'll admit to admiring it more than a few times, but consider it a mercy as well as a compliment. It's one of the few spots on you that Chamtivos didn't pummel black and blue."

"Don't let any of that stop you from touching wherever you

please," he said. He captured her lips once more, unable to resist their allure. She responded enthusiastically, her soft moan in harmony with his as she learned the shape of his lips and he learned hers.

No longer satisfied with the closed-mouth caresses they exchanged, he coaxed her mouth open with a gradual seduction. She stilled in his arms, arching deeper into his embrace, the stillness one of curiosity, of anticipation for what he might do next.

The glide of his tongue along the slick inner skin of her lower lip made her shiver, but she didn't stop him or pull away. He repeated the caress, this time on her upper lip, and her shiver strengthened to a shudder punctuated by a thin, surprised whine and the tightening grip of her arms on his back.

He drew back a second time. "The Kai don't kiss this way, do they?"

Anhuset shook her head. "No," she said in a breathless voice. "Though I've seen the *herceges* kiss the *hercegesé* in such a manner. She must have taught him." Her gold coin eyes shone in the darkness. "Do it again. Teach me how."

Her command sent another wave of desire purling through him. "I'm happy to oblige, mistress."

She was an eager student and a quick learner, mimicking his endeavors to ignite the same fire in her that she did in him. He massaged the curve of her waist and her long back as she teased his lips with her tongue.

Certain now she would welcome more from him, he deepened the caress, slipping his tongue into her mouth, past her teeth to taste her even more, no longer caring if she scored him bloody.

His concern came to naught. Anhuset relaxed her jaw, widening the space between her natural bite so that he could make love to her mouth without injury. Purrs rumbled in her throat, sounds of pure pleasure that urged him to hold her ever tighter, kiss her even deeper.

Serovek had kissed many women in his lifetime, kisses that ultimately led to a roll in the sheets, the grass, or any convenient place offering a modicum of privacy. Those kisses had been pleasurable, lustful, and forgettable the next hour, the next day. These ephemeral moments with Anhuset in his arms would remain burned in his memory until he died—which might well be as soon as the inevitable dawn.

The reminder of their circumstances only served to sweeten the kiss and all those that came after it. When they finally halted to take a breath, they discovered they held each other so tightly, a leaf of the finest parchment wouldn't fit between them.

"You're a marvelous teacher," she said between shallow pants.

"And you're an exceptional student." He stroked her silver hair with one hand. "I could spend all night tasting you," he said, thrilled that with her instinctive help, he'd discovered a technique for making love to her mouth without losing his tongue.

Anhuset caressed his lower back with both hands. "If we had the whole night, I'd want that and more, but we have only this short time. I must leave you to keep watch on the shore. For all we know, Chamtivos lied and will be here before dawn." She gave him a wry look. "You may not survive me, margrave, but I'll do all in my power to make sure you survive this stupid hunt."

His heart raced even faster at her words. That was an invitation, a declaration that he was welcomed into her bed and into her body. But this was Anhuset, and he never made assumptions regarding her, no matter how sure he might be. "So my reward for living will be dying from swiving you at a later date?"

She tapped his shoulder with one claw. "Don't presume. It will be me swiving you." She stroked his matted hair, fingers catching in the strands stuck together with dried blood. "A reward for the pair of us. And I'm not in the habit of killing my lovers. You'll live." She winked. "Barely."

One more brief kiss before they set to work, she to gather those supplies and weapons she'd take with her, he to retreat behind the bramble wall and build a small heap of kindling for a signal fire later. If he was to be bait, he'd make it easy for Chamtivos to find him, if not necessarily easy to kill him.

Before Anhuset left, Serovek caught her hand, entwined his fingers with hers, and lifted her palm to his mouth for a kiss. She reciprocated by pressing her lips to his knuckles. "Be careful," he said. "Fight as if you're the only one they hunt. If you worry about me, they'll take you."

She nodded. "Stay alive, margrave. I carried you up this hill. You owe me a long, hard ride." Their shared laughter eased the grimness, and she gave him a brief nod before leaping the bramble wall to sprint down the hill where she was soon swallowed by the heavy darkness.

He longed to go with her, to fight side by side, but his injuries prevented him. He was strong but at the moment too slow to be anything more to her than a burden. He served her and himself best by acting as the distraction for the hunters, focusing their attentions on him so that she might ambush them, one by one.

He built the fire from the kindling they'd gathered earlier, igniting it with the eating knife as his striker against a piece of flint, and bits of the tattered cloth as both char cloth and tinder. The fire provided welcome warmth, but more importantly it gave off light, a flickering, dancing luminescence he had no doubt those camped across the lake could clearly see, even through the battalion of firs covering the island. If things went as they planned, Chamtivos would mark the location of the light, assume his prey were foolish in their desire to stay warm, and head directly for the spot as soon as they landed the boats.

Pain exhausted him, and boredom made him sleepy as he waited alone for dawn to arrive. He was as armed as he could be with knife, sling, and two of the three spears he'd made. Anhuset had taken the third spear and her pair of throwing spikes.

The sling would serve him best, then the spears, and finally the knife. If he was fortunate, he'd kill any hunter who approached long before they got close enough for hand-to-hand combat.

Anhuset was right when she said they'd come at dawn. The sun had barely washed the sky a pale yellow when he heard her signal whistle in the distance. The boats were in sight.

Serovek dropped several stones into a pouch he'd made from the hem of his shirt and took up the sling. He slipped his index finger into the looped end to his knuckle and pinched the knotted end between that finger and his thumb, creating a loop. He'd wait to load the pouch until he spotted his quarry.

Time crawled in the forest's deceptive quiet. Even the birds remained silent, sensing the presence of predators. Only once was the quiet broken by a distant splash of water followed by screams for help and more splashing, then silence once again. For a moment Serovek's breath seized in his lungs and his nostrils until he heard the cries. A male voice, not Anhuset's. Whatever happened to the man who fell into the water, Serovek was certain the hunters now numbered one less.

Were he uneducated in the value of patience in battle, he might have abandoned his spot to seek out his enemies as Anhuset had done instead of letting them come to him. His patience, however, was finally rewarded as was his and Anhuset's planning the previous night. Three shadows, purposeful in their creeping ascent toward the bramble wall, solidified into a trio of men. Two carried swords and spears, the third a bow. Chamtivos's betrayer had warned Anhuset there'd be at least four skilled bowmen in their group. Serovek wondered if the traitor himself was among their number. It didn't matter if he was. A man who sneaked a knife to his opponent because he believed in the fairness of a fight was still an adversary, just a nobler one. To Serovek's way of thinking, Anhuset was his only true ally in this deadly game.

He eased two stones into his free hand, loading one stone into the sling's pouch. The three hunters didn't hear him, and judging by their actions, they hadn't seen him yet either. The topography worked to his benefit for the moment but not for long. Soon they'd be high enough up the slope to spot him behind the bramble camouflage.

It had been some time since he'd hunted with a sling, but Serovek practiced regularly anyway. One never knew when they might have to fend off a pack of wolves, furred or human.

The rush of battle fever surged through his body, pushing aside the pain of his injuries. He stood, swung the sling overhead in a fast arc and released the knotted end. A soft thunk followed, and the archer fell wordlessly into the underbrush before rolling down the slope to rest against a tree. He didn't rise.

The remaining two hunters barely had time to leap for cover when Serovek hurled the second stone, this time taking down one of the spearmen. His companion scuttled through the underbrush back down the slope, making a thrashing racket as he went. Serovek didn't bother taking aim or reaching for one of his spears. The fleeing hunter was too well-hidden and too distant now for a sure hit, and he didn't want to lose either of his spears in the attempt.

The second man he'd hit fell where he stood and didn't slide or roll down the slope as the archer had. Still armed with the sling and carrying one of his spears, Serovek made his way toward the dead spearman instead. "Better than falling down the hill," he muttered.

He didn't have to worry about fighting or finishing off the second man. His had been a kill-shot. The rock had smashed one side of the man's face, caving in cheekbone and eye socket. The other eye stared sightless at the tree canopy.

Serovek made short work of stripping the corpse of its weaponry to arm himself with a more respectable arsenal: a less primitive spear, short sword, and two knives. He left the body for scavengers and turned his attention to the archer while keeping an ear open for any movement from the distant brush and wishing one of the three had thought to bring a shield.

Senses riding a blade's edge of anticipation at taking a volley of arrows in the gut and chest from a revived archer, he approached more cautiously. Reason told him that were the archer still alive, he would have shot Serovek several times as he stripped the weapons off his dead comrade, but reason wasn't always right and caution had its virtues.

The man was as dead as the other, though far less mangled. The sling stone had struck him in the temple. Serovek had aimed for his head and released the sling just as the archer turned to signal to his companion. His death was instant.

Serovek glanced behind him. His sanctuary looked far away, and any other hunter headed in this direction would know where he was, especially with two bodies sprawled in the brush and one survivor to warn the others not only of his location but that he was far from helpless prey. Still, it was a safer retreat than lingering here.

Once again, he took all available weapons, including the bow and quiver of arrows. Halfway back to the relative safety of the overhang and bramble wall, he suddenly pivoted, pushing his back against a stately conifer with a trunk wider than his shoulders. A thump sounded behind him, and he recognized the noise—an arrow striking the tree on the opposite side. A second archer, and if he wasn't misjudging the rustling behind him, the bowman wasn't alone.

"We should have beat you harder in camp, margrave, and you should have killed Anagan before he could find us and tell your whereabouts." Chamtivos's voice silenced the emerging birdsong. "You can't hide behind that tree forever, and your sling won't do you any good now."

The surviving spearman must have crossed paths with his master in his flight and wasted no time in telling him where to find his dead companions and Serovek. "It would take a lot more than the clumsy affections from the runt of a cur bitch's litter to break me, you piece of shit," he told the warlord in a conversational tone, as if the two were friends discussing their day over a tankard of ale in a tavern.

Another thunk into the tree. Serovek wondered how many arrows the archer planned to waste turning the big conifer into a pin poppet. He glanced out of the corner of one eye, noting the gradual lengthening of a shadow only half a shade darker than all the others, easing toward him from the right.

Chamtivos's voice no longer held its gloating note. "Where's the gray whore?" he said in a guttural tones, the words hardly more than an incoherent snarl.

"Gone." And with any luck alive and spilling the blood of this bastard's minions across the entire island.

The warlord's voice changed again, taking on a cajoling note. "I'm a reasonable man."

Serovek snorted and regretted the action instantly as agony shot through his broken nose and into his skull.

"Bryzant paid me a small fortune to get rid of you, but I wager King Rodan would pay an even bigger one to have his valuable margrave returned to him," Chamtivos said

Serovek might have laughed at so obvious a ploy had he not been reminded of his steward's murderous treachery. He watched the shadow coming closer, one silent step at a time. "I don't wish to indulge in another round of your hospitality while I wait for the king's ransom," he replied. He turned perpendicular to the tree, bent, and scooped up a handful of dirt and brittle pine needles.

"I've no more reason to use such *persuasion* on you," Chamtivos argued. "The Kai woman told us only the Khaskem can reverse Kai magic."

That was true and probably the only truth Chamtivos spouted among his negotiations of ransom and promises to let Serovek live.

The hunter easing in from the right paused for a moment. Afraid he'd done something to alert him of his quarry's awareness of his presence, Serovek employed the same trick of distraction, continuing his conversation with Chamtivos as if ignorant of the approaching danger.

"What assurances do I have that your archer won't put three arrows in me the moment I step out from behind this tree?"

If there was one thing he'd learned during the long grueling hours bound in Chamtivos's tent, having his teeth loosened and his ribs caved in, it was that his captor loved to talk. Mostly about himself and his imagined greatness, as well as his puzzlement over why King Rodan hadn't bequeathed the valley to him instead of the Jeden Order or why he couldn't be king of Belawat himself instead of the "old fly bait" currently sitting on the Beladine throne. During the less torturous moments, when he spat out blood or breathed its iron scent through his broken nose, Serovek came to the conclusion that Chamtivos had bid farewell to intelligence, or sanity, or both long ago, trading them for the delusional dreams of a madman.

Chamtivos laughed. "Considering your current situation, I don't have to give any assurances, but just for the sake of argument..."

Serovek didn't hear the rest. He'd judged the quiet hunter's height based on his shadow—a shorter man than himself with a slimmer build. One more step and Serovek pivoted away from the tree, crouched down enough that his would-be assailant blocked the archer from a clear shot at him.

He caught a glimpse of the man's surprised face just before he hurled the dirt into his eyes. Anagan. The one who'd gotten away earlier to warn the others of Serovek's location. Anagan stumbled back with a cry, but not far enough. Serovek lunged forward with an upper jab, impaling him. The blade sank all the way through his chest wall and out his back. The man's eyes bulged, and a bubble of blood burst from his half open mouth.

Using the impaled man as a shield, Serovek hoisted him on the blade and rushed toward Chamtivos and the archer. The mortally wounded Anagan convulsed when two thumps sounded in quick succession. Serovek almost lost the momentum of his charge as the archer planted a pair of arrows into Anagan's back in the hopes of hitting Serovek as well.

"Kill him!" Chamtivos bellowed, his face pale with shock as he met Serovek's gaze over Anagan's drooping shoulder.

In the moment, time slowed to a series of vivid images: the archer reaching back for a third arrow, horror on his face at the sight of Serovek charging them with a dead man as his shield, Chamtivos's mouth wide as he shouted to the archer, his body leaned forward in the act of lunging toward Serovek.

Serovek had one chance—only one—to survive. He let go of the sword and the dead Anagan, freeing both his hands, and pulled one of the pilfered knives from his belt. He flung it hard, praying for accuracy.

The gods answered. The blade took the archer in the throat. He dropped to his knees, letting go of the bow to clutch the hilt as blood streamed over his hands, then fell face first into the dirt. Fueled by battle fury and pain, Serovek spun back, braced a foot on Anagan's corpse and yanked the sword free just in time to block a skull-cleaving strike from Chamtivos.

He deflected a second blow, delivering three of his own which Chamtivos defended against with ease.

The two fought on the uneven ground, through the maze of trees. Serovek, vision graying at the edges, felt the strength draining from him like water from a cracked ewer. Chamtivos, sensing his foe's diminishing prowess, renewed his attacks with even greater force and speed. And with more boasting.

"I will take your head, margrave," he said between pants. "And parade it through my stronghold for all my followers to see. I'll do the same to the monk and to the gray bitch. The people will cheer and praise my name, and the Jeden Order will fear me again. I will rise to my rightful place in these lands, not as lord but as king."

Fury, cold and resolute, cleared Serovek's vision and pumped renewed vigor into his limbs. He beat back Chamtivos's next attack, fierce enough that the other man staggered, nearly losing his footing. Serovek saw his opportunity, pulled one of the rocks from the pouch at his belt and pitched it straight into Chamtivos's face. Bone cracked. Blood sprayed. The warlord screamed and staggered, clutching his face with one hand.

Serovek followed him, circling to the side to slash at the warlord's leg, severing the tendon behind his right knee. Chamtivos howled and fell, holding his crippled leg.

The ragged gray edges once more began their creep across Serovek's vision. He struggled to maintain a grip on his sword. He stared at Chamtivos, feeling no pity or mercy for this creature who murdered his own family to rise in the world.

Every breath he took felt as if he inhaled broken glass, and he spoke between exhalations that made a mule's kick seem gentle. "I rode into battle against the *galla* with a man who is king in all but name. A man who stood tall under the weight of a heavy crown. Who sacrificed much to save many. That man understands the meaning of kingship." He raised the sword, heavier than a blacksmith's anvil now. "You know nothing of kingship."

He swung the blade with the last vestiges of strength still in his arms. The sword, slick with Anagan's blood, offered mercy in its sharpness. It effortlessly cut through flesh and tendons, bone and arteries, with one strike. Chamtivos's body fell to one side while his head bounced once on the ground before tumbling in the opposite direction.

The scenery in front of Serovek melded together in a watery mural of greens, grays, and blacks. He blinked several times, ignoring the sharp agony in his eyelids each time he did it. He wove a meandering path to Chamtivos's head, lifting it up by the hair before staggering to the closest tree where he dropped down to recline against the trunk.

Footsteps sounded nearby, but he remained where he was, finished. If this was more of Chamtivos's lackeys, he was easy pickings. At least once he was dead, he wouldn't hurt or feel like retching up his insides.

He peered at the two figures striding toward him, one a tall gray-skinned woman with yellow eyes and a mouth he'd sell his soul to kiss one last time. The other figure he didn't know but recognized the clerical garb. A Nazim monk. Before passing out, Serovek lifted Chamtivos's head and tossed it toward the monk. "A gift," he said, slurring the words. "You're welcome."

ELEVEN

The island's rugged terrain provided numerous opportunities to hide, to slip away unnoticed, and especially to ambush. What it didn't offer was the ability to easily escape its confines. It boasted only one patch of beach and sat in the middle of a lake patrolled by large serpentine shadows, discouraging anyone from swimming in the waters.

Anhuset shrugged off her grim thoughts and took up a lofty post that gave her a bird's-eye view of the beach where she expected Chamtivos to return with his party of bloodthirsty minions in a couple of hours. She'd used the time to create false traps, lay down more misleading spoor, and make a strap in which to keep the makeshift spear Serovek had made for her tied to her back until she needed it. Three throwing spikes were tucked into her tunic for easy reach.

Things could be worse, she thought. She could be waiting on an open plain, easy pickings for anyone who could draw a bow and hit the side of a castle wall. At least the warlord liked a challenge when it came to stalking his quarry, and she intended to give him one he wouldn't forget. Or survive.

Leaving Serovek behind to act as a distraction didn't sit well with her, even when she acknowledged—and he agreed—that it was the most practical thing to do. He was too injured to go running about the island like she could. He was also more valuable to Chamtivos than she was. Killing the Beladine margrave of High Salure was a notch on the belt and would raise his status among his followers. Killing the Khaskem's *sha* would only sweeten the triumph.

"I will bury you, warlord," she said, watching as long, sinuous shapes glided just below the lake's surface, following the paths of fading moonlight plating the water.

If she knew how many men would come and what weapons they'd carry, she could plan her attack better. However, all she knew for certain was where they'd land the boats and the time they'd arrive, and she didn't trust Chamtivos to tell the truth regarding the latter.

She checked her small cache of hastily made weaponry. Half dead, with only an eating knife and materials Anhuset had scavenged, Serovek had done an admirable job of arming her and himself with weapons that would be useful in this environment, even against opponents with swords and bows. Archers presented the greatest threat, and Karulin had warned Anhuset there were four among Chamtivos's group who were exceptional. They'd be her first targets to neutralize. She just had to get close enough to them without getting shot full of arrows.

Gods forbid one of them find Serovek. The bramble barrier she'd erected provided some camouflage for him, as did the island's topography. He was an exceptional fighter, especially on horseback, but these were different circumstances with unique challenges, including the injuries he'd sustained from a brutal beating. Anhuset hoped Serovek was as good with that sling as he boasted.

She ran a claw lightly along her lower lip, the memory of the kiss she'd shared with him still making her skin tingle. If they both emerged from this ordeal alive and mostly in one piece, she planned to scratch the itch he'd incited and swive him for days—once he healed, of course. She'd once told him he wouldn't survive her. An empty threat now. She hadn't carried him up a hill to save him only to kill him in her bed. The memory of his teasing her made her smile for a moment. Her humor fled as images of Serovek's battered features replaced the finer memories of his humor and his kiss, and by the time she spotted the pair of boats skimming across the lake at dawn, her fury had turned the blood in her veins to ice.

From her hidden perch atop a steep embankment, she watched the two boats come ashore, a half dozen men in each, with Chamtivos at the prow of one. They disembarked, allowing Anhuset to take stock of their numbers and the weapons they carried. Karulin wasn't among their party. Anhuset was glad for it. He'd betrayed Chamtivos by giving her the knife and decried the warlord's actions regarding the hunt. Anhuset had hoped she wouldn't have to fight him, but she'd been prepared to do so if forced.

She was too far away to hear their words or see their expressions, but their demeanor told her much. The coming hunt excited them.

Anhuset's eyes narrowed. She had never been, and would never be, a prey animal, and forest fighting was a defender's game. "Today is a good day for all of you to die," she said softly.

The party split into two groups of six men each. Four archers were among them, two in each group. Anhuset wondered if these four were the ones Karulin had warned her about. The rest, including Chamtivos, carried swords, spears, and knives. And one carried a sling.

One group began a hike into the treeline on the side of the island where Serovek waited. The second one traveled farther down the beach in the opposite direction. They were the ones Anhuset followed and would deal with first, starting with the archers and the slinger.

She'd had neither the time nor stamina to build real traps, but she made the appearances of some. Leaves mounded a certain way over half buried tree limbs hastily cut and sharpened, their exposed ends made to resemble hints of pit traps with their lethal spikes that swallowed and impaled their victims. The hunters might investigate them further and discover they were bluffs, but by then the damage was done. They'd be cautious after that. And slower.

The six who tracked her and whom she tracked in return, didn't split off in different directions but hiked through the trees in a short column, with one archer leading and the second one acting as rear guard. They stayed together, no more than six paces apart at any time.

Anhuset targeted the rear guard archer first, hurling one of the spikes at him from behind the barrier of a broad oak. The spike took him in the shoulder, spinning him so that he dropped the bow he held and fell with a pained yelp, clutching the injured spot.

She darted behind the tree again, only to reappear on the other side just as the front archer pivoted and fired the arrow he'd nocked. It struck the trunk close to where she'd stood. He already had a second arrow nocked in place when she threw another spike. It struck him in the hand, and while he lost the shot, he kept his feet and held onto the bow.

Bark shattered next to her ear, pelting the side of her face as the hunter with the sling returned fire with several stones. Anhuset bolted deeper into the foliage, using the forest's stately columns of trees and dappled shadow to hide from her pursuers.

The spikes had done their job in disabling one archer and injuring the second. She still had all six men to contend with, but she'd improved her odds.

Broken bark cracked nearby as the hunter with the sling hounded her through the forest. Anhuset sprinted past one of her false traps as she climbed the slope toward the island's peak.

The running footsteps behind her stopped abruptly. Alarmed yelps and expletives echoed through the trees. They'd spotted her trap and momentarily paused in the chase.

She sprinted even harder to put more distance between them, leaving more obvious spoor to lead them higher up the slope. She was far more careful on the way down as she circled back and ended up behind the hunters. She'd neutralized the archers enough that they'd resorted to their swords and knives. One of the spearmen took up the rear guard position now.

Anhuset bided her time, allowing the group to move farther ahead, their movements twitchy, faces grim as they realized they were not only the hunters, but also the hunted.

They paused a second time at the sight of another trap, and it was then she struck, this time to take down the spearman.

He made only a gurgle before she grappled him from behind and snapped his neck. He dropped the spear he carried. She caught it before it hit the ground. His limp body thumped once against hers as the slinger hurled a stone, and Anhuset blocked it with the spearman's corpse.

Anhuset hurled the spear. The slinger fell, still clutching his next round of ammunition.

"And now the hunt begins in earnest," she told the remaining three in Common tongue.

Her words and the shock of their comrade's swift death sent them fleeing in different directions. Anhuset caught one of the archers before he got far, using her stick to crack his skull open. His body rolled down the slope to disappear in a pile of leaves. She killed the second man in a similar fashion.

The archer with the injured hand was the only one remaining, and she chased him all the way to the island's peak, losing him twice when she had to dodge a clumsily shot arrow and again when he flung his knife at her.

She trapped him on the island's crown with its spectacular view of the dangerous waters below. Later, Anhuset could only guess why her opponent suddenly decided to charge her. Maybe in the hopes of throwing her off the nearby edge, into the water, maybe to tackle her with the idea of brawling to the death. Whatever plan he had, she'd never know it. He raced toward her with a war cry and his sword raised. She'd simply pivoted out the way at the last minute and kicked him in the back. His momentum and her kick propelled him over the edge and into the lake below. She thought he might drown until a long shadow sped toward him as he thrashed in the water.

Anhuset raced back down the slope, angling toward the place where she'd left Serovek, fearful that Chamtivos and the remaining hunters had found and butchered him. A glimpse through the trees at additional boats landing on the shore to deposit yet more armed men sent her heart hurtling into her throat. "Gods damn it," she snarled. "Will this never end?"

Serovek would have to fend for himself a little longer while she dealt with this newest problem. She crept closer to the shore, pausing at the sight of these newest invaders, heavily armed and wearing clerics' garb. Anhuset recognized their clothing. Megiddo had worn something similar when he first presented himself to Brishen at Saggara. Nazim monks.

They lingered on the beach for a moment, talking among themselves. Tired of waiting for them to do something other than chat, Anhuset edged out of the forest's shelter far enough for them to see her. She was too far away for them to shoot at her if they proved to be hostile.

Instead there was much exclaiming at the sight of her, though they didn't approach. One monk stepped toward her, hands out in a sign of peace. "Sha-Anhuset?"

Wary, Anhuset remained where she was. He knew her name. Had Erostis or Klanek made it to the monastery to get help? She didn't have time to question him or exchange introductions and idle conversation.

"Yes," she said. "And if you're through having a convocation on the beach, the margrave needs our help, and Chamtivos needs to die."

Her remarks galvanized them all into a rush toward her and the forest. Three monks remained behind while the rest raced with her through the forest toward the protected ledge where Serovek sheltered.

They found him sprawled against a tree, long legs splayed, head drooping so that his chin rested on his chest. One hand lay limply in his lap, the other by his side. Were it not for the bruises mottling his face, he'd be as pale as the moon. Even his lips had lost their color. He looked to Anhuset like a broken doll tossed aside by a bored child.

She hurried to him, skirting Chamtivos's head where it had rolled between her and the Nazim monk who accompanied her. The warlord's death mask was one of bafflement, as if wondering why his gaze looked upon such a skewed perspective. Anhuset crouched beside Serovek and pressed her fingertips against the side of his throat, trying to ignore the panicked thud of her own heart. She scowled, torn between relief and worry. His pulse thumped faintly under her touch but was unsteady. She searched his body, looking for new wounds, for blood. Her relieved sigh must have been loud because he twitched the tiniest bit.

"Anhuset," he said on a ghost of a breath before falling silent again. His eyelids fluttered but remained closed.

"Were Chamtivos and the margrave enemies before this?" The monk had joined her, his expression puzzled and sympathetic. "We've rescued others from the warlord's clutches. Those taken hostage were never brutalized this way."

"I don't think the two even met before the attack," she said, gently tucking a lock of Serovek's hair behind his ear. With Chamtivos dead, they'd never know why he'd visited his malice on Serovek's body, but she could guess. Jealousy and envy made even good people ugly at times. For those like Chamtivos, murderous and petty, with a streak of madness and a thirst for power a league wide, it made them monstrous.

"I'll return with two of my brothers to help carry him to the boats. Or I can stay with him if you wish to go." The monk gestured to the slope below them. "We could try to carry him ourselves, but it would be a slower trip, and we might injure him even more if we jostle him too much."

Anhuset held back a wry smile, recalling the grueling climb up the same slope with an unconscious Serovek draped across her shoulders and back. "You go; I'll stay." The monk, unburdened by fatigue and the exertions of a battle, would be much faster than she anyway in rounding up his fellow monks for help. And truth be told, she needed to be here, beside this resilient warrior who'd managed to kill six men, including their leader, by himself while injured and barely able to stand. He defied every assumption she'd ever made about humans, and Anhuset was heartily glad he'd proven her wrong.

She watched the monk, who'd introduced himself as Cuama, sprint back the way they'd come. He paused long enough to snatch Chamtivos's head from the leaf pile where it landed and soon disappeared into the trees. No doubt he'd present the head to the others as proof the warlord was indeed quite dead and no longer a thorn in their side.

She didn't try to wake Serovek. As long as he still breathed and showed no outward signs of distress, she'd let him be while they waited for Cuama to return with help. She used the time to strip the dead of all their weaponry, including the knife she pulled from the archer's body. The only things she left were the pair of arrows still lodged in the back of the man Serovek had obviously used as a shield in a charge toward his enemies. She braced her foot on the corpse, using the leverage to break the arrow shafts in half. By her initial count of the hunters who'd landed on the island, she and Serovek had dispatched all of them, but she wasn't taking any chances by leaving retrievable, repairable weaponry.

Chamtivos's headless body lay crumpled in the dirt. Anhuset poked it with her toe. "Scum with visions of greatness but no character to achieve it. Consider yourself privileged to have died by the hand of one whose boots you weren't fit to lick." She gave the corpse a hard shove, sending it tumbling down the slope in a flail of arms and legs before it came to a thumping stop against a big conifer. "May the scavengers eat well," she said and turned away to head back to Serovek.

By the time Cuama returned with three more monks, Anhuset had amassed a small arsenal of looted weapons and laid Serovek on his back in a cushion of leaf fall. The monks wasted no time constructing a sledge with fallen tree limbs and a pair of cloaks to carry Serovek down to the shore. She helped them lift, then lower him into one of the boats and climbed in with him.

Dark water lapped against the boat's sides, and the vessel yawed right, then left as Cuama and two of his brothers climbed in as well to take up oars. One more monk shoved the boat away from the shore, wading deep into the lake before hoisting himself into the vessel. Anhuset gave the island a brief glimpse before setting her sights on the opposite shore. "Goodbye and good riddance," she muttered.

Those same arrowing wakes that had followed Chamtivos's boats to the island now moved parallel to the monks' boats for the return trip.

She now knew what created the big wake, had caught a clear glimpse of a giant sinuous body with the head and skin of an eel, a great milky eye and a double set of jaws filled with curving fangs that had clamped down on one of Chamtivos's men and dragged him beneath the water.

Anhuset didn't count that hunter as one of her kills. She'd merely dodged her attacker's charge and given him a shove that propelled him off the cliff on the island's windward side. She'd assumed he'd drown, weighted down by armor and weaponry or simply because he didn't know how to swim. The lake monster, though, had other ideas.

Unfortunately, it looked as though this one did as well. The wake's arrow point increased in speed and decreased in distance as it turned perpendicular and shot straight toward the boat's side. "Brace!" she called to the others, gripping Serovek with one arm while she reached for one of the looted swords with her free hand. The thing was either going to ram the boat so that it capsized and spilled its occupants into the water or breach, hurling itself down on top of them. She and Serovek had survived the predation of more than a dozen hunters. She refused to be devoured by a snake in the water when they'd just defeated one in men's clothing.

One of the monks leaned over the boat's side and plunged his hand into the water. He bellowed two words in a language Anhuset didn't understand, and two bolts of lightning forked across the water's surface to light the ripples of waves just below the surface. They illuminated a colossal shape whose length stretched far and away from the wake point. The fine hairs on Anhuset's arms rose, and her scalp tingled.

A lake monster, much like the one she'd seen earlier, only bigger, broke the surface in a towering flume of water. The creature writhed and convulsed, trapped in a net of lightning that turned its milky eyes blue, red, even lavender in its reflective arcs. The muscular body, its girth greater than a draft horse's, shivered as muscle contracted under sleek gray skin. The vicious jaws snapped together once, twice, like steel traps.

Another monk joined the first, adding his invocation, and more lightning scorched fern-like roads into the creature's hide before it plunged back into the water with a splash whose deluge threatened to swamp the boat and gave them all a thorough dousing.

Anhuset wiped her eyes and immediately checked the unconscious margrave in her arms. He sputtered once, mumbled something unintelligible, but didn't wake. She gently brushed water droplets from his cheeks and turned her attention to her companions.

Awe and admiration battled with bitterness for supremacy inside her. Warrior monks with formidable sorcerous powers. What the Kai had once possessed generations ago, what they possessed to a much lesser degree only a year earlier before the Shadow Queen of Haradis had tossed her people to ancient, voracious wolves in her bid to seize a power she could neither control nor understand.

A growl settled low in her throat. "Secmis, you vicious bitch," she muttered in bast-Kai. "If there's any shred of you left, I hope it suffers for all of time and existence."

The fading of the Kai and the ascendancy of humans—an inevitable future. Anhuset grieved inside even as she held a human male protectively in her arms and thanked every god whose name she knew for each breath he took.

The monks in her boat and the ones occupying the other three vessels ignored her, intent either on rowing as hard as they could for the safety of land or watching the water for any signs of more of the great eel monsters. In Anhuset's opinion, the boats couldn't reach the shore fast enough, especially after one priest pointed out the breach and plunge of serpentine humps and the wave crests and troughs not far from them.

Were she not acting as Serovek's pillow and support, she'd have been in the water with those monks pulling and pushing the boat on land. As it was, she blew out a grateful breath at the sound of the keel scraping along rock as they beached the boats and left the lake and its hungry denizens behind them.

A young acolyte, left behind to guard a small herd of saddled horses, bowed to their group, his gaze darting repeatedly to her as the monks eased Serovek from her embrace and out of the boat. She followed, once more taking his heavy weight into her arms so that he lay across her lap instead of the unforgiving rocks covering the beach.

She almost laughed aloud at the acolyte's wide-eyed shock when Cuama retrieved Chamtivos's head from one of the boats and shoved it into an empty satchel tied to one of the saddles. The monk tugged on the bag, testing the knot's hold. Satisfied, he patted the horse's neck and approached Anhuset.

"The two of you riding pillion won't work. Hard on the horse and far too slow. And I don't think you want to risk draping him over a saddle and tying him down," he said. Anhuset shook her head. Whatever internal injuries Serovek might have would be exacerbated by such a transport. Cuama continued. "We can construct another sled. All of our horses are trained to pull one if necessary. We'd only have to get as far as Chamtivos's camp before we can put him in the wagon with our brother Megiddo and take him to the monastery that way." At her scowl, he held up his hands in a reassuring gesture. "Those who remained at the camp have been subdued and taken prisoner. They're no longer a threat."

Anhuset wondered if Karulin was one of those taken prisoner or if he'd fought and died in a fight with the monks. She didn't dwell on the question. "I want to ride the horse that pulls the sled."

"As you wish."

The return ride to Chamtivos's camp took twice as long as the ride to the island for which Anhuset was both frustrated and grateful. The monks were mindful of Serovek in the makeshift sled and kept their pace leisurely. Anhuset didn't bother counting the number of times she twisted in the saddle to check on her passenger. They were many and often.

The warlord's raider camp was a different place from the one she'd left: shelters broken and strewn about along with supplies, Chamtivos's tent a pale puddle of torn canvas in whose midst those raiders left behind now knelt, hands bound behind their backs. She spotted Karulin among them, his resigned expression changing to fleeting relief when he saw her and Serovek. He didn't call out to her or beg for clemency from her. His quick nod was one of acknowledgment and respect.

"Cuama." The monk turned his horse around and halted it beside hers. Anhuset gestured to Karulin. "Do you know that man?"

His gaze settled on Karulin. "Chamtivos's second. A much more reasonable sort than his master. The Jeden Order has attempted to negotiate with Chamtivos through him. Unfortunately, Chamtivos rarely listened to his more rational minion." Cuama frowned. "I was disappointed to see him here, though not surprised. I think he struggled under Chamtivos's command, but he was loyal to him."

His eyebrows arched when Anhuset said, "Maybe not as loyal as you think." She lowered her voice so that only the monk heard her. "He betrayed Chamtivos by giving us a knife that allowed us to make weapons. He also argued against the hunt at his own personal risk. And his presence here means he managed not to participate in the hunt despite Chamtivos's disapproval." She glanced at Karulin, who watched them intently. "If what I observed is correct, he's as esteemed among Chamtivos's followers as Chamtivos was. Even more so I think, because as you say, he's a more reasonable man." A saner one too.

Cuama returned Karulin's regard just as intently. "With Chamtivos no longer an obstacle, we might finally achieve peace for this valley. Karulin is our prisoner for now, but his value to us may be in his freedom."

"I ask clemency for him in gratitude for his help," she said.

"Noted, and you'll have the chance to defend him to the abbot when we reach the monastery."

While the monks dismantled the remainder of the camp, confiscated weapons and horses, and prepared the prisoners for a march to the monastery, Anhuset checked Megiddo, who lay undisturbed in the wagon, then Serovek's stallion. Magas had trumpeted a greeting upon seeing his master, great hooves stamping the ground as he yanked on the lead line that tethered him to the ground stake.

The stallion eye-rolled when she approached, snorting a warning. Anhuset kept out of reach so as not to be nipped or kicked. He'd not acted this way before with her, but she was splattered in blood not her own and reeking of death. A careful visual inspection revealed that except for a flay mark across his left flank, likely inflicted during Chamtivos's initial attack, he was unharmed. Serovek had worried for Magas, and Anhuset was glad she could tell him all was well with his beloved horse.

Their party split into two groups. The smaller of the two included Anhuset, Serovek, and Megiddo, all sharing the wagon. Serovek lay beside his bespelled comrade on a bedding of blankets. There wasn't enough room for a third person in the wagon bed or Anhuset would have sat beside him for the remainder of the trip. Instead she recovered the gelding she'd ridden during their journey and paced alongside the wagon, ahead of Magas who followed docilely behind, tied to the rear hitch. They left behind the larger party with the prisoners and the dead.

Before they left, Anhuset paused in front of Karulin. "The monks know," she told him. His fellow prisoners eyed her with suspicion and Karulin with puzzlement. They were unaware of what he'd done for her. She kept her remarks enigmatic so he could choose what to reveal to the others. "What's given in fairness is repaid in gratitude. There will be no debt."

He stared at her for several moments, expression guarded. "One who equals three," he finally said. "You're a credit to your people. Farewell, Kai woman."

The second leg of their journey seemed even more interminable, but they made it to the monastery belonging to the Jeden Order of Nazim monks.

Cuama kept her distracted during the trip with a history of the monastery. "The old scrolls say the Gullperi built it for one of their gods," he said. "When the Gullperi abandoned it, the forest swallowed it whole in vines. Supposedly a sorcerer stumbled upon it and cleared away the foliage." He gave a disbelieving sniff. "When you see the monastery, you'll probably think that unlikely. I suspect it's more a matter of treasure hunters that came to explore and loot, with a few of them getting roasted by Elder magic for their curiosity."

His remark emphasized the potency of Elder magic still lingering in Gullperi holy places. Powerful, sometimes lethal magic. Anhuset had witnessed it firsthand atop the tor when Brishen invoked a necromantic spell to turn himself and four others into the deathless Wraith kings. It didn't surprise her that the same power pooled latent in an ancient Gullperi temple.

Cuama was right to predict her disbelief in the notion that one man had freed the monastery from its ivied prison. Its size alone made that impossible. The majestic structure rose from the valley floor in a series of rose granite walls that blushed pink in the sunlight. The Gullperi had carved it straight out of a hillside, a tribute of colossal arches, soaring columns and decorative flourishes made for a forgotten god. Strange symbols etched into the granite decorated its façade, and the temple towered above the tallest trees carpeting the valley floor.

As they rode closer, she noted details beyond the majesty and decoration. This was a fortress dressed up as a place of worship, possessing all the architectural hallmarks of any military stronghold. No wonder the Jeden Order had claimed it as their own. It was the perfect sanctuary for sorcerous warrior priests who walked the line of heresy in their belief in and worship of a single god they called Faltik the One.

A swarm of robed and armored clerics spilled from the monastery's entrance and crossed the bridge spanning a dry, shallow moat. They surrounded the arriving group. Anhuset bared her teeth in a warning snarl when one monk reached over the wagon's side to touch Serovek. He pulled back and dropped the same hand to the pommel of the sword sheathed at his waist. Anhuset mirrored his action.

"Peace," Cuama said in Common tongue. He then addressed the monk in Beladine, but in an accent too thick and too swiftly spoken for her to understand what was said. The other monk backed away from the wagon with a bow but kept pace alongside it.

"You're safe here," Cuama reassured her. "As is the margrave and Megiddo. Ulsten is one of our best healers. His lordship will be in good hands under his care."

Anhuset was prevented from asking questions about Ulsten and what the monk intended to do to Serovek by a voice shouting her name from the entrance gate. Erostis stood there, bandaged on one side of his body. He waved to her, face haggard despite his joyous expression. She left the wagon to guide her horse past the procession to where the Beladine soldier waited. She dismounted, offering her arm. "You live," she said by way of greeting, grasping his forearm in a firm grip.

He did the same to her, his smile widening at her succinct salutation. "I do indeed, and I'm glad to see you're still breathing as well." His gaze traveled to the wagon, the smile slipping away as he caught sight of the riderless Magas. "His lordship?" he asked, voice pained.

"Injured but alive." She ran her gaze over his bandages. He was up and walking without a stick or the help of another, though he wore the same sickly pallor Serovek did. "One of the monks boasts of strong healing skills. It seems it isn't empty crowing."

Erostis tapped his shoulder gingerly. "I took two arrows. Bodkin tips instead of broadheads, or I'd be long dead by now. These priests know a thing or two about healing magic." His grave visage saddened even more. "Klanek wasn't so lucky. The monks tried to save him but failed."

Anhuset had known Erostis and Klanek for a short time, yet it felt as if she'd lost a battle mate. "I didn't know him well, but he was your friend and a valued soldier. I offer my sympathies."

He nodded. "My thanks, sha-Anhuset."

Their conversation ended when the wagon carrying Serovek and Megiddo rolled past them. A monk among the group waiting for the procession to pass approached Erostis to coax him back to his room. Erostis shrugged him off, his expression pleading when he turned from watching the wagon roll by to Anhuset, who gathered her horse's reins to follow. "You'll tell me when he awakens?"

A good man, loyal to his liege. Anhuset was glad Erostis had survived the attack. "Of course, I'll seek you out as soon as he opens his eyes."

In the hour that followed, the monks took Megiddo's bier to one part of the monastery while sending her and Serovek to another.

"We reserve this wing of the monastery for visitors," Cuama told her as they followed a group of priests carrying Serovek down a narrow cloister and up a flight of stairs. They emerged into a hallway that reminded her of the barracks at Saggara. Plain doors on either side, unadorned walls and wooden floors that creaked underfoot.

When Cuama tried to separate her from Serovek at the entrance to one of the chambers, she planted her feet and glowered. "It's worth it to me to fight for the right to stay. Is it worth it to you and your brothers to fight to make me leave?"

Cuama gave a long-suffering sigh before ushering her inside the chamber where she took up residence on a small bench set out of the way in one corner of the room. A bed and table with an unlit oil lamp were the only other furnishings. She watched without commenting as the monks deposited Serovek on the bed, his feet hanging over the end, his broad shoulders taking up the entire width of the narrow frame. The chamber, already small when unoccupied, grew crowded with the arrival of more monks, including the healer Ulsten.

They surrounded the bed, blocking her view. Cuama sat beside her. "These are our healers. They'll examine the margrave, judge the extent of his injuries, and decide how they might help him."

"I'm not leaving," she reiterated.

He offered a brief smile. "None of us want to brawl in an effort to show you the door. You're welcome to stay as long as you don't interrupt or interfere."

"I make no promises," she said. If she thought they were harming Serovek in any way, she'd damn well interrupt and interfere.

Two hours later, and the healers were deep in their invocations. Serovek had been stripped of his clothes, and another monk had delivered basic physicking supplies including bandages, hot water, drying cloths and small pots of salves. Anhuset was glad to see the monks didn't just depend on spellwork to help their patients.

Ulsten and the other monks had been chanting nonstop since they completed an examination of Serovek's injuries and cleaned his skin of dirt and blood. Their hands glided over his body without touching, leaving behind a soft glow that enveloped him and pulsed to the chant's cadence and rhythm.

"How much longer?" she whispered to Cuama, who'd stayed with her.

Her companion observed the proceedings for another moment before replying. "Soon. His injuries beneath the skin were worse than those we could see." Her heart stuttered at this new revelation. "My brothers are focusing all their power on healing those. When they're done, his lordship will still look ragged, and he'll still ache, but his bones will be knitted, and if Faltik the One deems it so, any bleeding inside will be staunched." He shook his head, wonder creeping into his voice. "The margrave must be very strong. To fight with such prowess while so wounded is impressive."

The dull ache of regret beat under Anhuset's breastbone at his words. Serovek was strong, exceptionally so, but he wasn't invincible. Her own faith in him and his ability to hide how badly he was hurt had enabled him to fool her into thinking otherwise. She shouldn't have agreed to the plan of using him as bait, no matter how effective it had been; shouldn't have left him to fend for himself or succumbed to a moment of weakness and kiss him until her knees turned to water and her blood to a molten river where desire overwhelmed caution and sense.

Were he awake and heard her thoughts, he'd scoff. She knew it in her bones. Still, it was difficult seeing him like this, vulnerable yet somehow still undiminished. Anhuset thanked both fortune and any gods paying attention, including this Faltik the One, for the monks' timely arrival on the island.

The chanting finally halted, trailing off to a heavy silence. Everyone in the room stared at the margrave as the glow around him pulsed once before fading away. He looked unchanged to her, still bruised and battered, but his breathing was no longer labored, and his chest rose and fell in an even rhythm. He looked like a man sleeping off the effects of too much drink and a hard night of brawling in a rough tavern.

Ulsten approached her. He wore the serene expression of a religious devotee and the sword of a soldier. "Don't be alarmed if he doesn't wake for a few hours. Sleep is his kindest friend right now and a better healer than any spell."

"He's out of danger, then?" Anhuset battled back a surge of euphoria as well as a wide grin. No need to make everyone in the room jumpy.

The monk nodded. "You may remain here with him if you wish. Someone will bring tea and food for you. The room next to this one will be yours and ready when you wish to rest." He pointed to the scabbed cut on her arm, visible through the slash in her sleeve. "We can heal that." He touched his own face to mark where her bruises were on her features. "Those too if you wish."

She declined the offer. Human magic wasn't Kai magic in her opinion, and she was wary of it. Besides, her injuries were minor and nothing a poultice couldn't cure. "If you can send more water and cloth along with the food and leave the salves, I can take care of them myself."

Once the monks left, she approached the bed and its sleeping occupant. Despite Ulsten's assurances, she set her finger under Serovek's nose, taking comfort in the draft of his breath tumbling over her knuckle. Thanks to the monks' spells, his bruises had faded from purple and red to shadowy blue, and the swelling had subsided. Bits of dried blood still glued his eyelashes to his cheeks, but beneath all that his handsomeness shone through once more.

The thought brought Anhuset up short and she backed away from the bed. Her own breathing stuttered. She stared hard at the margrave. Hard enough and long enough that her eyes began to burn. His features didn't alter under her intense scrutiny. Still handsome, still refined.

As they had always been, at least to human eyes. And now to Anhuset's. She crossed her arms and turned her gaze away, refusing to acknowledge the fear tightening around her chest like a vise. She recalled Brishen's expressions when she caught him watching Ildiko. How they'd changed over time from fascinated revulsion to lustful adoration. In that moment she would have bartered all her possessions for a mirror so that she might gaze upon her own reflection and discover whether or not she wore the same look. The vise wrenched tighter against her ribs.

She turned away but didn't go far, taking up residence once more on the narrow bench. She closed her eyes to ease their dryness and shut out the sight of Serovek, peaceful in his slumber. Her thoughts whirled and her heart raced, but not for long. Sleep she thought impossible to capture crept up on her and soon her pulse slowed and her mind calmed as she leaned her head back against the wall and drifted into slumber.

The squeak of a hinge brought her instantly awake, dagger ready in her palm as the door eased open, revealing first a bar of light from the lamp-lit corridor beyond, then a silhouette poised at the threshold. The windowless room she shared with Serovek lay in darkness, its lamp guttered out while she napped. It was a darkness she saw well enough in but one that blinded the visitor. She kept her eyes slitted so their tell-tale luminosity wouldn't betray her position. Likely a monk to deliver sustenance and the water she requested, but she wasn't relaxing her guard.

"Don't just stand there, man," Serovek said, his deep voice tired and raspy. "Come inside or leave, but shut the damn door."

CHAPTER
TWELVE

Serovek shielded his eyes from the bright bar of light that spread to a wedge as the door opened wider. A second silhouette joined the first, and the two figures merged with the darkness as they entered the room.

A familiar voice brought him more awake. "I thought you done for, my lord."

He levered himself up on one elbow, bracing for agony that never came. "Erostis. Damn, it's good to hear your voice, man."

"Same, my lord, but it would be nice to see you too, instead of stumbling around this room in the dark."

His complaint conjured a crackle and the spreading glow of light from one corner of the chamber, revealing Anhuset seated next to a now-lit brazier. Serovek couldn't tell where her gaze rested by sight, but he felt its weight. "Anhuset."

She offered a brief nod. "Margrave. Welcome back." She unfolded her tall frame from the bench to help the monk accompanying Erostis place a pitcher and goblets on a nearby table.

Had she watched over him while he slept? The idea warmed him more than the brazier ever could.

Erostis limped to his bedside and Serovek frowned at the sight of his liegeman swathed in bandages on one side of his body from shoulder to hip. He grasped Erostis's forearm and gave it a squeeze. "The gods were kind. I feared you were a dead man."

"I wondered the same about you." Erostis scrubbed his face with one hand. "Kind to a point. Klanek took arrows. The monks tried to save him, but to no avail." His face, haggard by injury and convalescence, became even more so with sorrow.

Grief settled on Serovek, a suffocating blanket. He'd lost men before in battles and raids, each death a wound that healed and scarred. He'd buried or burned most of them and delivered the news to the families himself when he could. A grim duty, but one he never shirked if he could help it. "The monks have his body here?"

"Yes, my lord."

"We'll bring him to his family when we return home."

"He was a decent sort, my lord. If you don't mind, I'd like to be the one to tell his wife. We grew up together in the same village. I think it'll be easier if she hears it from me."

That small bit of knowledge made Klanek's death even sadder. Soldiers serving at High Salure came from all parts of the Beladine kingdom, but most were local, sent from the surrounding towns and villages High Salure protected. Many of them were friends from childhood or even related to each other. Those bonds only strengthened their loyalty to Serovek and High Salure but also made the loss of each man harder to bear. Brother losing brother in battle, friend burying friend.

He sighed. "I think I met her once. We fetched Klanek to ride with us while we retrieved stolen cattle. She was chasing him around the chicken coop with a rolling pin, or maybe it was a cleaver." He smiled at the memory of the ridiculous scene.

Erostis grinned, blinking hard to hide tears. "That's Lederza all right. Klanek probably ate the pie or pastry she'd made and was saving for supper."

Both men chuckled, and Serovek caught the faintest chuff of amusement from the corner of the room where Anhuset stood listening. He suspected she'd like Lederza, should the two ever meet.

"If that's your wish, I'm happy to oblige," he told Erostis. "News like that is always better coming from a friend, though if you wish for me to accompany you, I will."

He wasn't surprised or offended when the other man declined. As margrave and ruler in his own right of the Beladine hinterlands bordering Bast-Haradis, he was treated with the same deference by the people living there. Klanek's wife would accept his condolences with a stiff, dry-eyed formality and die a little inside with every word he spoke. With Erostis, she could embrace her grief in that awful moment and weep on the shoulder of someone she knew.

The door opened once more, and this time he saw in detail a monk enter, bearing a tray containing covered platters wafting the delectable scent of food to his nostrils. His belly rumbled a greeting. The newest visiting monk scowled at Erostis.

"You're not supposed to be out of bed, Erostis. This is the second time I'll have to chase you back to your room."

Erostis returned the scowl. "If I have to lay in that bed any longer, I'll grow roots." He emphasized his frustration by stretching his arm in a sweeping gesture and yelped in pain for the effort.

The monk's expression lacked any sympathy, though he was gentle in helping Erostis lower his arm. "I believe I've proven my point." He ushered him to the door, pausing to ask Serovek, "By your leave, Lord Pangion?"

Serovek waved a hand to send them off. He'd winced when Erostis extended his bandaged arm, imagining a tear in the stitched wounds and the scream of torn muscle barely beginning to heal. "Get your rest!" he called out as the determined monk nudged Erostis into the hallway. "We'll talk again when we're both feeling better."

Erostis waved and disappeared with his escort. The second monk soon followed, closing the door behind him. The room's light dimmed to a tenebrous murk with only the crackling brazier and Anhuset's glowing yellow gaze to relieve it.

She circled the table where the dishes the monks brought had been set. The scents filling the room made Serovek's mouth water, and he chuckled at Anhuset's wary inspection of the offerings. "I don't think any of it's still alive, Anhuset, and I doubt the Nazim feast on scarpatine pie the way the Kai do."

"True," she agreed, cautiously lifting the towel off one plate with the tips of her claws, nostrils flared to catch any warning odors. "But there might be one of those vile potato maggot things lying in wait under these cloths."

He grinned, his joy at finding her here, at bantering with her, at still being alive to do so, chased back his sorrow over Klanek's death. The fact he wasn't in pain helped as well. "I'm happy to eat your share if there is."

"No one can accuse you of lacking heroism," she said wryly and continued with her inspection.

"And here I thought I had to kill a warlord to garner your admiration."

She glanced askance at him, her firefly gaze a dance of golden luminescence that darkened and lightened according to her emotions and even the play of light made by the brazier. "It helps," she said. "Though I find human suppers more challenging adversaries."

He laughed outright, surprised that it only brought a deeper ache to his fatigued body instead of the sharp agony he expected. The monks must have worked their magic on him while he was unconscious. Had Anhuset stayed and kept watch while they did? He hoped so. "I'm glad you're here, Anhuset."

She gifted him with another hint of a smile. "Likewise, margrave."

Considering her natural reserve and prickly nature, her response was akin to a declaration of love. His heartbeat sped up at the notion. While he was tempted to tease her, he thought better of it. He might not be completely bedridden, but neither was he a picture of nimble prowess. In this small chamber, he was at her mercy. Provoking a hornet promised a nasty sting.

She rearranged plates, putting a few back on the tray and filling the two tankards from the pitcher. "Ale," she told him. "Unless you'd prefer water."

"Ale every time," he said as she brought the tray to the bed.

"Do you need help sitting up?"

He shook his head and lifted himself into a sitting position, once more bracing for a pain that never came. "The monks must have extraordinary healing powers. I shouldn't feel this good right now." He offered her a short bow. "Then again, maybe it's the company."

She sighed and set the tray carefully on his lap. "You're obviously feeling better judging by your incessant teasing."

"I think you missed it."

"And I think you should be quiet and eat." She shoved a spoon and hand cloth at him. He was grateful she left the eating knife on the tray.

"Will you join me?" Sharing a meal while in bed with Anhuset was a fantasy whose current reality wasn't quite how he'd imagined it, but he'd take what he could get and be glad of it.

She sat across from him, legs folded under her to fit on the bed's narrow confines. There were no maggot potatoes or even the pan-fried ones she actually liked, but she shared the dishes with him, picking through heaps of roasted grains, eggs boiled in spiced tea, and fish baked in salt. He watched her from beneath his lashes, hiding his amusement at the various expressions that chased across her face: surprised delight, mild disapproval, but none of the outright revulsion he'd expected.

She glanced up once to catch him regarding her. As if she heard his thoughts, she shrugged and said, "I'm growing used to how humans cook."

He took a swallow of ale to smother his laughter at the faintly horrified note in her voice. Never before had he known so fearsome a martyr.

While he wanted to savor this time with her and speak only of pleasant things or tease her until she threatened to stab him with her eating knife, he needed to know what happened on the island and how they'd ended up with an escort of Nazim monks to the monastery he feared they'd never reach alive. Most of all, he needed to know Megiddo's whereabouts.

She reassured him of that one first. "He's safe, the spell protecting his body intact. The monks have placed him in a special chamber reserved just for him. They say you can see for yourself when you feel up to it."

All the tension locking his muscles with dread over Megiddo's fate bled away. There was nothing he could do for now about the monk's tortured spirit, but he'd accomplished what he'd set out to do: return him to the arms of his order. Serovek's success had come with help and at a steep price, and while he couldn't resurrect Klanek and restore him to his widow, he'd make certain she wasn't left destitute.

"What about Chamtivos's men? The ones who stayed in the camp as well as those who hunted us?"

When she relayed the events on the island and told him of the monks' arrival and how they learned of their predicament, he exhaled a long sigh. "Be it luck, fate, or a god's intervention, the monks' timing couldn't have been more fortunate. Erostis wouldn't have survived and who knows how we might have fared if we even made it off the island alive."

"The Nazim would say it was the mercy of Faltik the One that had them find Erostis at the right time." She shredded a roasted chicken wing with her claws before spearing the slivers of meat and popping them into her mouth.

Serovek raised his tankard in a toast. "I'm happy to credit whoever was responsible and pay tribute, whether they be the One, the Two, or the Three."

"Careful," she said. "You're a wounded man convalescing in a monastery populated by warrior monks who might think you just committed blasphemy against their god."

"I'm not afraid." He tapped his drink against hers. "I have you to protect me. A woman who can take down a pack of raiders by herself… these monks are no match for sha-Anhuset."

Her lids lowered and one of her eyebrows slid upward as she leveled a disbelieving look on him. "You might be handsome but your flirtation skills need work."

Serovek froze with his drink halfway to his mouth. He inhaled to point out what she'd just said, afraid he'd misheard her. She realized her slip before he could speak, and her yellow eyes narrowed to slits. Lavender flags of color painted her cheekbones and the claws on one hand tapped a warning staccato beat on the tray's wooden bottom. "Is it really worth it to you to say it, margrave?"

They stared each other down for several moments before Serovek sighed and cheerfully said, "Yes, Anhuset. Yes, it is. I always knew you thought me handsome. About time you admitted it."

Those slender white eyebrows crashed downward, and the tray made a screeching noise where she dragged her claws across the surface. "Do you always court death?" she asked, a growl underlying her question.

He dabbed the corners of his mouth with his napkin. "Rarely, though some might consider courting you one and the same."

"You aren't courting me," she snapped, the blush riding her cheekbones now spreading across her face. He'd flustered her.

"So sayeth you," he replied. "And only you."

"You assume a great deal just because I kissed you on that hillside."

"No, I simply hope for a great deal more." That kiss had sustained him through the pain and given him the impetus to fight past it, fight hard, and do whatever it took to stay alive just for the opportunity of experiencing all of Anhuset's consuming affections.

A knock at the door interrupted them before they could argue further. At Serovek's bid to enter, a monk slipped inside and offered the Beladine military salute to Serovek and a bow to Anhuset. "I'm here to collect your supper plates and tell you if you feel well enough, you're welcome to bathe in the springs below ground. They have healing properties that work alongside our magic." He glanced at Anhuset, gaze touching on her own contusions, cuts, and bruised skin. "You're welcome to do the same, sha-Anhuset."

"A most excellent invitation," Serovek said. "And one I accept." He set his emptied tankard on the tray just as the monk swept it from his lap. Anhuset rose nimbly to her feet, more watchful than annoyed now. She looked for any weakness in his demeanor that might belie his assurances of strength.

"Join me," he said. "I'll prove to you I'm more than capable of taking a walk to a pool." When she hesitated, he slyly suggested, "It will be your chance to drown me with no one the wiser." A rattle of dishes sounded at the table as the monk cleared them away.

Anhuset's lips twitched. "Well, when you put it like that, I'd be a fool to refuse."

Soon, they followed a novice monk through quiet corridors, descending empty stairwells until they were indeed below ground where the monastery kept its root cellars and buttery. Bundled in borrowed woolens and heavy cloaks, they passed another group of chambers, their doors shut, before entering a short hall surrounded entirely by mortared stone with an archway at the end. On the other side, the space opened up to a cavern carved out by nature and time instead of the hand of man. Two small, interlocking pools bubbled quietly, a light veil of steam floating over both.

"It isn't drinkable," their guide said. He set down the drying cloths he carried on a flat expanse of rock far enough from the pool to keep dry in case of splashing. "The minerals give the water a strange taste, but it's good for healing shallow wounds and easing the ache of bruises."

"And it's warm," Anhuset said in an almost reverent voice.

The novice nodded. "Stay as long as you wish. I believe your comrade Erostis will be here later to soak his own injuries, so you'll have company."

As much as Serovek liked and admired Erostis, he didn't greet that news with any enthusiasm.

Once the novice left, Anhuset wasted no time in shedding her borrowed garb and treating Serovek to a breathtaking view of her body before stepping into the first pool and submerging up to her neck. Her white hair floated around her like spider silk and she gestured to him with a wave of her hand. "Are you coming in or do you need help?"

Had he any plans to hide his desire from her, his aroused state would give him away the moment he pulled off his clothes. Luckily, he had no interest in hiding how much he lusted for her and hoped such obvious proof might convince her he was sincere in his passion.

He didn't miss the admiring glint lightening her eyes when he waded into the water. She didn't look away or keep distance between them as he swam toward her, the water sliding around him like warm silk.

"How many bruises did you count as I walked into the water?" he asked.

To his delight, she floated toward him, only halting when her body bumped against his and her arms slid around his waist. "What bruises?" she said, a hint of her teeth flashing white behind her partial smile. Her laughter, low and sultry, seduced him almost as much as the feel of her pressed against him. He returned her embrace, drawing her close so that no empty space existed between them.

Sleek and muscled, she was the epitome of the Kai warrior humans feared and respected, physically powerful, very aware of her many strengths and how to use them. Serovek savored those aspects of her, indulged in the way his blood pumped hot through his veins at how she fit to his body, how her buttocks curved taut in his hands and the muscles in her long back flexed under his caress. She was slim-hipped with legs that went for leagues and could break him in half if she wrapped them around his middle and squeezed. The forbidden and the dangerous had always been the lodestones of humanity, and he was no exception. And while Anhuset was still dangerous, the language of her silent affection told him that she was no longer forbidden to him.

They held each other in the water, doing nothing more for the moment than learning each other's shape and texture in the quiet of the pool, without the threat of death hanging over them or the sense that one kiss might be a first and also a last exchanged. It was a moment to prolong.

"Are you going to kiss me again, margrave?" she said. "Or have you lost your courage and fear for your tongue?" She didn't challenge him by baring her teeth, but he sensed a subtle shift in her body, a fine tensing of muscle as if she expected him to refuse her invitation.

He cupped her face, beautiful even with its purplish marks, and tilted her chin up with his thumb. "I finally have a naked sha-Anhuset in my arms. I fear nothing."

Her sigh became a moan when he captured her lips with his and explored their contours anew, relearning the giving terrain, the way she tasted, how she slanted her mouth under his and caught his lower lip between both of hers to suck and nibble. Her memory of that first exploration while they stood beaten and bloodied on the island hillside was as clear as his, for she slowed the kiss and opened her mouth wider to invite him inside. He didn't hesitate, swooping in to caress her mouth with his tongue and expertly avoid the sharp points of her teeth. She returned the caress with the same fervor and less caution, her tongue tangling with his before swiping along the top and sides of his mouth.

They broke apart to breathe. Serovek pressed his forehead to Anhuset's, only to retreat when she jerked away with an "ouch!" She touched her brow and he remembered the contusion she'd gained, courtesy of a nasty head-butting that left her with a painful lump and her adversary with a shattered nose and missing teeth.

"Forgive me," he said. "I'd forgotten about that spot."

She waved away his apology. "You can make it up to me," she said with a sly grin, obviously no longer worried that her toothy amusement might scare him off.

Those flashes of vulnerability reminded him that for all her physical prowess and ferocity, there were still aspects of Anhuset that were unsure, self-doubting, even fearful. They were as much a part of her character as all the rest, just buried deeper and only revealed to those she trusted most. She trusted him.

The realization of such a gift bestowed upon him spiked his passion for her even higher though he hadn't thought such a thing possible. He cradled her hips, lifting her a tiny bit. The water's buoyancy made it effortless, and she wrapped her legs around him, anchoring herself in place, thighs wide. Inviting. Tempting. Teasing. Her eyelids dropped to half mast, lending a sleepy come-hither expression to her features. Her back arched, legs tightening on his torso.

He bent his head to nuzzle her throat, then nibble the elegant cords of her neck, and move on to her shoulder, where he bit down gently and was rewarded with a gasp and the sting of her claws raking lightly across his shoulder blades.

He lifted her higher, arched her back a little more and took one firm breast in his mouth. Her nipple, a lavender-gray, surrounded by an areola of similar shade, hardened in his mouth, and he suckled it to an even stiffer peak. Anhuset's panting moans echoed in the chamber and likely down the narrow corridors where others could hear. Serovek didn't care and doubted she did either.

His plan to lavish the same attention on her other breast was curtailed when Anhuset's legs flexed so tight around him, it was his turn to gasp. "Anhuset," he rasped. Her eyes, a burnished gold glittering with sparks, stared at him for a moment before widening when he gasped again. "Release." She loosened her grip, and he inhaled a grateful breath.

While she might have relaxed her hold, she didn't let go entirely. Thigh muscles contracted as did her calves, forcing him forward with a hard push. Her pelvis tilted and in one quick motion he slid partially inside her. "Gods," he groaned as she squeezed his shaft, her inner muscles flexing to grip the head of his cock and tug.

"Enough teasing, margrave," she said in a guttural voice. "Show me what it is to be pleasured by the Beladine Stallion."

Her words set him afire. If he were younger and less experienced, he would have come inside her right then, still only halfway embedded in her. He remedied that with a full thrust forward, burying his entire length in her, shuddering at the shockwave of sensation that followed.

Her eyes rounded for a moment, and her mouth opened but no sound escaped. Afraid he'd hurt her, he tried to withdraw only to have her increase the vise-like grip of her legs on him to hold him in place.

"Gods be damned," she blasphemed in a thin voice. "The rumors are true. You're a fucking horse."

"Am I hurting you?" he said, ready to withdraw if needed, though he was nearly delirious from the pleasure of being inside her.

She shook her head. "No." She lunged forward to steal a hard kiss. The tip of one tooth raked his bottom lip. He felt the sting and tasted the tang of copper. "Again," she said, her own lip dotted with his blood.

He obliged, pumping hard into her as the water in the pool purled back and forth in waves. It was a mating, fierce and hungry, with the rake of claws, the thrust of hips, the bite on a shoulder or neck, a sweet nipple in his mouth, his cock deep inside her body. His name on her lips in a chant that was part command, part begging, part gasping, and all praise as she fucked him into oblivion and drained his bollocks dry.

He suckled one breast, teasing the other with his fingers as he continued thrusting into her. Anhuset's claw tips pressed into his back, almost breaking skin as she climaxed in his arms and nearly cracked his newly healed ribs under the grip of her legs. His heartbeat thundered in his ears and pounded against his breastbone. Sweat trickled down the sides of his face, beading on his skin along with the water.

Anhuset inhaled great gulps of air and slowly peeled her fingers off his back. Serovek was certain if he were to look in a mirror now, he'd see divots in his skin. She stared at him, her features slack with a wonder that made him want to preen and also sent a rush of relief through him. He hadn't disappointed her.

"You are one amazing ride, Stallion," she said, and this time it was she who teased him.

Serovek's laughter echoed in the cavern. He hugged her to him. This magnificent woman, who wouldn't know coyness if it kicked her in the gut, never ceased to charm him with her unadorned honesty. It was a charm unique to her. He suspected it wouldn't appeal to most, but he'd fallen for it willingly and hard.

He scraped her damp hair back from her face, smiling as she blew an annoying strand out of the way. "You were wrong," he said. "I survived you."

She answered his smile with a provocative one of her own. "So you did. This time, but can you do it a second time or a third?"

"The only way to find out is to make several attempts."

"That is a very good plan," she said, reaching into the water to cup his softened cock and stroke his balls. For an instant his legs instinctively tensed at the proximity of her claws, but she was careful, only her palm and fingers caressing him. She raised an eyebrow. "You don't trust me?"

He snorted. "Of course I trust you, but there isn't a man breathing who wouldn't be wary when daggers surround his bits."

She chuckled. "That's true. Even a Kai man would be alarmed." She lolled in his arms. "Kiss me again and then I'll wash the blood from your hair."

Serovek didn't need to be told twice and spent the next several minutes availing himself of Anhuset's taste, not only of her mouth but her neck and earlobes, the crooks of her elbows, her nape and her temples. She did the same to him, her tongue a wet caress on his skin that pumped the blood hot and fast into his loins again. His cock swelled, eager to experience the delight of her body.

She slipped out of his arms, motioning for him to follow her as she waded to the pool's edge where their clothes lay in a heap. The monk who'd led them to the pool had left not only towels but a small jar of boiled soap weed and a comb.

Good as her word, Anhuset soaped and rinsed his hair while he partially reclined in front of her, in a near torpor as she patiently combed the bloody mats out of his hair. Even with the occasionally painful tug of the comb, he relaxed so much under her grooming he nearly fell asleep.

When she was finished, she handed him the comb. "My turn," she said.

Eager to touch her in the same way she'd touched him, he happily traded places with her. Combing her hair was an easier task than combing his. She wore it a similar length but the texture was different, thick as his but straight as a spear haft and coarse enough to discourage tangles. The comb glided easily through her locks until hitting an unexpected knot.

It caught the comb hard enough to jerk her head back. "Ow!" she yelped, staring up at him as if he'd lost his senses. Her eyes widened, and she jerked forward only to fall back with another yelp, the comb still entangled in her hair.

"Hold still," he ordered, letting go of the comb. "You have a bad tangle back here." She ignored his command, trying to wiggle away, only stopping when he said, "A ribbon?" Anhuset made an odd noise, something between a growl and a mortified squeak, and went still.

Serovek pried the comb loose from the knot that was actually a frayed white ribbon twined around some of her hair. He slowly uncoiled it, surprised by its presence. She wore a few tiny braids at her temples to keep recalcitrant strands out of her face, but he'd never seen her adorn her locks with beads or other ornaments, and especially not ribbons.

This one had seen better days. Ragged at the edges and more gray than white now. He ran this thumb down its length, teased by a memory that skated along his consciousness. Anhuset sat in front of him stiff and silent as a marble pillar.

"Feel free to cut it out if necessary," she said. "I tried to tie it the right way but had to knot it to make it stay."

"I wouldn't know what to do with a hair ribbon."

His heart paused its beating for a moment as the memory finally revealed itself. A conversation at High Salure less than a month earlier but seemed a lifetime ago. "Where did you find the ribbon?"

She waited so long to answer, he almost gave up on getting one. "When you brought back staples from that market to replenish our supplies. There was a ribbon tied to a bunch of herbs. It fell to the ground. I took it."

I wouldn't know what to do with a hair ribbon.

She'd asked why he never married, and he'd told her of his wife, describing her beauty and love of hair ribbons. He barely recalled the face of the flirtatious woman in the market who'd given him the flowers, but staring at the ribbon still tangled in Anhuset's hair, he remembered the bouquet and his eagerness to get back to the camp and the Kai woman waiting for his return. "I can comb around it."

"No. Take it out. No one can see it anyway, and it's just a nuisance."

He didn't cut the ribbon out but spent extra time unraveling strands of hair until it came loose. As much as he wanted to keep it, he offered the ribbon to her when he was done. She held it for a moment before tossing it to the side. "Remind me to grab it before we leave," she told him. "I'm sure the monks have a midden I can toss it into on the way back to our rooms."

There was no way that treasure was going into a midden if he had anything to say about it. He kept the words behind his teeth, finished combing her hair, and scooted around her to slide back in the water. She stayed on the pool's edge, her expression a study in stoic reserve, her yellow eyes unblinking as she watched him. She held an invisible shield in front of her, a defense against embarrassment at him finding the ribbon and the belief that surely, surely he understood why she'd tried wearing it properly, and worst of all, why she had failed.

He did understand and fell even deeper in love with her. It wasn't the right time to tell her either of those things or even dwell on the symbolism of her wearing the ribbon at all. She would only lash out and close off even more. Instead, he steered the conversation in a different direction.

"You," he told her in a teasing voice, "have the most delicious breasts."

As he hoped, the outlandish remark worked its magic. The shield went down and her eyebrows went up before she laughed her raspy laugh. "Is that so?" She stared down at her chest before turning to one side and then the other, displaying the objects of his admiration like fine wares. "What makes them so delicious? And which one do you prefer?"

He rose half out of the water, and she leaned forward so he might sample. She slid her fingers into his hair, claws massaging his scalp while he tasted each breast and she moaned her approval.

"It's impossible to choose," he said after moving from her breasts to her mouth. The small interlude served to heighten his need to taste all of her. He coaxed her to stretch out on her back, her legs splayed so that he wedged between them, his head resting on her knee. He kissed the sensitive skin behind that knee, smiling when her toes on both feet curled. He continued up her body, bypassing her thighs despite the protesting throb of his cock, to kiss her belly, placing a ring of kisses around her navel.

Anhuset's breasts rose and fell with her ever quickening breaths as Serovek retraced his path to the place he'd purposely bypassed, settling between her thighs, nudging them farther apart.

The taste of a Kai woman, he soon discovered, was similar to that of a human woman, but that's where the similarity ended. This was Anhuset whom he made love to with his mouth and tortured with his tongue, and there was no other like her in all the world.

Her climax was a beautiful, thrashing thing to behold, even if he risked having his nose broken again by one of her knees. When she no longer arched and bucked and growled, he slid up her body, cupping his hands around her face. This kiss was leisurely, deep, luxurious.

"You taste like me," she said when they paused to take a breath.

"And you taste better than the finest wine."

"Such a honeyed tongue you have," she said before clasping him tight in her arms and rolling so that he lay on his back atop the clothes and she sat astride him, perched on his thighs. Her hand wrapped around the base of his cock, sliding up and then down, pausing to capture the drop of semen beading its crown with a fingertip. His hips thrust upward and he gasped. She brought her finger to her lips and licked. "Honeyed tongue, honeyed cock," she proclaimed.

Bewitched by the sight, Serovek grabbed her hips, steadying himself more than her as she shifted positions just enough and sank down on him again, his cock buried to the hilt inside her. His eyes rolled back no matter how much he tried to keep them trained on Anhuset's face and the ecstasy in her expression.

She rode him hard, harder than any woman he'd had before her. She embraced her pleasure and his, enthusiastic and unapologetic in her appreciation of his prowess and love of his touch. For the first time in his life he made love to a woman he wasn't worried about hurting, a woman whose own strength equaled his, who gave as good as she got and then some, who demanded every last drop of his ardor and kissed him until his lungs were on fire.

She'd told him he wouldn't survive her. Serovek was beginning to think she was right. At least he'd die a very satisfied, contented man. His orgasm didn't wash over him in a gentle rush, but slammed into him like a storm wave. He chanted Anhuset's name in his head even as his mouth struggled to emit more than groans and growls as feral sounding as hers had been. He kept thrusting until he was emptied and his bones turned to water. She loomed above him in all her naked majesty, a deity, and he her supplicant beneath her.

It was a very fine place to be.

Erostis never appeared to interrupt their interlude. They finally dressed, which took much longer than needed thanks to several interruptions of kissing and caressing.

"Remind me to send the monks a sizable gift for their monastery once I return to High Salure," he told her. "Without their considerable healing talents, this..." he gestured to the cavern and also her, "would have never happened." She gave him a dubious look. "At least not now."

They gathered their things. Anhuset might have forgotten about the ribbon but Serovek had not. He tucked it into the cuff of his tunic's sleeve. A ribbon but also a treasure beyond price. Just like the woman who'd worn it.

THIRTEEN

T heir journey to the monastery had been rife with obstacles, violence and tragedy, its very purpose the grim delivery of a man's living but soulless body into the safekeeping of his fellow monks. Yet Anhuset knew when they all returned home, Serovek and Erostis to High Salure and she to Saggara, she'd hold close the memory of her time with the Jeden Order and with Serovek most of all. He was no longer simply the annoying, intriguing margrave, but her lover now.

She stood on one of the balconies overlooking the Lobak valley, washed in the new green of early spring. Patches of snow still lingered in sheltered places, and her breath hung misty in the brisk morning air. She kept her back to the rising sun and the hood of her cloak pulled far forward to protect her eyes as she surveyed lands bequeathed to and controlled by the Jeden Order.

It looked peaceful, but its appearance was deceptive. This valley remained embroiled in conflict, though she hoped with Chamtivos's death, those who balked at being under Jeden rule and had their lands confiscated for it, might finally come to a truce with the monks. She recalled Karulin's words when he challenged Chamtivos, reminding the warlord that they'd veered from their purpose of fighting for their lands to preying on innocent travelers.

Chamtivos, cruel and ambitious, retained the loyalty of most of his followers through fear or under the guise of pursuing a just cause. Some remained devoted because they could revel in their own brutality under his command. Those had been the ones who beat Serovek so brutally—more for sport than for extracting information from a recalcitrant captive. They were also the ones who volunteered to join Chamtivos's hunt and met a just end.

Karulin and the others had stayed behind, and Anhuset wondered if Chamtivos's second had used that time to sway those with him to turn on their leader. In his place, she would have done so. Loyalty given had to be loyalty earned in her opinion, and Chamtivos had forfeited his reputation when he became a brigand instead of a rebel. From what little she'd learned of Karulin himself, she believed his leadership would offer a chance for peaceful coexistence if the monks were smart enough not to kill him first.

Footsteps sounded behind her, quiet ones, especially considering the size of the person to whom they belonged. Anhuset smiled, her heartbeat speeding up in anticipation of Serovek's company.

"I'm surprised to find you still awake, firefly woman," he said, stopping next to her. Cloaked as she was against the cold, he'd foregone a hood or cap. The sun lit red highlights and silver strands in his dark hair and even in his beard, which had thickened during their stay with the monks. After a sennight with the Order, their bruises were fading.

He noticed the focus of her regard and rubbed one cheek with a sigh. "I'll shave it off soon enough," he said. "Definitely before the hot weather arrives." He matched her stare with one of his own. "You prefer me clean-shaven?"

With the rare exception, Kai men didn't wear beards. It was more a cultural preference than a physical limitation as they bore the shadow of a beard when returning from days on patrol. Serovek bearded or clean-shaven, he was striking. Either look suited him, though the beard added years to him and a certain forbidding dignity.

"My preference shouldn't matter," she said. "It's your face."

"Your preference will always matter."

They stood side by side, arms pressed against each other. He'd always seemed to correctly guess her quirks and read her moods. It was uncanny, and in this he remained unfailing. Another lover might have come up behind her, wrapped his arms around her and pulled her into the cove of his body. She would have shrugged him off instantly. Serovek did none of those things, understanding in some instinctive fashion that while her devotion ran deep and intense for a loved one, she didn't display her affection in overt ways and never in a public setting where others might note it and use it against her later. Some might think her overly cautious. She preferred that to being overly dead. Still, she reveled in his nearness, the heat rolling off his large frame to warm her side this chilly morning.

The monks had given her a room to use at the monastery, a space as spartan and basic as any of the barracks at Saggara. She used it only to store her things. Otherwise, she was with Serovek in his chamber, and while she avoided public displays of affection, private ones were a different matter.

Their intimacy was intense, rough at times, and also lighthearted. Even now, she wore the marks of his passion for her on her skin, and her thighs pleasantly ached from the hard ride he'd given her a couple of hours earlier. He lived up to his reputation as an experienced lover with endless stamina, and he expected her to keep up with him, which she did with great enthusiasm. They'd broken his bed twice, apologizing to the monks each time. Serovek finally told them bedding on the floor would suit them better. They'd both grinned at the smothered guffaws from the Nazim who'd taken away the remains of the broken bed frame.

With him, she learned to unbend, to laugh more easily, though she'd never see in herself the beauty he swore she possessed. Her lovers had found her a challenge to conquer, a notch in the belt at having bedded the formidable sha-Anhuset and lived to tell of it. Serovek had found her a challenge as well, though not in the same fashion. The way he looked at her when they first met was the same way he looked at her now, as if he'd just discovered the most sublime of all the gods' creations. Sometimes it puzzled her; other times it overwhelmed her.

While he might see her as some lovely flower, albeit with razor-sharp thorns, the monks saw a golden opportunity to train with a renowned Kai fighter. Several times now she'd accepted an invitation to spar in the training yard and came away from the bouts exhilarated and sometimes bloodied.

For his part, Serovek spent the hours in conference with the abbot of the order, a man named Tionfa, who'd once been an Ilinfan sword-master. Anhuset's interest in the monks soared, and at her first meeting with the abbot, she commented on his history and the fact that the Ilinfan brotherhood was well known, even among the Kai.

"Do you still fight, Excellency?" she asked. Tionfa was an elderly monk, old enough to be her father or even Serovek's father. She didn't make the mistake of assuming his age made him any less an adept and dangerous fighter.

He smiled at her in a way that told her he predicted what her next question would be. "I still train," he said. "And teach. Before you leave us, I hope to spar with you. I've heard many things from my brothers about your martial skills."

She'd thanked him, offering him a low bow. Much to Serovek's amusement, she'd practically skipped out of the chamber.

"I'm still awake," she told him now, "because the abbot has invited me to train with him in an hour, and I won't miss such an opportunity for the sake of something as silly as sleep."

He made an odd strangled sound, and she glanced at him to discover a fleeting look of dread cross his features. "Promise me you won't accidentally kill the man. He seems a voice of reason, like your ally in Chamtivos's camp. Between them, they may reach a truce and end the fighting in this valley altogether, but they both have to be alive to negotiate."

She snorted. "Either you think me more bloodthirsty than I am or more skilled than I am. Remember, margrave, he was once an Ilinfan swordmaster, and we're only sparring. Maybe you should ask him to show me mercy."

"A swordmaster old enough to be your father." He held up a hand to forestall her argument. "I know age isn't the limitation many foolishly assume. I've seen enough grandfathers wipe the floor with an upstart pup with more brawn than sense. It happened to me when I was younger and had my arse handed to me by a man more than twice my age at the time. But you're a Kai. He'll have a challenge on his hands."

"So will I." Like him, she'd seen an older, more experienced warrior take down a younger, stronger, more foolish one. She looked forward to this sparring session. "You worry for nothing," she said, slipping her hand into his where they were hidden by the folds of their cloaks.

"The monks obviously know we're intimate," he said. "And there's no one else here but us, them, and Erostis who, by the way, recently informed me he'd won a bet with another liegeman regarding our relationship." Her eyebrows snapped together in a scowl. "You're a soldier, Anhuset," he said with a half smile. "You know soldiers wager on anything and everything." Her disapproving "hmpf" only widened his smile. "As I was saying, all here know we're lovers. No one will care or use it against us if I kiss your hand."

That was true, and she surprised him when she lifted their clasped hands and kissed each of his knuckles. His gaze rested on her, a soft, living thing, and caressed her as lovingly as his hands. Those deepwater blue eyes blazed from within, brightened by the fire she'd kindled there. "Or if I kiss yours," she said and winked at him.

She would miss this banter when they left. She couldn't help but wonder what might happen when they parted company and returned to their respective homes. Until now, her lovers had been brief connections without commitment or even interest beyond a night or a week. Anhuset refused to lie to herself. She wanted much more than a week with the margrave of High Salure.

He'd punched through every barrier she put in front of him, broken down every wall. It was hard to remember she once thought him ugly. He still annoyed her at times, usually right before he made her laugh. Her respect for him equaled that which she had for Brishen, a near impossible feat by her standards. He was good company in or out of bed, and the hours she'd spent with him during this journey, and especially in the monastery, had flown by. Never in her life had she imagined she'd fall in love with a brash human with his strange, laughing blue eyes and stout heart. She closed her eyes against the terror of that realization.

A distant thunder rumbled, not above them but below. Serovek's voice held a wary note. "That can't be good."

Anhuset opened her eyes to the sight of a large company of armored cavalry riding toward them, easily numbering a hundred or more. They galloped across the valley's flat expanse, carrying with them a flag sporting a gryphon devouring a snake. The banner of the kingdom of Belawat. She glanced at Serovek. "Why isn't this good?"

"Because a visit from the Beladine army never is. Those are King Rodan's troops, and a company that size isn't here for a social or diplomatic visit."

His response was punctuated by the sound of bells, either rung as a signal or a warning. It was soon followed by running feet as monks raced down the corridor behind them.

He backed away from the balcony. Anhuset followed. They joined the crowd of monks running the length of the hallway to disappear down the stairwells. Some were fully armored, others partially so. All carried weapons. This indeed was not a social visit.

The outer portcullis at the single entry gate to the monastery slammed down with a bang. The inner portcullis followed. Anhuset glimpsed it all as she sped by slotted windows and murder holes on her way to her chamber.

The monks had recovered most of her armament when they dismantled Chamtivos's camp and took his followers prisoner. As many times as she'd donned her gear by herself, she didn't need a squire or page to help her and was soon dressed in full harness with her sword strapped to her hip. Serovek met her in the hallway, likewise attired.

"Why do you think they've come?" she asked.

He shrugged. "Who knows? But relations between the Jeden Order and King Rodan have always been delicate, and Rodan is a mercurial sort. It may well be he woke up one morning recently, decided the Nazim were indeed heretics and sent his army to arrest them."

Disbelief made her sputter. "A hundred men? Trying to arrest a near equal number of fighting monks who can wield magic and are protected in a fortress like this? That doesn't make any sense."

His grim expression turned even grimmer. "No, it doesn't."

Before he could say anything else, the abbot himself came striding toward them, bedecked in armor as well, an arming sword belted on either side of his hips. Anhuset had no doubt his skill with both was unmatched by any of Rodan's soldiers fast approaching the monastery.

He addressed Serovek first. "If they've come for the Order, don't linger. Your horses are waiting in the stables. Someone is saddling them as we speak. There's a rear gate big enough for a pony cart to get through and leads directly into the woods. No one can see it from the path leading to the main gate. You'll be gone before the fighting starts."

"You have our sword arms if you wish them," Serovek said. "We'll stand with you." Anhuset nodded her agreement.

Tionfa's wry smile belied the resolute flatness in his gaze. "You know as well as I do that the margrave of High Salure cannot fight with the Jeden Order against his own king." He turned to Anhuset. "And you are an ambassador for the Khaskem. Joining us would be seen as a declaration of war from Bast-Haradis."

Serovek's shoulders drooped. "I'd hoped you might say something different, but I'm not surprised."

"You knew you'd have to remain neutral."

Serovek nodded. "Allow us to stay long enough to learn what they want."

The abbot nodded. "So be it. Come with me. You can stand out of sight near one of the battlements and hear both parties."

Anhuset stayed next to Serovek as they followed the abbot and a contingent of monks up three flights of stairs and onto the monastery's roof with its high, crenelated walls. The Beladine troops had crossed the bridge and paused outside the gate, their armor and weapons flashing in the bright morning sun. Their commander nudged his horse forward. The creak of wood as bows were drawn sounded loud in the tense silence.

Tionfa kept his profile to the company below as he showed himself at the battlement's edge. He carried a shield to duck behind in case of arrow fire.

"Pray some idiot archer doesn't lose his grip on the string and fire off an arrow," Anhuset muttered to Serovek.

"Now would be a very good time to pray," he replied.

The troop's leader gazed up at Tionfa. "Abbot Tionfa, we haven't come to fight."

"By the look of you, you haven't come to have tea either," Tionfa said. "What business does the Royal Beladine have with the Jeden Order?"

"We come on command of King Rodan for Serovek Pangion, margrave of High Salure." There was a short, gravid pause. "He is under arrest."

Tionfa glanced briefly at Serovek, who'd gone pale and scowling. "On what charge?"

Anhuset's unease exploded into outright fury when the troop captain replied, "Treason against the kingdom. Sedition against the crown."

CHAPTER

FOURTEEN

Serovek heard the words as if from a far distance. Treason. Sedition. Words that were the antithesis of everything that defined his life as a faithful military governor to the Beladine kingdom. He'd never much cared for the wily old king, and he'd exercised his leadership of High Salure in ways His Majesty might not approve, such as his friendship with Brishen Khaskem, but he'd never been disloyal to his country or his king.

"What madness is this?" Anhuset's eyes were like torches, her lips drawn back to expose her teeth as she demanded an explanation.

His thoughts racing, Serovek stared past her and didn't answer.

This was Bryzant's doing. Of that, he had no doubt. His steward, excellent with accounts, was also obviously a fair hand with strategy. He hadn't relied on one plan to get rid of Serovek. He had two. If an upstart warlord with delusions of kingship failed to do it, then a king consumed by paranoia and jealousy just might.

Popularity wasn't a sin unless it bought one the admiration of a kingdom's populace. Then it became a threat, at least to the current ruler. What venom had Bryzant poured into the king's ear to convince him his suspicions were not only founded, but so much worse in truth? Another thought made Serovek's blood run cold. He was currently in a stronghold, just not his, and if a contingent of the king's men had ridden this far to capture him, what was going on at High Salure?

"Say the word," Anhuset continued. Her hand dropped to her sword pommel. "I will fight with you against this idiocy."

This woman, parsimonious with her displays of affection, willingly courted her own death to defend him. A romance unlike any other, he thought with an inner smile. He stroked her arm.

"Ah, firefly woman, how I wish such a situation might be solved with the hard swing of a blade and some bloodletting," he said. "Unfortunately, this isn't one of those times and will require a lot more delicacy if we don't want to start a war on two fronts."

The abbot employed an old but effective tactic of delaying any acknowledgment of the commander's statements, allowing Serovek time to plan what he might do. He shouted over the battlements, "Why would you think the margrave of High Salure is here?"

"Let's not play games, abbot," the troop's leader shouted back. "Half the valley knows he's here, along with a Kai ambassador from Bast-Haradis."

Tionfa glanced at Serovek, one eyebrow raised in question.

"Tell him sha-Anhuset is no longer here. That there was no reason for her to stay once we brought Megiddo safely to you, and she's returned to Bast-Haradis."

"What are you doing?" Anhuset practically hissed the question.

When Tionfa relayed Serovek's words, the troop leader shrugged. "She isn't our first concern. We're here for the margrave. If you don't turn him over to us, we'll simply return with a larger force and take him."

Serovek had expected just such an answer and was ready with one of his own when the abbot said, "What do you wish to do?"

"Give myself up, of course."

This time Anhuset shoved him. "Are you mad, too?" she snapped. "That's an admission of guilt, and you aren't guilty."

He grabbed her shoulders. She was stiffer than a pike stand. "Listen to me. I hoped something like this wouldn't happen, though I'm not surprised it did. This is Bryzant's doing. I know it. A secondary plan in case Chamtivos didn't successfully complete his task. I can explain more later."

Not at all appeased, she lashed out at him. "You say that as if you'll live to do so."

He'd have to step carefully and present his argument posthaste, before she decided he was too much of a dimwit to understand his own dire circumstances and take the decisions out of his hands. He wouldn't put it past her to suddenly pull back and punch him hard enough to knock him unconscious.

"That's certainly my intention." He stroked her arms, speaking urgently. There was only so long the troop's captain would be this patient. "Rodan is a suspicious bastard who sees a threat to the throne in every shadow behind every tree, but he's also clever and a good strategist.

"He has two advantages in play at the moment. I'm away from High Salure, in the territory of a rebel warlord, and enjoying the hospitality of priests many in this kingdom consider heretics. If I remain behind these walls, Rodan will raze my fortress to the ground and arrest those he considers loyal to me. He'll then send a full army to attack the monastery and declare the Nazim heretical." Tionfa's nod and grim face lent strength to his argument. "This valley finally has a chance for peace. It doesn't need another conflict created by a one man's ambitions or, in my case, one man's innocence. I'm no more guilty than you or the abbot here, but if I don't willingly turn myself over to them, the repercussions will be far greater than my arrest. War started, lives unnecessarily lost. And you need to be well away from any of it. You know as well as I do that Rodan has been spoiling for war with Bast-Haradis since King Djedor signed that trade agreement with the Gauri."

"Abbot," the captain bellowed from below, "I don't have all day. Give us the margrave."

Serovek jerked Anhuset in his arms and kissed her scowling mouth. She returned the kiss just as hard and was still scowling when he let her go. He joined Tionfa at the battlements, leaning out so those below could clearly see him. Anhuset's expletive-rich snarls about staying out of arrow range singed his ears. "Keep your boots on, man. I was just fetched from my bed. I'm coming down now."

He retreated from the wall along with Tionfa and discovered Anhuset nearly standing on his heels.

"What do you want me to do?" she said.

I want you to become my wife and share my bed for the rest of our lives. Instead he gestured to the abbot. "Follow Tionfa's first suggestion. Use the back gate. Take Erostis with you. If Rodan's man asks, I'll say he didn't survive his wounds and his body was burned. Return to Saggara on Magas." He'd turn himself over to his captors without struggle. Magas, though, was his and his only. "Rodan has always coveted him. He's out of a mare from Nadiza's lightning herd. The king doesn't get my stallion as a bonus."

"He shouldn't be getting *my* stallion either." She glared at him as if he were the one who instigated all of this.

A euphoric swoop of joy at her words bottomed out his stomach. He considered pulling her into his arms a second time but as that glare turned even hotter, he thought better of it. "So I'm yours now?"

Before she could blister his ears about the poor timing of his teasing, Tionfa interrupted, motioning to the hall where his escort waited. "Margrave."

He and Anhuset followed them down the stairwell. They'd split off from each other at the bottom. "Tell Brishen to keep an eye on his borders and a tight net on any Kai raiders trying to cause trouble on the Beladine side," he instructed her. "Rodan is just looking for an excuse."

"And I'm just to forget about you being led off in shackles to face a traitor's fate?"

He wouldn't pay her the insult of patronizing her by saying all would be well. No one could predict such a thing. "That honeyed tongue you said I had? Not only useful in seducing a prickly Kai woman. The king knows my value to him. I'll talk my way out of this one."

"You are far too sure of yourself sometimes," she said as they reached the last step and this time it was she who grasped his arms as if trying to resist temptation and hold him prisoner herself.

He kissed her forehead and the frown there. When he pulled back, he smiled. "Maybe, but here you are in my arms, so I must be doing things the right way."

Their goodbye kiss was as swift and intense as the one on the battlements. Serovek set her from him and stepped out of her reach. "Go. If I were the captain of that troop, I'd send men to scout the surrounding area just to see what might be found. Fetch Erostis and get out of here quickly. Don't be found."

She nodded and bolted down the hall leading to the stairwell that would take them to the wing of the monastery where guests were housed. Another pair took off for the stables at the abbot's instructions. If Magas and Anhuset's horse were already saddled, she and Erostis would be galloping away from the monastery before Rodan's men could clap Serovek in irons.

Tionfa stayed beside Serovek as they crossed the bailey toward the gate with its double portcullises. Serovek unbuckled his sword and some of his armor, handing it to the abbot. "Will you keep these for me until I can return for them?"

Tionfa nodded. "Or send them to whomever you choose."

They both paused not far from the inner portcullis. Serovek bowed to Tionfa. "I and the Khaskem owe you much for keeping Megiddo safe until we can find a way to unite his soul with his body, and I personally am in your and your brothers' debt for saving me, Erostis, and sha-Anhuset. And for trying to save Klanek."

The other man returned the bow. "The world is a better place with the brave and compassionate in it, margrave. We hope you all walk this fair earth for many years to come." He glanced at the Beladine contingent waiting on the other side of the gates and lowered his voice. "Should you ever decide to take the throne, I think you'd find more support than you realize. The Beladine kingdom would thrive under your rule."

Serovek darted a glance at his waiting escort and spoke just as softly. "Don't say that too loud, abbot, or you'll be joining me on the journey to Timsiora, wearing a handsome pair of shackles of your own. Besides, I've no interest in such a thankless duty. Kings who were once free soldiers become prisoners of diplomacy and administration. That is a slow death."

Tionfa accompanied him to the inner portcullis and gave the signal to have it raised, then lowered again once Serovek walked under it to stand before the outer portcullis. He nodded once to the waiting troop commander, who nodded back in recognition of a peaceful surrender of a prisoner. Serovek didn't look back when the outer portcullis struck the ground with a bang and rattle of chains.

Two more soldiers joined their leader, each one reining their mounts on either side of him. One led another saddled horse behind him. The commander dismounted to meet Serovek halfway. He saluted, surprising Serovek with the gesture of respect. "Lord Pangion," he said. "I'm Captain Ratik. I served at High Salure for a season when I first joined the army."

A young captain, maybe a dozen years Serovek's junior with a familiar face under his helmet. He searched his memory for a green recruit newly arrived at High Salure and found what he was looking for. "I remember you. Your sister married Lord Canotkin's youngest son."

Ratik cracked a smile until he remembered his duty and whom he addressed. "She did," he said in a solemn voice. "Very good memory, my lord."

One of the things Serovek had learned early in his years as a military leader was the importance of remembering faces, names, and some small personal detail tied to them. These were men who rode into battle together, sometimes died together, and defended each other. They followed the orders of a superior, most of the time unquestioning, and to Serovek's way of thinking they deserved some recognition from that superior that they were more than just a sword or a spear or blood to be spilled in pursuit of an objective. That philosophy had earned him a fierce loyalty among the men who served High Salure. His thoughts turned briefly to the treacherous Ogran. There were exceptions.

At Ratik's gesture, the soldier holding the irons came forward and stopped when Ratik held up his hand a second time. "Give them to me." Once he held them, he stared at Serovek with a resolute expression, as if he was about to do something unpleasant or against a personal code. "Will I need these?"

Serovek had no intention of trying to escape. There was much more at stake here than his freedom. If that's all it was, he would have sneaked out with Anhuset and Erostis. But the manacles were more than just devices of restraint, they were a symbol, and he had no doubt Rodan expected him to ride to the capital and be presented to his king wearing them. "Probably," he said.

The captain sighed, nodded, and clapped the manacles on his wrists. "You understand my opinion of this means nothing. I'm doing my duty."

"As a Beladine margrave, I expect no less from any Beladine soldier."

Once he was mounted on the borrowed horse, the troop turned as one and galloped back the way they came. Serovek glanced over his shoulder to see Tionfa once more on the battlements, a hand raised in farewell.

Their journey to the capital took four days through mountainous terrain and paths still knee-deep in snow in places. Serovek calculated their travel time against his trek to the Jeden Order and guessed his perfidious steward had sent a message to the king before Serovek was barely past the gates of High Salure. He'd hedged his bets on getting rid of his liege through a murder pact with Chamtivos, and if Serovek survived, then he'd exploit the king's suspicions about Serovek and turn Rodan against him. He hoped once they reached Timsiora, he'd find Bryzant there so he could kill him.

Unlike his imprisonment under Chamtivos, his only hardships

were the annoying manacles, the watchful eyes of his escorts at all times of the day and night, and a horse whose trot threatened to shake his teeth loose no matter how much he adjusted his seat to the animal's gait. Ratik and his troops were respectful to him the entire time, some even deferential. He ate what they ate and slept on the ground as they did, huddled in blankets. Sometimes he slept; other times he stared up at the night sky, worried for Anhuset and Erostis, worried about those at High Salure. Had Rodan sent more of his army to wrest control of the fortress from the High Salure troop? Gods forbid there had been any fighting. He prayed not. His reason told him he didn't have to fear for Anhuset or Erostis. Neither was a wilting flower. Still, he hoped they'd made it to Saggara without mishap and Magas with them.

They reached Timsiora at midday when the streets were packed with foot traffic as well as carts and other assorted livestock. The crowds parted for Ratik and his men, and several people who watched them as they passed exclaimed in shock, and even outrage at the sight of Lord Pangion, margrave of High Salure, hero in the *galla* war, once a Wraith king, manacled and escorted as a prisoner to the palace.

"I don't believe it," he overheard one man say. "I hear his fortress is finer than the royal palace."

"I believe it," another said. "Why stop at governor when you can become king?"

Serovek winced inside at the reactions. This would only make things worse for him. No doubt there was a spy at every corner who'd report back to the king about the crowd's response and fuel Rodan's belief that he had a potential usurper on his hands.

Ratik turned him over to a troop of palace guards. He and his men all bowed from their saddles and saluted. Ratik even offered a sign that Serovek recognized as a blessing of the creator god Yalda. "May the sun not abandon you to darkness, Lord Pangion. Good luck."

Serovek nodded his thanks and followed his new escort into the palace itself. More stares and surprised exclamations, frantic whispers from courtiers lingering in the various corridors to gossip and plot or hope for an audience with the king. By the time he was led to Rodan's audience hall, he was certain the entire royal court was behind them.

The doors closed on their curious faces and Serovek strode toward the throne on its high dais at the chamber's other end. An old man perched upon the chair, gaze sharp as a raptor's and just as predatory. He didn't blink the entire time Serovek closed the distance between them or when he genuflected before the throne.

"Your Majesty," he said

King Rodan reclined in his seat, one finger tapping the side of his cheek as he regarded Serovek silently for several moments. "So, the traitor has returned," he finally said. "I'm told you didn't try to escape." Once more a prolonged quiet. Serovek knew better than to speak without invitation. "Have you nothing to say, Pangion?"

"I'm innocent of the charges of both treason and sedition, Your Majesty," he said, knowing such a simple defense would have no bearing on the king. "I have no reason to escape."

Rodan reached for something on the small table next to the throne. A square of parchment with a wax seal broken open to show whatever the parchment contained, it had been read. "That isn't what this missive from your steward says," he said. "Shall I read it to you?"

If he were honest, stupid, and suicidal, Serovek would have told him not to bother. He could guess at what pile of horse manure had been written there. "I would appreciate it, Your Majesty."

Rodan moved the parchment away from him as far as his arm would stretch and cocked his head back so he could read. "I fear his lordship has changed, and not for the better, since his return from his battle with the *galla*. His time as a Wraith king has altered his view of his own role as a margrave who serves the will of Your Majesty, especially since his popularity has grown and expanded far beyond High Salure. I write to tell you that he is now en route to the Lobak valley, ostensibly to return the body of the monk Megiddo Cermak to the Jeden Order. I believe, however, based on an informant's knowledge, he is meeting with the warlord Chamtivos. All in the Beladine kingdom know of this insurgent and his desire to wrest the lands from the Nazim despite Your Majesty's decree that the valley belongs to them. Two such men, with military knowledge and the leadership prowess that persuades other men to follow them, would be a force to reckon with should they decide to form an alliance. You may also find it of interest that a high-ranking ambassador of Bast-Haradis has accompanied Lord Pangion on this trip, though there is no reason why such a representative of the Kai kingdom is needed."

When he was done, he refolded the missive and dropped it back on the table. "There's more, mostly groveling praise of little consequence. I won't bother reading that part. I've known you long enough, Pangion, to know you have no more patience for that sort of thing than I do. But what your steward says here." He tapped the missive with a fingertip. "And the information he has paints a grim picture of a man with aspirations that are… problematic to say the least. What do you say to all of this?"

I'd say you're a blind fool for believing the words of an upstart steward with ambitions far beyond his capabilities instead of looking at years of unswerving loyalty. Instead, Serovek replied with "You're correct, Your Majesty. You've known me a long time, and in that time, I've served your interests faithfully, kept your borders secured and the kingdom of Belawat safe from man and demon alike. My steward's *concerned* message consists of crumbs of truth wrapped in a layer of lies, a toxic cake with no substance except its poison."

He proceeded to relay the events of the trip from the time Anhuset arrived at High Salure to when Ratik arrived with his troop, leaving out the parts about his intimacy with the Kai woman and changing the story line from Anhuset standing next to him on the battlements to her leaving for Saggara the moment they put Megiddo into the monks' safekeeping. He wanted to leave out the part where they visited Haradis, but suspected Ogran or Bryzant had already relayed that information to whatever go-between messenger they used to relay information to the king.

Rodan's harsh features didn't change through the narrative or when it ended, nor did his raptor gaze turn friendly. "What happened to your horse?"

The question confirmed for Serovek the wisdom of having Anhuset ride Magas to Saggara. He adopted a pained expression. "Lost in Chamtivos's raid on us. I didn't recover him, nor did the Nazim."

A flicker of disappointment caught in Rodan's eyes. "A loss. He was a magnificent animal."

And one that will never be yours, Serovek thought. *Even if I don't survive this ludicrous circumstance.*

He bowed his head in a supplicating gesture. "May I speak more, Your Highness?" The action must have appealed to the king, for he nodded. "If you want absolute proof that my journey to the Jeden Order wasn't to open negotiations for an alliance with Chamtivos, then bring one of the monks to Timsiora to witness in my defense, or better yet, have them bring Chamtivos's head with them. I was the one who took it off his body. I'm content in my role as margrave. I visit the capital only upon your summons, not because I'm enamored with court and its trappings. Belawat already has a king who rules the kingdom with a deft hand."

"So does High Salure," Rodan replied in a voice gone icy. "All you lack is a crown, and I find it hard to believe that a man of your standing with a powerful and loyal army of your own might remain content to govern a backwater. Especially one so far from the seat of real power. You understand if I'm convinced of your treachery, you will be executed for your crimes."

"I do." It wasn't Bryzant's letter and machinations he'd have to conquer, but the king's own perceptions of his influence and his ambitions. They, more than some falsely histrionic letter from an unimportant steward, would determine his fate.

Rodan motioned to something behind Serovek, and the rhythmic march of boots grew louder as they neared. Serovek tensed but remained kneeling. "I'll speak to other witnesses over the next few days," the king said. "I may even wait a little longer with my decision and do as you suggested, summon a Nazim monk or two and have them bring Chamtivos's head. Until then, you are a prisoner of the crown." He gestured again, and this time the guards behind Serovek hauled him to his feet. "Take him to the Zela. Prison accommodations won't be as fine as those in the palace guest wing, but you're a soldier. You've quartered in worse."

Dismissed without further word, Serovek was escorted from the audience room and greeted by a sea of curious onlookers. This, he thought, would be his fate if he ever wanted to take the throne. Every door opening to a mob like this. He didn't know which was worse, the cell waiting for him in the Zela because the king considered him a traitor, or the cell constructed by the very nature of the kingship he didn't seek. In that moment, and for the first time, he truly pitied Brishen Khaskem.

CHAPTER
FIFTEEN

Anhuset was afraid she'd have to sling Erostis over her shoulders the way she had done with Serovek on the island, but he managed to keep up with her as they raced behind the monk leading them to the stables. There they found Magas and the horse she'd ridden on their journey saddled and ready. With only a wince and a short expletive, Erostis swung into the saddle on Anhuset's gelding and guided it into the stable yard, leaving Anhuset and Magas to eye each other.

"Now isn't the time to play the spoiled princess, Magas," she said. "I'd leave you behind for convenience's sake and take a more agreeable horse, but your master has asked me to do otherwise. Don't make me regret agreeing to his request."

Whether it was the tone of her voice or even if the stallion actually understood what she said, Anhuset could only guess, but Magas snorted once and stepped forward of his own accord to wait for her to mount, docile as a sheep. Anhuset swung into the saddle and followed Erostis into the stableyard.

The monk who led them there stood closest to Erostis. "Have you heard of the old trader way?"

She shook her head, but Erostis nodded. "I have. All the caravans used it before they built the bridges across the river to reach the valley. It takes twice as long to get anywhere." His scowl matched Anhuset's.

"Only if you're pulling a wagon," the monk argued. "Go that way. You won't cross Rodan's troops. They came here from the main route and will return that way to head north for the better mountain passes."

That was good enough for Anhuset. "Let's go."

The back gate the abbot described was actually a tunnel carved through the hillside into which the monastery was built. It looked even older and more mysterious than the monastery itself, its rock walls lit from within by an unknown luminescence. Strange murals and sigils decorated its ceiling. Whoever had carved out the tunnel expected a great deal of traffic to pass through it at one time. The passage was wide and the ceiling high, with a dry floor on which the horses' hooves clopped dully with every step. It went farther than she anticipated, and they moved slower than she wanted, but they dare not risk laming a horse that had lost its footing on the rock floor. A sheer wall greeted them at the tunnel's end. If not for the faint draft and scent of outside air reaching her nostrils, Anhuset would have thought it was a dead end. They turned almost at the wall, discovering a natural cave with a short ascent onto flat ground.

"How is it no one's discovered this entrance?" Erostis wondered aloud.

He had his answer as soon as his horse set down the first hoof onto the cave's wetter, more uneven floor. A visible ripple of air stirred around him as if he and the gelding had parted a veil and stepped through. From Anhuset's vantage point in the back, they disappeared only to reappear on the other side of the shifting curtain. Magic, she thought. Either the monks' or the Elder race's.

She coaxed Magas through after Erostis, skin prickling with the otherness passing over and around her. Her soul clenched for a moment, grieving the loss of her own meager magic. This sorcery didn't belong to the human monks. It was far older, definitely Elder, much like the remnants the Kai once possessed.

Erostis had paused to watch her pass through the invisible wall.

"Look behind you," he said. She did, staring at what appeared to any who might glance inside or even explore the cave, a wall of ghastly looking vines the color of boiled intestines covered in formidable thorns and twining so thick around each other, they presented an impenetrable barrier to the viewer. "I wouldn't go near that if I'd stepped in here for some shade or shelter from the rain," he said.

Curious, she reached out to touch one of the vines, expecting her hand to pass through. Instead, the vine's solid mass quivered under her fingers, cold and damp. Even stranger, the thorns closest to her hand extended, like those of a cat's claws. The tip of one grazed the knuckle on her forefinger, drawing blood. "A powerful illusion," she told Erostis, and held up her finger. He whistled and backed the gelding farther away from the wall.

They left the cave, entering directly into the woodland Tionfa had described. The trees grew so tall and close together, they blocked out much of the sun, leaving a stunted undergrowth of lichen and mushrooms to thrive in the encompassing shade and damp. Bars of sunlight still managed to get through, but Anhuset didn't have to raise her cloak to protect her eyes, even with the late morning light pouring down bright and blinding on the treetops.

"We need to find a clearing," she said, "so we know where the sun sits and can find our way out of here."

They rode for several moments before finding a place where an ancient oak had finally succumbed to rot and toppled, taking some of the surrounding smaller trees with it. Its demise and fall had created an oblique pathway of light that pierced the woodland's tenebrous world. Anhuset let Erostis stand in its brilliance and look up, his hand at his eyebrows to shield his eyes. "We head that direction," he told her, pointing north and into an even more shadowed part of the wood.

They rode most of the day through the forest, emerging from the trees at sunset onto a road rutted deep and overgrown with grass. "Do you recognize any of this?" Anhuset asked her companion.

Erostis stood up in the stirrups to survey their surroundings, and to her relief, gave a certain nod. "Yes. If we keep to a steady trot, we'll reach a spot where the road splits into two. One leads to High Salure, the other curves west toward Saggara."

If the road wasn't in such poor shape, she would have urged Magas into a full gallop to eat up the distance and shorten the time it took to reach Saggara. Her patience had worn thin as they'd picked their way through the wood, every moment spent there punctuated by the memory of Serovek's face when he told her and Tionfa that he intended to turn himself over to Rodan's troops without a fight—grim, resolute and worst of all, accepting of the possibility of a death he didn't deserve for crimes he didn't commit. She admired his nobility and still wanted to punch him for it.

That mocking inner voice spoke up once more to vex her. *You're afraid.*

"Of course I'm afraid," she muttered under her breath, but fear had never slowed her down, much less stopped her. It was only a weakness if one allowed it to lead instead of follow, and the only two things Anhuset followed were her reason and Brishen Khaskem. Gods be damned if she was going to race to Saggara only to wait there, pacing a trench into the floor wondering what was happening to Serovek. She set a faster pace for Magas, and Erostis matched her, taking his horse on the other side of the path where the grass had rooted and the ground beneath was more level than that rutted by countless wheels.

Erostis predicted correctly and they reached the split in the road close to nightfall. Anhuset pulled back her hood, no longer plagued by the bright light of day. Erostis nodded in the direction of Saggara. "Methinks we'll part company here, sha-Anhuset."

She wasn't surprised by his announcement. If he were still in poor shape from his injuries, she'd insist on him returning with her, but he looked none the worse for their journey except for a bit of stiffness in the way he held one shoulder. Still, she'd offer him the option of accompanying her if he wished. "The margrave wanted you to travel with me. If Bryzant is in control of High Salure or even acting the puppet to another controlling it for your king, you'll be imprisoned if caught. Or killed."

He shrugged. "I'll take the risk. I'm more useful to his lordship there, and I can help without going anywhere near the fortress itself. I know enough people in the surrounding villages who'll help and feed information to me. I can even send someone to Saggara with news if you wish it, and no one at High Salure will know."

It was a good idea and one she embraced. She tossed him the pack, weighted with a supply of road rations. "Take this."

He caught it neatly in his arms. "What about you?"

"I'm not the one still convalescing and getting my strength back. You need it more than I do, and I can hunt." She offered him the Kai salute. "Good luck to us both."

He returned it with a Beladine one. "Sha-Anhuset, it has been a privilege to travel and fight alongside you."

With a last wave, he turned the gelding and continued down the path that would eventually take him to High Salure and its surrounding territories. Her vision sharpened with the falling light. The less traveled path she took leveled out, and she put Magas back into a steady canter, feeling the earth beneath them gently descend toward the distant plain below.

The days it took to reach Saggara stretched for eternity, though her reason told her she made good time. She rested Magas when necessary, foraged or hunted only when her belly tried to gnaw its way to her backbone, and dozed for no more than an hour or two during the day, resolutely shoving back the memories of her time with the margrave at the monastery and the worries that plagued her now over his fate.

By her best guess, she was a day out from Saggara when she spotted a lone rider taking one of the roads that led to the ferry Serovek's original party had used to get them down the Absu. She recognized the rider's posture and as they rode closer to where she watched, half hidden by an outcropping of rock and trees, she recognized the rider himself. Ogran.

"You murdering piece of shit," she said through clenched teeth. Cold fury washed over her.

Her claws bit into her palms with the urge to split the lying, betraying bastard from gullet to bollocks. She had no doubt he'd turned on his unwary traveling companions the instant they were out of Serovek's sight, killing them without hesitation. The gods only knew where he'd tossed their corpses.

Had he returned to the valley to ascertain the fate of the rest of Serovek's party and report back to Bryzant? Anhuset smiled thinly. His unfortunate comrades wouldn't be the only ones never to reach their destination.

In no hurry, he kept a leisurely pace on the road. Anhuset eased Magas back into the trees before dismounting and tying his reins to a low branch. She'd cover more ground and make less noise on foot. Keeping parallel to the road, she raced through the forest, descending the slope so that by the time she was even with the road, she was ahead of her prey, waiting.

She hurtled out of the concealing tree line so fast Ogran only had time to jerk in the saddle and grunt before she leaped on him, her weight and momentum throwing him clear of the horse to land on his back with Anhuset atop him. The horse bolted, leaving its stunned rider behind.

Ogran howled when she struck him, breaking his nose. Blood spurted from his nostrils, and she shoved his arms down when he grabbed for his face, pinning both under her knees. "Who paid you to betray the margrave, maggot?" Anhuset knew the answer, but she wanted to hear him say it.

He struggled under her, glaring and spitting expletives at her. She grabbed his head by his ears and slammed it back into the dirt, hard enough to make him see stars but not enough to crack his skull. His breathing turned to gurgling gasps when she laid her palm against his throat and pressed just enough to feel his larynx spasm. "I will break every bone in your body, one by one, Ogran, and then I will gut you like a fish if you don't answer me. Who paid you?" She wanted to hear him say it so she could force-feed the words back to him.

"Bryzant," he finally said on a wheezy gasp. "High Salure's steward."

Anhuset lifted her palm, and Ogran inhaled a deep breath. Even bloodied and pinned with a vision of Death looming over him, he still glared at her. While she couldn't always read emotion in the bizarre movement and coloration of human eyes, she recognized hatred when she saw it. "Figures you'd manage to survive, you yellow-eyed hedge whore," he spat.

If he thought to offend her with vulgar disparagement, he was sadly mistaken. She'd played drinking games with her fellow Kai soldiers that centered around the exchange of creative insults that would set his ears on fire. "Worse luck for you, isn't it, maggot?" she said. "What did you do with the bodies of the men you killed?" She didn't bother asking *if* he killed the other three Serovek sent with him. She knew he did. She struck him across one cheek. "Weson?" A second strike on the opposite cheek as he spewed even more invectives. "Ardwin?" A third strike. "Jannir?" She raised her hand, threatening a fourth.

"Enough!" he shouted, cheeks stained scarlet from her blows. "I'll take you to them if you promise not to kill me and get off me."

Liar, she thought.

She stood up, stepping out of the range of a swinging fist or kick. He scrambled to his feet, and she waited to see if he'd try to run. He didn't, and that told her what she needed to know. "Who's the closest and where did you leave him?" she asked. The question simply bought time. She was saddened and angered to have her supposition about the fate of the three men verified, but she couldn't recover their bodies, not now, even if Ogran had actually told her the truth.

His lip curled into a sneer. "Weson," he said. "We teamed up together." He pointed down the road where his horse had bolted. "Another two leagues that way. I left him in the trees."

After all this time there probably wasn't much left of Weson thanks to the elements and scavengers, but Anhuset pretended to consider. "My horse isn't far," she said. "I ride there; you walk ahead of me." She deliberately turned her back to him, ears perked as she put four steps between them and quietly pulled one of her knives from its sheath. Ogran was right-handed, like everyone in their earlier party except Erostis. She'd noted those details for each man, knowledge that always came in handy whether or not you fought with a comrade-in-arms or an adversary.

The warning sound came as she expected, the soft hiss of steel sliding against leather, the shift of dirt under a boot with a step forward. She twisted fast to the side, caught the twinkle of a blade as it flew past her and flung her own weapon in an underhanded throw that took Ogran in the belly hard enough to knock him off his feet. He lay on his back, hand gripped around the knife's pommel, the blade sunk to the hilt. Blood trickled out of his mouth as he stared first at the knife and then at her in disbelief.

Anhuset felt no pity for him. No doubt he'd dispatched his trusting companions in just this way. She crouched beside him and stared into his rattish face, his once-ruddy complexion turning pale. "It takes a long time to die from a gut wound," she told him. His eyes widened. "And I want my knife back." She wrapped her hand around the pommel and yanked hard. The blade slid free with a jerk and a gout of blood. Ogran tried to scream, but Anhuset cut off the attempt with a quick swipe of the bloodied knife across his throat. He was dead before his head hit the dirt.

She dragged his body off the road and out of sight, wedging it against a pair of young saplings so it wouldn't roll. The forest scavengers would pick his bones clean in no time. In her opinion, he didn't deserve a burial any more than the men he'd killed deserved their deaths. She stripped him of the money he carried. If any of the three he'd murdered had families, they could use the coin, and if fate were kind, she'd have a chance to return it to Serovek to give to them. She also recovered the knife Ogran had thrown where it lay in the road and returned to Magas waiting patiently where she'd tied him.

A more peaceful person might say her killing Ogran wouldn't bring back the men he killed or save Serovek from an execution, but in her mind, it was justice, and if circumstance had seen fit to let her deal that justice, so be it. She hoped the same might happen with Serovek's steward Bryzant.

She reached Saggara a day and a half later, tired, filthy, and ready to switch an equally tired Magas for a fresh mount so she could ride to the Beladine capital after relaying her news to Brishen. She galloped through the gates of the redoubt and had barely reined the big stallion to a halt before she was out of the saddle and striding toward the doors of the expansive manor house that had once been the long-ago summer palace of Kai royalty. She spotted Brishen's steward, Mesumenes, as he emerged into the main bailey from the manor. His eyes rounded when he spotted her. "Where's the *herceges*, steward?"

She handed Magas's reins to a nearby soldier. "Take him to the stables. Have the stablemaster give him the best care." She patted the stallion's neck before he was led away. "Good horse," she said. The horse rolled an eye at her as if to say he was indifferent to her good opinion, then followed the soldier to the stables.

Mesumenes had disappeared back into the manor. Anhuset strode after him, only to be greeted at the threshold by Brishen, who burst through the doors and swooped her into his arms.

"Lover of thorns," he said into her hair, squeezing her until she gasped. "I was about to send all of Saggara out looking for you."

She briefly returned his embrace, noting the pinched worry lines around his mouth. "I'm fine. There's much to tell and messages to give, but I have to make it fast. Serovek needs my help. As soon as I give you my news, I'll ride from here with rations and a fresh horse to Timsiora and..."

"Sha-Anhuset." Brishen's voice was calm but implacable, addressing her as his *sha* instantly focusing her attention back to him. His features softened. "Enough." He squeezed her arm. "Enough. Come with me." He nudged her toward the door, inviting her inside.

She exhaled a frustrated sigh, entering the house at his side. "*Herceges*, I mean no disrespect, but I don't have time for friendly chatting."

"But you will make time to plan instead of racing off with no idea in mind as to how you'll break Serovek out of a Beladine prison for treason and sedition."

She halted, caught by surprise. "You know."

Brishen nodded. "A messenger from High Salure managed to sneak out of the fortress and ride to Saggara. Rodan sent troops to arrest Serovek at the monastery. High Salure is currently under the command of one of King Rodan's military advisers. The messenger told me it was seized by royal troops and will be held until Rodan decides what to do with Serovek."

Her anger at the injustice of Serovek's predicament had simmered in her blood from the moment the troop captain had announced the charges. It heated to a boil now. "He's innocent of both charges. His fucking steward tried to have him killed by a warlord and now by his own king. The warlord himself admitted it as did the steward's henchman, before I cut his throat and left his corpse to the crows."

Brishen's eyebrows rose. He gestured for her to keep up with him as they made their way through the busy great hall to one of the more private chambers he used for meetings and set in a short wing of the house. "When we aren't trying to figure out how to help our friend, you'll tell me that story."

He ushered her inside one of the rooms—familiar to her and one she disliked. It was in this room they and the Elsod had hatched a plan to defeat the *galla* and change the Kai nation forever. Brishen was closing the door when a bright-haired figure darted inside.

Ildiko blew a strand of hair from her face and tucked it behind her ear. "You found her! Thank the gods."

Anhuset bowed. "*Hercegesé.*" It was an odd thing to hear the relief in Ildiko's voice. She and Anhuset got along well enough, and Anhuset's admiration for Brishen's ugly human wife grew a little more each day. She was a worthy consort to the regent and devoted mother to a child not her own.

Ildiko didn't try to embrace her as Brishen had, but she smiled a wide, square-toothed smile. "I think the worry took a decade off Brishen's life."

"I assure you that was never my intention," Anhuset said.

Brishen leaned against the closed door and crossed his arms. "Since we're obviously pressed for time, tell me what happened, and we'll go from there."

She didn't waste a moment recounting their journey to the monastery, starting first with what she knew would displease him—their side trip to Haradis. Brishen's expression, usually mild, turned harsh, every angle sharpening with his growing scowl, especially when she told him of the *galla* still lurking behind the walls and how she believed it had been a manifestation of Megiddo that had saved them. Anhuset glanced at Ildiko. The *hercegesé* didn't scowl as her husband did, but her face was even paler than when she first rushed into the room.

"Serovek should have never brought you there," Brishen said, voice flat. Angry. "And neither one of you should have gone into that cursed place."

"The decision was mine, Brishen. I would have gone alone if he refused to accompany me." Anhuset lifted her palms in a supplicating gesture. "I know why you refuse to revisit Haradis or allow others to do so. I understand. Truly. But had I not done so, we wouldn't have known about the canals dug or the fact there was a *galla* trapped in there. Maybe more." Saying that sent a shiver through her, and Ildiko hugged herself as if warding off the cold.

Brishen's expression only hardened even more. "Be that as it may, I am ordering you as your regent and your commander to stay away from Haradis. You will not go back there without my express permission. Is that understood?"

Mild-mannered and jovial most of the time, though less so since the *galla*'s ravages, Brishen angered was a formidable sight to behold. The few times Anhuset had seen him like this, he'd reminded her of both his parents. Ruthless, implacable, dangerous to cross. She bowed. "Yes, *herceges*."

"Continue," he said, and his voice was no longer as chilly as before.

She told him of the bridge that shouldn't be there and the haunted city with its phantasmal queen and her entourage of ghosts, of

Bryzant's and Ogran's betrayal of Serovek, of Chamtivos and their ordeal in the camp as well as the fight on the island and the monks' arrival there.

Brishen raised a hand to halt her narrative. The yellow of his eye flickered from dark to light with the change of his emotions. Swirling ribbons of fear laced with shock and, worse, guilt. "Are you all right?" That one-eyed gaze passed over her slowly, looking for signs of injury.

Anhuset nodded, quick to quash any notion that she blamed him in some way for Chamtivos's actions. "I've been in worse shape coming back from patrol. The Nazim monks are good fighters, even better healers, and impressive sorcerers." She winced inwardly at the note of envy she couldn't hide when she said the last and winced again at the faint sadness in Brishen's face. "The Beladine king would do well to keep them as allies instead of proclaiming them heretics and turning them into enemies."

She finished with a retelling of the royal troop's arrival and her and Erostis's flight. She kept her encounter with Ogran even briefer. He didn't deserve her time or Brishen's ear.

She said nothing at all about the halcyon days at the monastery while Serovek recovered—in her arms, in his bed.

Brishen gave a low whistle. "After all of that, it's hard to believe you and the others managed to get Megiddo safely to his brothers."

Anhuset recalled Serovek's dreams, the ethereal blue light in his gaze just like the one she'd seen in Brishen's. The same light that some-times flared around Megiddo's bier. There was no better time than now, with Ildiko present, and the three of them alone in this chamber where others couldn't hear.

"*Herceges*," she said, and saw him stiffen at the tone in her voice. "You should know that while I traveled with the margrave, I witnessed more than once what looked like remnants of Kai magic on him." Ildiko's short gasp sounded beside her. "He dreamed of Megiddo, but it was more than a dream. A vision was more like it, of the monk tortured in some cursed place swarming with *galla*. I woke him from one such dream, and when he opened his eyes, they glowed with the blue light of Elder magic. Megiddo's bier glowed the same way at the time." She paused as Brishen's skin turned the lackluster shade of fireplace ash. "The margrave told me he's had such dreams since returning home from fighting the *galla* and says they're worse, stronger, sharper, and more numerous when he's in close proximity to the monk's body."

"Brishen," Ildiko said softly. He held up a finger to stop her from saying anything else, making Anhuset wonder if the *hercegesé* had finally confronted her husband about his own visions and the azure glow in his eye.

"We'll attend to that later," he said. "For now, Serovek has more to worry about than visions of Megiddo. The messenger who came here said while there's a military adviser controlling High Salure for now, this Bryzant you mentioned has left High Salure to speak with the king at Timsiora, no doubt to argue for a sentence of guilt and the punishment of death for his erstwhile lord."

Anhuset growled. "That treacherous pus bucket wants High Salure for himself or a reward of equal value from the king. He set all of this in motion the moment Serovek left for the monastery. I'm going to kill that bastard just like I did his minion." She caught Brishen's half smile. "It isn't funny, Brishen," she snapped. "I've given my report. I need a horse and supplies so I can ride out again. I don't have time for more talk." Her reason told her such recklessness would do no one any good, but her emotions ran high and hot at the moment, verging on an uncharacteristic panic that also made her waspish.

"Make time," he replied, undaunted by her anger. "By the look of you, you haven't slept or eaten for a couple of days, have half the forest stuck in your hair, and you smell worse than a bog. You want to help the margrave? Start with a bath and some food." It was his turn to offer a placating gesture at her glare. "If you march into King Rodan's court demanding an audience or worse, that Serovek be set free, it's a certainty they'll execute him. He's highborn and high-ranking. He'll be granted a trial and the right to rebut his accusers."

"A mock court and a mockery of justice." She paced in front of Brishen.

"Guaranteed, but a trial, even the sham of one, buys more time. Give me the chance to remind myself of the details of Beladine justice and form a plan. He's my friend too. Use the time to map your best and fastest route to Timsiora. If you want an escort, take whomever you think will benefit you best."

"That would be you," she said, already knowing his answer and knowing too she'd make the journey to Timsiora alone.

His eyelid slid down, covering his eye while the one over his empty eye socket fluttered. He opened his eye once more to study her, such fondness in his features that it made her heart ache for this prince of no value who had saved a world. "I only wish I could," he said. "But we both know that isn't possible."

Ildiko, only an observer and listener during their time in the room, finally spoke. She brushed Anhuset's elbow with her fingers. "Come with me," she said. "I already sent Mesumenes to find someone to prepare a room for you and bring up food, drink, and water for a bath." Her nose wrinkled to emphasize the need for the third.

"I can just go to the barracks," Anhuset said. She was always more comfortable there than here with its echo of ancient royal Kai splendor, a splendor not for her.

"I think not," Ildiko replied, and her voice had taken on the same resolute tone her husband's had only moments earlier.

Brishen chuckled. "Go on, cousin. You won't win."

"Hold that thought for when I return, husband," Ildiko said to him, and the grim promise in her reply chased his half smile away.

The two women were halfway to the room reserved for her when Anhuset said, "You're going to confront him about his own visions and the light flare of sorcery you've seen with him, aren't you?"

Ildiko nodded. "Count on it. You did me a favor by describing Serovek's own experiences. If you'd told Brishen in confidence, he might not have told me, afraid I'd worry."

"But you're already worried."

"Such is the reasoning of men, Anhuset," she said and rolled her eyes, making Anhuset take a step back.

She soon followed Ildiko into one of the spacious chambers usually reserved for guests at Saggara. True to her word, food, a pitcher of wine and a hip bath filled with steaming water awaited her. Towels and soap were stacked on a chair next to the bath, along with a rinse pitcher, and clean clothes were laid across the bed. A cheery fire danced in the hearth to chase away some of the room's cold.

Ildiko gestured to the chair. "It appears they forgot a comb, and you're in desperate need of one," she said, more matter-of-fact than insulting. "I know you well enough by now to know you'll refuse a maid, so I'll send someone up to drop the comb off to you." She left Anhuset standing next to the table of food, pausing on the threshold, one hand on the door. "We're glad you're returned, Anhuset. I don't think I've ever seen Brishen afraid until you didn't come back when expected." She closed the door softly behind her.

Anhuset stared at the surface of planking studded with nails and bound with strap hinges. "Then you never saw him when he feared for you, *hercegesé,*" she said softly.

With no choice but to give Brishen the time he requested, she ate the food brought and drank the wine, though if someone were to ask her what she consumed and how it tasted, she couldn't say. It was sustenance, nothing more. Her mind was elsewhere, or specifically, on someone. Every worst-case scenario played out in her mind regarding Serovek's fate. A cursory or bypassed trial, an even faster execution via the gallows rope or the headman's ax. She shoved aside her half-finished plate and downed the rest of the wine.

Steam no longer wafted off the water's surface in her bath, but it was still warm enough. Besides, she wasn't using it to relax but to wash away days of road dirt and sweat, not to mention the spit and blood Ogran had managed to splatter on her. She was thoroughly sick of being splashed with bodily fluid from human males.

What about Serovek? the small evil voice inside her mocked.

That's not even in the same realm, she thought as she peeled off her filthy clothes and kicked them aside before stepping into the bath. She sank to her knees, allowing the water to rise to her chin and lap at her earlobes. The memories of making love to Serovek chased away the less pleasant ones of battles and beatings and blood. They blunted the sharp edges of the panic that threatened to suffocate her.

He'd lived up to his reputation as a superior lover. He'd made her body sing under his hands and mouth. Even now it hummed at the memory of him inside her, the stretch and swell of his cock as he thrust into her, a slow up and back motion that increased in speed as he cupped her buttocks in his hands and suckled the sensitive hollow where her neck curved to her collarbone.

Her body missed him, but her spirit missed him even more. Anhuset had taken lovers before who, while maybe not as well endowed, knew how to please their partners as well as Serovek did. She didn't miss or crave them, didn't linger on the recollections of their intimacy, wouldn't remember their faces if some of them didn't serve under Brishen's command here at Saggara. The margrave, though… she missed it all. The sex, yes, but just as much or even more, the time they spent together in conversation or the completion of mundane tasks, even the fear and thrill of fighting. Those previous lovers had never looked at her beyond the intimidating *sha* who had the regent's trust and was good with a sword. The margrave had, from the very first moment he met her, made it plain he was very much enamored with what he saw. Not just sha-Anhuset, the Kai warrior, but Anhuset, the prickly, guarded woman who knew her way around a blade but couldn't conquer a hair ribbon if her life depended on it.

"Don't you dare die on me, you arrogant bastard," she said, glaring at the opposite wall as if Serovek stood there watching her with one of his bold smiles.

Dwelling on those lovelier moments made her heart ache, so she pushed them down into the recesses of her mind and tended to her bath. By the time she was finished, the water was murky, and she still hadn't washed her hair.

Ildiko returned with a procession of servants in tow carrying a smaller tub and several buckets of more warm water. A pair of burly servants hauled in her chest of clothes. They set their items down where she instructed and shooed them out when they were done. Ignoring Anhuset's dour scrutiny, she peered at the water and curled her lip. "As I thought. No longer fit for getting your hair clean. Are you done? If so, step out and I'll help you with your hair."

"I don't need help, and why did you bring my chest?"

"Have you seen your hair?" Ildiko eyed her as if she were a little dim. "You need help." She pointed to the chest. "You know best what you'll want to wear for your journey to Timsiora. You can dress and pack in here, then come downstairs when you're finished. Now, out of that bath."

Muttering to herself about wasting time and being just dirty and not an invalid—all which Ildiko blissfully ignored—Anhuset stepped out of the larger one to kneel in the smaller one and allowed Ildiko to wash her hair for her.

"This is wrong," she protested after the first dousing with one of the water buckets to thoroughly wet her hair. "It's my task or even the task of a servant since you think I need help, not that of the *hercegesé*."

"Don't be ridiculous," Ildiko replied. "I'm washing hair, not scrubbing floors. Besides, I don't want you terrorizing the servants with all the glaring and scowling and snarling."

While Ildiko might not have been scrubbing floors, she set to scrubbing Anhuset's head with the same zeal until the strands squeaked when finger-combed and her scalp stung. Anhuset remained undecided if she'd just been groomed or tortured. It was a far cry from the leisurely washing and combing Serovek had given her.

"Done!" Ildiko finally, blessedly pronounced and handed Anhuset a comb and a towel. "You can finish the rest."

Anhuset held both and stared at Brishen's wife, wondering why she'd forgotten that this weak, human woman was the same one who once bludgeoned a Kai assassin to death with a shutter pole. "This is revenge for all the bruises I left on you during our sparring sessions, isn't it?"

Ildiko's laughter didn't persuade her otherwise. "If I wanted revenge I would have sent you a plate full of roasted potatoes for your dinner and lied by saying that Brishen ordered you to eat them."

"Like he did at your wedding." Anhuset still hadn't forgiven him for pulling rank in that manner.

"Just so." Ildiko walked to the door, her shoes making wet, squeaking sounds on the floor from being splashed. She paused with her hand on the handle and turned back to give Anhuset a long look. Any amusement had fled her expression. "What is Serovek to you now, Anhuset?"

Everything.

The word thundered in Anhuset's mind, and for a moment the world shifted beneath her feet before she steadied herself and returned Ildiko's stare with a guarded one of her own. "He is Lord Pangion, *hercegesé*," she said in an indifferent voice. "Beladine margrave of High Salure and friend to the *herceges*."

Ildiko's gaze didn't waver for long, excruciating moments. A tiny smile flitted across her lips. "I thought so." She opened the door, closing it behind her with a quiet click.

Anhuset stared at the door for a long time while water dripped from her skin and hair to puddle at her feet. She finally toweled off, combed out her hair and dug through her chest of clothes until she found what she wanted —sturdy tunic and trousers, a padded hauberk and riding leathers. The first two she'd wear now as she met with Brishen. She'd don the hauberk and leathers before she left for Timsiora. The servants had also delivered her worn travel satchel to which she added one change of garments in case the others weren't fit to wear by the time she reached the Beladine capital.

A servant waiting in the corridor instructed her to meet the *herceges* in the library. Anhuset climbed the rest of the stairwell to the third floor where the knowledge amassed by previous Kai kings was stored in a room nearly as big as the great hall, with tall windows that looked onto the redoubt below and the lands beyond that fell under Saggara's protection.

She expected to find both Brishen and Ildiko there, but only

Brishen waited for her, his back to her as he stared out the windows. "*Herceges*," she said, announcing her presence and bowed when he turned.

He motioned for her to join him at the windows. A small table and chair were nearby, the table's surface covered with unfurled scrolls. Brishen pointed to them. "Beladine law, or at least as it was when those scrolls were added to this library. I don't think much has changed since then."

She drew closer to the table to peer at the scrolls, reading what was surely the dullest accounting of anything ever written and pitying Brishen for having to make sense of it. "What did you find?"

His brow furrowed, whether from concentration or concern, she couldn't tell. "A way to save the margrave if you can't convince the king of his innocence. You may still have to employ it even if you do convince him, and from what I know of Rodan, I wouldn't be surprised if he forced you to do just that." His frown deepened. "It's dangerous, cousin."

Every time he addressed her by their familial ties, he revealed his worry for her. "What is it?"

"According to Beladine law, the accused has two choices—stand trial before the king, in which witnesses to his guilt or innocence plead their case and the king decrees final judgment or the accused may name a champion to fight for him. If the champion wins, the accused will be declared innocent. If he loses, the accused is declared guilty, no matter the testimony of witnesses." The corners of Brishen's mouth turned down. "It's a fight to the death."

Anhuset swayed, lightheaded from relief. She could act as Serovek's champion. Diplomacy was not her strength unless it was practiced with a weapon instead of words. She had everything to lose or everything to gain in such a scenario. She didn't even have to think twice. "I'll get my things."

She'd pivoted for the door when Brishen snapped out, "Wait." He set his hip against the table's edge, the casual pose belying his troubled gaze. "If only it were so easy to send sha-Anhuset in to wipe the floor with an adversary and emerge the victor."

Her triumph was momentary, defeated by his enigmatic statement. "What else, Brishen?" A sudden thought occurred to her. "I can't go without your leave. Do I have it?"

He blinked, obviously taken by surprise at her question. "What?" He shook his head. "That's of no importance."

"It's of every importance, Your Highness." She wielded the most formal of addresses to impress upon him the importance of his approval, how it impacted everything she'd adhered to as a *sha*. He was her cousin, yes, but he was her liege.

Brishen sighed. "Of course you have it. I leave all but one choice in this matter up to you." Her stomach somersaulted as relief washed through her, though she held her breath waiting to hear what the one choice was. "When you go, you go as Anhuset, not sha-Anhuset. You will not stand before Rodan as the second of the Khaskem, as an ambassador for the queen regnant or a representative of Bast-Haradis. You go as a Kai woman who just so happens to be a friend of Serovek and a witness to his actions during the journey to the Nazim monastery in the Lobak valley. Anything else will look like the meddling of a foreign power in the affairs of the Beladine nation, and that has all the elements for inciting a war." His features saddened. "Serovek Pangion is my friend and my battle brother, but Bast-Haradis has sacrificed enough, suffered enough. I won't send it into a war for one man, not even him. It's on you alone, cousin."

Why he thought she might balk at such restrictions or the heavy weight of such a responsibility, she didn't know and groaned inwardly when he said, "One more thing, and this will be your greatest challenge in this endeavor."

As if facing King Rodan and winning a fight to the death while in a human kingdom wasn't challenge enough.

"A victory in an arena will guarantee a single reprieve for a single instance. I doubt Rodan believes a word Bryzant has told him about Serovek allying himself with an insurrectionist like Chamtivos. He could raise a rebellion of his own at any time if he wanted to without help from a backwater cur like that. Bryzant gave Rodan what he was looking for: an excuse to get rid of a perceived threat that wouldn't outrage his people over the execution of a man who'd helped save them all."

Dread darkened her hope. "If I win, the king will simply find another way to arrest him again. There will be no trial. No second chances." It was a grim consideration, one she couldn't dwell on. Her purpose was just to help him survive this imprisonment and pray another wasn't forthcoming later.

Brishen nodded. "Serovek is a threat because he's a viable usurper who could win support among Rodan's restless nobles. He's from a respected Beladine family; he's wealthy, and he's proven himself an exceptional fighter. His rise would benefit other powerful families through popularity, money, and heirs. He's the stuff bards weave tales from when they speak of heroes. Men of great place."

"He doesn't want any of that."

"We know it, but we're not the ones who need convincing. Serovek has to be diminished, become lesser in the eyes of the Beladine people and therefore no longer a threat to their king." Brishen paused, frowning as if searching for the right words. His hesitation tightened the knot of trepidation in Anhuset's belly. "The Anhuset who left Saggara to journey with Serovek Pangion isn't the same Anhuset who returned. Ildiko saw it. So did I. You love the margrave enough to will-ingly—eagerly—act his champion in a fight to the death. Do you love him enough to marry him?"

CHAPTER
SIXTEEN

The prison known as the Zela housed every manner of criminal, from the debtor to the murderer, the thief and the traitor alike. It wasn't the crime that determined where in the Zela one was incarcerated but the status of the criminal. A troop of palace guards had turned Serovek over to the warden and his men with instructions that he be put in a cell on the topmost floor.

This one lacked the comforts most Beladine nobility was accustomed to, but it had a chair and table and a bed that looked free of fleas. The sliver of window set high in the wall allowed in a small bit of light and a great deal of cold wind. There were no tapestries or rugs to warm the cell, and the blankets folded on the bed looked threadbare. Serovek was thankful he wore heavy clothing to ward off the worst of the chill.

The warden blew on his fingers before tucking his hands under his arms. He peered at Serovek from the other side of the cell bars. "Never thought to have the margrave of High Salure as my guest here at the Zela," he said. There was genuine puzzlement in his voice instead of mockery, and even a touch of disappointment.

"Home it is not," Serovek replied, keeping his answers noncommittal. Everything he said to anyone in this place would be immediately reported back to the king. He didn't believe a word of Rodan's statement that he would take time to consider Serovek's guilt or innocence. It didn't matter which he was. What mattered to Rodan was the possibility of his margrave usurping his throne and how best to neutralize that threat. This little interlude of hospitality was just his way of making Serovek stew, to increase his fear and panic. At the moment, all it did was stir the deep-seated fury burning hot enough inside him to make him sweat despite the cold. Too bad his steward wasn't in here with him right now. Serovek would cheerfully tear off Bryzant's arms and beat him to death with both.

"Prisoners are given dinner in an hour," the warden said. "And being who you are, you can have visitors, though they stay on this side of the bars. Is there anyone you want to see?"

Serovek almost declined, then changed his mind. "A king's chronicler," he said. "There's one I've spoken with before. Jahna Uhlfrida. If she isn't available, then another will do."

He'd manage to find a way out of this disaster with his head still attached to his shoulders and High Salure returned to him. Serovek had watched Rodan's expressions while he read Bryzant's letter. Mocking disbelief, contempt—each expression flickering across the king's face as he read aloud. If there was to be a true trial, then it wouldn't be so much a matter of convincing the king of his innocence but of convincing him of his loyalty and disinterest in the throne. By his estimation, he had three days at most to plan what he'd say. In that time, he'd make use of the Archives and their purpose in chronicling major events in the Beladine kingdom to recount his journey to the Lobak valley and the death of Chamtivos.

The idea hadn't occurred to him until he considered how he might get a message to Anhuset. Not a plea for rescue but a note of reassurance that he was still alive, not to worry, and to take care of Magas. Serovek smiled as he imagined her scoffing at reading such pap. He could only assume she and Erostis had successfully made it to Saggara and warned Brishen. As Serovek Pangion, his death would be meaningless, just another criminal put to death at the king's pleasure. As margrave of High Salure though, his death would have an impact on the stability of the hinterlands and Bast-Haradis that bordered them. He had no doubt both King Rodan and the Khaskem were very aware of that and likely why Rodan had been quick to arrest but slow to condemn him.

As the warden had noted earlier when he first arrived, a prison guard brought dinner, sliding the tray through a narrow slot at floor level that didn't require opening the cell door to hand him his meal. The cell bars themselves were narrow, allowing a half hand's span of room between them but that was all. While the bars offered no privacy, Serovek was glad they weren't the doors set into the stone walls, with only a spyhole in the wood for a guard to check on a prisoner, if they even remembered to do so. Those were tombs.

His meal was plain, tasteless fare, and an hour later he remembered nothing about it. Other less hardy noblemen incarcerated like him might complain, but he'd had worse and less. At least, based on the fact he was still standing and not writhing on the floor in pain and foaming at the mouth, it wasn't poisoned.

He'd just shoved the empty tray back through the slot to be retrieved by another guard or servant when approaching footsteps— one in heavy boots, the other, soft shoes—alerted him that he had another visitor. When they finally came into view, he was surprised to see an old woman of queenly bearing accompanying a guard. At Serovek's cell, the guard bowed to her and retreated to a spot where he could see—and hear—the visitor.

Serovek didn't know her, but he recognized the insignia on her heavy cloak and the concealing headdress that covered her from the top of her head to her shoulders, leaving only her lined face bare. Her sunken cheeks were ruddy with the cold and her eyes as sharp as any hawk's. A dame of the Archives.

She stood close to the bars, watching him in silence as he came toward her, her gaze measuring as it swept him from head to foot. "Lord Pangion," she said. "I am Dame Stalt. A messenger arrived at the Archives. We don't usually receive requests for an audience from the Zela."

He offered a brief salute. "Madam, I expected a chronicler, not one of the exalted dames herself."

One faded eyebrow rose and her lips twitched at the corners. "I admit to the failing of too much curiosity, though it's a necessary one considering what I do. Of the nobles who've passed the hours in this place, I never expected to find one of the men who fought the *galla* doing so."

The warden had said something similar. At least people acted surprised instead of expectant at finding him here. "A remark I imagine I'll hear many times over the next few days. I'm sure I'll echo the refrain of every person in the Zela when I say I'm innocent of the charges." He gestured to the bars. "I'd invite you in and order wine or ale, but as you see, there are restrictions."

Her expression told him she was aware of his attempt at charm and utterly immune to it. In a small way she reminded him of Anhuset. "How may I be of service to you, Lord Pangion?"

"While I recognize the honor of your presence here, I asked for Jahna Uhlfrida."

Dame Stalt's expression softened at the edges. "Ah, Jahna. Lady Uhlfrida is Lady Velus now, wife of an Ilinfan swordmaster. She no longer abides here in Timsiora though she remains a chronicler."

Serovek had found Jahna intelligent, engaging, and lit with an inner glow that bespoke a love of knowledge. The news of her marriage gladdened him. Among the many unable to look beyond the birthmark staining her cheek and neck like a splash of red wine, an Ilinfan swordmaster had seen a beauty of both flesh and spirit and claimed her as his wife. "My congratulations to her. I wish her well. I received a copy of her chronicles based on our meeting. Very good work. She was detailed, and most important, accurate without unnecessary embellishment."

The dame nodded. "She's one of our best chroniclers. However, as she's not here, you'll have to make do with me."

He was perfectly happy with the substitution, and this was a dame with a certain power even the nobles didn't possess and of which all kings were made wary: the ability to frame history in their records according to their own biases. "As you've recorded the events of the *galla* war, are you interested in any of the aftermath?"

"Of course," she said with a shrug.

"I can recount the journey I and others took to the Jeden Order to deliver the body of the Wraith king and Nazim monk Megiddo Cermak. It might seem a journey like any other, but the warlord Chamtivos died during this excursion, and it's why I'm here now."

A shrewd look replaced her curious one. "You wish to record your innocence."

"I wish to record facts." No doubt Bryzant was trying to spread rumor far and wide of Serovek's supposed misdeeds. Serovek wanted what really occurred recorded where it counted most.

"You understand King Rodan may request to see any and all notes and that I'm bound to turn them over to him?"

"Yes." She might consider it her duty to turn over all written items to Rodan for review if asked, but he had no doubt there were things written and recorded and hidden away for later generations that current sovereigns would prefer no one knew. If he didn't survive Rodan's paranoia, his own accounts of the truth and his innocence just might.

Dame Stalt regarded him for several moments, her gaze direct, piercing. "I'm an old woman, Lord Pangion," she finally said. "And the cold here is hard on my bones. My chroniclers are also very busy with assignments already given. However, I can provide you with ink and quill and as much parchment as you need to write down an account of your trip. I'll request that a small brazier be delivered to you as well, so the ink doesn't thicken too much and your hands stay warm enough to keep your writing legible. I will send someone to the Zela twice a day to take what you've completed. Will this suffice?"

He hadn't expected that level of generosity and offered her a low bow. "Very much so. I thank you, Dame."

She returned the bow with a brief nod. "It's well known the Beladine hinterlands thrive under the guardianship of High Salure. May it continue, margrave." Supportive words carefully framed to give an appearance of neutrality.

"May the gods favor it so, Madam."

When she left, he restlessly paced the room. Until someone returned from the Archives, there wasn't much to do but worry, recall, or wonder, and he did all three—not about himself but about Anhuset and Erostis. Had they made it to Saggara without delays or problems? Was Magas being taken care of? Those questions and concerns birthed others—the fate of High Salure and those soldiers who considered themselves loyal to him more than to the crown. If they had any fear for their own skins, they would declare loyalty to Rodan, even if they had to lie through their teeth.

At least he didn't have Megiddo to worry about any longer, his body anyway. Safely ensconced in the monastery under the protection of his fellow monks, he wasn't at risk from the perils of the road. Safe unless Rodan decided the monks weren't useful Beladine citizens but heretics to be purged from Beladine society. He paced even faster. Madness, he thought, wasn't born out of fear; it was born out of boredom.

The dame was as good as her word. A clerk arrived at the same time a guard brought food to break his fast—more of the same gruel he'd eaten the night before, only cold. Serovek didn't care and passively submitted to a temporary shackling at the opposite wall while the clerk set up parchment, ink bottles and wells, and a generous supply of quills for him to use. Someone else brought a tabletop brazier, and it was the warden himself who looked it over, pronouncing it acceptable. Once only a single guard remained in the cell, he released his prisoner from the shackles.

Serovek wasted no time lighting the brazier to warm his hands. His face felt frozen, and he'd spent an uneasy night shivering in the bed under the woefully thin blankets. If the warden expected him to complain of a lack of pampering, he would be sorely disappointed. The small brazier was a luxury in itself.

He dragged the table and chair to the least drafty part of the chamber and moved the mat under the bed so as not to start a fire from a stray spark. It didn't take long to warm his hands and face, and while the rest of him creaked from the cold, he could write and make the words legible. And thank the gods, he was no longer bored.

Unlike the previous evening, time flew as he wrote, and he had several pages completed and ready for the Archives clerk who arrived to take them. "Dame Stalt will see to it these are copied and the originals sent to King Rodan if requested, margrave," the clerk assured him before she left. Serovek wondered how much of what he wrote would remain the same in the original Rodan saw. He suspected that even if the king demanded exclusions or significant edits to suit his whims or purpose, the dame would leave the copy as it was and stash it away for safekeeping.

He continued working through the afternoon as the stack of blank parchment and supply of ink steadily diminished with the scratching of his quill. He didn't look up from the current page at the sound of a pair of footsteps pausing outside his cell, expecting the clerk's final return of the day.

"I see they're treating you well, margrave."

Serovek froze in the middle of a word, quill tip leaving a spreading ink spot where it pressed against the parchment. Bryzant. One of only two people who could make him forget the cold because they made the blood run hot in his veins, and unlike Anhuset, who made him run hot with desire, his steward ignited him with fury. He casually laid down the quill, brushed his hands together to wipe off any sand and slowly rose from his chair.

The reason for his current predicament stood on the other side of the cell bars, watching Serovek with a satisfied half smile that tipped toward gloating the closer the margrave came to the barrier between them. Serovek wondered what had incited him to travel to the capital. A hostile environment at High Salure? Worry the king would change his mind if Bryzant wasn't there to spin more lies? Or maybe just satisfaction at witnessing his liege's downfall and execution. All three suppositions had merit.

He hoped his voice sounded much milder than he felt inside. "I wondered if you'd stay at High Salure or come here to fill the king's ear with more poison. Couldn't resist paying me a visit to see what your plan wrought, Bryzant?" He allowed a sneer to creep into his tone and curled his top lip upward to emphasize it. "Or is this some kind of memorial to crushed hopes over the fact that Chamtivos is the one dead instead of me?" The steward's gloating expression melted away, revealing the true emotions he'd managed to hide for so long: Envy, jealousy, ambition. Three things that drove some men, like Chamtivos, to commit heinous acts of familicide, abduction, and torture and others like Bryzant to ally themselves with monsters in order to climb the ladder of power.

The steward glanced briefly at the guard nearby, listening to their conversation. A sly malice veiled his features, at odds with the injured tone he affected. "You were my liege until you turned traitor, Lord Pangion. While I'm crushed by such revelations, it seems only courteous to inquire after your health. Can we not at least converse civilly?"

"I don't have chats with treacherous lickspittles like you," Serovek scoffed, scoring a hard hit with his contempt as Bryzant's nostrils flared and his eyes narrowed. "All those years of faithful service and you were merely biding your time, making your plans, for what? Becoming margrave yourself?" Serovek snorted. "What do you know of governance or even battle?" He didn't give Bryzant a chance to answer. "Maybe, like Ogran, you were motivated by monetary gain. You're the youngest son of a lesser nobleman. Without holdings or inheritance. A generous reward from the king would buy the first and take care of the second. Blood money always helps a belly crawler stand."

"So high and mighty, even locked in here," Bryzant snarled, abandoning his woeful demeanor and forgetting the watchful guard. "The Beladine people might have hailed you and that pathetic monk as heroes, but you'll not die a hero's death or be remembered as such."

Serovek had held onto his fraying temper, taking pleasure at the small cuts he delivered against his erstwhile steward. That grip slipped the moment Bryzant insulted Megiddo, a man whose boots Bryzant wasn't fit to lick. Too intent on their conversation to notice how Serovek gradually moved closer and closer to him, Bryzant gasped when Serovek suddenly shoved his hands through the gaps between the bars, grabbed the other man's tunic and yanked him forward to slam his face against unforgiving metal.

The spaces were too narrow for Serovek to get his hands through past his wrists, otherwise he would have snapped Bryzant's neck. A part of him not submerged in white-hot fury recognized that restriction was likely a good thing. He didn't need murder added to his charges. It didn't stop him from smashing Bryzant's face ever harder against the bars where he mewled and struggled in his captor's grip.

"Be grateful for the bars, little man," Serovek said, bringing his own face against them so Bryzant could see the promise of retribution in his eyes.

It took the nearby guard and two more to finally pry Bryzant from Serovek's grip and only then after a hard rap with a sword pommel across one of Serovek's hands. He retreated from the cell door while the guards dragged Bryzant out of grabbing distance. The steward shook them off to straighten his clothes. His cheek was red with an imprint of the bars, and his glare bore a hatred fueled by the same envy and ambition that made him betray Serovek in the first place. "I'm glad I came to Timsiora," he said between stuttered breaths. "Your death will be sweet to watch, and I will celebrate when it's done."

Serovek gave a humorless laugh. "Do you think me the only one who'd avenge an unjust death? Enjoy your triumph while you can, Bryzant, for you'll soon see a shadow lurking in every corner and behind every tree, wondering which one of them might be an assassin with your name engraved on their blade."

Bryzant paled.

There were no vengeful assassins waiting to exact vengeance against Serovek's enemies, at least none that he knew of. It was a bluff, pure conjecture, but the steward didn't need to know that, and Serovek capitalized on the other's man fear of him and his jealousy. Judging by Bryzant's reaction, he believed every word. With a snarled epithet hurled Serovek's way, he strode away, watched by the three guards whose scornful expressions likely mirrored their prisoner's.

The guard originally assigned to the watch approached the cell, making sure not to make the mistake Bryzant had, though Serovek would have been happy to assure him he had nothing to worry about. "I'll have to tell the warden what happened, Lord Pangion. He might restrict your visitors."

Serovek cursed inwardly, regretting his momentary loss of temper. "I'm more than willing to apologize to the warden and swear on my family's name that what happened won't happen again."

The following morning brought not a clerk but Dame Stalt herself once more. She handed him new parchment, trading with him for the completed pages. "Word about Timsiora is there are already people lined up in the king's receiving chamber waiting for an audience with him to give character testimony in your favor."

Serovek flinched. "I don't know if that's a good or bad thing." Popularity had its pitfalls. This was one of them.

Dame Stalt nodded. "I wondered as well." She lowered her voice. "King Rodan is threatened by your popularity among the Beladine military as well as its civilian population.

"I have no interest in raising a rebel army," he said.

She flipped through the pages, sending an occasional glance at the nearby guard. "Let's hope His Majesty believes you and those who want to testify on your behalf."

Before she left, the dame tilted her head to the side and once more regarded him with her all-seeing gaze. "I've read much of what you've written so far. You write very favorably of the Khaskem's *sha*. She sounds both intimidating and admirable." A tiny smile hovered around the old woman's mouth, and her gaze turned knowing.

Serovek wasn't moved to disavow any assumptions she made. He wouldn't verify or expand on them either. "She is."

That smile widened a little more. "Should you live but lose High Salure, come to the Archives, Lord Pangion. We might have work for you there." She surprised a laugh from him with the quick wink she bestowed on him before she left.

It might have been better if the warden had restricted visitors, he thought later in the day. Hand cramping from the feverish pace he'd set for himself recording the details of the trip to the monastery, he paused to rest and fell asleep on the bed, huddled under the covers. A guard banging on the bars jolted him awake. "Another visitor, margrave."

Serovek peered at the figure standing on the other side of the cell bars and blinked twice to make sure he wasn't seeing things. "Gaeres?"

Of all the people he would guess might come to see him, a fellow Wraith king wasn't one of them. The Quereci chieftain's son had ridden away with his entourage once they escorted Serovek and Megiddo to High Salure. As isolated as the Quereci were, Serovek wasn't sure he and Gaeres would ever cross paths again, and if they did, it would be by chance on the summer plains when the nomadic clans grazed their herds of sheep and goats and horses across his territories. He never imagined facing Gaeres here in the heart of the Beladine kingdom.

Gaeres didn't smile. His dark gaze passed over the bars and his features, hawkish and severe, tightened with disapproval. "Serovek," he said in the clear, precise voice Serovek remembered. "I'd hoped to see you again one day, but not like this."

Serovek left the bed and walked to the bars. He shoved one hand through, watching askance as his guard tensed. "What are you doing in Timsiora?"

Gaeres clasped Serovek's hand with both of his. "There's an apothecary here well known for creating cures that actually work." His austere face turned even more so. "Many in our camp have been struck with a sickness. The old and the young are of course the first to succumb. I heard the news of your imprisonment when I arrived and couldn't believe it. I had to see for myself."

Serovek frowned at the news. For the Quereci's sake, he hoped it wasn't plague. For everyone's sake, he hoped it wasn't plague. "What did you tell the gate guards to let you in?"

"The truth. I'm a chief of the Quereci." He finally smiled. "The clan matriarchs decided that my feats as a Wraith king earned me the right to be named a chieftain."

Serovek chuckled. "Quereci women expect a great deal of their men, don't they? It's good to see you, friend."

Gaeres's rare smile faded. "You as well but not in these circumstances. What happened to put you in the Zela?"

"It's a long story," Serovek said. "One I'm writing now for the king's chroniclers. You'll be able to read it when it's done if you wish to visit the Archives one day. For now, though, I think you have more important things to attend to if there's sickness among the clans."

"I'm told I can present myself at the palace as a witness for you. I'll be glad to do so. As a Wraith king, I know firsthand your honor and courage."

Of those who might appear before the king to offer their support of Serovek, he couldn't think of anyone more detrimental than a fellow Wraith king, except maybe Brishen himself—a Wraith king *and* the Kai regent. "I appreciate the gesture, but you're better off making yourself scarce here in the capital. Get what you need from your apothecary and go home. King Rodan isn't too fond of Wraith kings at the moment, and you may end up sharing this cell with me if you present yourself to his court with the purpose of defending me."

Gaeres's frown was fierce. "Are you certain? I'll take the risk."

Serovek nodded vigorously. "Very certain. Your duty is first and foremost to your people who obviously need you right now." If the young chieftain insisted, he'd have to abandon civility and demand Gaeres to stop helping. Fortunately, the other man didn't press and gave silent acquiescence with a nod.

Exhaling a relieved sigh, Serovek turned their conversation to something a little lighter. "Have you married?" He'd been astounded to learn the lengths Gaeres would go to for the chance of gaining a wife from among his clansmen. Quereci women must be exceptional if a man was willing to fight a demon horde just to increase his chances of impressing one of the clanswomen enough to consider becoming his bride.

Gaeres's expression turned more guarded. "No, not yet."

"Surely you've proven yourself worthy of the privilege of taking a wife? Herding *galla* is a little more difficult than herding sheep or horses."

The other man shrugged, his eyes no longer meeting Serovek's. "That isn't the problem. I've just decided to wait for now. When do you stand trial?"

Serovek recognized a feint when he heard one and abandoned his questions to follow Gaeres's new path. "I don't know. I'm sure if and when the king decides to actually have a trial, I'll be the first to know."

"I pray the gods will be merciful and show the king that you're a loyal subject."

"You and me both, my friend," Serovek replied.

They spoke another few moments before Gaeres bid him goodbye. Serovek saluted him. "I wish you good health and to your kinsmen," he said. "Come to High Salure when this is done. I'll take you hunting." He wasn't dead yet and wouldn't plan his future as if he was.

The other man nodded, then paused and returned to his spot in front of the cell, much to the guard's disapproval. "Serovek, do you dream of Megiddo?"

Serovek glanced at the guard. So far there was nothing said here that would alarm or offend the king. No secret to be kept if spoken of in the right way. "Yes. Often. You?"

A troubled look, rife with a guilt that Serovek instantly recognized and that made his stomach knot, chased across Gaeres's face. "I think they're visions more than dreams, and I think his soul suffers."

Did Gaeres's eyes glow the ethereal blue Serovek's did when he awakened from those nightmares? Did he hear Megiddo as if the monk stood beside him, alive and whole? He kept the questions to himself. These were the things that would alarm Rodan. "I think it does too," he replied, wishing he could say otherwise, tell Gaeres he was wrong.

A terrible sorrow aged Gaeres's face for a moment. "What can be done?

Serovek had worn that same look in a mirror's reflection. "I wish I knew." And if the gods willed it, he'd live long enough to find out.

SEVENTEEN

A nhuset braced herself to make the last leg of her journey across snow-covered terrain toward the walled city of Timsiora. Behind those walls, a sea of humans with their strange eyes and mollusk skin lived, worked, and traded under the rule of Rodan, King of Belawat. And somewhere in there, Serovek awaited trial. For a moment the breath thinned in her lungs at the enormity of the task before her, the stakes involved, and the likely disaster if she failed.

She tapped her heels against her mount's sides, urging it forward, and they picked their way down a gentle slope toward the city where it nestled in a box canyon under a blanket of early spring snow. Heavily bundled against the cold and hooded against the glare of a midday sun, she pulled down the cloth mask protecting the lower half of her face from the cutting wind. Cold air stung her cheeks. She ignored it, used to the bite of old Winter as it clawed for purchase in the high places where Spring had not yet gained a true foothold.

Her primary purpose here was to gain an audience with the king. Giving every resident of Timsiora a clear view of her features guaranteed word of a lone Kai's arrival would travel through the city faster than a brush fire, attracting the king's notice and, hopefully, his curiosity. She shoved back her hood as well, slitting her eyes against the blinding brightness.

Unlike the denizens of High Salure, who were used to seeing the Kai and even teaming up with them on the occasional patrol, the Beladine in Timsiora were no more accustomed to a Kai's appearance than those humans who lived in the Gauri capital of Pricid on the southern coast. Just as she expected, the scant number of guards at the entry gates tripled in an instant once they got a good look at the approaching rider.

Anhuset halted in front of the portcullis, keeping a casual pose atop her horse even as a half dozen soldiers spilled out of the wicket adjacent to the gate. They gathered before her to extend a welcome of frowns and drawn bows.

One man stepped forward. "A single Kai?" He leaned to the side, peering around her as if looking for a Kai army to suddenly appear at her back. When none did, he gave her a confused scowl. "Are you lost?"

Keeping a wary eye on the archers and wishing she held her shield in front of her, Anhuset leaned forward to rest her forearms on the saddle's swell as if she and this guard had all the time in the world for a casual chat. "I'm not lost," she said. "I'm here to visit my lover, Serovek Pangion, margrave of High Salure."

She fancied she heard every jaw go slack and every eyelid snap upward. The shock value of honesty was always greater than that of the most convincing lie, and if the reaction from the welcoming committee was anything to go by, there was no lie more spectacular than this truth. Gasps and sputtered laughter met her statement. Even some of the bowmen wavered in their aim, and the guard acting as spokesman gaped at her like a landed fish drowning in air.

Anhuset waited, features composed, while he finally overcame his shock to glare at her. "The Kai have a strange sense of humor, and I don't have time for stupid jokes. State your business, Kai woman."

Before she left Saggara to ride to Timsiora, Brishen had given her a piece of valuable advice.

"Be patient," he'd said. "It'll be your greatest weapon and greatest strength while you're there."

"My greatest challenge as well," she'd replied. "Especially where humans are concerned."

Brishen's eye had darkened to gold with amusement and no small amount of worry. "Just keep in mind what you're there for in the first place."

She drew upon that advice now. Instead of baring her teeth and trying to intimidate the guard, she merely shrugged and repeated her statement. "I don't joke. I'm here to see the margrave of High Salure. I know he's a prisoner of the crown."

If she and Brishen were right in their assumptions, Serovek would be the last person any of the Beladine would take her to see. They'd take her straight to the king. It didn't matter that she hadn't announced herself as an ambassador for the Kai regent or the queen regnant, her appearance alone at Timsiora's gate was so unusual, the guards would assume what she'd never stated.

They did exactly as Brishen predicted. Anhuset waited outside the gate as a growing crowd of curious onlookers lined the battlements above her to point, stare, and gossip. Soon, a soldier of higher rank than those barring her entry into the city joined them. He stared at her without the curiosity and distaste the others had shown. He surprised everyone, including her, when he gave a short bow. "I'm Captain Droginin, sha-Anhuset," he said, addressing her by her title as well as her name, though she'd offered neither to this point. "I was assigned for duty at High Salure for a short time. You may not remember me, but I was one of the margrave's men who helped rescue the Khaskem when he was abducted and tortured by raiders."

Anhuset's eyebrows lifted, and she almost forgot not to show her teeth. She noted that Droginin avoided saying "Beladine raiders." Brigands paid by some wealthy patron to end the marriage of Brishen and Ildiko before it truly began, they had displayed a breathtaking cruelty against their captive, leaving Brishen disfigured and partially blind. She might have hated all the Beladine for the crime were it not for the fact several of their countrymen had allied themselves with the Kai and endangered their own lives to rescue the *herceges*.

She didn't remember this man, but he knew enough about her on sight and had no reason to lie. She returned his bow with one of her own. "Then you have my and his Highness's eternal gratitude, Captain."

"Raise the portcullis!" he shouted, still watching her. "Lord Pangion is currently being held in the Zela," he said. "I can't take you to him, but I'll escort you to the palace. I've no doubt the king will want to see you."

Just as she'd hoped.

Captain Droginin walked beside her horse until they passed through the barbican where he then swung onto the back of a waiting mare. Anhuset followed him through the city toward the palace, traveling down a central boulevard lined with hundreds of hideously ugly humans. It reminded her of her foray into Pricid as part of Brishen's escort where they'd faced the same ghastly curiosity from humans as horrified by the Kai's appearance as the Kai were by theirs. That visit to a human city had been for a wedding, as was this one.

The irony wasn't lost on Anhuset.

The royal palace was a large structure, though smaller than Saggara and designed in a more blunted style that spoke strictly of function over aesthetics—built of stone to withstand siege and fire, except for its vulnerable wooden roof from which flew numerous flags with house crests, and above them all the largest, most colorful flag belonging to the Belawat royal family in residence there.

More guards at more gates, along with a crush of courtiers who made no attempt to disguise their gawking or their commentary on the Kai woman's frightful appearance. Anhuset swallowed down laughter when the more squeamish among them flung themselves against the walls as she passed them in the open-air cloisters or fell into the thorny embrace of dormant rose bushes lining the snowy gardens. The urge to smile wide and long almost overcame her, and she gained an appreciation for Ildiko's enjoyment of crossing her eyes in front of Kai nobility.

She followed Droginin down several hallways, their boots striking a tandem rhythm on the floors. Behind them, the Beladine nobility followed in a wave of chatter. They kept their distance but shadowed the two and their small contingent of soldiers all the way to a set of narrow double doors three times as tall as they were wide and flanked on either side by a pair of guards in royal livery.

"Sha-Anhuset of Bast-Haradis to see His Majesty," the captain said.

Word of her arrival in the city had obviously reached the palace before she did for there was no hesitation or questioning before two of the guards opened the doors for her to cross the threshold. Droginin offered another bow. "This is where I leave you, sha-Anhuset." He pivoted sharply before cleaving a path through the crowd of court butterflies waiting to follow her through the doors.

Their protests sounded loud behind her when the guards crossed glaives to prevent them from filing into the chamber, and she caught a glimpse of disappointed faces when the doors shut. This chamber was not so grandiose as the one she saw through the space made by another set of partially open doors. This was obviously the antechamber before the great hall with its elevated throne at the far end. A man heavily garbed in expensive woolens and silks greeted her with a sly and disapproving expression. His critical stare took in her riding leathers and tough woolens made to withstand the rigors of the road and weather.

"His Majesty will see you now," he said without preamble. "Follow me." He led her through the second set of doors and into the great hall.

It was a grand space simply for its size and the height of its roof. Tapestries whose details were lost in the gloom hung on the walls at regular intervals, providing warmth in a room colder than a sepulcher. Her breath fogged in front of her as she crossed the cavernous chamber, noting the countless number of swords, polearms and shields used to decorate those places the tapestries didn't cover. Trestle tables and benches were pushed against the walls, kept out of the way until meals were served. Small clusters of people stood in various spots watching as she approached the dais upon which the throne sat and the old man who hunched there like a vulture.

Grateful for the lack of numerous windows that would have flooded the throne room with light this time of day, she stopped squinting and focused her gaze on Rodan, monarch of the kingdom of Belawat. The man she was certain had Brishen abducted and mutilated, the man who sought Serovek's death thanks to fear and paranoia of having his throne usurped. Her upper lip began to curl with the loathing and contempt swelling inside her. She forced both down. Now wasn't the time to allow for temper or obvious dislike. This would be her greatest test in patience and diplomacy, two things no one had ever praised as her strengths.

She genuflected before him, bowed her head and gave the Kai salute of a soldier to their commander. She raised her head to meet his eyes, revolted by the sight of his bloodshot sclera and the milky scale covering one of his faded green eyes. She hadn't thought human eyes could be uglier. She was wrong.

"Sha-Anhuset," he said in a voice nearly as harsh as his lined and weathered features. "Lord Pangion has written favorably of you in his account of the journey you shared to the Lobak valley. It seems Chamtivos and his men weren't quite prepared to fight a Kai."

Serovek had been allowed to write an account? Anhuset hoped her expression remained bland while inside she wondered how he'd managed such a feat while imprisoned. She also wondered how much of that account would remain in its original state and how much the king's scribes would alter it. "I don't think the warlord or his men were prepared for Lord Pangion, Your Highness. It was he who killed Chamtivos and hopefully put an end to the fighting in your territories there." He'd provided her with the opportunity to impress upon him Serovek's loyalty. She had no intention of squandering it. The quick narrowing of his eyes told her he recognized her reply for what it was.

He continued his questioning. "Why has the Khaskem sent you all the way to Timsiora? Alone?" Within that simple question lay a wealth of growing suspicion.

"He hasn't sent me, Your Majesty. I come as one woman in support of a friend."

One of his hoary eyebrows slid upward. "According to those at the gate, he's also your lover." His mouth turned down a little and his nostrils flared as if he tasted something unpleasant.

"Just so, Your Majesty." He might find it distasteful that Serovek had shared a bed with her, but Anhuset pitied every poor woman who'd shared a bed with this bilious sack of bones.

He snorted. "I wonder if Serovek would confirm such a declaration."

"Only he can answer that, Your Majesty." Surely she would choke on this forced graciousness before she completed her task.

"And the Khaskem has nothing to say about his *sha* riding to Timsiora for a visit with a man accused of treason and sedition?"

Brishen had been right to insist that if she went to the Beladine capital, she couldn't do it as an ambassador. Rodan poked and prodded, looking for something he could latch onto that might be interpreted as Kai interference. "No, Your Majesty. The Khaskem hasn't sanctioned this visit. While he considers Lord Pangion a personal friend, he feels this is a Beladine matter, not a Kai one." How many times would she have to rephrase the same answer before Rodan stopped asking?

The king slouched in his seat, eyeing her with a combination of distaste and fascination. "You realize that as Lord Pangion's self-proclaimed lover, you're hardly an objective witness for his innocence, even if your account of the trip agrees with his."

The prickly feel of sweat broke out on her back, despite the icy temperatures in the cavernous chamber. This was where she had to make every single word count, make it logical, sincere, and most of all, of benefit to the king *and* to Serovek. Her weakest skill set highlighted in these most important moments. What she wouldn't give right now for a sword and a good, bloody fight. "I'm not here as a witness, Your Majesty." The address grew more bitter on her tongue every time she uttered it. "I come for other purposes."

Rodan must have heard a certain tone in her voice for he abruptly straightened, the mild curiosity transforming to intense interest. "Continue. I'm listening."

Anhuset exhaled slowly, choosing her words carefully on that long, drawn out breath. "I know for a fact the accusations made by Bryzant the steward are false and motivated by envy, greed, and the desire to rise by any means necessary. Chamtivos's interest in Lord Pangion was only the money his death would bring him, money promised to him by Bryzant. The warlord told me so himself. For Bryzant, the margrave was simply an obstacle to be removed and Chamtivos the tool to do it. Such a man who'll betray his liege puts no value on loyalty and will betray anyone." She let that last word linger in the air for a moment. "But as you say, I'm not objective in this matter. Bryzant wanted all of us dead. No witnesses."

She had set the framework of her argument, and in that moment she desperately wished Brishen were here to make it instead of her. He'd do so with ease and a naturalness that didn't come to her without immense struggle. The perspiration beaded on her back now trickled down the valley of her spine. "I believe wholeheartedly in Lord Pangion's innocence. I will stake my life on it." Rodan's eyes narrowed, and she saw within his face a hint of burgeoning understanding for what she was about to say. "Beladine law states the accused may prove his innocence by choosing a champion to fight for him in judicial combat. If the champion wins, the accused will be acquitted and allowed to go free."

An image of Brishen's ashy face, with his mouth thinned in worry, and his eye a yellow paler than an early autumn moon as he stood by her horse to see her off, rose in her mind. "Win that combat, cousin. Paint the city red with your opponent's blood if you have to, but win that fight and come back to us alive."

Rodan steepled his fingers together and peered at her over their tips. "I'm familiar with our laws, Kai woman." A small frown stitched a line across his brow. "You realize this would be a fight to the death? You lose, you die, and so does the margrave. And there may not be anyone to accept your challenge; therefore, no fight."

That very thing had been Brishen's greatest fear while they hatched this plan. Anhuset had a reason, a motivation, to lay down her challenge, but there had to be one of equal importance for an opponent to accept it and step inside the arena with her knowing they might well die there.

"Someone always accepts, Your Majesty, if the prize is great enough."

A grim smile darkened the king's face, and his expression turned flinty. "I sense the Khaskem cleverness in all of this. What prize do you think is worthy enough to lure someone into the arena and risk their life to fight a Kai warrior?"

Brishen's voice echoed in her ears. "Will this steward face you in the arena if he was offered something of immense value? High Salure itself? Serovek controls it because it's his family's demesne, not because he's a margrave. This steward could be offered the holdings and let the king appoint a margrave to handle the actual governing."

Anhuset had laughed at the suggestion. "From what I saw of Bryzant, he's a milksop who pays others to spill blood for him. The last time I saw him he practically wet himself while standing on a kitchen table to avoid a loose scarpatine. He wouldn't come near me."

But Brishen's idea had merit with some alterations, and she presented it to Rodan now. "High Salure is a jewel in your crown, Your Majesty. It belongs to the Pangion family, which has no heirs except his lordship to claim it. While it may lie at your far borders, it's wealthy and strategically important. There are other brave, fighting men among your nobles who'd surely be tempted to make High Salure theirs." Thank the gods Serovek wasn't in the same room to hear her say those words. He'd try to strangle her.

"This gets more interesting by the moment," Rodan said. "Approval of judicial combat is at my discretion according to those same laws. You winning doesn't mean Serovek is absolved; he only earns his freedom to cause trouble for me at a later date." Jealousy, envy, and poisonous suspicion which had turned the king against one of his most loyal subjects, practically radiated from his body. Anhuset inwardly flinched. Brishen's predictions had been dead accurate so far regarding Rodan's every move and the motivation behind them.

"It's why I submit my second proposal, Your Majesty." How in the gods' name she managed to keep her voice this calm so far, she'd never know. "Should you agree to a trial by combat and I emerge the victor, then I will extend an offer of marriage to Lord Pangion. A union of Kai and Beladine human made in good faith."

When Brishen first made such a suggestion to her, she had no doubt she'd looked at him the same way Rodan was looking at her now —speechless from shock.

"Don't look at me as if I've lost my senses," her cousin had said with a humorless chuckle. "I assure you I haven't. The greatest dangers to Serovek are his reputation and his standing. He's a prime catch for every Beladine noble family with a marriageable daughter–powerful noblemen with large estates who can field personal armies and make alliances. You can win a dozen judicial combats and Rodan will find a way to have Serovek arrested again, and I fear the next time he'll resort to torture to wring an untrue confession out of our friend."

Anhuset's stomach had plummeted not only at Brishen's words but at the shadow of memory behind his eye. If anyone knew the horrors of torture, it was him. His reasoning lay heavy on her shoulders, layers upon layers of hard choices that would directly affect the rest of her life in great and small ways if she followed the line of his thinking and agreed to it. "He's no longer a prime catch if he marries someone like me." A bastard Kai woman who couldn't bear him children, who was neither Beladine nor recognized as noble, who lost her magic and couldn't tie a hair ribbon properly, who knew much of war and little of feminine graces, who would never be a sought-after widow or gain an inheritance. A woman of no value at all to a Beladine nobleman seeking to rise in power.

Brishen had nodded. "Not someone like you. You specifically. Such a marriage would only be tolerated if Serovek remained a margrave. The Beladine people will never accept a Kai queen consort, even if she were the wife of a popular usurper."

She had instantly accepted the risks and dangers of acting as Serovek's champion in a fight to the death. Done so without a second thought. But a marriage...

Brishen had encouraged her to take an entire day to consider it before she gave him her answer, and she'd used the entire day to ponder over her choices. She had never stooped to coyness and loathed it in others. She'd faced death without looking away many times. Facing life and doing the same was much harder, but she didn't turn from truth, and the truth was she'd fallen in love with a handsome-ugly human man of immense courage and unwavering integrity. If Serovek was worth dying for, he was certainly worth marrying, and once past the upheaval of her own heart and thoughts at the realization her life would irrevocably change if she became his wife, she embraced the idea. Only the question remained if he'd embrace it as well.

"Of the many things I might have expected you to say, I didn't expect that," Rodan said. "Let me ask you this first. Why would you want to marry Serovek? Surely, the Khaskem wouldn't approve of such a match between his *sha* and one of my noblemen?"

The words stuck in her throat for a moment, but she forced them out and past her lips. "I would no longer be his *sha*, nor will I be allowed to remain in the Kai army."

His frown deepened. "Surely you'd give up more than that. Are you not third in line for the throne after the queen regnant and the Khaskem?"

The question surprised and sent a spike of unease through her. How had he known she was related to Brishen through his father's line? Even most of the Kai only thought of her as his *sha*, nothing more, and those who knew otherwise didn't discuss it, especially with humans. "I'm not in any line, Your Majesty. I'm a bastard; the illegitimate daughter of King Djedor's sister and a stablehand." She described her heritage without embarrassment. She didn't place her personal value on her bloodlines. "Kai inheritance laws bar bastards from succession of any kind."

"Interesting." Rodan's face had soured even more with her explanation. Anhuset prayed it wasn't because he didn't believe her but because he suffered from the same prejudices against illegitimacy many of noble birth possessed. Disdain in this instance was of no importance. Disbelief was a problem. "Why," he said, "would a high-ranking Beladine like Serovek choose to bind himself to you? Granted, his debt to you for saving him should you win the trial would be immense, but such debt can be satisfied with payment, and he's a wealthy man."

Disdain it was, and Anhuset almost fell to her knees to thank the gods for Rodan's prejudiced haughtiness. "I believe he desires such a bond as I do, Your Majesty," she told him with a shrug. "And what is the harm in asking? If he says no, I still offer myself as his champion."

And for your sake, you better say yes, Stallion, she thought.

The king stared at her for so long, she began to wonder if he'd fallen asleep on the throne with his eyes open. Did humans sometimes sleep that way? She hadn't witnessed such a thing before, but those strange eyes did things no Kai eyes did. With any luck, he was still wide awake and concluding what she and Brishen had hoped to impart: that with a Kai wife destroying any chances of Serovek pursuing the throne, it would benefit Rodan more to keep his capable margrave alive and governing the hinterlands.

Finally, he spoke. "Fascinating. I'll consider your words and take council with my advisors regarding the request for trial by combat as well as a marriage." He tilted his head to the side, regarding her with the intensity of a man trying to figure out a baffling puzzle. "I'm undecided, sha-Anhuset, if you're very brave or very reckless."

"One can be both, Your Majesty."

For the first time in this unending audience, Rodan gave up a small huff of amusement. "Very true. You're welcome to take lodgings in the palace if you wish it."

Anhuset couldn't think of any place in this entire city she'd rather not spend an evening than under the king's roof. "I consider it an honor, Your Majesty, but I'm an unexpected visitor and don't wish to rob one of your courtiers of space. I have a place to stay just outside the city, though I would ask a boon of you." She didn't lie. That space was a narrow tent pitched in the conifer forest covering the canyon walls surrounding Timsiora.

"What is that?" he asked, the slight narrowing of his eyes warning her that he was tiring of this meeting as much as she was.

"That I may see Lord Pangion."

The narrowed eyes went to slits for a moment, reminding her of a feral cat. He stared at her, then shrugged. "One visit. On the other side of the bars, and accompanied by guards and at least one of my sorcerers." He still believed the Kai possessed their magic and was taking precautions. Anhuset had no intention of enlightening him.

She bowed low. "Of course, and you have my thanks." Excitement bubbled inside her, anticipation and no small relief. Soon she'd be gone from here, and while she'd never before delighted in a visit to a prison, she'd engaged in many firsts today. One more made no difference, except in this case, she'd see a man whose face and touch had haunted her dreams since she left him in a monastery, prepared to give himself over to royal troops as a prisoner.

"A messenger will find you when you have my answer," Rodan said and dismissed her from his presence with an abrupt shooing motion.

His guards wasted no time escorting her out, though it was they who jogged to keep up with her as she left. The flock of courtiers were still outside, their faces avid. Word of what she'd said at the gate had obviously reached all corners as many in the crowd wore smirking expressions, even horrified ones. Anhuset ignored them all, striding through their midst and threatening to stride over them if they didn't get out of her way.

Droginin was waiting for her outside the castle. Anhuset hadn't expected to see him again. "I've volunteered to take you to the Zela, sha-Anhuset."

Once at the prison, he spoke with the guards there and was met by the warden, a refined-looking man whose appearance seemed at odds with his grim profession and even grimmer surroundings. Droginin offered to keep an eye on her horse while she was inside.

"I'll take you back to the city gates once you're through here," he said.

Anhuset studied him before offering a closed-lip smile. "So you're to be my nanny while I'm in Timsiora, captain?"

He gave a small laugh. "I prefer to think of it as your escort. So you don't get lost here in our beautiful capital."

There was no obvious sarcasm in his words, but she heard it just the same. Escort, nanny, whatever one might want to call his role, he'd been assigned to keep an eye on her while she was here, an unwanted and unexpected guest that everyone was sure would cause trouble during her stay.

The warden greeted her with a half bow and a knowing glance. "It seems the Beladine Stallion casts his seed far afield. I wouldn't have believed it if you weren't standing in front of me." She stared back at him, unmoved by either anger or amusement at his lewd banter. He cleared his throat and looked away. "Come. This way."

They passed through a small antechamber into a narrow hallway that led into a labyrinth of other dark, narrow hallways. The Zela looked enormous and imposing on the outside but was suffocatingly cramped on the inside. She welcomed the gloom but guessed for humans who sought sunlight, those imprisoned here found the Zela a sepulchral place and chillier than any tomb.

The warden led her up flights of stairs until they reached the topmost floor. Here the hallways were only a little wider and the cells on either side spaced in a staggered fashion so that the occupants couldn't see each other across the way. As they moved farther down the corridor, the warden called out, "Margrave, you have a visitor most eager to see you."

A swarm of butterflies erupted into flight in Anhuset's belly. Worry. Anticipation so fierce she almost shook with it. Her ears strained to hear a voice but no one replied. The warden halted at one cell door, a latticework of metal with openings large enough to see through but too small to do more than put a hand through the spaces. She spotted a shadowy figure seated at a table, limned in the meager light of a small brazier. The scratching noise of a quill on parchment was the only sound.

"You have a short time only and will be watched." He tipped his chin toward the small audience behind her and she glanced over her shoulder. She'd known they were there. Footfalls growing in number as they climbed the stairwells and traversed the hallway. Four guards in armor and one man in robes decorated in sigils. The sorcerer Rodan sent to counter any magic she might try to wield in helping Serovek escape. His presence was superfluous now, and the thought sent a melancholy twinge through her.

The warden banged on the cell door. "Margrave, do you want to chat or should I send her away?"

Serovek straightened in his chair and finally stood to stroll toward the door. He halted abruptly and a muscle tic jolted across his cheek once, twice even as the rest of his face froze. "Sha-Anhuset."

"Margrave," she replied in an equally cool voice. Those butterflies spun in a whirlwind through her ribcage. He looked uninjured, if a little haggard around the edges. Still handsome in the way humans defined handsomeness and handsome to her in the way her heart dictated she see him. She slid her fingers through the openings in the bars, the metal freezing in her grip.

"I'll leave you to it then," the warden said. "Say what you need to. I need to retrieve something from my desk. When I return, you leave." He paused to say something to the group clustered within hearing distance before disappearing down the hall.

Serovek's demeanor didn't change though he nearly broke her fingers in his grasp. His voice was low, no longer indifferent. "What are you doing here, firefly woman? Does Brishen know?"

Obviously a refrain she'd hear often while in Timsiora. When had Brishen exchanged the role of her liege for that of her parent? She sighed. "He knows." For the first time since she arrived she was in the presence of one who wouldn't flee in alarm at the sight of her toothy grin. "I'm here to make you the subject of idle gossip in every tavern, brothel and court gathering in Timsiora," she teased.

The lines at the corners of his eyes deepened with his answering smile. "You've never done things by half measure, though I can't guess what you did to make me even more a target for gossip mongers than I already am."

While her public declaration to all and sundry that she and the margrave of High Salure were lovers had been done for a specific purpose, she wasn't ashamed that others knew. She didn't know how Serovek might feel about it. "I announced at the entry gate that I was your lover and had come to visit you. I'm afraid I've diminished you in the eyes of your countrymen."

Sincere confusion and puzzlement settled over his face. "How would such an announcement, a true and glorious one I might add, diminish me?" She must have made an odd noise because his eyebrows crashed together. "What's wrong?"

If she weren't made of hardier stuff, her knees might have buckled. No practiced charm or seductive quip would ever equal in power what he just said to her. It was a punch to the gut in the best way. "Nothing," she said. "Now that I'm here." She twined her fingers hard with his, careful to keep her claws from digging into the backs of his hands. "I've come to tell you the return trip to Saggara was mostly uneventful. I met up with our friend Ogran on the road."

Those deep-water blue eyes went nearly black for a moment. "And how is our friend?" he said in a tight voice.

"Taking up worm farming when we parted ways." The flit of a smile across his mouth told her he understood her allusion to Ogran's death. "We didn't speak long. My horse was tired, and we were both eager to get home." She didn't mention Magas's name, knowing word would get back to the king who, according to Serovek, coveted the stallion.

He stroked her knuckles with his thumbs. "You were always patient with your steeds," he teased.

She snorted. "This one, like all stallions, requires it, but they do the job adequately if you ride them hard enough and keep a steady hand." His sputtered laughter made her grin.

"Gods, firefly woman," he said softly in bast-Kai, "how I have missed you." He switched back to Common before their audience grew suspicious. "Did you really tell all and sundry I was your lover?"

"Practically shouted it from the rooftops."

He pressed closer to the bars, and she did the same. "Well then, since the word is out..." He kissed her, his lips cold against hers but no less seductive for their chill or the fact a wall of steel separated them so that it was more the brush of a moth's wings across her mouth than the passionate play of lips and tongue she wanted from him and wanted to share with him.

When they parted, he let go of her hands to trace the juts of her cheekbones with his fingertips. His features were solemn, mouth drawn down with worry. "Why did you come? Surely Brishen didn't approve."

Brishen had been very clear about his opinion of her journey. "This decision is yours, cousin. I have no say in it, therefore I don't sanction for or against it."

"I didn't come as the Khaskem's second," she told Serovek. "Only as Anhuset. I represent myself, not the kingdom of Bast-Haradis."

His eyes closed for a moment. "Thank the gods," he said and opened them again. "I figured Brishen would know how to handle this. I didn't want to be the spark that started a war between two kingdoms." The grim lines in his face didn't ease. "Even so, you shouldn't be here."

"Neither should you," she said. "Yet here we are." She eyed the guards and sorcerer askance before turning a telling look on Serovek, hoping he could read in her expression the message that he go along with the charade she was about to enact.

She relaxed her body, draping herself against the bars. Her voice, usually clipped turned breathy. "I have many things to say to you, my love." Serovek's eyebrows shot to his hairline. "How I've thought of you and missed you."

He looked just like the gate guards when she announced she was his lover, and Anhuset would have laughed out loud if she was doing this out of jest. But this was a serious game, one with stakes too high to lose.

She switched to bast-Kai, keeping the breathy tone of a lover's pillow talk but speaking fast before the guards put a stop to it. "I don't have time to explain," she said. "If you want to walk out of this with your head still intact or your neck not stretched, don't argue or protest what I do or say. And if the king asks you if you'll marry me, you say yes. Understood?"

Jaw slack, he gave a single nod, and as Anhuset predicted one of the guards snapped out a warning. "Speak Common or you're done."

She immediately complied. "Do you not feel the same, my darling?" When this was over, she was going to wash this false sweetness off her tongue with a dram of hot lye.

Serovek contributed wholeheartedly to her sham. "I can't begin to express how I feel at the moment, my dove, but I understand," he cooed. Anhuset almost gagged.

"Time's up," one of the guards said, and she turned to see the warden moving down the hall toward them, returned from his foray downstairs to his office.

"What are you up to, Anhuset?" They were both so close to the bars, Serovek whispered the question in her ear.

She looked back at him, memorizing his face and the play of shadows across its angles and hollows. "Saving your life."

"Why?"

Anhuset stared at him for a moment, flummoxed by the question. Surely she didn't just hear doubt in his voice? This man of supreme self-confidence who'd been able to read her with stunning, frightening ease?

The warden motioned for her to join him, and the guards drew closer to physically drag her away from the cell if she didn't come of her own accord. She was out of time. She reached through the bars to slide an errant lock of his hair through her fingers before pulling away. "Is it not obvious, margrave?"

The two guards closest to her jumped back when she spun on her heels, their hands dropping to their sword pommels. Warning bolts of lightning passed over the sorcerer's hands. Anhuset raised her hands in surrender and walked away to join the warden waiting for her in the corridor. Serovek's gaze, piercing and intense, rested heavy on her back.

CHAPTER

EIGHTEEN

Serovek paced the breadth and length of his cell, wondering how many other prisoners before him had done the same, their enforced confinement weighing heavier and heavier on their minds and spirits with each passing day. He'd done well enough until now, using the task of chronicling the journey to the Jeden Order's monastery for the Archives as a way to occupy his mind and stave off boredom while he waited for the king to summon him to trial.

Some might consider it simply an exercise in futility. No doubt Rodan had ordered Dame Stalt to turn over everything he wrote and had his scribes alter key facts that turned a well-intentioned journey of mercy into a sinister plan of sedition fueled by treasonous ambition. Serovek, however, suspected Dame Stalt was a stickler for accuracy in historical records. She may have given the king what he asked for, but he wouldn't at all be surprised to learn there were at least two copies of Serovek's original recounting hidden away for posterity's sake somewhere in the mysterious depths of the Archives.

The writing had helped him hold onto his patience, and except for the confrontation with Bryzant, the anger over his imprisonment. One more day in this cell might be humiliating, but it was also one more day he didn't face the gallows or the chopping block. One more day that he could refine the argument he had prepared in his own defense when he would finally stand before Rodan and whatever tribunal the king called.

And then Anhuset showed up on the other side of the cell bars and destroyed his equanimity in an instant. His patience evaporated, his anger burned hot, and his worry threatened to consume him. For what purpose had she come? And what plan had she hatched? Her enigmatic warning that he not protest or argue whatever it was she said or did had set off every alarm, alarms that rose to deafening volumes inside him when she mentioned the king and marriage. He'd wanted to interrogate her, but their time was short, their audience composed of guards and sorcerer avid in their attention as they listened to them converse. Anhuset had given her warning in bast-Kai in a voice so at odds with her very character, he'd been taken aback at first. All to fool those listening who would assume the conversation between them was merely blandishments exchanged between lovers. They might not have believed the part about the lovers had she not announced it very publicly when she first arrived at Timsiora.

Serovek paused in his pacing and allowed himself a faint smile. How he would have loved to hear her make that declaration and see the faces of those who heard it. His smile faded and he resumed wearing a trench into the floor.

Two days had passed since she visited and no word from her or the king since then. Dame Stalt came to retrieve the last set of parchment from him and shared what she knew.

"There's work being done at the forum," she said. "It looks like a disturbed hive of bees when you walk past it. Digging, hammering, and cutting. One of the clerks has a brother working there. They've been told to build a wall between the seats and forum floor to go around the entire forum. You'd have to sit four rows up to see anything going on inside the enclosure."

Serovek pictured what she described. A ribbon of nausea encircled his stomach. Had the king decided his fate without waiting for judgment from the tribunal? And if so, was his execution something more epic than a quick beheading or the slower but ubiquitous hanging?

He thanked the dame for her help, the supplies and the use of the small brazier.

"I will tithe at Yalda's altar in your name, Lord Pangion," she said. "And pray that he may look favorably on you."

"I'll take any prayer you can spare, Madam." He bowed to her, watching as her stately, narrow figure disappeared from view. Then he began to pace and hadn't stopped since.

He did pause when he caught a glimpse of one of the guards out of the corner of his eye. The man had been slouched against the wall, half asleep at his post. He abruptly straightened, snapping to attention at the sound of footsteps. Serovek recognized the tread. The Zela's warden.

Serovek's heart jumped a beat at the jangle of keys. He stepped back to the center of the room, waiting while the warden unlocked the cell door and opened it wide. Behind him, the previously slumbering guard kept a steady aim on him with a loaded crossbow.

"It seems your stay with us at the Zela is at an end, Lord Pangion," the warden announced. "Though you aren't free." He raised two sets of shackles. "Hands out first, and then we'll deal with your ankles." He stood to one side as a second guard shackled Serovek's wrists, then looped a connecting chain to the ones encircling his ankles. Even if he thought to try something stupid like running, the irons made it impossible. His normally long stride was reduced by a third and he followed the warden down the hallway, descending the stairwell at a careful shuffle. Guards hemmed him in on all sides. He might be on his way to his death, but he muttered "Thank the gods," once he stepped outside into cold, open air and morning sunlight.

Grown used to the Zela's gloom, he closed his eyes for a moment, opening them only when one of the guards nudged him toward a cart with planks built for seating on either side. Iron rings were fastened to the side boards and the floor. He stepped into the cart and sat down, watching as his escort attached the chains to two of the rings. A guard sat on either side of him with enough distance to keep out of reach.

Two more sat across from him. The warden nodded once to him and then to the cart's driver who gave a sharp whistle. The pair of horses harnessed to the cart lurched forward, and they were on their way to the palace.

Serovek didn't look down or look away from the citizens of Timsiora as they watched the prison wagon roll past. If Rodan thought to humiliate his margrave by parading him down the main avenue in chains, then he would be sorely disappointed. Serovek was a prisoner, but he wasn't guilty of the crimes laid against him. There was no reason to hang his head in shame.

As they rolled closer to the palace, the streets grew even more crowded until the wagon came to a standstill. The driver cracked his whip over the heads of those in front of him, and the horses rattled their traces as they stomped their hooves and tossed their heads. The crowd didn't budge until one of Serovek's guards stood up and bellowed, "Make way for the lord of High Salure."

He might as well have uttered an invocation because the wall of people surrounding the cart shifted back and out of the way in a massive ripple, and the transport lurched forward once more. Serovek suspected his expression was as round-eyed and amazed as those who watched him from the crowds, though for different reasons.

The people had obeyed the guard's shouted command as if he announced the passage of the king himself. Unless he'd missed a coronation someone forgot to inform him about, Serovek didn't think he'd just succeeded Rodan as monarch of Belawat. So why the deference? He'd expected the curiosity. Trials, beheadings, and hangings always drew a crowd who found entertainment in death and bloodletting. He'd seen that in several faces, but something else as well, a fever-pitch excitement that audibly hummed in the air.

His unease grew when the cart turned off the boulevard leading to the palace onto the one leading to the amphitheater known as the forum. Public events of all kinds were held there: events for the festival of Delyalda, plays, exhibition games and displays of martial prowess such as wrestling, archery, sword-fighting and horseback riding. Colloquies between justiciars and defendants over petty crimes were held in the forum once a week as well. All of these drew crowds, but he'd never seen a turnout as large as this one.

Serovek's thoughts raced. Tribunals for imprisoned noblemen like him weren't typically held in the forum but in the palace itself in one of the larger chambers reserved for matters of state. All executions took place in another part of the city. So why was he brought here?

The forum came into view, unchanged from the outside, with its high curved walls and three sets of gates through which long lines of people waited to pass and find seats on one of three tiers. Another larger gate meant for those who worked at the forum or participated in any of the events held there lay on the opposite side where Serovek couldn't see. The driver guided the cart there, cracking the whip in warning to clear the way. They finally rolled through the fourth entrance, its towering arch soaring over them, the horses' hooves making loud echoes as they trotted across brick and stone and finally stopped close to an alcove.

"You get out here, Lord Pangion," one of the guards next to him said.

He shook off the offers to help. "I'm a prisoner," he said, "not an invalid," and jumped to the ground with a rattle of iron. He was glad they hadn't dragged him out of the cart, but there was a difference between deference and coddling. He'd been a prisoner twice in the past month, and the two experiences stood out in marked contrast in his mind. Chamtivos's minions had beaten him badly enough that it had taken the skill and magic of the Nazim monks to heal him, while the guards and the warden who served the Beladine king treated him with a wary respect. They would stand by and watch him die if it came to that, but at least they wouldn't spit on his tomb when it was done.

They led him toward the alcove which, from this new angle, revealed a short flight of stairs that led upward and out of sight. A private stairwell for the select few to reach the more expensive seats on the second floor without having to mingle with the common crowds jostling each other in the cloisters open to the public. Serovek recognized it. He'd been here twice before as a guest of the king for a play and a mock battle. The hall he shuffled down now was lined with torches, the wooden floors covered in rugs at intermittent spaces to soften the footfall. Not as crowded as the corridors on the lower floors, it was hardly empty. Servants raced to and fro doing the bidding of their noble masters, arms full of furs, blankets, and pillows, or carrying trays of food and drink.

Serovek's mouth thinned. King Rodan was hosting a public spectacle of some type, and Serovek doubted he'd been brought here as a guest of the event. Part of the spectacle most likely, one which no doubt involved blood, violence, and his imminent death. He wondered what wild creature the king planned to feed him to.

He emerged from the cloisters into a large box decadently outfitted for maximum comfort. In its center a small throne draped in furs had been elevated on a dais. This was the monarch's private space in the forum—high enough for the best view and far enough away from any dangers or the blood that sometimes splattered those occupying the lower seats. Smaller, less opulent boxes on either side of Rodan's were filled with the nobility who stared at Serovek as he entered the royal enclosure and turned to face his king.

Rodan wore the intense look of a hawk that had spotted prey and waited for just the right moment to swoop down and smash the creature into the ground with its talons. His faded eyes burned with a dark glee that ignited even more at the sight of Serovek in shackles. "Welcome, Lord Pangion." His smile was merely a baring of yellow teeth.

Serovek was tempted to return the expression in a like manner but thought better of it. For now. Instead he genuflected, mastering his balance under the shackles' weighty restrictions. "Your Majesty," he said. Behind him the noise of the crowd grew in volume. "Is there to be no trial? Only an execution epic enough to make it a spectacle?" His question carried the edge of contemptuous insolence.

The nobility watching the exchange gave a collective gasp. Serovek didn't apologize or drop his eyes. He had never liked Rodan, considering him too mercurial at times and plagued by a suspicious nature that only grew worse as he grew older. The monarch had left the governance of his eastern borders to Serovek with little interference, and Serovek had served in that capacity to the best of his abilities. It had been a beneficial exchange until the margrave of High Salure had joined Brishen of Bast-Haradis to become a Wraith king and save a world. People loved heroes and hero kings even more. Rodan wasn't a hero king and everyone in Belawat knew it. His margrave had become a threat to the throne.

While the nobles shifted uneasily at Serovek's question, Rodan's features didn't change. He even chuckled at the question as if he and Serovek shared some favorite joke. "Oh, there will be a trial, margrave. I've simply chosen a more public venue to have it so that all may participate after a fashion and enjoy the day." He motioned to one of his servants standing next to a drape of cloth that hid another entrance to the side and behind the throne. The servant twitched the curtain back, said something Serovek couldn't hear and shoved the curtain fully aside.

Serovek's breath locked in his lungs when Anhuset strode through, beautiful, proud, her features set and her eyes the palest yellow, signaling her anger. He doubted anyone else in this space could translate the message in that citrine gaze like him. He wished he could tell them she was likely imagining how they'd all look with their heads on pikes.

The tiniest pause in her step told him she'd spotted him standing there, though she didn't turn to look directly at him. Instead, she stopped where the servant indicated, and saluted the king. "Your Majesty."

Serovek consumed her with one slow, sweeping gaze. She was taller than everyone in the king's box except him, towering over the servant standing nearby who eyed her claws and backed away by incremental degrees. Dressed in armor with her hair scraped back hard and wrapped in a knot so tight it stretched the skin at the corners of her eyes and lent a sharpness to her already prominent cheekbones, her presence loomed large. Even the king looked as if he shrank a little in his chair until he remembered himself and snapped straight-backed once more. He lost that avid gleam in his eyes, only to have it replaced by the shadows of dislike and distaste as he stared at her.

"Anhuset," he said, and Serovek started a little at the absence of her title of *sha*. "I've taken all that you said into consideration. I think you'd be a very suitable wife for Serovek Pangion."

Had the king suddenly sprouted wings, he couldn't have stunned the witnesses to this tableau any more. Serovek was thankful for Anhuset's earlier enigmatic warning. Only he and she didn't gape at the king as if he'd grown a second head from his shoulders. What in the gods' names had she negotiated with the king? Not that he was complaining. If an arranged marriage with the woman who haunted his dreams was the punishment for his supposed crimes, he was more than happy to proclaim himself guilty.

Delighted by the reactions, Rodan flashed his yellow-tooth grin. Anhuset's upper lip curled the tiniest bit. "As I consider myself a fair man, I will grant your request for trial by combat and accept your bid as Lord Pangion's champion."

This time Serovek couldn't help his shocked inhalation. This he hadn't expected, and his blood froze in veins turned to filaments of ice.

Don't argue or protest what I do or say.

He'd thought at the time her comment had related to the odd remark about marrying him, assumed she'd concocted some bizarre plan with Brishen that might convince Rodan not to kill him if he was offered some beneficial alliance with Bast-Haradis. Every fiber of his being shouted at him to do exactly the opposite of what she demanded.

The king's sinister smile went even wider at Serovek's obvious distress though he kept his attention mostly on Anhuset. "I've already chosen your opponent, one less concerned with the possession of things such as inheritance and far more interested in the basic needs of life."

"What have you done, Anhuset?" Serovek forced the words past clenched teeth.

This time Rodan did turn to him. "Lord Pangion, Anhuset of the

Kai has invoked the law of trial by combat on your behalf and offered herself as your champion." The smirk he wore turned even more gloating. "I've accepted on your behalf."

Judicial combat. A fight to the death. If she won, he'd go free. If she lost, she'd die, and he'd die with her. Rodan hadn't gotten Magas. He wouldn't get Anhuset either if Serovek could help it. He knew the law, knew it had been generations since it had last been invoked. The accused was not allowed to fight for himself. There had to be a champion, and the requirement of a fight to the death had a suppressing effect on any would-be volunteer saviors of the accused. Of course, Beladine law hadn't taken sha-Anhuset into account. Neither had he.

"I refuse the champion," he said. He'd rather face Anhuset's wrath or the ax than watch her die in the arena for the sport of a king and the entertainment of the masses on the pretext of justice meted out for a crime committed. She was a superior fighter with a martial prowess hard to match, but Serovek was familiar with Rodan's machinations, the way he bent the rules and reinterpreted the laws to suit his purposes. He'd make certain to weight the odds in favor of her opponent, whoever that was.

A low growl emanated from his right. Anhuset's eyes were the palest yellow and her lips had drawn back just enough to expose the points of her teeth. The servant, fearing for his skin more than offending someone, took an obvious step back. If the force of her glare could set fire to things, she would have immolated him on the spot.

An unmistakable note of malicious glee entered Rodan's voice. He was enjoying himself at Serovek's expense. That was obvious to all. "You can't refuse," he said. "I've accepted on your behalf and her opponent awaits her." He turned to Anhuset. "Are you ready?" She nodded. "The forum is yours, the weapons there for your use."

Still reeling and horrified over what just unfolded in front of him, Serovek took a second, closer look at Anhuset. She was armored but unarmed. Breast plate and greaves, pauldrons and vambraces, plackart, and beneath it all, a mail hauberk and padded gambeson. With a helmet tucked under her arm, she was fully harnessed but confoundingly enough, lacking a single weapon—if one didn't count her teeth and claws. He'd only glanced at the forum floor with its covering of sand and its high walls but remembered the weapons rack occupying one part, mostly empty except for a few polearms, a sword or two and a solitary shield.

He reached out as she passed close to him, a pair of soldiers behind her to lead her down to the forum floor. The chain connecting his wrist and leg irons rattled as he grasped her arm. "Don't do this," he begged her in a low, fervent voice. "Stand down."

She lowered her head to stare at his shackles before lifting it once more to gaze upon him. Her eyes were no longer like the white heat of twin suns but the pale yellow of a harvest moon. Her mouth softened, and for the span of a breath, she leaned into him. "We live for those we love," she told him in bast-Kai. "We die for those we love. This is a privilege, Serovek, not a sacrifice."

She pulled away before he could tighten his grip and pivoted out of his reach. He stared at her departing back, shouting her name inside but silent to all others. She would give them their spectacle in the forum. He refused to give a second as a private performance here. He would toss aside that prideful assertion without a second thought later, willing to play the puppet to any of Rodan's demands.

Every seat in the forum was taken, with more people sitting in the aisles leading to them. Serovek stood adjacent to Rodan's chair, not close enough to reach him and do harm without ending up a pin poppet for his archers, but close enough to hear Rodan's commentary to his queen and his closest advisors, his fawning favorites and his most trusted servants. The few occasions he tried to lure Serovek into an argument or commentary, he received only a "Yes, Your Majesty" or "No, Your Majesty," or the slightly longer "As you say, Your Majesty." Giving up after several rounds of coolly abbreviated responses, Rodan ignored him.

When the crowd's eager voices reached a dull roar and many began to chant, "Begin! Begin!" Rodan finally rose and stepped to the wall that acted as a balcony. One of his sorcerers placed a shimmering stone in his hand and backed away with a bow. An awning stretched over the king, casting him in shade, but the people still saw him and cheered when he raised both arms for their attention. "People of Timsiora," he said, his voice a sonorous blast that reached every part of the forum, obviously the work of the enchanted stone he held. "Of Belawat and her territories, a man we all know as brave, heroic, fierce in battle, loyal to me for many long years, has unfortunately been accused of treason against the kingdom and sedition against the crown."

Another roar went up, this one a mixture of disbelieving boos and disapproving whistles. As before, it faded when the king raised his arm. "Serovek, Lord Pangion of High Salure and one of my most valued margraves stands accused of these crimes. Witnesses have come forth to argue against him." Serovek wondered who these mysterious witnesses were. To his knowledge, only Bryzant had slandered him to Rodan.

"According to Beladine law, he may be tried before a tribunal or..." Rodan paused for effect, and the crowd held its collective breath. Serovek rolled his eyes. "have his innocence or guilt decided in judicial combat. A fight to the death." This time the crowd held its silence, and the silence pulsed like a beating heart. "Long has it been since we in Timsiora have witnessed trial by combat—a fight to the death—but today we will. A champion has come forth to fight in Lord Pangion's name and Lord Pangion has accepted."

It was Serovek's turn to growl, and Rodan glanced over his shoulder to flash him a wolfish smile at his obvious lie. The crowd erupted once more, this time with cheers and calls for a fight to begin. The king gave a signal and a gate at one end of the amphitheater opened up, admitting Anhuset, who, from this distance, looked small but not at all diminished as she strode toward the center of the arena. "My people," Rodan shouted above the din of unsure cheers, "I give you Anhuset of the Kai kingdom of Bast-Haradis, champion of Lord Serovek Pangion." The cheers, which had been quieter at first as the crowd gawked and pointed at the formidable silver and gray Kai woman standing tall in her heavy armor, rose to even greater volume when she pivoted sharply to face the king and offered him the Kai salute reserved for a monarch.

Serovek nearly choked on his own spittle when he saw it. He'd made it a point to learn more about his Elder race neighbors over the years, becoming mostly fluent in their language. He'd fought beside them on patrols, fought against them in raids, and diced with them in their barracks. He'd danced with their women during their festivals, rode with their regent into battle against demons, and fell in love with one of their high-ranking officers. The Kai salute was dramatic, sharp, and forceful. A thump to the chest with the fist before the arm straightened and was held stiffly to the side. It was also very similar to a much more vulgar Kai gesture in which the fist opened up to a spread hand before the arm straightened. A subtle change gone unnoticed by those unfamiliar with Kai gestures and lingo, which the king and likely every soul in Timsiora could count themselves. An obvious change to the Kai and to Serovek. Anhuset had just told the king in front of thousands of his subjects to go fuck himself.

She might well lose this fight and die this day as his champion, but she would do so undefeated. Serovek swore in that moment if she perished, he truly had nothing to lose, and Rodan would pay a heavy price for his paranoia.

Rodan gave a regal nod, accepting her insult with all the pomposity it definitely didn't deserve. Serovek clenched his jaw to keep from laughing out loud. His amusement was short-lived when the king told Anhuset, "Choose your weapons, Anhuset, for you are about to meet your opponent."

Dread replaced humor but Serovek's jaw stayed clenched as he leaned to the side like everyone else in the king's party when he signaled and another gate matching the one Anhuset came through opened on the opposite end. The tension in the forum was thick enough to walk on as they waited for someone to enter the arena. Anhuset stood by the weapons rack to make her choice once she saw her adversary.

Some*one* never emerged but some*thing* did.

A monstrosity the size of a small horse, encased in hard black scales, scuttled into the arena on multiple fast-moving legs that sent showers of sand into the air with its passing. Its long, segmented tail was equal in length to its body and arched over its back, tipped with a barb as big as a dagger and dripped a black liquid which left smoking puddles in the sand. A pair of massive front pincers, serrated along one inner edge, curved in front of its body, acting as both shield and weaponry guaranteed to rip apart anything they managed to grab. The crowd screamed together, and several people abandoned their seats, trampling over those in the aisles in a bid to escape.

Serovek's own bellow stayed trapped in his throat, though his eyes ached from bulging from their sockets. A scarpatine, but one of a size straight out of a nightmare, something he'd expect to see in the world of the *galla*, where surely they would run screaming too if something like that scuttled across their accursed landscape. The colossal insect danced one way and then the other on its eight bent legs, its belly carving lines in the sand as it reacted to the movements of the crowd surrounding it.

Anhuset had wasted no time choosing her weapons. A straightforward pairing of round shield and long spear with a leaf-bladed spear head and weighted at its butt end by a ferrule for balance. She put on her helmet, pulling it low over her brow. Surely, she was half-blind under so much light.

The massive scarpatine paused in its dance as if waiting, its armor-plated body gleaming dully in the sun. Its tail curved forward even tighter, the tip twitching back and forth as it shifted position, its movements starting to match those of Anhuset, who slowly began to circle it. Suddenly the scarpatine pivoted and lunged, its many legs eating ground faster than any gallop as it attacked her. She leaped out of the way just in time to miss a blow from one of those pincers. Her shield took the hit instead, the strike glancing off its rim with a loud thud. Anhuset jabbed with the spear from the side, aiming for a closely guarded soft spot—the top of the insect's head where numerous black eyes on short stalks covered the expanse. She missed in favor of dodging the downward plunge of the barbed tail.

"What do you think, margrave?" Rodan asked in a voice thick with gloating triumph. "The culmination of my sorcerers' hard work and many experiments. Human magic at its finest though we've cleaned the city of every stray dog and cat keeping the thing fed this long."

And will you start with children next? Serovek kept the question behind his teeth, saying instead, "I beg Your Majesty to allow me into the forum to participate in this fight." His leg muscles were practically twitching with the urge to break for the exit and race for the down stairwell. He watched as Anhuset made a second attempt at finding a chink in the scarpatine's armor for her spearhead. She and the creature circled each other, lunging and feinting at intervals.

He forgot Rodan altogether when the insect surged forward so fast, it almost landed atop Anhuset. It missed her by a hair thanks to her reflexes and the fact she was close enough to the weapons rack to shove it in front of the scarpatine. Its pincers caught and broke the rack apart, dropping polearms and swords into the sand like the inedible bits and pieces of consumed prey. Anhuset bent to fling a shower of sand over it, confusing its sense of movement long enough for her to put distance between them. The crowd roared its approval, chanting her name.

"How much does this woman mean to you?"

Rodan's question worked to pull Serovek's horrified attention off the fight and onto him. He didn't immediately answer. Such a question was a trap on numerous levels, an invitation to step into a pit full of spikes. Considering the circumstances, he had no choice but to answer and do it quickly. "I would take her place in an instant. Still shackled. Without armor or shield. Without a second thought. I never wanted a champion. You chose her. Not me."

Fevered with the same bloodlust as the crowd he sought to entertain, Rodan motioned for one of the guards forward. "Unshackle his legs but not his wrists." He pointed to the archers in the room. "Shoot him if he does anything more than stand there."

Serovek's heart thundered in his ears, but he stood still as a pillar while they removed the shackles from his ankles, switching his attention back and forth between Anhuset fighting for her life in the forum and Rodan staring at him with the cold malice of a serpent.

"Never let it be said I don't cater to my margraves," he said. "I won't take you at your word, Serovek. You'll have to prove it. Anhuset came to me asking to be made your champion. I agreed. She stays in there until the fight is over. If she loses, I'll let the scarpatine feast on her corpse. You however… I'll give you the chance to make good on your boast. You can join her in the arena, help your champion win the day, but you'll do just as you described. You'll go in there without armor, without shield, and still shackled."

"Then I beg you allow me to go now, Your Majesty," Serovek replied, sickened by the idea of Anhuset being fed to the abomination she now fought. "Every moment I'm here, I'm not helping her."

It was the perfect scenario for Rodan. The chances of Anhuset emerging from this fight were slim, Serovek's practically non-existent. The Beladine would have their bloodsport and the heroic margrave would die fighting in the forum helping his champion defend his innocence instead of under an executioner's ax blade at the king's orders. A potential usurper removed as a threat, a king unblemished for ordering the death of a hero. The king barely got out a nod of permission before Serovek was striding for the door, his escort of guards struggling to keep up with him as he raced for the stairwell.

The crowd's cheers reached deafening volumes when he jogged into the forum. He didn't dare call out to Anhuset, whose full concentration was centered on the scarpatine at the far end. He scrambled to find a suitable weapon for himself among the wreckage of the weapons rack. There was no shield. Anhuset held the only one provided. Blades and polearms lay scattered in the sand. A sword would be useless against a creature with a carapace that worked like plate armor and was impervious to a sword's slash. He could take out its legs, but he'd have to come in close to do so. No shield meant no protection from that barbed tail which would impale him in an instant. His hand closed around his prize—a crow's beak with its hook on one side, ax blade on the other and spike crowning the top. A two-handed weapon with the long reach to keep him out of the way while he chopped away at the insect's legs. The limited reach caused by his shackles wouldn't stop him from effectively wielding such a weapon against the scarpatine.

He sprinted to where Anhuset and the scarpatine faced off, neither one getting the advantage over the other, though Serovek saw signs of Anhuset tiring. Her adversary remained just as quick, just as agile, and just as intent on making a meal of its annoyingly nimble prey. This close to the thing, his skin crawled at the sight of segmented legs, multiple eyes and bizarre jaws that extended and retracted over and over behind the protective wall of pincers. The spiky hairs covering its legs quivered at his approach, and the scarpatine spun to face this new threat, pincers clicking and snapping a warning.

Anhuset shouted at him over the boom of the audience's cheers. "No armor, no shield, and still in shackles." She nodded to the crow's beak. "That will help if you can stay out of the way. I'll try to keep it trained on me while you hack away at it."

She didn't question his presence or admonish him for it. She'd sized up his weaknesses and the challenges they presented and offered a solution for how to minimize both. She might strip off a piece of his hide later if they managed to survive this melée, but for now it was about the fight and only about the fight. It was one of many things about her that enthralled him.

The audience in the stands yelled his name and hers now, baying for blood, whether it was the scarpatine's or theirs. Anhuset balanced on the balls of her feet, ready to dart away the moment the insect lunged at her. "The plan is to stay alive," she yelled. "But if you have a strategy, I'm listening."

Serovek's only strategy until now was to convince the king to even let him on the forum grounds. He dodged the vicious tail, easing toward the creature's right side while Anhuset jabbed at its face behind the equally lethal pincers. They were effective shields, batting away the spearhead with ease, almost knocking it out of her hand.

A grim thought occurred to him as he watched Anhuset counter her opponent's moves—a memory of the sly triumph on Rodan's face when he gave permission for Serovek to enter the arena. Serovek didn't dwell on it. Couldn't dwell on it as he threw himself to the side when the tail swung toward him in a sweeping arc of venom droplets. A hot burn sizzled in spots along his arm and he glanced down to see scorch marks in his sleeve where the venom had struck the fabric. Somehow, they'd have to immobilize that tail or he'd never get to the legs.

"Are you burned?" Anhuset flung herself back from the swipe of a pincer, knocking it aside with her shield for good measure. "Take the shield!"

Were he not shackled, he'd accept her offer. She was better protected than he in her armor while he wasn't protected at all. But the chains limiting the reach of his arms made the shield more of a hindrance than a help, and he needed both hands to wield the crow's beak with any efficiency. "Keep it." He saw an opening on the scarpatine's left flank and took it, darting in to hack at one of its legs. He only managed to cut off the tip of one before the creature swung so fast, its movement lifted Serovek's hair away from his face.

The edge of its outside claw caught Anhuset on the side, hurling her off her feet to slam into Serovek. He hit the ground in a cloud of blinding sand and an explosive exhalation that emptied his lungs of air. He heaved a gasping Anhuset off him, caught the edge of her dropped shield and raised it just in time to block a strike from the powerful tail. The barb slammed into the shield and through it, driving it toward Serovek's chest. Splinters of pain shot through his bones as he strained to hold the shield away from his body and watched a drop of venom pearl at the barb's tip, hanging there like a deadly raindrop.

He caught a flash of movement from the corner of his eye before another jarring shock juddered up his arms. He was slung to the side, the venom drop splattering in different directions. "Fuck!" he shouted as a sizzling heat blistered its way down his side. The world somersaulted in his vision as the scarpatine's tail, still stuck to the shield, whipped one way, then the other. Serovek let go of the shield, waiting to drop and roll away as fast as he could.

Instead, his shackles clacked as they slid down the scarpatine's tail, taking him down as well. When he'd raised the shield to block the creature's strike, the chain connecting his wrists had looped over the tail, trapping him as surely as the shield still trapped the barb. The edge caught him hard in the shoulder twice and almost in the head once as the tail flailed and whipped, trying to arch over the insect's back so the pincers could grab what the tail had caught.

For all its size, the scarpatine wasn't strong enough to fling its heavy prey over its back. Serovek twisted the chain even tighter on the tail and dropped to his haunches, bent his knees and dug his heels hard in the dirt beneath the flyaway sand. "I have the tail down!" he shouted to Anhuset, who battled the pincers with the crow's beak he'd dropped. More venom splattered in a wide arc. "Climb it! Climb it!"

He didn't know if she heard him. The crowd's screaming nearly deafened him to everything except the skittering noise of numerous legs scrabbling through sand, the hard clicking of pincers, and the grating sound of insectile double jaws sliding across each other.

The muscles in his back, thighs, shoulders, and arms cramped as the scarpatine dragged him across the ground and tried to raise its tail. Its back was a landscape of square plates as hard as any armor he'd ever worn, protecting the creature's vulnerable insides. Beyond the view of Anhuset dodging the pincers, he saw the people standing in their seats, faces almost bestial in their zeal for the fighting. Anhuset suddenly swung out of sight only to reappear with a leap and stand on the insect's back.

She slid to one side, nearly losing her balance when the scarpatine arched, its body rippling under her feet in a roll of smooth armored plates. The movement threatened to wrench Serovek's shoulders out of their sockets and pull him to his feet. Anhuset widened her stance and held her balance. In one hand she gripped the crow's beak, in the other the leaf-blade spear. "Hold that tail," she barked at him.

"Not going anywhere," he shouted back.

Her trust in his abilities humbled him, for she turned her back on the barb still impaling the shield. She almost lost her balance a second time avoiding the upward swing of the pincers as the scarpatine tried to reach its unwelcome rider while protecting its head. Serovek imagined her furious expression as she belted out expletives that made even his ears turn hot with a blush. Using the hook side of the crow's beak, she wedged the steel into the sliver of space between plates and jerked upward, exposing a patch of soft insides. She raised the arm holding the spear, slamming it down and at an angle, driving the spearhead past the steel and up the spear haft. Black liquid spurted out of the wound in a smoking, viscous sludge, the smell so foul, it made his eyes water. No savory scarpatine pie ever smelled this bad.

Anhuset leaped off the scarpatine's back, but not before the sludge splashed across her greaves and the top of her boots. The scarpatine's legs collapsed, its body dropping flat and the heavy tail falling hard enough to knock Serovek onto his back under its weight. It no longer so much as twitched. The champion had won, and judging by the crowd's ecstatic cheering, all knew it.

She suddenly loomed over him, without the spear but still holding the crow's beak. "How did you manage to get yourself in such a bind?" Sand dusted her perspiring face, and she squinted hard in the unforgiving daylight.

"I seem to enjoy embracing things that can easily kill me," he said and grinned. The urge to laugh soon followed, no doubt fueled by the miraculous fact they were both still alive to jest with each other.

Instead of severing the tail to free him, she shoved it aside to hack away enough of the shield with the ax side of the crow's beak, allowing him to slip the connecting chain of his shackles carefully up and over the lethal tip. He grasped her offered hand and gained his feet. She didn't let go when he stood to face her. An obvious expression of relief flitted across her face when his shadow spilled over her to block the sun's brightness.

"You're smoking," he said, watching as gray tendrils of smoke wafted off her armor where the scarpatine's blood had splashed the metal.

"And you're blistered," she replied, her claws plucking at the burned spots in his sleeve and the inflamed skin exposed there. She lifted his arm to inspect his shackles and froze when the metal cuff at his wrist slid back just enough to expose the now filthy but still recognizable length of once-white ribbon tied there. The yellow of her eyes deepened to gold. She didn't say anything. Instead she let go of his arm to grab a fistful of his tunic and yank him closer so she could kiss him senseless in front of half the population of the Beladine capital and its king.

Serovek barely registered the shocked gasps intermingled with cheers and catcalls from the crowd in the stands. If she wasn't painted in places with scarpatine blood and he with scarpatine venom, he'd gather her in his arms and hold her tight enough that her ribs creaked. They stepped back, he wearing a full grin, she a close-lipped smile. Nearby, the dead scarpatine baked in the sun as black blood oozed into the sand, creating small pockets of foul-smelling ruin.

"Come," he said, speaking close to her ear so she might hear him above the crowd. "You must present yourself to the king. No doubt he'll be disappointed that you killed this new toy of his."

Her silvery eyebrows crashed together in a ferocious scowl. "Fuck him. I won. You're innocent."

"And I doubt there's a soul in the forum who'd argue that fact," he said, tipping his chin toward the crowd, who cheered even louder. "But considering your temper at the moment, let me do the talking."

As he predicted, King Rodan was indeed disappointed at the loss of the abomination his sorcerers had made for him. No doubt he'd hoped for a vicious spectacle of his new pet's prowess. Something to display to all as a new weapon or simply to cow his own people in case any were planning insurrections. Serovek prayed the disappointment came mostly from the fact that Anhuset had killed the only one made and that more weren't forthcoming.

And while Serovek couldn't be sure, he'd confidently wager the king's discontent also sprang from the fact it was Anhuset, not Serovek who killed the scarpatine. He wasn't versed in the laws the way Rodan's administrators were, but he knew the importance of their interpretation. It was a fight to the death. The champion won by killing their opponent. If Serovek had killed the scarpatine, then Rodan would have had grounds to forfeit the match. The king had willingly sent him in there, betting Serovek wouldn't just help Anhuset, he'd interfere.

He might well have been right. Serovek would have killed the scarpatine himself defending Anhuset if she could no longer defend herself. The match would be called forfeit and he'd cheerfully stand trial before a tribunal whose purpose wasn't the pursuit of justice but to please the king. He'd said nothing to Anhuset, afraid if she knew the ramifications of anyone but her killing the scarpatine, she would have taken unnecessary risks to win, even if it meant dying to do so.

We live for those we love. We die for those we love. Her statement rang in his mind, a peek into what it was like to be cherished by this fierce, steadfast woman.

She stood beside him now below the king's box and squinted up at the Beladine monarch, her face as sour as his as they stared at each other. Rodan finally stood and approached the balcony's edge once more. His gaze settled on Serovek, grim and resolute. Serovek wondered what excuse or twisted interpretation of the law he might use to revive the charges against Serovek and keep him prisoner until Rodan chose to kill him.

One of the royal sorcerers stepped forward and handed him the same piece of stone, infused with the magic of sound. It amplified Rodan's voice again so all in the forum could hear him. "I've always known you to be an exceptional fighter, Lord Pangion, and your champion certainly equals you in skills. You've both provided us with worthy entertainment." He paused as the audience's cheers overwhelmed the magic. Once the noise died down, he continued, his features tight with dislike. "And your champion is victorious. The charges against you no longer stand. You are acquitted." He gestured to someone behind him. "See to it he's unshackled."

The crowd again erupted into cheers and clapping, many calling out Serovek's name. He winced, wishing they wouldn't. He was in this spot because Rodan already thought he was too popular. The king held up a hand for quiet. "There is, however, the matter of High Salure. How you answer my question will determine whether or not it's returned to you."

Serovek braced himself for another trap.

"Will you bind yourself to Anhuset of the Kai as her husband?" Rodan said.

The question silenced the crowd more effectively than any spell. The weight of thousands of stares settled on Serovek's shoulders and back, and beside him Anhuset stood rigid, staring straight ahead at the arena's high wall.

This was what she referred to when she told him to say yes to the king's question of marriage. At the time he thought it odd, spoken as it was out of context and as a quick warning before the prison guards interrupted them. He'd probably disappointed her when he refused to stand quietly aside while she faced certain death to prove his innocence. He couldn't find it within himself to regret that, though he planned to apologize later. A marriage proposal though, even one spurred on by a ploy or strategy, was altogether a different matter. A personal one. One that shortened his breath, made his heart beat fast and his soul light with joy.

"Yes," he said. "A thousand times over. Yes."

Anhuset's stance didn't change, but Serovek still felt her wilt with relief. Rodan's smile was a thin slash and his brief nod to her a mysterious one. "The margrave has said yes," he repeated for the crowd's benefit. A few cheers and applause met the announcement. Even more curious speculation arose among the stands. "Is this still your desire as well, Anhuset?"

She nodded emphatically so all could see her answer even if they couldn't hear it. "Yes."

"So be it." Rodan spread his arms to encompass all in the forum, raising his voice even though the stone with the spell to amplify it did its work without his help. "By the laws of this land and the approval of this monarchy, the kingdom of Belawat recognizes the marriage of Serovek, Lord Pangion, margrave of High Salure and Anhuset of Bast-Haradis. So may it be. So may it remain."

The crowd answered back with one thundering voice. "So may it be. So may it remain."

It was the shortest, strangest wedding ceremony Serovek had ever attended and by far his favorite, highlighted by the irony of exchanging one kind of binding for another when one of the king's servants removed the shackles from his wrists. Were he alone with Anhuset, he'd pull her into his unchained arms and spin her about in celebration, even if it did earn him a hard punch to the shoulder for his antics. He merely bowed to the king instead, and she followed suit.

Rodan tossed the enchanted stone back to the sorcerer so only those closest to him could hear. "Gather your things," he ordered the newly married couple. "And attend me in my antechamber."

"Yes, Your Majesty," they replied in unison.

The king turned his back, dismissing them without another word. Serovek grabbed Anhuset's hand and the two hurried through the gate from which they both first entered the forum, the audience cheering their exit.

This part of the corridor was quiet for a moment, that brief hush before the first crush of people filled it as they too left the arena. With Serovek declared innocent, he was no longer a prisoner of the crown and no guards followed him and Anhuset into the corridor's gloom.

Fueled by the euphoria of still being alive and now being wedded to the woman he desired most in the world, he was desperate to hold her. She didn't resist or protest when he nudged her toward a corner and wrapped her in a hard embrace. Anhuset returned it with a bone-cracking one of her own, claw tips pressing into his back, almost breaking the skin as Serovek captured her mouth in a consuming kiss.

A kiss of gladness tinged by the terror of a shared fight for survival. Their first kiss as husband and wife. Serovek breathed her in as he savored her taste and the feel of her in his arms. She was hard muscle and power, made of unbreakable courage and unshakable devotion. Armored inside and out except in those rare, magical instances when she'd offered him a glimpse of vulnerability.

They paused to catch their breath, and he leaned his forehead against hers. "I'd swive you against this wall if you weren't armored to your back teeth and there wasn't a mob of thousands about to descend on us."

She smiled, her eyes bright with a firefly's glow in the dim hall. The smile faded a little. "It doesn't have to be real. This hasty marriage. It was Brishen's idea to lower your standing among the Beladine people. A formality only. We can figure out the rest when we leave..."

She paused when he placed a finger across her lips. "I want it to be real in every way. Do you?"

Even the fear of having a scarpatine barb impale him didn't compare to the terror of waiting for her answer. The smile returned. "Yes. Very much."

They kissed again, lost in each other until the thunder of numerous footfalls reached their ears. "The crowd," Serovek said.

"And the king awaiting us," she replied.

They fled the forum ahead of the surge of humanity filing out of there and hurried to the palace. A few hailed them as they passed, offering shouted congratulations, but no one stopped them. An entourage of guards led them to the antechamber where they waited for Rodan.

He didn't make them wait long. He wore the same sour look he'd given Anhuset at the forum, and he didn't waste time on good wishes or congratulations. "Whether or not this marriage is a sham is of no concern to me, but here's how it will work from now through the end of my reign and those of my heirs, margrave." His eyes narrowed, their murky irises glittering with threat. "If you put aside your Kai wife to marry a human one, you forfeit High Salure. If your Kai wife dies, and you take another human wife, you forfeit High Salure. If you die before your Kai wife does, she inherits nothing and will return to her people. If some strange sorcery makes it possible for you to sire children off your Kai wife, you forfeit High Salure." He paused and his brow lowered even more in a scowl. "And if you ever ally yourself with Bast-Haradis against Belawat for any reason, you forfeit High Salure, because I will have you put to death without trial. Are we understood?"

Serovek didn't hesitate. "Perfectly, Your Majesty."

The king stared at him and then Anhuset in grim silence as if he weighed the sincerity of Serovek's answer. Seemingly assured, he spoke again. "I've already sent a message to my regiment at High Salure. By the time you arrive, they'll be gone and on their way back to Timsiora. You may even pass them on the road."

A small voice urged Serovek to accept the king's terms, bid him farewell and leave the capital with all speed, Anhuset by his side. A greater voice pushed him to request a favor. "Your Majesty, I would claim redress of the false charges made against me by my steward Bryzant." His fury over Bryzant's treachery hadn't gone away; it merely settled in his gut like a stone, pushed down while he tended to more urgent matters.

One of Rodan's eyebrows arched, and the same gloating half smile from earlier played across his mouth. "Were they false? Truly? Maybe in practice but possibly not in spirit." He shrugged, obviously savoring what he was about to say. "You'll have to get your revenge on Bryzant another day. I've sent him home to his father's estate. I suggest you put aside your desire for vengeance for now and return to yours."

Were he not the king or if Serovek didn't value his own skin, he would have flattened Rodan in that moment with a punch to the face. He reached out to hold Anhuset's arm, feeling the quiver of muscle there, half fearful that even if he restrained himself, she might not do the same. "Of course, Your Majesty," he said, his voice calm. "Then if you require nothing else..."

Rodan dismissed them with a short "Go," and turned his back on them.

Anhuset waited until they were halfway to the stables where she'd left her horse before speaking, and her tone would have curdled milk.

"Spiteful old bollocks bag," she spat. "He did that on purpose. He knew you'd want Bryzant's head on a pike. *I* want Bryzant's head on a pike."

Her outrage for him made Serovek smile inside though he didn't dare display it. "He'll not get away with his treachery. There's always consequences. It's just a matter of when, not if."

At the stables, Anhuset traded her mail hauberk to the stablemaster for a second horse. Serovek groused over the trade all the way to the gate. "He'll resell it in the market and get four times what this nag is worth."

"Think of it as one less thing you'll have to strip off me for a good swiving," she said. And with that, he no longer complained about the trade.

They put Timsiora behind them without looking back and Serovek followed Anhuset to a place deeper in the conifer wood, on a rise that gave a view of the road below but was hidden by the trees. A tent stood within the shadows, its gray canvas blending in with the patches of snow and the understory of winter-dead brush. The remains of a fire lay in front of the tent.

"Home for now," Anhuset said. "Unless you'd rather return to Timsiora for a day of rest."

If he never saw the Beladine capital again in his lifetime, it would be too soon. He was exhausted, in pain, lusting for his wife, and desperate for true sleep. The tent seemed the most inviting place in the world to him, even though it did look rather narrow. "Are we both going to fit in there?"

Her eyes shone golden in the shadows. "One of us will probably have to sleep atop the other."

"As I'm still recovering from having the breath knocked out of me when you fell on me, I call top." She laughed at his wink before urging him to dismount so she could see to his blistered skin.

He sat patiently while she physicked the blistered patches of flesh where the scarpatine venom had burned him. Bare to the waist, he shivered in the cold, skin pebbled with gooseflesh under her touch as she made a quick salve from supplies she kept in a satchel. "It's just a comfrey ointment," she said. "I'm sure there's an apothecary in Timsiora who can sell a better concoction, but this will do for now unless you want me to ride back." She spread the ointment with careful fingers, pausing at intervals to brush her lips across the uninjured places on his body.

"This will do fine," he said, shivering, unsure if it was from the cold or the sensual pleasure of her affection. That, more than the ointment, made him forget his discomfort.

He soon forgot everything except the weight of her limbs on his, the smoothness of her skin, her scent in his nostrils, and her heat as she sheathed his cock deep in her body and rode him into oblivion, reaching her climax before he reached his. Her moans and the grip of her thighs coaxed him to join her, and he uttered her name in prayer as his eyes rolled back and he came hard inside her.

The tent was indeed narrow and half collapsed on one side thanks to their exertions, but neither cared. While Serovek had claimed his place atop Anhuset, they ended up on their sides facing each other, legs and arms entwined, skin to skin, breasts to chest. He kept an arm around her hips, holding her close to stay inside her. Her lamplight eyes burned softly, and Serovek wiped away a streak of sand granules from her cheek with his thumb.

"How are you, wife?" he said, savoring the term.

Her features gentled even more, and the corners of her mouth curved upward. "Slippery."

He chuckled, then stopped when he felt himself sliding out of her. He gripped her hips even tighter, not ready to leave that sweet place just yet.

Anhuset encircled his wrist in her hand and raised his arm. Her claw traced the dirty ribbon still wrapped there. "I thought this went into a monastery midden. Why did you keep it?"

Serovek could list a hundred reasons for why he kept it, but he gave her only the most important one. "Because it was proof your feelings for me had changed. There is no finer gift in all the world than the love of sha-Anhuset."

She gave a tiny, inadvertent flinch. "I'm no longer a *sha*."

He'd wondered what she sacrificed in order to offer her marriage proposal. She'd give up much to remain his wife. Regret filled him at the thought of her losing her position as Brishen's second. She was born to it, and he'd seen firsthand how she defined herself by it. As much as he wanted her, it wasn't under circumstances like these.

"You risked your life for me," he said. "I'm losing count of the number of times now. I don't want you for my wife just to keep High Salure. It's just stones and mortar. Forfeiting it wouldn't be the end of the world. I want this marriage because I've loved you since I first set eyes on you in Saggara, so grim and beautiful." He stroked a lock of her hair where it draped on her bare shoulder. "But I won't rob you of those things that mean the most to you. We can live separately if you wish. The king's restrictions don't demand we occupy the same household together."

His mind raced. They could visit each other every week or even twice a month. Brishen still wouldn't allow her to remain a *sha* for reasons that were strictly political and diplomatic. Serovek understood that, as did Anhuset, he was sure. But she didn't have to leave behind her people and her home just to remain his wife. They could make it work; it would just take some planning.

Anhuset sighed, and the small smile she'd worn before their conversation turned more serious returned. She stroked his back, tickling the dip of his spine with a fingertip. "Oh, I don't know. Margravina has a more stately ring to it than *sha*, don't you think?" She continued mapping a path down his back to his buttock before giving it an appreciative squeeze. "And High Salure has comfortable beds with soft blankets and warm hearth fires. Your furnishings are quite princely too."

The clamp around his heart eased a little, one he'd refused to recognize as he made the offer to send her home to Saggara while he returned to High Salure, married but still without a wife. "You didn't mention the food," he teased.

She gave a disdainful sniff. "We can debate that unpleasantness later."

He kissed her and she him, their mutual caresses becoming more urgent, more passionate. Serovek pulled back to stare into her eyes with their swirling citrine shades. "None of that matters. There is no bed I want to be in more than the one I'm in now with you, and we're far away from High Salure."

Anhuset swatted him on the buttock she'd cupped a moment before. "You have to be the chattiest individual I know," she said. "Do you want me as your wife in every way?"

An easy question to answer. "Yes."

"Do you want me to live with you at High Salure?"

"Yes."

Her voice became a loving touch that stroked his soul. "Do you love me even half as much as I love you?"

He pretended to consider. "Well...you did fight a giant scarpatine for me." He yelped when her claws dug into his flank. He abandoned the teasing. "I love you with all that I am and for all the days of our existence, firefly woman."

Her pointed teeth gleamed white in the growing darkness and her embrace tightened as if she would meld him to her. "Then for gods' sake, man, shut up and prove it."

Serovek laughed and set about doing just that.

EPILOGUE

Anhuset stood atop the berm that encircled Saggara's training yard for its soldiers and watched the sun break the horizon toward dawn. Behind her the manor house and its bailey buzzed with activity and sound as those who'd attended the celebration of sha-Anhuset's marriage to the human margrave of High Salure continued with their revelry into the coming daylight hours, even after the guests of honor had taken their leave. The training yard itself was empty, offering her a quiet place to recall the hours she'd spent there in practice melées, training both newly minted Kai soldiers and veterans alike. Her favorite memories were of the mock combats with Brishen, even the grimmer ones where she'd helped him relearn how to wield ax and sword as a partially blind fighter.

She had no true regrets at leaving Saggara to live at High Salure. She'd miss its rhythm, its silent voice, but that had already begun to change with the influx of displaced Kai from Haradis and Saggara's renewed role as the kingdom's capital. The training yard, though, was still the same. She'd miss it even though she was growing comfortable in the yard at High Salure.

Her marriage to Serovek was a month old, a happy one though she still woke some mornings startled to see the Beladine Stallion sleeping next to her, his features sometimes peaceful in slumber, sometimes scowling as he battled through a dark dream of Megiddo while the ethereal blue light of ancient Kai magic seeped from under his closed eyelids. During those times she'd eased him awake, not with a touch, but with a low-hummed tune she'd learned as a child. He'd still gasp when he woke, but he didn't flail or strike out. She'd envelop him in a tight embrace while he breathed hard and gripped her with desperate hands and shook off the remnants of whatever horrific visions plagued him. He didn't speak about them, and she didn't ask, offering comfort instead with silent affection and the unspoken promise that she'd fight his demons alongside him.

A light footfall she recognized made her glance over her shoulder to see Brishen crest the berm, looking every bit the regal regent of Bast-Haradis. Unlike her, he wore his finery with ease and had smiled earlier that evening when she clawed at the high collar of her formal tunic and complained of having to wear such nonsense.

"This is your wedding celebration," he said. "You can't show up in hunting leathers or armor, cousin."

"I don't see why not," she snapped. "Serovek doesn't care."

"You have him so bewitched he wouldn't care if you showed up wearing nothing."

Knowing her new husband, he'd wholeheartedly prefer it. Anhuset had kept the thought to herself.

Brishen came to stand beside her. "I thought I'd find you here."

She eyed him askance. "And why is that?"

"Because I always thought this was your favorite place in Saggara. The gods know you spent many an hour in this training yard bruising and blooding new and experienced soldiers alike. Me included."

He wasn't wrong. "I wasn't sure if you'd ever be the same fighter you were before you lost your eye, but you surpassed my expectations. I think you're even better now." She gave him an approving once-over glance. He'd worn an eye patch this evening in deference to those guests not used to seeing the mutilated socket where his eye had once been.

Brishen offered her a bow in recognition of her praise. "I had motivation and an excellent mentor." His features sharpened, and his mouth turned down. "You should know I've spoken with Serovek about his visions of Megiddo and the glow of his eyes. I told him I deal with the same. I think the monk is trying to cross worlds to reach us. To seek help. I just don't know how we can give it."

The grim turn of their conversation didn't surprise her. She'd seen the two men sequester themselves in Brishen's private study for an hour or so the previous day. Both had emerged wearing identical expressions of melancholy, regret, and guilt.

"You have nothing to feel guilty for," she'd told Serovek after one especially bad dream. "Needs must, and he himself severed Andras's hand to break his grip and allow Brishen to close the gate."

Serovek had stroked her hair and kissed her forehead. "I said much the same thing to Andras, who hates us and himself for abandoning Megiddo. My reason knows what you say is true. My soul still won't accept it." Judging by Brishen's expression now and after his meeting, Serovek wasn't alone in his burden.

"What can you possibly do?" she asked. "You did what was demanded of you. There are always casualties in war."

Brishen shrugged. "You're telling me nothing I don't already know. Still, I think one day soon the four kings will have to meet again and find a way to free Megiddo from his prison."

"Serovek's visions are horrific. He doesn't have them as often now that Megiddo is far away in the monastery, thank the gods."

"It curdles my spirit even to speak of it." Brishen gave a small shudder as if to shake off a darkness crawling over him. His features relaxed and he gave her a smile. "This isn't how I wanted to end our visit or how I wanted to say goodbye. I actually came here to tell you your new husband had an especially voracious appetite for the scarpatine pie we served for dinner." His eye widened with a touch of wonder. "He ate the two he was served and most of Ildiko's with particular relish, even savagery. I knew he liked it but..."

Anhuset snorted. She'd witnessed Serovek's concentration on the Kai delicacy. It was no secret that he liked a dish even many Kai abhorred. She suspected his gusto for it now had more to do with symbolic revenge than culinary preference. "Expect such enthusiasm in the future every time you serve one to him."

She changed the subject, pivoting to point at the activity in the bailey. Horses being saddled, oxen and mules hooked to their traces in preparation for pulling wagons loaded high with goods. "You were too generous with this dowry you've given," she told Brishen, frowning.

He sniffed. "Hardly. You're my cousin, my friend, and at one time, my *sha*. I won't have it gossiped about the entire kingdom that the Khaskem was a skinflint with his relatives."

Anhuset wasn't sure she deserved such munificence from him. She didn't at all regret marrying the man she loved, but she battled her own guilt at deserting the man she'd grown up with and served all her adult years.

Brishen had always been very good at reading her, and that particular talent didn't fail him now. "What's wrong? I sensed you were troubled the moment you rode through the gates."

Never one to mince words, she came to the point. "Do you think me disloyal?"

His eyebrows arched in surprise. "What?"

This was harder than she anticipated. "I surrendered my role as your *sha*, packed my possessions, and will leave Saggara to live permanently at High Salure, even though Serovek has willingly offered for us to live apart and take turns visiting. That isn't the marriage I want, but I must abandon you to embrace the one I do want. Am I selfish? Disloyal?" She'd asked these questions of herself numerous times since she left Timsiora as Serovek's wife. She'd considered asking Serovek but knew he'd instantly come to her defense, not in the least objective in his opinion on the matter.

Brishen sighed. "Considering it was I who suggested the marriage in the first place, no, I never thought your loyalty to me was in question. I'm pleased beyond words for you. Serovek is an exceptional human. He'd have to be to deserve you."

She blushed at his praise, relieved by his words but still unconvinced. "I can't help but feel as if I'm abandoning my post, abandoning you, abandoning the royal house of Khaskem entirely."

He stared at her without replying, finally coming to some inner decision about what to say. His quick glance around them to make sure they were still alone on the berm told her whatever it was, it remained between the two of them. "Because it would take an act of the gods to make you reveal a secret, I'm going to tell you something. Something only Ildiko knows until now." He exhaled a slow breath as if bracing himself.

"Good gods, Brishen," she said. "What is it?" She kept one of the darkest secrets of all for him—the knowledge he'd stripped the Kai of their magic in order to save them. Surely, this couldn't be worse than that.

Brishen held up a hand, silently asking for her patience. "When everyone thought my line had died in the fall of Haradis and before I was crowned king, Ildiko came to me. She, more than I, has always understood court machinations, whether they're human or Kai. She understood immediately what it meant for the two of us when I took the crown. She was an able regent while I was away fighting the *galla*, especially with you standing behind her."

Anhuset didn't think her support had that much impact but agreed that Ildiko had done a more than capable job of holding the Kai kingdom together while her husband was away fighting the *galla*.

He continued. "But her role was temporary, or so the Kai people assumed. A regent until I returned to Saggara. They accepted her as such for that time frame. But they would never accept her as queen consort." Resentment over that fact flitted across his features. "She is and will always be human, no matter how fluent she becomes in our language, how quickly she absorbs our culture, or how much Tarawin thinks of her as her mother. Ildiko will never bear me children, and even if it were possible, no Kai would consider a half human, half Kai child a fit heir to the throne."

The inability of the very rare Kai and human couple to bear children wasn't unknown. Like Ildiko, Anhuset couldn't give Serovek a child. He'd been quick to assure her such a thing didn't matter to him. She believed him. Had it mattered to Brishen? Considering his change of status after the rest of his family died in Haradis, carrying the line would become of utmost importance. "Did you suggest the marriage be annulled?"

He scowled. "No, she did." A kind of melancholy humor replaced his scowl. "She even had her replacement picked out for me. I told her I would abdicate in order to keep her."

Anhuset gasped. She'd known none of this during those dark, desperate days. She hadn't even sensed it. Brishen and Ildiko had been somber, worried, fearful—just like everyone else. A marriage in jeopardy was a small thing compared to a kingdom in jeopardy, though the failure of this marriage would have had far-reaching consequences. And abdication to save it even more so.

Brishen offered her a brief smile lacking any amusement. "Ildiko was beside herself, afraid of civil war breaking out as the remaining noble families would fight each other for the throne. As fate would have it, Tarawin survived." He closed his eye for a moment. When he opened it again, its yellow depths swirled with emotion. "I owe those who brought her safely to Saggara a debt of gratitude I won't be able to repay in ten lifetimes."

"My gods, *herceges*," she said. "Abdication? Tell me you searched for another way."

He didn't even flinch, and a resolute hardness settled over his features. "I knew the risk of civil war, knew the monumental struggle Bast-Haradis would have to endure to recover from the destruction the *galla* visited on it. I had contingent plans and fail-safes and capable ministers in place to hopefully ease the transition of power, but even if

I hadn't, even if Tarawin had died with her parents and siblings at Haradis, I would have still abdicated." His face looked carved from rock. "There are those who, if they knew what I just told you, would say I'm not to fit to rule as either king or regent because I didn't put the kingdom first. You may well think so yourself. Unlike me, the woman whom no Kai would accept as queen put the kingdom of Bast-Haradis before all else. I suffer no guilt, no regrets. I will give up my life for Bast-Haradis. I will never give up Ildiko for anyone or anything. Now ask me again if I think you disloyal."

His revelation had thrown her over a cliff, and for the moment Anhuset was still in free-fall, grappling with her changing notions of what loyalty meant, what duty demanded, what love inspired and what one would sacrifice in the service of all three. Her admiration for Brishen didn't change, though her admiration for Ildiko grew by leaps and bounds. Faced with similar circumstances, would she be willing to give up Serovek for a greater good?

Brishen stayed silent as she worked through the cascade of thoughts and questions, ready to face whatever condemnation she might rain down on his head for what he perceived as a failure in his role as regent. Anhuset did none of that. Instead, she bowed low and saluted him, not as a vassal to her liege but as one Kai warrior to another after a battle won. "Thank you, Brishen," she said, infusing her voice with all the affection she held for him. "This is why you were certain the marriage between me and Serovek would convince the king his margrave was no longer a threat."

His shoulders sagged for a moment and his grin held an obvious relief. "Partly, though I wouldn't have suggested it if I didn't believe you already in love with the man or if I thought him unworthy of you."

"I understand better now why you love your wife."

"And why I think she's beautiful?" He winked.

Now that she too saw Serovek in a different way, she understood his teasing question. "That too."

He reached out to squeeze her arm. "You may no longer carry the title, but you will always be sha-Anhuset, and Saggara will always welcome you for however long you wish to stay. Besides, I want you back here in the summer to train our newest recruits, so talk Serovek into giving you up for a week or two."

Footsteps warned them they were no longer alone, and Serovek topped the berm, dressed for departure in cloak and gloves. His glance darted between Brishen and Anhuset. "Tell me now if I'm interrupting so I can stay longer and make a nuisance of myself."

Brishen laughed. He gripped Serovek's forearm in both greeting and farewell. "I'll leave you two alone and meet you in the bailey when you're ready to leave." He offered him and Anhuset a short bow. "Margrave. Margravina."

"Your Highness," they replied in unison and watched as he strode down the embankment toward the bailey.

"I like the way he said that," Serovek said.

"Said what?"

"Margravina." Serovek slipped an arm around her waist to draw her to him. The rising sun cast a red patina on his dark hair. He'd shaved his beard off when they returned to High Salure, revealing once more the refinement of his features, with his elegant jawline and the slant of his mouth when he smiled.

"It's taken some getting used to," she admitted. During her first week at High Salure, everyone there must have thought her hard of hearing because she'd ignored them when they addressed her by the title.

"You carry it easily," Serovek assured her.

"That's because you haven't forced me into hosting fluttery human women at social gatherings where the brutality of pouring tea and making small talk will surely be the death of me." She stroked his back through his cloak, admiring the play of muscle under her palms, even through the fabric.

He laughed. "We'll have to face that at some point. No getting around it, but I'll be at your side, protecting you from the vapid and the stupid."

"My hero," she said, both mocking and serious.

He planted a hard kiss on her mouth before saying, "Always. Until then, we'll leave it to the new steward to field the occasional unexpected visit from a curious neighbor. She seems a capable sort, good with accounts. Quiet but unflappable when it matters most. I'd much rather have you in my training yard demonstrating to my troops how a Kai can use their sorry arses to mop the cobblestones."

Wary of bringing any more overly ambitious younger sons of lesser noblemen into High Salure as a replacement steward, the margrave had surprised everyone except Anhuset when he'd given the role not only to a woman but to a woman of common birth whose father was a merchant in Timsiora and who considered his daughter's new role the pinnacle of all pinnacles. Anhuset had discovered the new steward to be all the things Serovek praised her for and was glad to have her at High Salure. Her husband stood behind his philosophies. He liked strong women, soft or not. "She'll be busy enough cataloging the entire village's worth of goods Brishen decided was my dowry."

He nodded. "A generous man, the Khaskem." He caressed her hair, twirling one of the tiny braids at her temple gently around one finger.

She captured his wrist and tugged at the ribbon still tied there, more frayed than ever. "This will fall off soon," she said.

Serovek shrugged. He slid a hand into her hair to where another newer, whiter ribbon lay hidden. He'd woven it there himself when, after returning to High Salure, he'd presented her with a small box filled with many white ribbons. "Then I'll just take this one to replace it." He pulled her close. "Are you ready to go home?"

"I am home."

Serovek flinched, even as his arm tightened around her for a moment before going slack.

She, on the other hand, held him even tighter. "Are you not here beside me?" He nodded, a smile blossoming across his mouth and his deep-water blue eyes turning almost black. "You will always be home, no matter the ground I stand on," she said.

The kiss they exchanged stole the breath from her lungs and made her knees tremble.

Serovek pulled away to cup her face between his hands, thumbs stroking her cheeks. "So may it be," he said in a reverent voice.

She hugged him until his back audibly cracked and he grunted, making her grin. "So may it remain."

~END~

ACKNOWLEDGMENTS

Long grueling hours went into writing this book, and I wasn't alone in the labor. More grueling hours of work were put in by the intrepid Evil Editor Mel and R.J. Blain. With their support, dedication, and much-needed help, I staggered across the finish line. Thank you.

ABOUT THE AUTHOR

Grace Draven is a Louisiana native living in Texas with her husband, kids and two doofus dogs. She has loved storytelling since forever and is a fan of the fictional bad boy. She is a winner of the Romantic Times Reviewers Choice Awards for Best Fantasy Romance and a USA Today Bestselling author.

gracedraven.com

facebook.com/GraceDravenAuthor/

instagram.com/grace_draven/

ALSO BY GRACE DRAVEN

Also by Grace Draven

World of the Wraith Kings

https://gracedraven.com/world/4

World of Master of Crows

https://gracedraven.com/world/3

The Bonekeeper Chronicles

https://gracedraven.com/world/2

The Fallen Empire

https://gracedraven.com/world/5

Other Works

https://gracedraven.com/world/1

www.ingramcontent.com/pod-product-compliance
Lightning Source LLC
Chambersburg PA
CBHW060314100726
47907CB00002B/395

9 7 8 1 6 4 1 9 7 2 2 4 6